Praise for

# *The Wilkes Insurrection*

"A timely, must-read thriller with rich characters and a plot full of unexpected turns. Get ready to fall in love with Tamika Smith."

—ROBERT DUGONI, international bestselling author
of the Tracy Crosswhite series

"Compelling characters, dark web intrigue, and a wonderfully twisted plot. Pull this timely thriller to the top of your reading list."

—FORMER US SENATOR BYRON DORGAN,
*New York Times* bestselling author

"Robbie Bach has expertly woven a thrilling plot into the hard truths that shape our world. Tamika Smith is the hero we need right now. Her struggles and ambitions amidst the challenges of a divided country are inspirational. This narrative cleverly breaks down social stereotypes in a way that exposes not only our own struggle for identity, but the parallel struggles of our society. This novel is an absolute must-read!"

—RETIRED US NAVY OFFICER BRAD SNYDER,
five-time gold medalist, Paralympic Swimming

"Robbie Bach has built on his Xbox credentials to spin a great, contemporary thriller. *The Wilkes Insurrection* takes you on a roller coaster ride through the back alleys of the dark web, around several explosive curves, into the depths of anarchy to a stunning final confrontation. Like any great video game, the storytelling is engaging, the evil is visceral, and the forces of good must unite to rise to the occasion."

—PETE PARSONS, CEO and Chairman, Bungie Studios,
creators of *Halo* and *Destiny*

"Just when you think you have the plot figured out, Bach delivers a breathtaking twist. Inhale *The Wilkes Insurrection* for its timely relevance, then linger in its promise for humanity. Bach is an exciting talent to watch for readers who love authors like Jeffrey Archer, Tom Clancy, and Nelson DeMille."

—JUSTINA CHEN, award winning author,
*North of Beautiful* and *Lovely, Dark, and Deep*"

"*The Wilkes Insurrection* gave me a lot of what I love—gritty military drama, exciting plot twists, and insights on the inner workings of government, big tech, and counterterrorism. It also gave me something I haven't seen enough of—a Black female protagonist who has strength and resiliency, tempered by empathy and very human responses to love, duty, and trauma. A thrilling read, and an important one."

—LORRAINE ORR, Chief Operations Officer,
Boys and Girls Clubs of America

"More plot twists than a bobsled run. Tamika Smith's sprint to the finish is Olympic worthy. The 'Faster, Higher, Stronger' of thrillers."

—STEVE MESSLER, Olympic gold medalist, Bobsled;
Founder, Classroom of Champions
&
—KIKKAN RANDALL, Olympic gold medalist,
Cross Country Skiing; motivational speaker & entrepreneur

"In this masterful, roller coaster ride of a novel, Robbie Bach grippingly describes an America that is imploding, one that is wracked by deep partisanship and social divisions while confronting an unprecedented assault from a sophisticated home-grown terrorist. Amidst the mayhem, the personal stories of an unlikely collection of heroes come to life. Through the decisions they make and the actions they take, these characters remind us that America remains a fragile experiment but there is more that unites us than divides us. *The Wilkes Insurrection* is both a top-notch political thriller and a heart-felt plea for saner, less polarized politics. Bach is a great storyteller and a messenger of hope."

—PAMELA PATENAUDE, former Deputy Secretary, US Department
of Housing and Urban Development (2017-2019)

## Also by Robbie Bach

*Xbox Revisited: A Game Plan for Corporate and Civic Renewal*

# THE
# WILKES
# INSURRECTION

A Contemporary Thriller

# ROBBIE BACH

GREENLEAF
BOOK GROUP PRESS

Published by Greenleaf Book Group Press
Austin, Texas
www.gbgpress.com

Distributed by Greenleaf Book Group

For ordering information or special discounts for bulk purchases, please contact Greenleaf Book Group at PO Box 91869, Austin, TX  78709, 512.891.6100.

Design and composition by Greenleaf Book Group and Sheila Parr
Cover design by Greenleaf Book Group and Sheila Parr
Cover Images: Colorful explosion with fire and smoke on light background; Washington, DC, United States: Abraham Lincoln Memorial at night; Abstract tech background. Floating Numbers HUD Background. Matrix particles grid virtual reality. Smart build. Grid core. Hardware quantum form; used under license from Shutterstock.com
Permissions credits continue on page 351, which is a continuation of the copyrighted page."

Publisher's Cataloging-in-Publication data is available.

Print ISBN: 978-1-62634-888-2

eBook ISBN: 978-1-62634-889-9

Part of the Tree Neutral® program, which offsets the number of trees consumed in the production and printing of this book by taking proactive steps, such as planting trees in direct proportion to the number of trees used: www.treeneutral.com

TreeNeutral

Printed in the United States of America on acid-free paper
21 22 23 24 25 26   10 9 8 7 6 5 4 3 2 1
First Edition

*To Nani and Papa, loving parents who demonstrated the strength and courage of the Greatest Generation.*

# Prologue

# DAYS TO COME

IN THE NEXT FEW MINUTES, the FBI, ATF, local cops, and probably a few other acronym police would show up at his front door.

They'd followed him home at last.

It would have been better if he'd had a bit more time, but his careful preparations were about to pay off.

He stepped through the secret passageway in the right wall of his living room, and with some extra effort, pulled the hidden door shut behind him. This special escape hatch had not been easy to construct—building a fake bookcase and cutting through the wall into the next apartment quietly and without assistance was no easy task. He'd gotten the idea from *The Chronicles of Narnia*. Now he was the terrorist in the wardrobe, an irony not lost on him.

Once in the closet on the other side, he took an electric razor to his hint of a beard, just to be sure. He put on a shoulder-length bushy wig with a touch of gray, and a slightly out-of-style dress. He added tinted eyeglasses, a large overcoat, a handbag, and low-heeled shoes. With a quick swipe of lipstick, he walked into the adjacent apartment, awaiting their first move.

After years of planning and field work, it was time to exit stage left. So be it.

He was tapped into his enemy's radio frequencies—he could hear them talking on their headsets. It hit him that they were all there to capture him.

*Finally.*

"Radio check," came a gravelly voice clearly in charge. "Team 1?"

The next bit of instructions came in a whisper. "In position—top of the stairs, visual on the doorway."

"Team 2?"

Another quiet response. "In position. Back stairs are blocked."

"Sniper team?"

"In position—sight lines on windows and both alleys. No place for him to run." The sounds of street traffic could be heard in the background.

"Team 3?"

"In position—back of the building covered."

"Detroit police?"

"In position—ready to seal off the block." He smiled at the thought of the Detroit police catching him.

"Choppers 1 and 2?"

Through some static came, "Standing by."

There was a pregnant pause. Then the magic words: "Teams 1 and 2, move in."

Time for his grand performance. He unlocked the deadbolt on the door to his second apartment, slipped out the entrance, and walked toward the steps that came up the center of the building. He was glad he'd practiced the subtle wiggle-walk of a woman. Right on schedule, FBI agents rushed into the hallway from the stairs.

"Lady, you need to get the heck out of here," whispered the first agent with pointed urgency. "Cole, hold her in the lobby. She may know something."

Fat chance. He scurried down the steps, his new FBI friend helping him, all the while listening to the action in his earpiece.

The best was yet to come.

He heard the smash of the door being knocked in with shouts of "FBI" ringing in his ear. The inevitable calls of "clear, clear, clear . . . all clear." And then he heard the words that made his heart sing.

"Fuck. Goddamn it. Where the hell'd he go? Johnson, you saw him come in, right?" Without waiting for an answer, he went on. "There's no other way out—keep looking."

"Agent Phillips, you better come here and see this." Pause. A long pause.

"Holy shit. Another attack. Seal this off and get the Director on video. NOW!"

Then some words from the gravelly voice that might make things a bit more complicated. "Detroit PD . . . close down the streets. Cole, make sure they search anyone inside the perimeter. Hell, search anyone standing anywhere near the perimeter. He *has* to be here."

Did they really think he wasn't prepared?

With a satisfied smile, he reached into his handbag and pressed the button. The car explosion reverberated across the block, shaking the building and nearly knocking him down. The bomb sent his escort Cole running out the lobby doors. Temporarily freed from FBI supervision, he walked outside and across the street, right through a barricade vacated by a muffin-topped policeman, also scampering to the car that was now on fire.

He chuckled to himself—it had all gone perfectly. Stupid pigs. Beginning with the first airplane attack over a year ago, they'd only seen what they wanted to see. Now they had everything . . . and nothing. His day with destiny was finally coming.

He whispered wistfully, "Allahu Akbar . . . God is Great, indeed."

And the stage was set for his final act of destruction.

# PART 1

## THE FIRST DEADLY DAY

Just goes to show that you never know
Just what tomorrow may bring
But I'll tell you this that what it is
Is seldom what it seems
'cause life is a curious thing
Life, ooh life is a curious thing . . .

**—Wayne Kirkpatrick, Amy Lee Grant**

# Chapter 1

## FLIGHT 209, APRIL 16, 2019

JOHN QUINCY HUMBOLDT was used to the Rube Goldberg exercise of Newark Liberty International Airport. Not that there was anything liberating about its labyrinthine escalators and constant state of construction. The airport name honored those who had died on Flight 93 on 9/11—a thought never far from Johnny's mind. He quickly passed an elderly couple, chuckling at their pile of luggage, and navigated to the TSA PreCheck line.

Thirty minutes later, he was lumbering down the drafty jetway, trying to get himself psyched up (or was that "out"?) for the flight home. Despite hundreds of thousands of miles spent in the air, he still hated and feared flying. He knew it was irrational. But all he could do was endure it.

Over time, he had developed a checklist to get him through the airport morass and the flying anxiety.

1. Print your ticket—paper over battery life.
2. Never, ever check a bag—and don't travel with people who do.
3. Make sure all devices are fully charged—and hope your seat has power.
4. Get snacks and a bottle of water—coach-class chow is worse than fast food.
5. Board early—let the fight for overhead bins begin.
6. Window seats only—if you fear flying you want to be able to see where you're going.

7. Put on headphones and music quickly—conversations with others are dangerous.

8. Never use Wi-Fi—that is how more email gets delivered to your PC.

9. Always keep your seatbelt fastened—turbulence can start before the sign is turned on.

The last item in his pre-flight routine was a prayer he muttered as he walked into the plane: "Dear Lord, protect this flight, its crew, and passengers. Please take care of Maggie and the kids. Keep us safe." Would the weather on the route be okay? What about the possible thunderstorms and tornados over Kansas that he'd read about? What if this was the flight he was meant to miss? Did praying to a God he didn't believe in make him feel better?

*Shit.*

Flight 209 to San Francisco was an old 757. The long, narrow tube with way too many people in it. This venerable but ill-conceived Boeing plane was the airborne version of the proverbial "cattle car" from the stockyards of the Midwest. And it was going to be a full flight.

Johnny slid into his exit-row seat near the front of the plane, just one row back from the bigger service door behind first class. Without a seat in front of him, he'd have plenty of legroom but no place to put his bag and lots of cold air from the door when they reached altitude. At least he could stretch out.

Out came his cell and headset for the quick check-ins that would buy him some time. Office or home first? That was easy.

After asking his assistant to rearrange his schedule for the next few days, he hit the speed dial for his wife's cell.

"Hey, Maggie. How was your day?" Absently listening, he made the appropriate "mmmm," "uh huh," and "wow" sounds, settling deeper and deeper into the steel reinforced airplane seat. He finally said the obligatory, "Don't wait up. I'll be home late." Then, "I love you" and disconnected.

Love? Who was he kidding?

As Johnny pulled out his laptop, a couple in their mid-sixties paused just outside his row. They had two big carry-ons and no clear means to get them into the storage bin. "Social" was not Johnny's middle name, but he recognized them from the security line. He could hardly ignore their puppy dog looks.

He put his laptop on the floor and took off his headphones. "Sorry . . . I'm a little slow. Can I help you put those overhead?" After the two tons of bricks were safely stored (what else could weigh that much?), the elderly man introduced himself as Charles Roscovitch. His wife's name was Shea. The last name was somehow familiar, but Johnny couldn't quite put his finger on it.

"Nice to meet you. I'm Johnny."

"We're headed out to California to see our daughter—she just gave birth to our first grandchild." Shea's excitement lit up the sterile interior of the plane.

"Did she have a boy or girl?" Johnny figured he should at least be polite.

"A boy—he has my red hair." She beamed with pride.

Shea continued chatting with Johnny, asking him about his trip and whether he was headed home. Charles eventually reached across. "Shea, leave the man to his work. I've been trapped in the window seat before with too much to do." And with that blessing, Johnny was released back to his laptop.

First things first—a trip update to Paul. He and Paul Hayek had co-founded Cybernoptics, a new entry in the burgeoning virtual-reality market. His meetings earlier that day had yielded encouraging news on raising money but would require significant changes in the company's strategy. His partner would probably blow a gasket.

Write for thirty minutes, choosing words cautiously.

Connect to Wi-Fi, violating a rule in the process.

Hit send. Email missile-fired to Paul.

Disconnect from Wi-Fi—returning tranquility to the flying universe.

As the plane navigated its way out across the Appalachians and with his email winging its way to San Francisco ahead of him, Johnny drifted off into an uneasy slumber.

• • • • •

*BOOM!*

The 757's service door blew out at 34,000 feet in a sudden explosion of air and debris. Johnny saw a flight attendant being sucked out the gaping opening. Anything nearby that wasn't tied down—luggage, books, piles of paper, and a sea of plastic cups—all hit his seat or the back of his head on their way out of the hole.

The plane lurched down and to the right. He was pushed forward to the point where he thought he was leaning outside into the emptiness.

Screams. Oxygen masks. Chaos.

# Chapter 2

# FALLING FROM THE SKY

AS THE PLANE'S DESCENT DEEPENED, Johnny clutched at the seat armrests, gasping for breath.

Then he remembered the flight attendant instructions he routinely ignored: "Pull the mask toward you, place it over your nose and mouth, and breathe normally."

That last part had to be some sort of FAA airline joke.

The older woman sitting next to him was now in a total panic. Her husband, too. Their eyes were wide, mouths trying to yell, with wrinkled hands clutching out in mid-air. What were their names? Shannon? Sherry? No . . . Shea and Charles!

Grabbing her hands, Johnny instructed as calmly as possible: "Here you go, Shea . . . put this over your head. Hold it tight here." He reached across and helped Charles get his mask on, too. He gave them a thumbs up, as if that would somehow make them feel better. Or maybe he was trying to steady his own heart rate. His nervous flying seatbelt rule had saved him. For the moment.

The plane was rapidly descending.

A pilot's voice crackled on the intercom: "Ladies and gentlemen, we've experienced an unexpected depressurization in the cabin." (Duh.) "Please stay seated with your seat belts fastened and your oxygen masks on. We are reducing altitude as quickly as we can and will update you when we know more. Follow the instructions of your crew fully and carefully."

Helpful. Except the only crew member he'd seen recently had been sucked out of the plane, the terrified look in her eyes now etched into his memory.

Johnny's mind immediately went elsewhere. Where's my laptop? Did that email get sent? I don't want to have to re-write that.

The ridiculousness of this thought pattern sunk in as the fragility of his situation became clear.

Screw Paul and Cybernoptics. His family flashed across his suddenly exposed conscience. So many things he wanted to say—the guilt of having focused on the wrong things at the wrong time rushing in. How could he get a message to them? Would they ever know how he felt?

"Ladies and gentlemen, we're flying at a safe altitude of 7,000 feet and have stabilized the plane as best we can. You should be able to breathe without the oxygen masks if you choose. Air traffic control has cleared us to land at Offutt Air Force Base outside of Omaha, Nebraska. Emergency personnel are waiting and I've asked the crew to prepare you for a rough landing. Again, please follow their instructions fully . . . those of us in the cockpit will do everything we can to put us on the ground safely."

Emergency personnel and crash-landing procedures were not what Johnny wanted to hear. Forget his fear of flying—now he was afraid to land. His hands were again clamped to the armrests, feet dug into the floor. The plane was flying like an amusement park roller coaster. Jerking up and down, left and right, with the occasional shudder thrown in just to keep him guessing.

The guilt of not being present for his family returned, and after a few moments of scrambling around, he realized his only way to communicate would be text messages sent just before they came down.

What could he say? Hell, with the plane bouncing, could he even hit the keys?

**Forgive me for not being there . . . so many times. I hope you find a deeper love.**

That one was for Maggie.

To his son Nathan:

**Time to grow up. Protect your mom and sister. I love you.**

Phoenix:

**You can do anything, be anything. Fight Song. Love to my precious one.**

Johnny loved both of his children, but his girl was special in so many ways.

Not to be forgotten:

**Simplify. Think small to be big.**

The idea of Paul narrowing the scope of the company brought a wry smile, even amidst the tragedy assaulting his senses.

Couldn't be more than a minute or two now. The plane was oddly silent, punctuated by the flight attendants' regular chant of "Brace! Brace! Brace! Heads down! Stay down!"

Johnny helped the couple next to him assume the crash position. Then he did the same, cell phone tightly in hand waiting for the plane to drop. His family had taken so many flights together—thank God he'd be the only one killed. Eventually, he saw one bar, then two bars of service. He sent each text message, hoping that they'd all get through.

Now there was nothing to do but wait.

"Brace! Brace! Brace! Heads down! Stay down!" He could hear the fear escalating in their voices.

Johnny felt the wind rushing through the opening and heard the occasional sob from somewhere behind him. The setting sun sent late rays of light across the interior of the plane, perhaps a welcome message from the angels beyond. He heard more than a few people praying, the elderly couple beside him included. Shea grabbed his hand.

"Brace! Brace! Brace!"

Was it truly as clinical as he'd always claimed: *We're born, we live, and then we die, the end?*

"Heads down!"

Dear God, could they please SHUT UP!

"Stay down!"

Too much time for his life to flash before his eyes. But more than enough for him to contemplate his sins.

"Brace for impact!"

The ground rushed up.

The first cacophonous jolt was a big bounce, and he was turning upside down. Then everything went dark.

# Chapter 3

# THE CRASH

THE CALL CAME AT 19:47. "What the hell are you waiting for?" Major Tamika Smith yelled into the phone. "Hit the damn alarm and scramble the team." She slammed down the receiver without waiting for an answer.

As a reservist, Tamika was scheduled to report to Offutt Air Force Base one weekend a month for training. At least that was the theory. With all branches of the military still heavily engaged in the Middle East, she was the acting Combat Search and Rescue leader (or CSAR in Air Force–speak) responsible for all emergency operations at the base. Practically speaking, she was stuck at Offutt—her law career and job as a Senate staffer in Washington, DC, on hold for the foreseeable future. Once in the Air Force, always in the Air Force.

Thankfully, her quarters were just two quads across from the CSAR facilities—directly past the flight line. The sprint to the hangar would have done her Air Force Academy track and field coach proud. Tamika arrived to see crews putting on boots and donning fire gear. She almost knocked down a captain coming around a corner.

"What's going on, Major?" he began a rapid-fire set of questions. "Who hit the alarm? Should I call the Commander? How can I help?"

Tamika recognized him as the base commander's senior aide—a tall, thin drink of water from Louisiana. "Slow down, Washington. Let me get on the mic and we'll go from there."

Breathe, Tamika.

She grabbed the handheld mic attached to the wall by an accordion cable. "Attention all crews." And then, "Hey . . . shut the *hell* up!"

Quiet, finally.

Now, more calmly, she began. "Listen carefully . . ." She tried to balance her sense of urgency with the need for people to take a deep breath and focus. "We've got an inbound civilian 757 with two hundred thirteen souls on board. Two hundred passengers and thirteen crew. They blew a door at 34,000 feet and have lost significant hydraulic control. They're trying to dump fuel, but we should assume that fire and smoke are in our future. They'll be coming in from the northwest on Runway 12. Tough to guess about touchdown, but the pilot will make sure he gets over the airfield. So let's set up on Ramp B. Five minutes out. Obviously, this is not a drill."

Air traffic control could have diverted the plane to Omaha or Lincoln, but Offutt had some decided advantages. In particular, its remote location reduced the likelihood of casualties on the ground. Her instructions would put the bulk of her team partway down Offutt's main runway. Given the likelihood of fire, getting stationed close to the scene would buy them critical seconds to douse any flames and pull out survivors. But too far down the runway might make them roadkill in the wreckage.

"Washington—you need to call Commander Jessup. But he's not going to be much help here until the press arrives." At that point, his unique pain-in-the-ass skills might be useful. "If you really want to help, you can pair up with me."

The look on the young captain's face had equal elements of excitement and terror. Kind of like a teenage boy about to get to second base with his girlfriend for the first time. To his credit, he didn't hesitate. "Major, I've done some training, but you'll have to tell me what I need to do."

Yelling above the sound of vehicles revving up, she kept her instructions short and to the point. "Grab some gear, Captain, and follow me. Keys are in the truck."

They jumped into a vehicle and raced out onto the field, with Tamika directing him down the ramp toward the middle of the runway.

Putting on her equipment, she realized she better prepare him for what was coming. "Look, if this plane comes down hard, there'll be shit everywhere. Plane parts, luggage, smoke, and probably body parts."

That did not improve the look on Washington's face.

"Just stay focused on our task and you'll be fine. Part of the team will jump on any fires, but our assignment is getting people out and away to safety. As the plane goes past us, we're going to go like a bat out of hell after it on the runway. Get as close to the fuselage as you can. Then stay with me. I've done this too many times before."

Once in position, Tamika looked back down the runway, mentally tracing a line out toward the horizon. Dusk was settling across the prairie sky in hues of blue, red, and purple. Through the haze, she spotted the 757 with its wing and belly lights blazing. This was clearly not your typical approach. It looked like a boat bobbing across a rough ocean—first up, then down, now left, followed by steep right.

"Rev it up, Captain, it looks like he'll be lucky to get it down somewhere on the field."

On the radio: "Listen up—stay narrow for now. I don't think they have much lateral control, and I don't want any of us to get hit. Once he goes by, we can spread out based on how lucky he gets. Let's make this count."

The growl of the truck engines filled her ears.

In that instant, memories of enemy attacks crashed in. The smell of smoke, the feel of heat, and the cacophony of sounds associated with battle. Tamika's ears rang with the crackle of her radio, the screams of wounded, and the continuing jackhammer sounds of machine gun fire.

Staring straight ahead, Tamika fought to stay in control. To push back the unwelcome memories that sometimes closed in around her.

"Major? Major Smith?"

"I'm here, Captain." Adrenaline brought her back to the moment. "Just drive the damn truck when the plane goes by."

With binoculars, Tamika could see the gaping hole in the right side of the fuselage as the plane shimmied back and forth across the approach vector. It crossed the outer boundary of the field, looming large as it sailed by.

"Go! Go! Go!" She screamed as the cavalcade of fire and rescue vehicles took off down the runway.

At the last moment before touchdown, the plane lurched down on its left side. It bounced once—and then broke apart. The mid-section flipped over and slid across the end of the runway. Both wings split off followed by a fireball. Sounds of destruction boomed across the field.

The initial strike had split the nose away from the main body of the plane. What looked like the first six or seven rows of the passenger compartment along with the cockpit slid all the way past the end of the runway but looked upright and relatively intact.

The main cabin, on the other hand, was in shambles. It went well off to the right side of the runway, settling upside down and facing backward. Smoke poured from gaps in the shell. The last ten rows of the plane had separated hard at landing and somersaulted into a ditch on the left side of the runway, surrounded by crushed debris from the tail.

"Let's get some foam on that main cabin to the right," Tamika yelled into her radio. "Crews one, two, and three, converge on the midsection of the fuselage. Four, you have the nose. Five, you're on the tail section. Let's move!"

She slammed down the radio and yelled at Washington, "Put us right next to that big hole at the front of the cabin. You're gonna want your oxygen mask on."

They screamed down the last stretch of runway then veered off into the sloped grass approaching what was left of Flight 209. As they swung around to the side of the plane, Tamika jumped out of the truck before it had rolled to a stop. She ran up to the opening with her heart pounding. She took a deep breath. Then leapt into the fire.

In that instant, she knew it would be for the last time.

# Chapter 4

# DETROIT

OBAID BIN LATIF allowed himself a small smile.

More than two years of training and planning had paid off. His original hope was to destroy the plane in the air. Perhaps cause some fatalities on the ground. But as he watched the early videos on Twitter, he realized this might even be better. The Air Force base location added intrigue to the story. The survivors would talk about their terror as the plane crashed, and the press could turn the "brave" pilots into heroes—as if those pilots had any other option.

He was sitting at a bare, wooden desk in the intentionally spartan apartment he called home. It was a one-bedroom affair, with one room serving as his kitchen, eating, and living space. The bedroom served as his "office" and "filming room," complete with a black flag and a solid white backdrop to prevent the authorities from figuring out his location. Outside the camera's field of view, "art" adorned the walls. A collection of photographs he'd taken during his preparation, along with some other planning materials that would become more relevant later.

After all, the whole idea was to leave nibbles for the FBI.

Bringing terrorism back to America was an essential step in the plan. The goal was to start a war—not exactly a jihad, but a war that would deeply scar a generation that had never learned what it meant to fight. A war that would divide the country permanently. And an airplane attack had seemed like a fitting place to start.

His backstory was not that special, practically lifted from a paranoid write-up on the Breitbart News Network or Infowars. The breadcrumbs said he was trained at an ISIS camp in Raqqa, Syria, where he learned the art, science, and faith of being a jihadist. Having no family in Syria, there was no history to protect—all he needed was a fake passport with a fake name and a good refugee story. For bin Latif, fake news was good news. Ironically, Michigan was the third-largest Syrian resettlement location in the United States.

Perfect.

Bin Latif was not your average radicalized ISIS suicide bomber. He had no real wish to die nor did he care for the conventional jihadist credos. He was not doing this for any glory or any desire to have a chat with Muhammad or meet a collection of virgins. He didn't have a prayer rug and there was no way he was getting up at dawn to fulfill the two Raka'at of the Fajr prayer.

What had drawn him to ISIS originally was its incredible ability to create chaos. In less than a year, the organization had infiltrated several countries, rewritten its own borders and then erased them, created a social and economic model, and scared the shit out of the rest of the world. That was some serious mojo and worth the trouble to make the connection.

If it meant he had to pretend, on occasion, to believe in some Salafist or Wahhabist Islamic teaching or act as if Sharia law mattered, so be it. Bin Latif's objective was purely political. Established governments were corrupt, self-serving, and elitist. ISIS meant chaos, chaos was good, therefore ISIS was good. The associative theorem of terrorism.

He was not in a rush—this was a deep mole mission. So as ISIS had deteriorated over time, he'd realigned himself—for the sake of optics—with a new group. One that was even more tightly tied to his blueprint for chaos and division. The world would soon meet the Islamic Brotherhood Front—and would learn to fear it as well.

With the plane down, it was time for Obaid bin Latif to take credit for the carnage on behalf of the IBF. He'd written a draft script before the crash. As he sat at his desk, he finished modifying sections to reflect the actual events. The beginning would be in Arabic and the rest in a heavily accented, stilted English. That would certainly keep them guessing. As long as he stayed two steps ahead of the authorities, he knew exactly where they were.

And that was enough for now.

"Okay, lighting looks good," he said out loud. "Let's check the sound . . . audio is clear. Field of view is right. Time to roll."

He donned his regular, drab Arab clothing, took his seat again at the wooden desk in front of the camera, and used the remote control to start the recording. He'd memorized the Arabic section and then read the English portions from boards he'd hung behind the camera. He especially loved the last line:

"Your president speaks with much bravado about making your borders safe from Islamic extremists abroad. In fact, he should look much closer to home."

Filming complete. The video would go live in time for the morning news cycle. Another mental checkmark on his terrorist to-do list.

But bringing down the plane and bragging about it on video was only the beginning. His mission required him to dial up the terror to achieve ultimate success, and the prospect of another attack sent a tingle up and down his spine. The planning had been in place for months. Now that the game was finally on, it was his job to strike anew, hard and fast.

The first attack, admittedly, had been chosen more for its drama and cinematic effect—as well as its echoes of 9/11. But his second assault would be deadlier, its lethal impact striking at the heartbeat of the nation. Since he had not known exactly when the bomb would bring down the plane, he had prepared the next attack in advance to ensure he could move quickly. He was already at the apartment and had all the video equipment running, so he returned to the same "set" and recorded a second message. Nobody would have to wait long to learn that Flight 209 was just the beginning.

"Let me be very clear. No one is safe. None of you are out of our reach."

He forced himself to pause and take a deep breath. Eagerness could lead to mistakes. He was paranoid about leaving DNA evidence. He had skintight gloves and a hairnet on anytime he was in the apartment, and never used the bathroom there. Bin Latif had always come to his flat disguised as a westerner, so he would emerge from the apartment as that person. There was more retribution and chaos to come.

He had to get to the airport quickly.

# Chapter 5

# RUNWAY 12

AIRPLANE CRASHES ARE impossibly violent. Tamika understood the physics involved—velocity, mass, materials, impact angle—but mostly she understood that when a hardened aluminum tube going 150-plus miles per hour hits an eight-inch concrete slab, the result is horrific. Add over two hundred people, seats, luggage, airplane equipment, and aviation fuel, and you have quite the recipe.

Think china vase in a washing machine.

With the light fading and smoke swirling everywhere, Tamika climbed through the hole at the front of the plane and immediately flipped on her head lamp so she could take stock of the situation. Her senses were assaulted by the chaos. But amidst the noise and furor from rescuers, passengers, ambulances, and the increasing chop of helicopters, a deep sense of calm came over her. The cold professional took control. The person who knew she could do this as well as anyone.

With the remnants of the plane upside down, she found herself walking on the former ceiling, which was buried in luggage that had exploded out of the overhead bins. Many people were still strapped into their seats, hanging from what was now the ceiling in a bats-in-a-cave formation. Some seats had exploded off their footings at impact and were mixed in with the luggage on the ground. Two small fires were still burning, filling the air with smoke, adding to the urgency for both passengers and rescuers. Tamika heard cries, screams, and moans. How did anyone survive this?

Back on the radio, she shouted, "Okay, crew one—get on those fires. Hot spots in the middle of the plane. Everyone else is on triage. Let's get the most critical out of the tube. Check for neck and spine injuries but get 'em out fast. Washington, I want you outside coordinating with the battle staff back at the hangar. Set up an evac area on the runway. Group them by severity of injury."

She paused to let him prepare for the next command.

"When we remove the dead, put them in a separate area. Use the sheets to cover them."

Triage at a crash scene was more art than science. Tamika saw injuries ranging from severe cuts and lacerations to some broken bones to first- and second-degree burns. The fireball had been intense but the wings breaking off had been a blessing, as they carried away much of the remaining fuel with them. And then there were those who did not make it—crushed by debris or mangled when they were thrown loose in the plane. Tamika knew their faces would revisit her that night. But for now, she had to let them go. Save those you could and move on.

Tamika knelt by a middle-aged woman. "Stay still. You're just going to hurt yourself more." She called for help, "Kaveh! Over here." A member of crew two carefully lifted the woman over his shoulder and scrambled out the cavernous hole.

Back at the front of the tube, near the gaping wound where a door had once protected passengers, she helped two elderly people down from their seats—carrying first the woman and then the man out on her back. In basic training, she could rock the unit in the sprints but got crushed by the men in strength drills. No longer. The combination of years of weight training and refining her technique enabled her to carry nearly twice her weight comfortably.

Age was catching up, but adrenaline was a powerful drug.

As she set the old man down, he became quite agitated. "The man next to us . . . where did he go?"

The woman jumped in, "My husband's right. He was there when we hit and when I looked around, he was gone. His name was Johnny. Clean-cut, brown hair, tall . . . with I guess what they call an 'athletic build.' I don't know what we would have done without him. I was so terrified, I didn't know *what* to do. He was a little angel for us."

"Hey, hey . . . take it easy. Everything is all jumbled in there. I'll go back and look. I promise. But right now, you need to take care of each other." With a look up and a grab for her radio, "Washington, we need some blankets here and a medic."

Back into the washing machine, Tamika continued her triage and evacuation work—now also looking for the missing seat and male passenger. The mangled footings told her the seat got ripped out in the crash, but she couldn't find any sign of it in the tube itself. *Shit.* The seat row was near two large openings in the wreckage. If the seat had come loose at the wrong time, it had gotten ejected out of the fuselage.

Another casualty. Back to the living.

•  •  •  •  •

An hour later, Tamika was satisfied that she could do nothing more at the tube. With night fully set in, the runway had taken on a new complexion. Big spotlights, multicolored emergency lamps, smoke, and shadows put her in a more reflective state of mind. As the rush eased out of her body, she hopped in a truck and did a survey of the rest of the crash site to see how her teams were doing. She was already replaying the early stages of the rescue effort and could tick off several things they would need to address in the post-mortem. But everyone had risen to the occasion and performed well beyond her expectations.

Passengers in the front of the plane had fared the best as the nose had slid down the runway rather than turning end over end. And no fire. Both pilots survived, soon-to-be heroes who had clearly delivered a miracle. Plenty of injuries in that part of the plane, but no casualties. Thank you, Boeing engineers.

The tail section was a different story. The whiplash-inducing impact of the back end of the plane crushed several rows of passengers and blew out the rest of the rows of seats. Tamika got out of the truck and walked through the wreckage, absorbing the sound and smell of death. Crew five would get extra attention from her in the post-mortem and follow-up training. The faces of the dead would stay with them for a long time.

Back at the main crash section, Washington had clearly taken command of the evac area and was in the process of moving the last of the injured onto ambulances and trucks and generating a casualty count. All things considered, he'd done an incredible job with minimal training—and Tamika told him so. "Anytime you want to get out of the Colonel's office, you give me a call and I'll put in a good word. You were awesome tonight."

"Thank you, ma'am. But honestly, I don't know how you do this. Moving the survivors into position and bossing the drivers around was easy. I felt like I was saving people. I went down to the plane a few minutes ago, and they're still clearing out bodies. I forced myself to look, but I wish I hadn't. And there was no shooting or fighting today. I don't want to think about what you went through during your tours."

There was nothing for Tamika to say. Welcome to the Air Force.

She motioned him to get in the truck—her job now shifting back to command and control. Lost in thought, Tamika took the wheel and whipped the vehicle around and down the runway with her foot all the way down on the accelerator, seemingly trying to outrun her thoughts from the crash site. All her life, running had been an escape of one form or the other, so why not now?

A glint of silver flashed in her eye and then, *bam!* She hit the brakes so hard that Washington slammed into the dash, just barely managing to get his hands up in time.

"Jesus Christ! Major?"

# Chapter 6

# PALO ALTO

"ARE YOU SHITTING ME?"

Paul's open hand flying through air, smashed the table for emphasis. "How can it possibly take that long?" His bronzed skin was trying to turn red in anger—his curly black hair flying up and down each time he hit the table. He was only five foot nine, someplace between a fireplug and a pit bull, but his small frame hid a furnace full of emotion and anger.

They were sitting in the dining room of the house that served as world headquarters for Cybernoptics. Climbing the ladder in the Silicon Valley startup world was nowhere near as glamorous as Paul Hayek had first imagined. They'd rented a beat up, one-story ranch house on the wrong side of Highway 101 to save money. Eventually, they'd added a nearby warehouse space, where much of the actual development work was done. But Cyber House was still home base and the heartbeat of decisions for the company. Posters, spaghetti wires, and portable whiteboards covered up the peeling paint but couldn't hide the poverty that must have lived there before.

The table looked like it was going to collapse when their spiritual leader slammed his hand down again to reinforce his point. The product management lead mounted his response carefully. "Paul, you know as well as I do that the silicon slip has downstream effects. We can spec APIs all weekend with you and it won't matter until we've got real hardware to work with. The team is trying to fix the EV-1 chips—and until that's done, we won't have a good target platform and developers won't have anything to test on."

"Wow . . . now we're just shoveling the shit around to see where it sticks." Paul made their old Polycom speaker phone pay the price for its insolence. Nobody was even on the line.

The argument continued for another forty-five minutes, delving into increasingly complex layers of technical goo. Paul loved the deep dive—this was where he was able to exercise his brain the most—but he hated their situation and the arguments between hardware and software that were fragmenting the team. Cybernoptics was too small to survive something like that. And despite his willingness to argue at the drop of a hat, he disliked making big decisions himself and forcing them on the team.

A psychologist would point to his upbringing as the source of so much angst. Sure, he'd been born in Lebanon and had seen more than enough conflict in his life. His mother was a Shia Muslim, his father a Maronite Christian, and that was a recipe for strife in the overheated cauldron his family had called home. His parents loved each other and would do anything for Paul, but seemingly all the rest of Lebanon, Syria, and Jordan hated the idea that a Muslim and a Christian could love and marry.

His vibrating phone forced a cease-fire on the development debate—an email from Johnny that he needed to read. "Chickens or Eggs" did not tell him much, but he knew the New York trip was about survival, so he opened the email.

**From:** Johnny Humboldt
**Sent:** Thursday, April 16, 2019 3:30 PM
**To:** Paul Hayek
**Subject:** Chickens or Eggs
**Importance:** High

I tried to catch you after my meetings today—I hope the product reviews are going well and that we finally have a firm beta date. More on that in another email. As you know, I had meetings with three VCs today. Here's the short answer:

1. Justin and Donovan: Forgetaboutit. I thought we were inexperienced . . . but this was amateur hour.

2.  The Hillfield Fund: I liked these guys, and they asked some really good questions. Most I had heard before, but they had some new insights. Tough thing here will be valuation and ownership. Their due-diligence list will also be super long.

3.  Lifeline Family Ventures: Wow . . . classic VC name. Not rocket scientists but not stupid either. Have a bunch of East Coast old establishment money they're trying to put to work, mostly in non-tech investments. But they have some Valley envy (which is fine by me) and are looking for a place to bet.

In the end, the real problem we have is one of "chickens or eggs." We can't "prove it" to investors without the product . . . and we can't finish the product without investor money. I know you don't want to hear this, but the shit show in development is killing us. If we can't set and then hit a date, there'll be no new money. We can talk (and yell) more when I'm back in the office tomorrow . . .

Johnny

Well . . . at least the email said there was a possible path forward. Paul had plenty of history with investors and most of it was not good. The sense of "been there, done that" brought back other painful memories, which is why he and Johnny had tacitly agreed that the white Protestant should raise the money. Paul's talents were more suited to focusing on the product. And he knew that Johnny was right about one thing: If he didn't get development back on track, the rest didn't matter. Screw the moneymen (gladly). If they could finish the right product, they would definitely win.

And then a few hours later, a text message came through, and all Paul could say was, "What the fuck?"

# Chapter 7

# OFFUTT AIR FORCE BASE

COLONEL JERRY JESSUP and his wife Pauline were enjoying a rare evening at home—they were binge-watching *NCIS* of all things—when his cell phone went off. Pauline sighed, hitting the pause button. He hesitated for a split second and then grabbed his phone from the coffee table where he'd propped up his feet.

"Jessup. What? Is this a Major Smith surprise drill? Shit. Okay, she certainly knows what to do. I'll be there in five."

"Problem at the base?"

"A commercial plane blew out a door and is making an emergency landing. This could be messy. I suspect I won't be back tonight." He'd said those last words far too many times. And then there was the follow on, which he tried not to make a throwaway line. "I'm so sorry—tonight was going to be just us."

"After twenty-five years, I know the drill. And never say you're sorry. You serve." She shrugged, gave a little smile, and offered a cheek, but he went for the full deep kiss. He really had looked forward to an evening alone with her. Her whispers in his ear brought a warmer smile. As he approached fifty, he still thought of himself as the tall, dashing fighter pilot she'd married out of the Academy. The pitch-black hair, the thick mustache, the swagger, and the chiseled physique all remained, even as his desk job nibbled away at the edges.

"Stay safe." She sent him off with a wistful look that said, *I'll be waiting when you get home.*

For the Jessups, this was just part of the deal they'd made with the

Air Force. When you combine patriotism with ambition you get a career military officer blind to the sacrifices that must be made. Proud of his service with the ego to match, Jessup would always say his family came first, but the country and his sense of duty regularly put him to the test.

"JJ," as he was called by friends, was Commander of the 55th Wing at Offutt Air Force Base. The Wing provided "intelligence, surveillance, and reconnaissance (ISR); electronic attack (EA); command and control (C2); and agile combat support"—at least that's the way it read on the website. Basically, they were air spooks who gathered information and used it for combat support.

When he yanked his car to a halt at the Emergency Services Hangar, JJ trotted inside to find a virtually empty, silent warehouse with flashing lights spiraling in the distance through the open hangar doors. This was about to go down. And he'd seen enough crash landings to know what it would be like. Then he heard the engine roar, the thunder, and the eruption.

"Shit. Where the hell is Washington?" Yelling that into an empty warehouse wasn't super useful, so he ran out to the flight line. Instantly, he felt at home in a world that had been his life. Choppers were already lit up and headed to the end of the runway, chased quickly by ambulances that were flying down the taxiway. Ground crews were getting equipment squared away and preparing for any casualties that wouldn't be flown straight to the hospital. For Jessup, there was an element of satisfaction—people knew their jobs and were doing them exactly as they'd been trained. He knew his shit and his team was on top of their game.

"Goddamn, where *is* Washington?" He ran into the operations office and grabbed a field radio. There was incessant chatter between the rescue teams trying to sort out the mess. He waited patiently for a break in the action. Finally. "This is Eagle-1." His call sign brought some quiet to the airwaves. "Falcon-2, come in, please."

"Falcon-2 here, sir. I'm in the main fuselage, evacuating survivors." At least Major Smith was where she was supposed to be.

"Status report?"

With some grunting, she said, "About what you'd expect when a

757 hits the runway hard. Everybody is beat up. Too early to tell on fatalities but too many. Team is on it."

"Anything you need from me, Falcon-2?"

"Negative. Birds and buses are here . . . expect incoming shortly. Washington is here coordinating with the battle staff."

"Roger that. I'll cover the back end." At least he knew his aide was following some protocol.

He switched to a security channel. "Eagle-1 for Hawkeye-2."

"Hawkeye-2 here." Major "Oggy" Ogginue was in charge of base security.

"Hawkeye-2, we need to get the base locked down. I don't want anyone other than Falcon-2's team near that plane. Nothing moves there that hasn't been authorized by me."

"Yes sir. The place is going to be crawling with press and looky-loos. I can stop them at the gate but that'll just send them to the perimeter, which might be worse."

JJ thought about how to manage the hordes that would descend on the base. His base. "Let's put credentialed press in one of the buildings out on Peacekeeper Drive—that's about as far from the crash site as you can get. Send Perry from Information Services over there to corral them. Have her tell those turkeys this is as close as they're going to get, and we'll have a statement for them when we're good and ready. And Oggy, make sure the gate guards are actually looking at their credentials."

Sigh. JJ felt like the ringmaster at a circus. "You should put some sentries around the rest of the perimeter. Active patrol. Arrest anyone who even comes close to the fence."

"Yes sir."

Part of JJ's security paranoia was about managing a crowd of people and enabling his team to do their work. That, of course, came first. But Offutt was not your average Air Force base. They were on a wartime footing with a significant amount of sensitive gear and the information that went with it. Security was always an issue, and a bunch of civilians running around was just unacceptable—especially the press.

He grabbed a chair to clear his head. The sirens and the lights radiating up from the airfield took him to another place and time. Ironically, that time he'd been in Captain Washington's shoes trying to create some order in the chaos—trying to save some lives. And he understood the manic motivation that drove Major Smith so relentlessly. He could still feel and smell the dust and the heat—his senses emblazoned permanently with an imprint of tragedy and death. The nightmares regularly woke him in a cold sweat. He blamed himself. He should have seen it coming last time.

He could have saved them all.

## Chapter 8

# FROM RUNWAY 12
# TO THE HOSPITAL

TAMIKA WAS OUT OF THE TRUCK before it had rocked back to equilibrium, running behind the vehicle and then full speed down the sloping grass bordering the runway. "Washington, get me some more light down here!" she yelled. Washington brought his head lamp around to the edge of the runway and looked down into the ditch. Tamika dropped down on all fours. She gently turned over something in the long grass and dirt. Amid the gloom she saw the bloody face of a man, still strapped into his seat, his leg hanging at an awkward angle.

*Jeezus*, she thought, *this had to be the missing passenger . . . Johnny.* As she touched his hand, she thought she felt the slightest of squeezes. *Holy shit.*

"He's alive but I don't think for long," she yelled up at Washington. "You don't bounce off a runway without internal bleeding."

Tamika cut him out of his mangled seat belt and checked as best she could for head or spinal injuries. Finding nothing obvious, and knowing that time was short, she hoisted him on her chest, bread-basket style. Then up the slope to the truck. Washington helped her carefully lay him in the back and climbed up to hold him in place. Tamika jumped in and hit the accelerator. Back to warp speed. At the same time, she got on the radio. "This is Falcon-2. I've got a critically injured male, early forties with a broken leg, facial lacerations, and likely internal injuries. We need an emergency evac to the trauma center—he's going to need surgery quick. Will be at the barn in thirty seconds."

She paused briefly, reflecting on the miracle of discovering Johnny in the dark, before speaking into the radio again. "Falcon-3, you there?"

"Yes ma'am." Laura "Lo" Velazquez was her second in command.

"What do we know?"

"Fifty-five confirmed dead—over a hundred and fifty injured. If the passenger and crew count was right, we still have three unaccounted for."

Tamika paused to absorb fifty-five more people dead on her watch. She wasn't going to allow another to be added to the list. "Falcon-3, triage and emergency services is your command now. I'm going to special deliver this one to the hospital."

"Roger that."

A Pave Hawk helicopter was returning from an evac run as they blew into the hangar area. Two corpsmen brought a stretcher over and they carried the injured man into the open bay of the bird. A modified version of the Army's well-chronicled Black Hawk, the Pave Hawk formed the bulk of the Air Force's combat search and rescue capability. Tamika had jumped into the belly of this beast more than once, and often under fire. Again, an uncomfortable feeling of déjà vu and a clear sense that this would be the last time.

"Hang in there, Johnny," she whispered to the unresponsive man. "Help is coming."

She yelled her plan to Washington as she hopped up, but he clearly didn't understand. Well, the Colonel would figure out where she'd gone eventually. Technically, she was supposed to lead the after-action process with her unit, but when "after" began was subject to interpretation. Velazquez knew enough to finish the recovery efforts and begin restoring some order to the facility without her. And Lo was going to have to do that on her own in the future, in any event.

Besides, Tamika was more interested in the miracle lying in front of her. She could not imagine him surviving the ejection from the plane. And how had she seen him out there in the dark while speeding down the runway? Whether she called it providence or serendipity, Major Tamika Smith believed extraordinary things happened for a reason—and she was going to find out why.

• • • • •

The bird rocked to a stop next to the parking lot at Nebraska Medical Center, one of two level-one trauma centers in the state and thankfully only ten miles due north of the Air Force base. Orderlies ran across the walkway connecting the helipad with Clarkson Tower, carefully lifting the wounded man out of the Pave Hawk and onto a hospital gurney. An attending female physician, who looked younger than Tamika thought possible, was immediately in conversation with the medics and ran with the gurney as it went into the hospital. Tamika followed along. She tried to get in a word with the doctor to let her know what happened.

"Major, I'm not new to the drill. We got this. Head inside and get cleaned up. You look as bad as he does." It was a polite way of saying "get the fuck out of the way and let me do my job." Pretty good bedside manner, given the circumstances.

Tamika sighed and trailed the gurney at a trot down the hallway as far as she could. They left her staring at two automatic swinging doors that made it clear she could not continue. She knew she probably shouldn't be here in any event—her real responsibilities lay with her team—but she was following an instinct. And her instincts were rarely wrong.

Taking the doctor's advice literally, Tamika went into the ladies' room to assess the damage. Yep, she looked like shit. Even by her own standards. Her helmet gear had turned her long, black hair into a wasp's nest, and her face was dark with soot, sand, dried blood, and several other gritty items stirred up by the crash. Just shy of six feet, and with strong, broad shoulders, she still looked like an athlete—but more of a decathlete now than the Olympic-class sprinter she'd been at the Academy. Though her brain was still high on adrenaline, the face in the mirror said "exhausted." Five minutes later, after an extreme scrub down and some straightening up, Tamika emerged from the rest room and went to the emergency room lobby.

She paused to look around and take stock.

For someone who had once considered a medical career and now spent her time triaging people, she hated hospitals. Tamika had spent way too many hours in one during her mom's cancer treatments and had vague but unpleasant memories of her father's stay after an ejection from a jet during carrier operations. Nebraska Medical Center looked a lot like the others. Out-of-date interior, lots of signs with different colors indicating various wings and departments, uncomfortable-looking chairs in the lobby. This one happened to have a big fish tank right in the middle.

Her cell phone suddenly sprang to life. Colonel JJ Jerkoff.

"Smith here. Yes sir, we found a survivor that was ejected from the plane. I just delivered him here at the trauma center. I'm checking in on other survivors . . . Captain Velazquez, sir . . . I'm sure she can handle the initial work . . . Yes sir, I know I don't work for the Red Cross." Her favorite commander was yelling at her for essentially deserting her post. Not technically true, but still.

She hung up—or more accurately he hung up, leaving her staring at "Call Ended." To no one in particular, Tamika said, "Four hours ago he didn't give a shit about CSAR and now he wants me following him around the accident site."

"We all have our masters, Major." The doctor from the helipad had somehow snuck up behind her. "I sometimes wonder if any of them remember doing our jobs." A tired smile on the physician's face showed that she was trying to make a connection.

"Doctor—good God, I didn't even get your name."

"Jansen . . . Lil Jansen. I thought you might like to know more about your Hail Mary patient. I understand he was ejected from the plane and you found him up the runway in a ditch."

"Yeah. I have no idea how I saw him in the darkness down in the gully. And I can't believe he survived the thrashing."

"Well, we sent him straight up for surgery," Jansen said. "He's got some broken bones which will heal, but his insides are all beat up and he has a grade three concussion. I just want to be real with you that his chances are less than fifty/fifty."

Tamika dropped her head and just stared at the floor. This one had already gotten under her skin. She thought of the elderly couple and what this would mean to them. She really did believe in providence and signs from God and was hoping this would be a positive omen somehow. Now it might just be another nick taken out of her already deeply troubled soul.

Composing herself, she looked up saying, "I'm sorry I was such an ass on the helipad. I know how things are supposed to go. I probably should've stayed on the helo and gone straight back to base. Or so my commander tells me. Thanks for coming out and letting me know his status. I'll . . ." Tamika floundered slightly. "I'll pray, I guess."

"Major, I'm just a second-year emergency room doc, but you and I are in the same business. Don't be ashamed of caring. The minute you stop caring, you need to do something else. Sounds like you've got to go back to the base in any event, but his name is Humboldt. John Humboldt. He won't be out of surgery for four or five hours, but you can check on him then."

Tamika managed a smile, which got her a quick hug from Doctor Jansen in return. She turned and walked out of the hospital with her head held up.

# Chapter 9

# NIGHT'S END

TAMIKA DROVE OUT to the crash site around midnight to meet with the Colonel. The runway was lit with large floodlights in preparation for the first Federal Aviation Administration and National Transportation Safety Board investigators who would sift through the debris. In the stark halos of light, the remains of the plane took on an eerie glow. The carcass of a giant dinosaur stretched out in the sand and grass surrounding the runway. Those who had perished were lined up in body bags ready to be taken to the morgue. Tamika had been on the front lines before, but this would leave her with a whole new set of images to visit her in the night.

The irony was not lost on her. The day had begun with an abortive meeting with Colonel Jessup to propose an emergency-preparedness drill for the base.

Jessup's response had been predictable. "Major, if you've done your job to train your team, they'll be ready."

Bullshit. It wasn't that simple. The data didn't lie. A full disaster drill had been put off for too long. But she'd been stopped short by her commanding officer's cursory decision only three slides into her presentation. "Sir, I have a mix of experienced personnel and new recruits who are just figuring out how to gear up. We need a live drill to pull the team together."

"Last time I looked, good teamwork was a function of the leadership. That's your job, Major. That'll be all."

"But—"

"Dismissed."

Why did he have to be such a prick?

Sure, she'd known that getting Jessup to shut down the base for a CSAR drill was a long shot. Earlier that morning Nebraska had seemed like an unlikely location for a military incident. And nobody got ribbons or promotions simply for being well-prepared.

Oh, and there was the reality that she was a reservist. A female reservist. Who had never flown a plane. Apparently, three Middle East tours didn't buy you much credibility unless you had wings and a penis.

But it wasn't just Colonel Jessup's dismissal of her plan that bothered her. She knew opportunities, roadblocks, and challenges were part of life. What she really hated was the Colonel's attitude—arrogance and pettiness were not traits she tolerated well. Nor were they attributes that led to great performance from the rest of the staff. She had seen far too much of that in Alabama, and her body gave an involuntary shudder at the mere thought. "Don't go down that rabbit hole now, girl," she said to herself.

God, she hated that she still couldn't rid herself of the guilt after almost twenty years.

Covering her ass (or her "6" as they liked to say) with the drill request was part of military life. But now that things had crashed and burned on Runway 12, *her* neck was on the line for any mistakes. Which had Tamika wondering about the Colonel's reasons for asking her to meet him now.

She pulled the jeep to a stop above the main body of the fuselage and joined Jessup for an inspection. As they walked together, Tamika watched him maneuver around the ruined hulk, his eyes constantly scanning. Colonel Jessup was ten years older than Tamika, with hundreds of hours in combat conditions, and, like most on the base, she respected him for his operational skills. But he had gotten stuck at the rank of Colonel, "Peter Principled" in the funnel that was the Air Force promotion list. Whatever the roadblock—and Tamika and others had speculated about that ad nauseum—it left the 55th with an experienced leader who was often bitter and had little patience for anything not related to mission status.

"Well, Major, looks like we were both right earlier today—your team got its training—and they were better prepared than you expected."

"In my training, nobody would have died." Dismissiveness implied.

"I know you think I'm an asshole, Major. But it'd probably be better if you hid your feelings just a bit. I was trying to pay you a compliment. And for the record, I know firsthand the trauma your team will face . . . and it sucks."

Tamika decided the best course of action was to keep walking. They moved around the main fuselage to the door that had failed. JJ crouched down to the remains of the door frame. He moved his hands around the entire structure, examining some marks on the ceiling of the wreck. No, she'd been wrong . . . that was the floor of the plane.

"Shit," he said. Tamika waited for an explanation but was greeted with a stone-cold stare. Just an expletive followed by silence.

"What is it, sir?"

Eventually, Colonel Jessup continued. "You and your team did the uniform proud. Make sure they know that."

"Washington stepped up and did some great work, too. He deserves as much recognition as anyone."

"Major, I wasn't aware he'd been transferred to your command—I will figure out how to deal with him later. I assume you can handle the after-action reporting without him. Use the opportunity to help your team develop. Take as much time as you need on the full report. If I'm right about this, your work is going to be reviewed by way more important people than me. No mistakes." He paused as a cloud seemed to pass across his face.

"Captain Washington, if he's still around, will get you on the agenda to report out to the full staff. I'll deal with the press and the aftermath—seems to be my role in life these days."

"Yes sir." Salute. Good riddance.

Tamika left the Colonel, wondering why he was so focused on the reporting. She jumped on a truck heading back to the hangar. Their CSAR workspace, which was more like a warehouse, was big and airy with plenty of metal and aluminum—so every small sound echoed, resonating up and down the building. And the quieter it got, the more you noticed the noise.

Most of her team was still there, some just sitting around staring off into the distance, others going through the mechanics of cleaning and reassembling gear, a few talking quietly. This was not the locker room after a big win on the field. Instead, it felt more like a memorial church service before the opening hymn.

None of this was new to Tamika or to the experienced members of her team. When you are in the business of saving lives, but also have to experience the reality of tragic death, there is no celebrating a job well done. All you can hope for is some sense of understanding and closure, and it was up to Tamika to bring that to her team. Speeches were not really her gig, but, for whatever reason, she had a lot to say on this occasion. Maybe it had something to do with the life still hanging in the balance back at the hospital.

"Okay, everyone, take a seat and listen up." How did the hangar get so quiet? Tamika sat down on the hood of a Humvee, put her helmet down beside her, closed her eyes, and let the words come out.

"I know we all thought today would follow the regular routine. But then something terrible happened to some innocent civilians. For them, what started as just another day turned deadly in a hurry. I will only say this once—because it is true and must be said. You did God's work out there tonight. You set aside your own safety and you saved lives. The shitty thing is that the people you saw dead or dying tonight will probably stay with you for a while. I'd like to say there is a magical cure for that—a way to wipe it from your mind and just move on—but that's not how it works. There's nothing easy about this. So don't be afraid to ask for help, and I mean professional help."

She paused, shifting her perch on the Humvee to buy some time. She looked down at her boots and brushed off some dirt. Her eyes closed and opened slowly, a deep breath taken. Then she looked up and began again:

"Forget everything about rank and chain of command and Air Force discipline. I hope you'll take what I'm about to say as thoughts from a friend. Because if you want to survive in this business, there are things you need to know." That brought some heads up and some odd looks.

Tamika continued. "I'm not a shrink, but I've been around this block. If you want to stay sane in search and rescue, it starts with faith. Some of you know I'm a Catholic, but I'm not here to sell you on the Church. I'm talking about a faith that is more about humankind. To do what we do, you must believe that good will come from it. You must know with conviction that you did everything you could to help others. Even when some you tried to save didn't make it. And you *absolutely* must have faith in humanity." The silence got deeper. Nobody moved.

"Even if your faith is strong, you'll also need a different type of strength if you want to survive disasters like today." Tamika's pace settled as she relaxed a bit. "You have to find the grit to confront the crises that are bound to come your way. Today was the last thing I needed in my life—climbing into that wreckage ripped open a bunch of old wounds—and yet that's what we're called to do. Persevere. Face the danger with heads up, bodies strong, and minds determined. When we do that, nothing can stop us."

Some of the veteran heads were nodding.

Tamika jumped off the Humvee and walked a bit, the movement releasing more thoughts. "If you have faith, if you persevere, the cosmic ball will roll your way. I believe that out of the good and bad of these tragedies, opportunities will appear that can change our lives for the better. Innocent people died today. We can't change that. But with the slamming of those doors, new doors will be opened. Lives will change, paths will shift, new directions will be found."

The hangar was deathly quiet. Tamika paused. She'd never said or done anything like that with this team or with any other team. She didn't even know she had it in her. But it felt strangely good to express her innermost thoughts—a release of pressure from the tensions bottled up inside. Maybe it helped the others at the same time.

"Again, I'm very proud of what you did tonight. And Colonel Jessup asked me to pass on his praise as well. End of speech. Get yourselves squared away and get the hell out of here. Team leaders—we meet at 1400 for after-action report planning.

"Dismissed."

# Chapter 10

# DAWN'S LIGHT

*I'M TOAST*, thought Tamika Smith.

The runner's burn felt good. Of course, it also reminded her that she was no longer on active duty. When did staying in shape become real work? She used to be able to whip most of the men on base. As an elite sprinter during her Air Force Academy days, she had scored at the extreme end of the competitive scale. Three tours of duty in the deserts and mountains of Afghanistan and Iraq had further steeled her body to deal with extremes. Now thirty-nine years old, age probably had as much to do with her exhaustion as her training regimen. Still, admitting defeat to Father Time just wasn't in her nature.

She put her hands on her knees and puffed out the excess carbon dioxide built up from several circuits on the flatlands surrounding her adopted home. Training in the semi-dark at 0600 was not your typical post-action experience, but somehow it had been the logical thing for her to do. No way she was going to get much sleep—better to take a long run around the base to put her mind and body back together. And her thoughts were a spaghetti plate full of tangled strings.

Beyond the trauma of the previous day and the stress of the performance evaluation that was sure to follow, her on-again, off-again role in the Air Force was front and center. The proverbial clock ticking on her career trajectory was a constant source of anxiety and frustration—and the purgatory of reserve duty made that worse. As willing to serve as anyone, the current disruption to her civilian career was driving a wedge between her personal goals and her patriotic sensibilities.

As she walked into her room in the Visiting Officer's Quarters (VOQ), Tamika picked up a thick letter next to her computer. She opened the envelope slowly, just as she had when it arrived two days ago. Tamika had turned to her father for advice—something she did with great trepidation, given his lifelong love for the Air Force and his extreme sense of duty and military correctness. When your father is General Frank Smith, you have to question his objectivity.

He had kept his distance since her shift to reserve status—another reason for her to wonder how he would respond to her latest thoughts. But the truth was, he was all she had left. The long (really long) letter he had sent in response to their short phone conversation was totally unexpected. Insightful and tender, it reminded her why he'd been so successful in his career. Most important, it made her think . . . especially those last few paragraphs.

> . . . *Old warhorses like me all face the question at some point in their life: "Am I ready to take on my next gig?" Some have made good choices and been able to walk away with their pride and integrity intact. Others have struggled with redefining their purpose and self-worth. When it comes to job and career re-alignment, timing is everything. Each of us must ask, "Am I self-aware enough to know when my time has arrived?"*
>
> *I think you know the answers to these questions and probably don't need my advice. You've always been your own person and that makes me smile inside. I know you'll make the right decision for you. And I will support you every step of the way.*
>
> *It's now 0200 so I should sign off. I will say a prayer for you— for your safety and for the insight you need to move forward. You know that Mom and Alex are watching and waiting.*
>
> *With love and hopes for your forgiveness,*
>
> *Dad*

As well as she knew him, her father always had a few surprises up his sleeve. The letter was classic General Smith stuff—complete with structure, bullet points (but never more than five), and carefully underlined catchphrases. He probably filed it in triplicate with a copy sent to military archives. Yet, for the first time in a long time, she saw the size of his heart. And that brought a warm feeling inside. Who would've guessed? Maybe that's why her mom had put up with all the military nonsense. Maybe that was the love she saw all those years ago.

Tamika put the letter back in the envelope knowing that her father was right. She knew she resented the way her current call-up was interfering with her civilian life. And now she knew the nightmares would return—complete with the faces of more people she had lost. Maybe it was time to put this phase of her life behind her for good. Declare victory and move on to her "Act II" permanently.

When she left her quarters to get some breakfast, the base was more alive than usual. Disasters will do that to a military post. Surprisingly, she was greeted enthusiastically by several people she did not know while walking across the courtyard.

"Congratulations!" "Nice biceps, Major." "Way to rock it, girl." And, "Damn how did you do that?"

Tamika knew her team had done some good work the previous day but could not figure out why everyone was focused on her—and the comments were so unmilitary, with a familiarity and lack of protocol that was unusual on base. She finally grabbed someone and asked what the hell everyone was talking about.

"Major, it's all over the internet: You're a hero."

Oh hell, what the fuck was that about?

# Chapter 11

# A MORNING BRIEFING

COLONEL JERRY JESSUP had watched in frustration as divisiveness took hold across the United States. The country had spent eighteen years at war with an enemy that it could not see, an army it could not effectively fight, and an opposition that kept developing new leaders to chase and kill. It was a fight that JJ took very personally. The nearly crippling recession in 2008 made matters much worse, exposing deeper problems that included racial tensions, gender bias, income inequality, an opioid epidemic, and police violence. All of this was reflected in the world of politics, where many people didn't want to vote for either candidate in the 2016 presidential election, with the result dividing the country in two.

Now Jessup had an opportunity to add his own agenda to the mashup that was the nation's fractured psyche. The NTSB and FAA folks were just getting started with their investigation and wouldn't talk to the Colonel or anyone else for that matter. But based on his initial inspection, JJ already knew the truth.

And it was the perfect opportunity for some redemption. Out of tragedy could come the rebirth of his career.

Before anyone in his command chain could get things organized or under wraps, he called an impromptu press conference at 0630. When news broke about the crash, the media had naturally flocked to the base, but Oggy and his security team had kept them at a distance. The press had done their best to report on the story by interviewing some survivors who were now off-base, talking to doctors, and trying to get information from other Air Force personnel. And while they'd had some success, they ultimately were left reporting random details from within an abandoned airplane hangar. Which meant the jackals were out for blood by the time JJ arrived. And he fully intended to give them some meat to chew on.

Lieutenant Sabrina Perry, who had been fending off press inquiries for almost ten hours, acted as a press secretary, asking everyone to gather in folding chairs that had been arranged in five semicircular rows on the concrete floor of the hangar. Cameras and the associated spaghetti and octopus set of cables and cords were set up at the back of the crowd. JJ, now in full uniform, had their attention as he came to the podium—and he had to admit it felt good to be relevant again.

"Good morning. My name is Colonel Jerry Jessup and I'm the commanding officer here at Offutt Air Force Base. I certainly wish we were here under better circumstances. As you know, a commercial 757 attempted an emergency landing last night at 2001 local time—that's 8:01 p.m. I know that all of you have been trying to get to the crash site but given the nature of our work here, that just won't be possible. Instead, I'd like to give you as much information as we have at this time."

A low murmur rose in the crowd restless with anticipation. JJ went on to provide details on the flight, the first responder response, and the status of passengers and crew. The record would show that the people on Flight 209 were remarkably lucky. Of the 213 passengers and crew on board, fifty-five died in the immediate crash, while 154 survived with injuries ranging from broken bones to various degrees of trauma requiring surgery. The lives of the remaining four, including Johnny Humboldt, hung in the balance.

"I want to emphasize the incredible skill of the pilots and crew of Flight 209. I've been a pilot all my life, flown combat missions in Bosnia and Iraq, and had to bring back damaged aircraft. Given the destruction I witnessed during my inspection of the site, only a heroic effort kept the plane aloft long enough for them to reach the airfield." Behind him, a picture of the crash site appeared—the same long-distance shot the Air Force had released earlier to the media.

JJ was reserving his best ammunition for last. "I also want to commend the first responders, especially our search and rescue teams here at

Offutt, for their incredible efforts to save lives. They went into the fuse-lage when it was still on fire and pulled over one hundred and fifty people to safety. And as some of you have seen on the internet this morning, we also rescued someone who was ejected from the plane over a thousand yards from the final crash site. A miracle indeed."

And with that he flashed the only other picture he would show during the press conference. On a pitch-black background lit by a head-lamp, a badly wounded and unconscious man was being carried up an embankment in the arms of a woman smeared in soot and blood with a look on her face that expressed extreme effort and great care. The han-gar went church-service quiet as people absorbed the image. It was like an angel carrying a martyr to his refuge—except it was a Black woman carrying a white man to safety.

"That's Major Tamika Smith—who not only saved lives but leads our entire Combat Search and Rescue effort at Offutt."

Colonel Jessup was not done.

"The NTSB and FAA have begun their official investigation, and of course will be responsible for that ongoing work because it involves a commercial airplane. But the crash also took place on an active US Air Force base, where we take our obligation to protect and serve very seri-ously. And this is a high-security installation. I've already reported to my superiors in Washington, DC, that I believe this crash was not the result of a failed door on an aging airframe as many of you have reported. The only thing that could produce the kind of damage I saw on the main fuselage is a bomb. The United States government will investigate this as an *act of terrorism*."

With that, all hell broke loose. "Has anyone taken responsibility for the attack?" came a yell from the back. "Is there a terrorist cell oper-ating here?" was the next question from a woman at the front. "Why didn't we have any advanced intel on this?" the Fox News correspondent demanded. The press corps just kept bombarding the Colonel, who sub-consciously enjoyed the fact that he was in control of the situation. He quickly declined all further requests for comment, citing national security. Reporters and crews thrashed around to get reports filed, to do live feeds to their local and national affiliates, and to find someone—anyone—who would comment on Colonel Jessup's proverbial bombshell.

• • • • •

JJ didn't see his wife until much later that day. Instead of heading home, he returned immediately to his office and pondered the chaos he knew would follow his announcements. He looked again at the photo he'd shown during the press conference. At the end of a long twelve hours, amidst all the violence and death, a photo of a Black woman rescuing a white man out of a dirty ditch was sure to go viral in one of those social media frenzies that now passed as news coverage. JJ's instincts told him the picture would join a short list of iconic images that somehow captures and personifies the state of the nation in a time of crisis.

Colonel Jerry Jessup had been here before.

Terrorists had brought the attack back to the homeland, demonstrating once again that no place was truly safe. Major Tamika Smith and John Quincy Humboldt were now symbols of an America at war with others and with itself. A war that had begun years earlier, on another fateful day.

# PART 2

## BACK IN THE DAY

They say that anger is just love disappointed.
They say that love is just a state of mind.
But all this fighting over who is anointed,
Oh, how can people be so blind?
Oh, they tell me there's a place over yonder
Cool water running through the burning sand.
Until we learn to love one another,
We will never reach the Promised Land.
There's a hole in the world tonight.
There's a cloud of fear and sorrow.
There's a hole in the world tonight.
Don't let there be a hole in the world tomorrow.

**—Don Henley and Glenn Frey**

## Chapter 12

# MONTGOMERY, YEARS EARLIER

*WHAP, WHAP, WHAP.* The rhythmic patter of the shoes on the red, Mondo-surfaced track at Alabama State University carried through the silent air. It was 0700 and Second Lieutenant Tamika Smith was well into a grueling workout of wind sprints stretching from 100 meters to 400 meters around a track that was beginning to heat up with the humid Alabama air. She hugged the corner, leaning into the curve as she flew around the far edge of the track, running with a grace and fluidity that seemed to absorb any sounds around her. This was just the steady effort involved in her daily practice routines. When races demanded, she could bring out a ferocity that ratcheted up the turnover in her stride and seemed to generate its own slipstream. At twenty-two, she was just coming into her prime as a sprinter.

The sweat felt good. The slightly labored breathing was a joy.

The intense concentration on her technique took her to a different place—a welcome break from a daily routine that was quickly becoming a nightmare. Her mind gladly went back to the recent World Championships in Edmonton and her 400-meter semi-final heat. As she had eased into the blocks, everything seemed to clear. The capacity crowd, clapping and yelling, faded into the background. Just white noise from a distant freeway. She leaned back and said a silent prayer to her mom. Then she carefully placed her thumbs and forefingers just behind the line on the track. She stretched both legs by kicking back like a ballet dancer who was lying on the ground. Finally settling back on her heels, she looked down the lane. All she could see was her path around that first curve. Relax, ease through the turn, set your stride.

Tunnel vision.

The chirp of the starter's gun propelled her out of the blocks in Lane 2. From there she could see most of the runners ahead of her on the stagger. The German in Lane 4, Grit Breuer, pushed the early pace, which was just fine with Tamika. Fast early meant dying legs at the end. Once out of the curve, she settled into a nice rhythm down the back stretch, focused on her breathing. She'd not made up any ground on the Russian in Lane 3, but just holding her own was a good sign—and the final curve would draw her closer just because of the shorter distance. Breuer continued to push the pace. All Tamika could do was hold her form and dig a bit deeper. The crowd was now swelling in the background, but the stony silence remained in Tamika's head.

The real pain began at the end of the second curve with 100 meters to the tape. As sprints go, the 400 is a run-hard-and-hold-on event and that was clearly Breuer's strategy. Strides got choppy, heads pulled back, and the fight for survival was on. Tamika could feel her lungs burning, but this was what she loved about the 400. She knew she was tougher than anyone in the field—maybe not as fast, but capable of pushing through the agony better.

With thirty meters left, Breuer was out of reach. But the Russian was fading. Second was a real possibility. And second meant an automatic spot in the final. And making the final was the difference between a great runner and an Olympic hopeful. Tamika had no acceleration left but she held her stride through the line, lunging a bit with her head bouncing down and legs struggling to stay upright.

Eight exhausted women just beyond the finish, each fighting hard to catch their breath. Some were bent over, while others leaned back with their hands behind their heads. In the end, it was a well-timed lean—something she'd practiced for the 200 again and again—that took her over the top. When Tamika looked up, her name was second in a personal best of 50.93. Her first time under fifty-one seconds.

Now back in the Alabama sunshine, she walked off the end of her workout and tried to focus on her athletic future. Competing in the Olympics was a lifelong dream for the newly minted Air Force Academy graduate, and the races in Edmonton had demonstrated that she had what it took to compete for a medal. With the military on a peace-time footing, she was accepted into the Air Force World Class Athlete Program, or WCAP, so that she could serve her five years of mandatory duty and prepare for the Olympics at the same time.

Tamika had been assigned to Maxwell Air Force Base in Montgomery, Alabama, to train as a Combat Search and Rescue specialist. She was excited about the CSAR opportunity because it mixed her interest in medicine with the ability to serve actively in combat zones. Her training would include parachute certification, dive training, SERE survival skills, as well as a full battery of leadership development classes. To Tamika, this was the all-you-can-eat buffet of military training.

It seemed like a perfect fit.

Her first few trips off-base into Montgomery had proven her wrong. She had grown up as a biracial military brat following her father around the world. But the Deep South was a totally new cultural experience. She quickly realized that the affluent and depressed parts of town were still racially divided. And she had this eerie feeling that whites were looking at her suspiciously when she shopped off-base, even when she wore her uniform.

Tamika didn't want to be a prisoner to Maxwell—that would not fit her style—and yet she felt totally out of place and unaccepted when she left the compound. The daughter of a Caucasian father and Black mother and the product of an ethnically diverse military, she was reminded that racism was alive and well in twenty-first-century America. Some things hadn't changed.

And then she'd ventured into town with a group of officers for what turned into a beer and pool bar crawl across the underbelly of Montgomery. What started as an opportunity to relax with some new-found friends had turned dark and painful in the blink of an eye. That night changed everything for her. It transformed how she thought about herself. It altered her outlook on the world. It brought bitterness and anger into the body and soul of a once eternally optimistic person.

She would never be the same.

With each step of her training, she tried to pound the bad memories from that night a bit further into her subconscious. Even though she'd finished fifth in the 400 final, Tamika knew that Edmonton was a jumping-off point for her running career. Whatever pain she was in personally, she needed to find a way to leave that in the barracks and on the base. To find a way of knowing that her Olympic dream was alive. Perhaps more challenged, but still burning deep and strong. She'd written a long letter to her brother, Alex, asking for his advice. He was her rock, and she knew his response would open the doors to a better present and a brighter future.

So began her day. One foot in front of the other. Tamika knew she needed to move forward and show she was the toughest of the tough. Just hustle back to the base. Shower. Eat. Parachute training. And do it again and again until she couldn't remember the rest.

But as she reached the base, the good Lord had another idea. Tamika watched Maxwell Air Force Base coming alive like a hornet's nest poked by a burning stick. Clanging alarms brought crews rushing across the hangars and pilots in jumpsuits moving with a singular purpose to the flight line.

Planes fired up. Weapons hot. What the hell?

# Chapter 13

# NEW YORK CITY

IT WAS 7:45 A.M. on a not-so-typical Tuesday morning, and traffic near his Gramercy apartment was brutal. As Johnny Humboldt stared out the window of his cab, he realized that "brutal" was the perfect way to describe his last few days. When you worked as a financial analyst at a Wall Street investment bank, you knew your schedule could be blown up at any moment. And this past weekend, his plans had been destroyed. "Financial analyst" was the title investment banks gave the best and brightest they could find from undergraduate schools, and while it sounded important, a better title would have been "grunt-in-residence." And shit definitely flowed downhill.

He'd planned a weekend away in the Hamptons with his girlfriend Maggie—a chance for them to spend serious time together after a crazy few weeks. Margaret Ashworth was a Teach for America teacher in Lower Manhattan, and the beginning of the school year meant starting with a new class of kids. It also meant starting her second year of grad school studies. Johnny had been working non-stop on a three-month aerospace industry project and had completed a big presentation for the head of the department on the previous Thursday. Johnny and Maggie had both been due for some time off—and some time together.

He replayed the weekend in his mind, ignoring the incessant honking of cars in the morning rush of traffic. Maggie had called him around 4 p.m. on Friday.

"Hey honey," she said sweetly. "I hope you're ready to show me a good time?" She liked to play the tease, and she knew Johnny enjoyed it.

"You bet. I hope you've got some special things in mind."

"That depends on how often you have to call in to work." She couldn't resist pushing his type-A buttons.

"Yeah, yeah. All work and no play. Let me finish a couple of things here and I'll be yours for the weekend. Want to meet for the 5:45 train?"

"I'll be the good-looking one trying to pick out her man. If you're late, you lose."

"You know I never, ever lose. See you soon."

Fifteen minutes later, Demi Wilson made him regret those words. As the assignments associate, it was her job to staff every project with the analysts that had the right skills for the scope and difficulty of the job. Johnny had been in avoidance mode all day. But she had a warm smile, nice curves, and a look that said she was available, even when she wasn't. Tough to say no to Demi.

"Jesus, Demi. I've busted my butt for the past month on that aerospace analysis. You can't possibly tie me up on something new already. I just got off the phone with my girlfriend and she's waiting for me at Penn Station. I don't have any way to call her to cancel. She's going to kill me."

"Look, I know it sucks. The firm will make up for it somehow. Dinner, the ballet, the Ritz, whatever. You were right about the smaller aerospace guys needing more capital . . . they're out looking to get financed or bought."

"Are we on the buy or sell side?" He couldn't help himself.

"Maclaughlin brought us in for the buy—our first time working with them in five years."

"Who's the target?"

"Patterson Electronics."

Patterson would have been at the top of his list financially, but Johnny was intrigued to find out why their quixotic founder had decided to cash in. "Wow . . . I didn't think he would ever sell. Everyone is going to want in."

"Including you, right? First meeting is in fifteen minutes in Midgley's office."

Johnny spent Friday night, all of Saturday, and the first half of Sunday playing with the numbers trying to see how he could make them sing and dance. The stated goal was to help Maclaughlin determine a fair price for the company and establish the financial structure of their bid, along with a strategy that would put them ahead of other potential buyers. His job was to make Jerrod Midgley, the senior partner on the deal, look brilliant.

In the midst of all of this work, Johnny had missed Maggie's first (and last) call, which went to voicemail. He should have phoned her at the bed and breakfast he'd reserved—or maybe taken the work with him and jumped on a late train. The truth was that he'd gotten deep into the analysis and by the time it crossed his mind to call it was too late. Calling on Saturday just seemed like a wasted effort. Maggie's message back to him was self-explanatory and confirmed the futility.

"You're an absolute asshole. Self-absorbed. Obsessed with money. Workaholic. And those are your best qualities. I meant what I said on the phone. You lose." Click.

It was time to man up or move on. Johnny enjoyed being with Maggie—she was smart, fun-loving, athletic enough, and plenty good looking. And her family had lots of money. This was the perfect Harvard match.

But did that mean he loved her? More to the point, what was love anyway? Could he commit to one person for the rest of his life? For someone who didn't believe in anyone but himself, that was an almost impossible thought. Where did Maggie fit in his holy trinity of Work, Status, and Money?

After he'd finished most of the Patterson analysis, he stepped back to put his thoughts into words. At 3 a.m. on Monday morning, he wrote Maggie a letter. He at least owed her that. He chuckled a bit at the thought of writing a self-inflicted "Dear John" letter. Naturally, he ended with a last-ditch pitch for forgiveness.

*Sadly, I can't promise that I'll change. In fact, I think it's pretty unlikely. I am who I am—and the good news is that you know what that means. I have no idea if that is enough for us to build a life together. I'd like to try. Who knows, maybe someday your God will reach down and whack me on the head. Maybe then I'll change my ways.*

*There is always hope, and I hope you'll give me a chance to at least say I'm sorry in person.*

*My love,*

*Johnny*

As he reread the missive, he realized that without even thinking about it, he was trying to find a way to win. Was keeping Maggie part of the conquest or was it what he really wanted? Sometimes he couldn't tell the difference. And mostly he didn't care. Losing her somehow just meant . . . losing. And failure was not an option.

"Hey, buddy, we're here." The cabbie's words brought him back to Tuesday morning and his present task. Johnny was at the Marriott Hotel on Liberty Street to get Maclaughlin's signature on an offer letter to buy Patterson Electronics for just over one billion dollars. He found the CEO with his team, eating breakfast in the obligatory restaurant just off the hotel lobby.

"Johnny, why don't you join us for breakfast?" the CEO suggested. "Jerrod Midgley is great at what he does, but we know you did all of the analysis. I hope we're going to be doing plenty of work together in the coming weeks."

Midgley had been brilliant making the pitch, but Johnny couldn't help but revel in the important role he'd played—regardless of the personal cost.

"Thank you for the offer," he replied, trying to sound grateful. "I'd love to stay, but I need to get this bid uptown to the DBC Bank offices and traffic looked awful coming down." As he left them with another wave of thanks, he briefly contemplated heading to the subway. It would undoubtedly be faster, but he just didn't feel like dealing with the crush of humanity. Now on the street, his hand went up to flag a cab.

He paused with the cab door open to marvel at a low-flying plane. At first, what he saw just didn't register. His brain rejected the image outright as being so absurd that it couldn't be possible. When he saw a landing gear wheel fall on the top of the Marriott, he knew it was real enough.

"Go, go, go!" he screamed at the cabbie.

# Chapter 14

# LOWER MANHATTAN

MAGGIE ASHWORTH WAS just a few blocks away at her charter school, already well into her first lesson of the day, reviewing basic computation skills with her fourth graders. Today she was sailing into the world of fractions, which was almost certainly the first concept her students had forgotten during the heat and distractions of the summer. But the only thing fractional on Maggie's mind was the gash in her heart left by a weekend of disappointment and anger. Sleep had never really come the previous night. She had given up early in the pre-dawn and finally decided to read Johnny's letter. It had been waiting for her along with a bouquet of flowers.

Her boyfriend was charming in person, and when he was motivated, he could convince most people that water flowed uphill and the sun rose in the west. One of the other financial analysts had described Johnny as "sometimes right, sometimes wrong, but always certain." He most definitely could make you question your own grasp on the facts. His note had proved the point, alternating between an apology and hints at a proposal. She thought about "for better or worse," "happily ever after," and "till death do us part." She was confident that Johnny did not appreciate any of that, only that marriage could be tallied as another personal achievement. And that would likely never change.

"Ms. Ashworth," interrupted one of her charges, with her hand in the air. "Why do you flip the fraction when you do division?" Maggie smiled ruefully. Her life was indeed being turned upside down and she didn't know what to do about it.

She had an open second period, so when the opportunity came, she went outside the school for a short walk to clear her head. Johnny always told her he had stayed a third year at the bank so she could finish up her second year with Teach for America. But Maggie knew the truth was almost certainly the reverse. She had followed Johnny to New York, using TFA to fulfill her goal of social responsibility while staying close to the magnetic heat source in her social life.

Now a five-year relationship was crashing and burning at her feet. Her emotions were a group of bumper cars banging into each other with no apparent means of control. She needed to breathe deep, sort through the mess, and get herself calmed down.

Her relationship with Johnny had always been a bit of an amusement park ride, but the excitement was the glue that kept them together. He was Einstein-smart, worked his ass off, had a mischievous sense of humor, and was already on his way to financial security. He'd grown up in a lower-middle-class neighborhood in Detroit—an only child with a father who worked in a Ford factory—but he was blessed with physical and intellectual gifts not found anywhere in his family tree. Pick a sport and he was good at it. Attend a class, he dominated it. Express an opinion, he had a point of view. High school valedictorian. Harvard scholarship. Captain of the rowing team. What was a girl not to like?

Okay . . . perhaps he was self-absorbed, competitive about everything, and lacked basic emotional skills like compassion, love, and faith. Oh . . . that.

The real question, of course, was why did she care? If he was such a self-absorbed, emotionless prick, why not just move on? Now that was a complicated question. One that went all the way back to introductory Spanish at Harvard.

"Mary, who's the hunk in the second row over there . . . the one with the ape shoulders?"

"His name is Johnny Humboldt. Rower, genius, and ego all rolled into one. I don't think I'd tangle with him. But if you want, all you need to do is give him a good look. He'll chase a prize."

By the end of class, he had lived up to his reputation.

"Hi, I'm Johnny. Did you understand anything he said in there?"

Not the most creative line, but the body and tone were good compensation. Her newfound attraction was tall, with brown eyes, brown hair, and a cocky smile. The look was "Harvard" but something about him also said "social climber."

"Not really but I wasn't paying much attention. Too many distractions." Smile.

After a few more pleasantries, he stopped beating around the bush. "And we're having a party tomorrow night at the boathouse," he told her, looking a little bit bashful for the first time. "Any chance you'd come with me?"

Mary was right. This wasn't going to be difficult.

Their first date was the beginning of a revelation for Margaret Ashworth. She'd lived for eighteen years as her socialite parents' daughter and now was realizing she could be whoever she wanted to be. Johnny opened her eyes to all kinds of new avenues for exploration and was her personal tour guide. He had just the right amount of confidence, patience, and irreverence to push her to find herself. By the time she graduated four years later, Maggie had rebelled against her parents' plans for her (upscale marriage, kids, and garden parties) and gotten serious about pursuing her own ambitions—ones that defined her as a populist woman intent on making the world a better place.

Margaret had become Maggie.

She tried to put all of that in the context of her current raging anger. Maggie was upset, yet reflective. Fuming, but appreciative. Ready to end the relationship, and still hopeful that he would somehow find a way to change. If she owed so much of her growth and development to Johnny, how could he be bad for her? Was he a total jerk, a good friend, or a future husband? Or maybe all three?

*BOOM!*

A resounding explosion echoed across the canyons of Lower Manhattan, interrupting Maggie mid-step. Looking up in the direction of the sound, all she could say was "Holy shit."

And then she ran for the school.

# Chapter 15

# THE BROOKLYN BRIDGE

A FEW BLOCKS FURTHER EAST, Charles Roscovitch's state of mind was not much better than Maggie's. He and Shea had arrived in New York the night before and consulted with the DBC Bank team before heading to bed. They'd told him they expected at least six companies to submit expressions of interest in his company, Patterson Electronics. While that was certainly good news from a financial perspective, it made the prospect of a sale that much more real.

His sleep that night had been disturbed by recurring nightmares loaded with alternating images of triumph and great regret. The flashbacks that visited him most nights were never the same and yet exactly alike. Scenes from his childhood as an immigrant's son. The first time he'd said a shy "hello" to Shea at Clarkson College. The years at Raytheon and his obsessive focus with getting ahead. The patents he'd used to create Patterson Electronics and the military systems it developed. He had fought against all the odds, beaten all the Ivy League types, and made millions in the process. But amidst this American dream was the stark reality that he'd put his trust in the wrong God and lost his family in the process.

He was blessed to be married to Shea—and his dreams included the moments of her love and care. She was brilliant in her own right but had sacrificed her career to raise two children essentially on her own—supporting a husband who was obsessed with creating products and making money. Their youngest child, Angela, was indeed an angel and had thrived without her father. But Bryce, well, Bryce was another matter.

Charles's nightmares included visions of his son's awkward youth. His goth years. The suspensions from high school. And the attempted suicide in college. All of it capped by his recent disappearance. Charles realized he'd lost his son—both figuratively and literally.

Now he and Shea were taking an early morning walk across the Brooklyn Bridge. A walk that should have been a romantic stroll for a loving couple about to secure their financial future. Instead, it was a silent slog in the sharp morning air, his head abuzz.

He was reviewing the choices he'd made and wondering about the combination of hard work and serendipity that had led to his success. Was he smarter than everyone else or just lucky? How could he have done it without Shea and her relentless faith in him? Had he really learned the right lessons along the way? Where was this bridge taking him?

Charles broke the silence. "I always said that family came first. But the truth is I had it wrong all along. Sure, I was proud of our family, but the work always came first. If I'd been around, Bryce would still be here with us."

Shea responded to his angst with the love of a lifelong partner. "I could explain to you how your work has provided for our family. I could point out that your heart has always been in the right place. That we'll search for him and somehow bring him home. But none of that really matters now. We can't undo what's happened, and even if we could, there's no guarantee the outcome would be better. Bryce was difficult for all of us from day one. All we can do—all you can do—is focus on the next step. The next decision. The next action. My love, we both know the time has come to stand up and take control of our future."

The next decision, indeed.

They needed to get to the bottom of the issue they'd studiously avoided thus far. Straight into the fray.

"Are you ready to sell?" she asked.

"In my heart, no chance. I love Patterson. I love the work and I'm energized by the challenges. Cashing in sounded easy at first, but the company means more to me than that. It's my home away from home. The employees are my friends and my responsibility. It's my life's creation."

He shifted his gaze to the horizon and then turned to look straight into Shea's eyes. "But I've concluded that whether I'm ready to sell is not the real question. The real issue is what's right for you and for our family. And that's a much easier question."

"But what about that heart you talked about? The heart I love. Am I going to lose that when someone else is running your baby?"

"God, Shea—I wish I knew. I hope not. All I can say is that I want our relationship to grow. I want to feel the love of my daughter. I want to find Bryce and make it right."

She wrapped her arms around him, providing some comfort that she really did understand and would always be there for him. It really was ironic that the company named after her, Shea Patterson, had stolen his attention for all those years. And now, that same company would provide for their financial future and enable them to be closer together than ever.

"Will that be . . ." began Shea.

". . . enough?" finished Charles.

The wind whipped across the Brooklyn span bringing a breath of cool air.

"I have no idea if it will be enough," he continued. "No idea at all. As strong as my faith has become, I suspect God is probably laughing at my anguish right now. No choice but to plow ahead."

They walked hand-in-hand back along the promenade under the giant stone pier that formed the Manhattan landing for the bridge.

"Charles, *look!*"

They stared into the distance between the monolithic towers . . . and then they both began to run.

• • • • •

In the blink of an eye, American Airlines Flight 11 blew away all of Charles's angst. He felt the explosion as the first tower shook on its foundations, not knowing exactly what had happened. He and Shea could see the smoke and flames rise as they returned to Manhattan. Together, they watched the videos, hearing the engines of the first plane rev at 450 miles per hour as it collided with the north tower of the World Trade Center. United Airlines Flight 175 hit the second tower shortly thereafter. Both buildings soon collapsed.

Over 3,000 people died that day and America would be changed forever.

Like others in New York City, Charles knew he and Shea would have to sort through the wreckage.

## Chapter 16

# THE PENTAGON, EARLIER THAT MORNING

AFTER PARKING HIS AGING Chevrolet Malibu in the black asphalt parking lot just south of the Pentagon, Captain Jerry Jessup paused to consider the very symbol of American military power and might. Sitting across from the Washington and Jefferson Monuments and next to Arlington National Cemetery, the Pentagon effectively connected elements of the country's civic and military history while being the functional command post for the Department of Defense. He'd done the tour and heard the stats: 17.5 miles of corridors, 6.5 million square feet, 25,000 people, and 6 zip codes. All in a classical stone fortress-like structure that included five rings and a total of seven floors, two of which were below ground. It was a shape turned into a building turned into an icon.

JJ knew it was intimidating by design.

As the Air Force's top officer on the Counterterrorism Security Group, or CSG, he was one of a gaggle of spooks trying to see through the smoke and fog of terrorist back-alleys to keep America safe. He felt the weight of that responsibility, especially as evidence mounted that the attack on the USS *Cole* almost a year ago was the work of an organized group. In the office early by habit, he was headed to an 0630 meeting with one of his intelligence analysts.

Corporal Juliana Aigner was approaching the entrance when he arrived. Dressed in fatigues, she had brought two cups of coffee and a couple of donuts for the meeting. They walked in together, navigating the hallways to JJ's office. It was a no-windows affair optimized for function over comfort or décor. The wall to the left of his desk was dominated by a huge whiteboard with names, dates, and locations connected by crisscrossing arrows. The opposite wall had a series of blown-up photographs from a variety of military facilities around the world. His desk had stacks of paper all piled neatly in specific places on the fake-oak surface. A credenza behind him had some family photographs and one of him in front of his F-18 Hornet on the USS *Abraham Lincoln*. A TV screen was mounted on the wall above the credenza. Even in crisis, Captain Jerry Jessup was about law and order.

"I know there's something happening," began JJ. "I can feel it in my gut. But the whiteboard just makes my eyes cross. It looks like one of those time-lapse photographs taken at night in a big city. So . . . what do you make of the two Khalids and their activities?"

Julie walked up to the whiteboard and traced some lines. "They've been all over the Middle East and in the US at least once. For that matter, so have our friends Mr. Khallad and Nawaf al-Hazmi. The Phoenix office is tracking some foreign nationals on the watch list who are taking commercial flying lessons." Her fingers moved across the board tapping on another name. "Then we have our favorite whack job, Zacarias Moussaoui in Minneapolis, trying to learn how to fly 747s."

"Most of the intelligence data points to another attack overseas. But then we hear whispers of 'calamitous,' 'spectacular,' and 'devastating' action in the US. We have no concrete evidence to share with anyone. Shit. What more do we know about these guys?"

Aigner jumped into analyst report mode: "Khallad is a shadowy badass that supposedly masterminded the attack on the *Cole*, but nobody knows exactly where he is now. He might have been in Kuala Lumpur and maybe he met with Khalid al-Mihdhar—another raghead with a jihadist background. Al-Mihdhar's been back and forth to Yemen at least twice, but somehow, he's now in the US on a valid visa. Whereabouts unknown."

"How the *hell* does that happen? Jesus, we're so screwed up."

Not knowing how to respond to that, Aigner continued. "The other

Khalid is basically a freelance terrorist, but we don't think he could pull off a major attack on his own. And by all accounts, the last of these kooks, al-Hazmi, is also still in the US."

And that was JJ's problem. "Why the hell are so many of the arrows pointing toward the United States? How many more of these camel jockeys are wandering around the homeland? Hell, they could have a convention." Unfortunately, he and Aigner could not make any direct connections. In the intelligence world, that did not happen all that often anyway. But he did not believe in coincidences either. There had to be a better way to nail these fuckers.

"Thanks for coming in early, Corporal. I've got a meeting with a source I met in the Navy during the *Cole* investigation. Maybe that'll give us some more to work on. I'll check in with you later." His mind was already back on the whiteboard.

JJ left his office at 0915 to make the hike over to the west wing of the Pentagon. The meeting was in office 1D315, which naturally meant the first floor on the D ring near corridor 3 in office 15. That part of the building was just completing renovations to fortify it in response to the Oklahoma City FBI office attacks—yet another wave in the terrorism tidal pool. Getting around the Pentagon was intimidating for some, but JJ had figured it out. You just take one of the ten vertical corridors to the central core, go around the clock on the A ring until you got to your corridor and then walk back out through the rings. Simple, right?

But the second he stepped out of his office into the hallway, he knew something was up. There was an unusual buzz of both sound and action. People were rushing in and out of offices. Others were dashing down the corridor.

Aigner came running down the hall. "Two jets just crashed into the World Trade Center," she said in between breaths. "Big explosions and fires in both towers."

Goddamn it! Too late.

Some of his questions had already been answered. The feeling in his gut exploded into a fireball. He shot back into his office and flipped on the TV. What he saw made him lash out at the guest chair, kicking it across the room into a filing cabinet. He stood there, trying to absorb the impossible. He looked up at the whiteboard, now magically decoded, all the arrows pointing to New York City. He was interrupted by the phone.

"Hey, can you believe this shit? These fuckers are trying to start a war. You still want to meet?" It was his contact from the Navy.

JJ paused for a split second before answering. "Yeah, I'll come right over. We still have to figure this out, one way or the other." He grabbed his notepad and went back out into the hallway melee. He moved quickly down the corridor to the center A ring. When he got to the west side of the building, he headed back out toward the outer rings and office 315.

He heard the rising whine as he came around a corner. He couldn't place it in his mind.

"*Oh, FUCK!*"

And with that, the walls in front and above him exploded—and he went dark.

•  •  •  •  •

Face as hot as fire. Lungs burning. A massive throbbing in the back of his head. JJ tried to open his eyes, but they refused to obey his initial commands. Deep down, a little voice told him to move. He began to crawl backwards because that was the only direction he could go. And then he ran into something and stopped.

"Open your damn eyes," he demanded out loud to himself.

As he did that, the volume was suddenly turned back on. He still couldn't see anything. But now he could hear screams from others, the banging of concrete as it continued to fall, and mostly the howling roar of a raging fire. With sight and sound back on, his other senses rebooted. Suddenly he felt the ripped-up nerves in his left arm and the now-doubled pain in the back of his head. Smoke was filling the small space of air in front of him and the pain began moving down into his lungs.

Survival instincts kicked in. As did the adrenaline of panic.

He tried to pull back from the heat again. Reaching around with his right arm, he was able to push some concrete debris aside and clear a small path to the back. A few seconds later, he felt someone pulling him out from behind and he was clear of the rubble.

A corporal's dirty face met him as he tried to stand up. "Come on, Captain—we gotta get clear."

JJ took two unsteady steps and then grabbed the corporal by the shirt. "Negative, Corporal. Start digging. There's others. We're gonna find 'em and get 'em out."

For the next twenty minutes, they pulled at the tangled mess of steel and concrete, listening for voices above the screech of the fire and the wail of sirens. JJ had trouble breathing and couldn't see for shit—not between the smoke and dust and darkness. His ears had to be his eyes. And he only had one usable arm. Still, they managed to pull four people out of the debris before a group of firefighters got to their part of the building.

"We've got it from here, Captain. Get yourself treated—that arm looks broken for sure."

The firefighters shouting commands and the background roar of the fire made his head hurt. Probably a well-earned concussion to go with his damaged wing. But all he could think about was the whiteboard. About the clues. About the intelligence he'd failed to figure out. He was thinking about his contact in the Navy whose temporary office was in the wrong place at the wrong time. Maybe he'd survived somehow . . . but probably not.

Mostly he was thinking about the assholes who had done this and what he would do to them once he found them.

Holding the crush of failure and guilt at bay, he embraced his new mantra: "Never forgive. Never forget."

# Chapter 17

# UPSTATE NEW YORK

ANGELA ROSCOVITCH SAT silently on the white couch in her parents' living room watching coverage of the attacks in New York City and Washington, DC. She had come home from nearby Syracuse University as soon as she heard the news—no way she was going to be able to study. For someone who always tried to do the right thing, she now had no idea how to act, who to call, or where to go. In the last week, her carefully ordered world had come completely undone—and the terrorist attacks were just the last straw. Like many things in her family's life, it all began with Bryce.

Her older brother Bryce was a junior at Boston University, struggling to complete a degree in political science. Angela knew he was unhappy in school—and in life generally—but, deep down, she saw a certain brilliance in him. Despite his poor grades, she assumed he would somehow muddle through, just like always. When her parents had brought Bryce home from Boston Medical Center a week earlier, they acted as if he was sick and just taking a break from school. But even from her dorm room at Syracuse, Angela knew it was much more serious. Then a few days later, Bryce disappeared. The carefully constructed Roscovitch household came tumbling down.

Bryce had called her a few days after his evaporating act.

"Where the hell are you?" Angela had demanded. Her parents were panicked and now that she had her brother on the phone, she wanted some answers.

"Ange, please don't fucking start in on me." The profanity surprised her, but the tone in Bryce's voice told her to remain quiet. "I think I made it pretty damn clear that I wanted out . . . and not just out of school."

Angela hesitated to dive in but realized she had little to lose. "Did . . . did you really try to kill yourself?" Just saying the words made her shiver. How could he have done that? Bryce?

A long pause on the line. Then a sigh. "I don't really know what I was trying to do. I guess I was desperate. You know I never wanted to go to college . . . that whole scene sucked. I've never felt so alone."

"Oh God, Bryce, I know that. But *killing* yourself? You could've called me. I would've been there in a second. You could have gotten help."

Angela had been terrified when she'd figured out why he was in the hospital. But now on reflection, she was also a little pissed at him. How dare he?

"I got so deep in a hole and just couldn't see a way out. I was so tired of trying to live up to everyone else's expectations. I know I should've called you—you know I love you so much—but I just felt helpless." Another pause. "I guess I couldn't do it. I took a bunch of pills but could've taken more."

Even though she was the younger sister, Angela was the responsible, "normal" child. Where she had always thrived academically and socially, Bryce was impossibly shy, with looks that made it worse. He had been gifted Charles's large, slightly hooked nose, Shea's round face, and some distant relative's dumpy body. Elementary school involved many parent-teacher conferences, middle school brought the inevitable trips to the principal's office, and high school was detention central. Bryce made it through the education system in part on pure talent and in part on system apathy—but that had come unraveled when he went to college in Boston.

Angela went back to the beginning of the conversation. "Where are you? Mom and Dad are a complete mess."

"So I guess trying to kill myself was the wakeup call it took to finally get their attention? I don't give a shit what they think—or how worried they are."

"Bryce!" came the reprimand. Her pissed-off mood returned.

"Please get real, Ange," came the even angrier response. "Look . . . all Dad's ever cared about is his stupid work. First Raytheon, then the GPS patents, and now Patterson. Those are his real babies. We're just inconvenient additions to his glorious family plan."

Angela wanted to defend her father—but there was some truth in her brother's words. And she knew her father cast a long shadow that Bryce could never quite escape. Her brother's insecurities and her dad's success and dominating character were a bad recipe.

"What about Mom? You know she's given everything for you." That brought silence. All she could hear was Bryce's breathing.

"I know Mom tries, but we both know she can take the mothering thing too far. I don't think either of them *sees* me for me. And when they brought me back from the hospital, they both acted like they had all the answers. Neither one listened. Shit, I don't have any answers either, but one thing I know is that I don't need another 'plan.'"

"But Bryce, where are you going to go? What are you going to do? You can't just run from this. I don't want to lose you—"

"I'm in New York. I'm okay for now."

"And then?"

"Haven't a clue. But I can tell you this. I know it won't be anything that will make Dad proud. From now on, the only expectations I'm going to live up to are my own."

And with that declaration, their call had effectively ended.

But Bryce's disappearance was only the beginning. Angela had come home the next weekend and was in the kitchen baking cookies (when in doubt, comfort food) when her father came back from one of his long walks with their dog, Frankie. She knew that the walks got longer when his mind was preoccupied. They'd been gone for almost two hours.

"Hey, Dad. Did you and Frankie have a good walk?" She tried a light, upbeat tone.

After putting his coat on the hook in the back hall, he wiped Frankie's paws one by one. "If you leave out the rain, the north wind, and wet dog fur, it was delightful. How's the baking? Is there a chocolate chip cookie there for me?" The walk seemed to have improved his spirits. Maybe now was the time to broach the call from Bryce.

"I think you got plenty of the dough before you left!" And then without missing a beat. "I talked to Bryce last week." Angela said this in a neutral tone, as if it was the most pedestrian topic.

Her mother came running in from the family room. "Honey, where is he?"

Her father stopped wiping Frankie's feet and threw down the towel. "Is he okay?"

"What did he tell you?"

"When is he coming home?"

"Slow down, both of you." Angela set down her oven mitt. "He made me promise not to tell you where he is. He doesn't want your help and he doesn't want anyone looking for him. Maybe he's ashamed . . . maybe he wants to prove himself . . . maybe he just doesn't know how to ask. But he's okay and wants to be left alone."

Charles let loose. "Angie! You just can't leave it like that. He's our son—*my* son—and I'll be damned if I'm just going to let him disappear from our family."

"I think the time for you to be a father has passed, Dad." She immediately regretted the words and tone. But her loyalty to Bryce ran wide and deep.

"Damn it, Angela. You know everything I do is to provide for the both of you . . . and for your mom. Don't go blaming this on me."

Not this time. This time, when her father pushed, she pushed back. "Holy shit! Really? Don't play that game with me. Is all your work about *us*, or your mission to prove you are better and smarter than everyone else? Screw your company and all the money. All Bryce needed . . . hell, all he ever dreamed about . . . was for you to care about *him*."

"Angela!" her mother interjected. "That is quite enough. You *will not* come into our house and yell at us about parenting. And you *will not* judge or lecture us because it's not as simple as you're making it out to be. You don't know everything that's happened. Bryce is complicated . . . he's always been complicated."

Angela tried to jump in. "Don't you think I know that better than anyone—"

But her mother was not done. "Look, somehow, we all failed him. I think about that every day. I wish it weren't true, but there's absolutely nothing we can do about the past. The only question is what we can do now? And you *will* tell us where he is and how we can reach him."

"Mom . . . I can't do that. You can yell at me all you want, you can kick me out even, but I will not violate his trust. It's the only thing I have left with him."

That was more than Charles could take. "So we're just going to leave him to fend for himself? You've got to be fuckin' kidding me."

Silence. No pins dropping. No clock ticking. Just the quiet that turns a room cold.

Everyone retreated to their corners. Charles said "shit" and walked out the back door, pulling Frankie along for even more walking. Shea sighed and went back to her desk in the family room. Angela left her cookies to cool on the warming tray, running up the steps to her bedroom and slamming the door.

Some twenty minutes later, her mom walked up to her door and whispered, "Angela? Please?"

An envelope came under Angela's door with Bryce's name on the front.

• • • •

Now as she sat watching the news coverage of the terrorist attacks, she fingered that envelope in her hands, as if it were some connection to the rest of her family. Bryce and her parents were both somewhere in New York City, and she had no way of knowing if they were all right, or even alive. Cell phone communications were impossible and calls to her parents' hotel went unanswered. She didn't even know how to address the letter to Bryce.

She patted the head of their longtime family pet. "Frankie," she said, voice cracking and tears on her cheeks, "Daddy always says that disasters are God's way of clearing the lint that accumulates in our lives."

Frankie's warm look provided solace but no answers.

# Chapter 18

# MAXWELL AFB, SEPTEMBER 12

"LIEUTENANT, WAKE UP."

"What the fuck? Who are you?"

"Sorry ma'am. You've got a priority call from South Korea in the Commander's office."

That would be the Colonel calling—even in the fog of sleep Tamika realized her father was the only person who would call her from Korea. But why in the Commander's office?

"Give me a second of privacy, Airman—if I'm going to the Commander's office, I'm not going looking like this."

The airman stepped outside, and Tamika put on a fresh shirt and fatigue pants. Her mind returned to the previous day. It locked on the images and sounds of the second passenger plane's engines revving as it hit the south tower, followed by the horrific aftermath as the colossal structure crashed down, crushing the buildings beneath it. Then an entire five-story wing of the Pentagon had collapsed amid the heat of a raging fire. United States airspace was closed to all civilian traffic, the US military was at DEFCON 3 for the first time in almost thirty years, Vice President Cheney was in a secure bunker, and President Bush was at Barksdale Air Force Base in Louisiana. She still had trouble comprehending how all of it could've happened.

Even though the base was reasonably well lit at night, there was still an unnerving haze hanging in the air. She felt a bit uneasy as they moved past each building. Her anxiety was no longer just about personal violation and humiliation—now she knew the country was going to war. She walked in silence with her airman escort—nothing really for either of them to say—but her mind was racing with possibilities. Had something happened to her father? Was he being called back stateside because of the attacks? She even wondered if word of what had happened to her in Montgomery had somehow gotten back to the Colonel. She'd told no one—but maybe someone had read the letter she'd written to Alex. There wasn't much privacy in the military.

She entered Commander Chase Weber's office and saluted. He shifted the tone quickly.

"At ease, Lieutenant. Airman—give us the room, please."

The commander cleared his throat. "Lieutenant Smith, I know about your running career and what we're doing to support you. I respect the double effort that must require. What I didn't know is that your father is Colonel Frank Smith. I served under him in my last command. I have great respect for him and his leadership, and I want you to know that I'm proud to have his daughter in my unit."

Tamika's mind was really racing now. What the hell was going on? She certainly didn't need this speech—in fact, given the events that had transpired, it made her a bit uncomfortable—and she definitely didn't need it at 0230 the night after terrorists attacked her country.

He continued. "I'm going to leave you alone with your father on the phone. Let me know how I can help." And with that, he left the room.

Wow. Psycho.

She picked up the phone. "Hello, Colonel Smith."

"Tammy, this isn't an official call. You and I need to talk."

"Daddy, what's going on? The Commander here is being all weird and you're calling me at O-Dark-Whatever. Are you all right?"

"Don't worry about me. I'll be fine. I'm sorry about the crazy hour, but you needed to hear this from me first."

The long pause was followed by a cracking voice. "You know that Alex was on special assignment." More emptiness with a few deep breaths. "He came back this week and was working at the Pentagon . . .

in an extra office . . . in the wing that was hit by the plane. Tammy, they haven't found his body but there's no way he survived." He hurried to continue, "I'm so sorry—I hate my job—I hate that I've dragged you and Alex into it. First your mother, and now Alex. You're all I have left."

Tamika collapsed into a chair, unable to speak. Barely able to breathe. Alex was her closest friend, her confidant, her role model, and her only sibling. She had lost her mother to cancer early in high school and her father was always on duty somewhere.

Alex had practically raised her . . . and now he was gone.

No, not just gone. Murdered by some crazy, stupid terrorists who cared so little about life that they killed themselves along with hundreds of innocent people. Jihad? Holy war? There was nothing noble or holy about it. Just more pain from a God who didn't seem to care. She stood up and started pacing back and forth, her breathing now deep and powerful.

"Tammy, are you still there? Please talk to me."

"Maybe he wasn't there. Or maybe he was in a meeting. Maybe . . ." Her voice trailed off as she reached for something, anything, that would keep her from falling into the sinkhole opening up under her.

"I wish that were true, Tammy. They have him on video walking down the hallway a few minutes before the attack. He was on the phone when the plane hit." His voice broke as he delivered the final verdict.

"Daddy, I'm just so fucking angry!" She was shouting through the tears. "Angry at the terrorists, angry at the Air Force, angry at God, angry at you! Angry that Alex is gone." She collapsed again into the chair and began to sob—and with the sobs came the urge to beat the hell out of the Commander's desk, knocking everything onto the floor in the process.

Commander Weber walked in carefully. He took the phone from her hands and quietly talked with Colonel Smith. By the time he hung up, Tamika was wiping her face with her shirt sleeve and cleaning up the mess she'd made.

"I'm sorry, sir. I shouldn't have lost it like that."

"You wouldn't be human if you hadn't. Nothing really important there anyway. Your dad asked me to give you a big hug. I know I can't replace him, but I can provide a shoulder." He reached toward her. But she turned to the side, pretending to pick up more papers.

"Thank you, sir, but I'll be fine. I just needed to vent. God, I hate being a female cliché."

"Has nothing to do with your sex, Lieutenant. I've seen men die in combat—friends, wingmen, husbands—and I've cried like you've never seen. You lost your brother. Sometimes we act all stoic, but even in the Air Force we grieve."

She released a long breath. "Thank you again, sir. Request permission to return to my quarters."

"One condition. Pack up some gear. You're going to DC at 0800. Your father will meet you there later tomorrow. We'll honor your brother—and then we'll hunt down the bastards and give them what they deserve."

# Chapter 19

# A NATION MOURNS

WITH THE TERRORIST BOMBINGS, the likelihood of war, and the death of her brother, Tamika's world had come unglued. Survivor's guilt and anger mixed together like a Molotov cocktail—an unstable concoction that was likely to explode at any moment. She could feel it coming. Her father was doing his best to support her, but he was dealing with his own demons, and his parenting skills were not great even on a good day. Their time in the nation's capital together was dominated by silence and tears.

As a celebration of Alex's life, they were invited along with other family members of the fallen to a memorial mass at the Washington National Cathedral on Friday, September 14th. On that day, they walked down the center aisle of the Gothic-styled church. Its thick, arched columns came down both sides of the nave and its soaring vaulted ceiling was supported by flying buttresses on the exterior. Wooden chairs had been arranged, beginning at the front of the altar and ending all the way back down at the entrance doors. Tamika could hear the loneliness in her walk as her steps echoed on the stone floor. The gathering crowd murmured in the background. She and her father found seats in the front right section with other Air Force officers.

Former presidents Ford, Carter, Clinton, and Bush were in attendance, along with the current President Bush and Billy Graham, both of whom would speak eloquently on that somber morning. She listened quietly to President Bush, fighting back more tears, trying to contain the fury that was building within. ⌣

*" . . . To the children and parents and spouses and families and friends of the lost, we offer the deepest sympathy of the nation. And I assure you, you are not alone.*

*Just three days removed from these events, Americans do not yet have the distance of history, but our responsibility to history is already clear: to answer these attacks and rid the world of evil.*

*War has been waged against us by stealth and deceit and murder.*

*This nation is peaceful, but fierce when stirred to anger. This conflict was begun on the timing and terms of others; it will end in a way and at an hour of our choosing."*

The Reverend Billy Graham's speech echoed some of the same themes but naturally was more spiritual. He talked about the reality of evil and the mystery of why God allows tragedy and suffering. He pointed out the importance of unity and how much we need each other. And finally, he spoke about hope—and with that Tamika's head fell.

*". . . but it also has been a week of great faith. In that hymn, 'How Firm a Foundation,' the words say, 'Fear not, I am with thee; O be not dismayed,/For I am thy God, and will give thee aid;/I'll strengthen thee, help thee, and cause thee to stand,/Upheld by my righteous, omnipotent hand.'"*

Hope now seemed so far beyond her grasp. A flickering light in the distance that she would never be able to reach. She held her father's hand tight—he was the last one in her world that could bring hope and love—but even he felt far away.

President Bush and Reverend Graham's words brought Tamika no peace, no solace, no reconciliation. But she did find the beginnings of purpose. A way forward. A path to channel her anger that might lead to some comfort. Perhaps it was revenge or maybe it was justice, but either way she was going to pursue it.

As they walked out of the service into a warm but overcast mid-September day, they were met by General Mac Trasolini who was the

Chief of Staff of the Air Force. Even though her brother was in the Navy, the Air Force was treating his loss as a loss to the whole family. Salutes were exchanged, but seemingly to dispense with the formality.

"Colonel Smith, Lieutenant Smith, I am deeply saddened by your loss. Frank—your family has given so much to our country, and I'm sure Alex lived that sense of service every day. I wish I had words that would change the way you feel—all I can offer is my prayers. If there is anything the Air Force can do . . . anything I can do . . . just say the word."

Tamika didn't hesitate.

She stepped forward right through Air Force protocol and asked for the one thing she now wanted. "Sir, for as long as I can remember, my dream was to run for Olympic glory. Those terrorist shitheads . . . they killed my brother and my dream."

She paused to wipe away the tears.

"Get me the hell to Afghanistan. Soon."

• • • • •

Second Lieutenant Tamika Smith struggled to find closure. For her, September 11th was a jumping off point—a line in the sand that denoted before and after. A date that would define her very existence for years to come. The violence of the crash and intensity of the fire made it impossible to identify accurately all those killed at the Pentagon, including her brother. With no body, there would be no personal burial service for Alex. No opportunity for her to honor him.

A year and a day after the attack—with Tamika on station in Afghanistan—the remains of those unidentified in the crash in Washington were buried under a pentagon-shaped memorial in Arlington National Cemetery along with the names of the 184 people who died in the plane or on the ground. That memorial would be Alex's final resting place.

Tamika would not see it for a long time.

# PART 3

## A SECOND LETHAL DAY

If you fall pick yourself up off the floor (get up)
And when your bones can't take no more
Just remember what you're here for
'Cause I know I'ma damn sure

Give 'em hell, turn their heads
Gonna live life till we're dead
Give me scars, give me pain
Then just say to me, say to me, say to me
There goes a fighter, there goes a fighter
Here comes a fighter
That's what they'll say to me, say to me
Say to me, this one's a fighter
Till the referee rings the bell
Till both ya eyes start to swell
Till the crowd goes home
What we gonna do kid?

—Ryan Tedder, Noel Zancanella, Disashi Lumumba-Kasongo,
    Matt McGinley, Travis McCoy, and Eric Roberts

## Chapter 20

# OFFUTT AFB, WEDNESDAY, APRIL 17, 2019

THE VIDEO JUST PISSED him off. Colonel Jerry Jessup was tired of the same old song. A bombing attack followed by yet another jihadist organization taking responsibility for the carnage. Like al Qaeda and ISIS before it, the Islamic Brotherhood Front claimed that the downing of Flight 209 was a brilliant masterstroke in the ongoing war with the western infidels.

Jessup pondered the terrorist's face on the TV screen of his office at Offutt Air Force Base. This latest incarnation of self-proclaimed terrorist agent had an unusually smug, self-satisfied look on his face, as if he'd just screwed his best friend's wife. Taunting the president was now somewhat of a national pastime, but the words were important to consider. JJ had called his best intelligence sources at the Pentagon immediately after his press conference. Nobody had ever heard of the IBF and Obaid bin Latif wasn't on any watch list or even anybody's radar. So who the fuck was he?

Sitting in his swivel office chair at 0730, he turned to stare out the window on to the tarmac that had seen so much activity the night before. His ever-prescient instincts told him he was not dealing with a typical sand-loving terrorist. For one thing, bin Latif was still alive—an unusual attribute for a jihadist. The IBF (whoever they were) would usually be praising the courage of a dead Islamic soldier who had sacrificed his life for the glorious cause. But this asshole had gone to great lengths to distance himself from the actual carnage. And he'd hinted there was more to come.

Just what the world needed—a newly discovered *serial* Islamic fanatic.

Captain Washington interrupted, "DC on the phone, sir. Colonel Brown's office." Only took them an hour after his press conference. Too bad they didn't move so quickly on things that mattered. What followed was not exactly a conversation. Brown was not JJ's boss, but he was a muckety-muck at the Defense Intelligence Agency, which was perhaps worse. And he was making it clear that he was not happy.

Listen, wait, sigh. "Colonel . . ." followed by more of listen and wait. Finally.

"Colonel Brown, with all due respect, all of this happened on *my* base and under *my* command. I'm sorry the FBI is pissed off, but the FBI isn't here. Once I knew it was a bomb, I had to put security above protocol." He also knew that every three- and four-letter agency in the government would try to own the investigation, and he wasn't going to give it up easily. This was personal.

Some more yelling, perhaps a bit less forceful this time. The usual BS about chain of command and then some nonsense about jurisdiction. JJ used the time to get some exercise, pacing back and forth in front of the window, taking mental notes on items to investigate further.

"Well, I have jurisdiction on this base. And what's left of the plane is here. My base, my plane, my case. This is a high security installation and it's going to stay that way. If somebody in Washington wants that to change, fine by me. But until I hear that from General Ewald, the FBI and the rest can wait." He sat back down in the chair, satisfied with his bluff.

General Arvin Ewald was the head of Air Combat Command—several levels up from anyone who even knew who JJ was or where he was posted. Using his name would slow down the process some, even if it was unlikely that Ewald would get involved directly. In the end, he'd likely lose jurisdiction to the FBI—if it was a terrorist attack on US soil, then the FBI and Homeland Security would get the lead. But like a dog with a familiar bone, JJ didn't want to let go until ordered.

This was his chance at 9/11 redemption. And perhaps some revenge.

JJ cut back in. "—Well your superiors aren't my problem. Right now, I'm dealing with a hundred plus press people, investigators who don't know how to work together, and over 200 dead or injured civilians. Not to mention a terrorist who managed to put a bomb on a US commercial airline without injuring himself. Let me know when you want to help."

With that he slammed the phone on the cradle. Then he went back to the small pile of evidence he had been reviewing. He'd get yelled at for his impertinence, but that wasn't new. What was new to him was an intelligent, unknown terrorist. That was worth his full and undivided attention.

● ● ● ● ●

The iconic photo of Major Tamika Smith rescuing John Quincy Humboldt from a ditch went viral, reaching a shocking 150 million views in less than a day. As befit the times, the picture struck a chord amid the background of cultural and political turmoil. Tamika was not surprised that the sound wasn't necessarily harmonious. A mixed blessing of hope and hate, of hero and villain. She rarely went on social media, but this was clearly a day like none other. Twitter—the Trump-blessed de facto news service of the country—was on fire:

From the Air Force: "In the finest tradition of service and sacrifice. Saving lives and protecting our country."

From Thomas Hanks: "An epic rescue. God bless those who serve."

From Senator Isabelle McSally: "Every pilot needs a guardian angel. Thank you, Major. You're a savior indeed."

And from a mother: "Such strength and character. A model for my daughters. #girl power."

Of course, there were those who saw the photo through an entirely different lens, and not coincidentally from an anonymous perch:

From gunrunner: "bitches in the military won't stop this from happening."

From supremacy7: "we've hit a new low in so many ways. whites need to rise up and protect ourselves. #AmericaFirst."

From majorityrules: "Another islamic attack. When will we learn? Kick em out or lock em up."

Most shocking, although in hindsight not surprising, were the tweets from the White House:

From @realDonaldTrump: "Proof that our immigration policy has FAILED. Build the wall."

And: "What the FAKE NEWS won't say. She couldn't protect us. Where was the FBI? Time to get out of the ditch. SAD."

*Goddamn him*, Tamika thought, after reading more than enough. And she wasn't referring to the president.

Done with protocol, she went right past Captain Washington, barging into JJ's office. "Just what the hell do you think you're doing?" She slammed the door behind her, shaking the thin walls to their foundations.

"A salute would be nice, Major."

"Write me up. Please." Now her hands were on the front of his desk and they were face to face, spitting distance.

"Just what has you so fired up? Or should I chalk this up to fatigue or PTSD and send you on your way?" He moved away from the confrontation and turned his back on her, pretending to look out the window.

"You thought it was cool to publish my photo? I don't need or want to be plastered all over the internet. Oh . . . and then there would be the small matter of announcing a terrorist attack to the media."

He spun around quickly with a pointed finger. "Sit your butt down, Major. First, it's not *your* photo. That photo belongs to the United States Air Force, along with everything you and your pretty little ass do. Second, last time I looked, you worked for me. I didn't ask for your approval, and I don't take insubordination lightly."

"Permission to speak freely, sir." Sarcasm added for effect. And she still hadn't moved her pretty little ass from the front of his desk.

"Actually, no. I'm done with you—in fact, I don't recall requesting a meeting with you in the first place. Your presence is required for a press conference at 1200. There's quite the clamor to talk with our new internet hero. Your favorite captain will take you there. Lieutenant Perry—she'll be your personal press secretary—can brief you on the basics." Fake smile.

*Damn it.* The last thing she wanted was a tooth extraction with a bunch of journalists looking for a story. Over the years, she'd become very protective of her personal life—she was sensitive to her dad's Air Force stature and to events she wanted buried forever—and this was not fitting with the program. She had a quick flashback to the crash the night before. Talking about that with the press was going to be scarier than diving into the burning plane. She spun on her toes like a prisoner going to the gallows.

"Major, aren't you forgetting something?" And before she could do anything he added, "Dismissed."

# Chapter 21

# NEWARK AND PHILADELPHIA

OBAID BIN LATIF KNEW Americans took so many things for granted. A bounty of natural resources, a common language, sufficiently shared history (some of it apocryphal or conveniently modified), and a diverse geography. More importantly to a terrorist, the United States had an infrastructure that supported and enabled the "land of opportunity." And it was an infrastructure that was rarely discussed—precisely because the shit just worked.

When bin Latif dug a bit deeper, of course, the situation was more complicated and significantly less rosy. The highway system was in dramatic need of upgrades. Water quality varied widely from region to region. The air traffic control system was designed in the dark ages. The power grid had capacity mismatches, inefficient production, brownouts, and single points of failure. Health care coverage was inconsistent and incomplete, with a fragmented network of hospitals and clinics ill-prepared for a widespread crisis. All of it reminded him why people used duct tape and bailing wire to hold things together. The shit worked, but it was very fragile. And while they talked about the problems, neither the Republicans nor the Democrats could muster the leadership to fix them.

In the end, Obaid bin Latif couldn't have cared less about the policy implications—that was for others to contemplate, evaluate, and seemingly ignore. What intrigued him about American infrastructure was its relative lack of security. Outside of airports—which post-9/11 had become a very special case—it just wasn't that difficult to gain access to important systems. Sure, there were fences, cameras, and some guards at various facilities, but most places were deemed not worthy of more advanced protection. Security was a function of the weakest link, and every one of these systems had obvious weaknesses that could bring down large, mission-critical services.

In terrorist terms, this was a target-rich environment.

Bin Latif's near-term goal was to create chaos. And what better way than to strike at the heart of the systems that make the country operate so well? If people begin to question whether the electricity will work, or whether they will have water, or if they can travel safely—if he could accomplish that level of doubt—he could open the doors to dramatic, radical change.

After all, he was a sane man. Chaos was a means to a very important end.

Now sitting in a corner of the main lobby at Newark's Penn Station, bin Latif watched a live video feed from a press conference at Offutt Air Force Base. A Black woman in Air Force fatigues was at the microphone answering questions about the airplane attack. *His* attack. He turned up the volume on his phone as she parried with the press, trying to answer questions without actually answering them. He smirked. *Hey, she's doing a pretty good job with those media hacks—and damn she looks mighty fine doing it*, he thought to himself.

Then her answers to the last few questions made him pause, as the chaos he was creating got personal. Well . . . sacrifices were necessary to drive change.

Bin Latif double-checked the time. He grabbed a backpack he had retrieved from an off-site storage locker on his way to the train station. He walked quickly to the escalator that led down to the tracks. Regardless of the cost, his mission was to strike before the dust had settled at the Omaha crash site.

13:05. It was time to get on the train.

• • • • •

The scene was all too familiar for the senator. People seated ten rows deep on foldout chairs arranged in an amphitheater semicircle with an aisle running down the middle. In the back was a phalanx of video and still cameras arranged on risers to allow for an unobstructed view over the crowd. Klieg lights shining brightly on a table full of microphones at the front completed the picture. This was a one-ring circus with an Air Force officer as the performing seal.

Senator Marianne Regan was the ranking member of the Senate's Select Committee on Intelligence, the upper chamber's legislative watchdog on intelligence activities and issues. She was in Philadelphia for a conference keynote speech on election security. Now sitting in the backstage green room having just completed her luncheon talk, she was watching a live press conference on C-SPAN. She had been conferring with staffers and other Intelligence Committee members on possible responses to the Offutt attack since eight that morning, and the events unfolding on the green room's TV screen were front and center in her mind. But her interests went beyond her professional duties—Tamika Smith was one of her senior staffers. She'd been called up from reserve status three months ago to serve at Offutt.

She watched as Tamika answered some general questions about the man she had rescued, the scene at the crash site, and the damage to the plane. Regan had thought highly of Tamika since the day she had hired her fresh out of law school. She knew her as a tough-minded but thoughtful staffer who cared deeply about the policy work they did—someone concerned about the impact she was having far beyond just earning a living. But the rescue story, the crash photo, and her current performance in front of the press was forcing the senator to think about Tamika in a different light. The person she saw fending off journalists and captivating people online could go places well beyond policy analysis.

On screen, a frumpy woman on the right clamored louder than the others: "Major Smith, in your opinion did it look like a bomb caused the crash?"

"Airplane crashes are incredibly destructive—and when you add fire and smoke, the result is hellish." Tamika paused briefly. "To be honest, we're trained to block all of that out. Our undivided focus is on possible survivors and getting them out quickly."

"And the damage?"

"It was a 757 going 170 miles an hour into a concrete runway," said Tamika with another timely pause. "That never ends well."

Senator Regan chuckled to herself. Wow—now *that* was a professional deflection worthy of any politician.

The next question came from a tall, slick-looking guy in the back yelling: "I don't know if you've been following this on social media but there are a slew of threads on the fact that this was a Black woman saving a white man. Any comments on that?"

"Shit," muttered the three-term senator from Washington State. "Did he have to go there?" But again, she smiled at Tamika's response.

"I try to stay off social media as much as I can, but my guess is that neither the ditch nor Mr. Humboldt cared about the sex or color of the person who pulled him out. I was just a reserve major in the Air Force doing her job. Nothing more, nothing less."

"But a symbol, yes?"

"Only for the dedication and skill of my fellow service men and women."

"Ha!" blurted the senator, looking around the green room as others gave her a funny look. Then to herself, *God, I had no idea she'd be this good.*

"Major," came another voice, "you've served two tours in Afghanistan and one in Iraq, and my sources tell me that you've been awarded a Purple Heart, amongst other commendations. Any comments on our involvement there or the ongoing fighting?"

The senator leaned forward in her chair, curious about Tamika's response.

"Generally, that's way above my pay grade. We saved a lot of people during those tours. But wars are ugly. Soldiers and civilians get hurt. Good people die. Still, it's our job to defend others. That's what we do."

"You lost your brother on 9/11."

This brought a murmur through the room. Senator Regan knew

about Tamika's excellent service record, including the Purple Heart, but her brother's death was new information. Somebody in the crowd had done their research. Clearly there was more to this story.

She saw Tamika pause and lower her head, then look up, trying unsuccessfully to hold back the tears. Quietly, she said, "God rest his soul." And with that, Tamika mouthed a thank you, as if on autopilot, and quickly walked out.

Senator Regan had a tear in her eye, too. Watching someone the same age as her daughter brought out the mother and grandmother in her. *Jesus Christ, I wonder what else she's been through?*

A staffer walked up to tell the senator it was time to head back to DC.

She would have to get to the station and call Tamika from the train.

## Chapter 22

# NEBRASKA MEDICAL CENTER

MAGGIE HUMBOLDT FINALLY pulled up in front of the hospital around 8 a.m. San Francisco to Omaha was not an easy flight under the best of circumstances. Now, after a red-eye and a six-in-the-morning connection through Chicago, she still had no information on Johnny's condition—just that her husband had made it into surgery. The twelve-hour whirlwind had left her both exhausted and frantic.

It had all begun peacefully enough. The teacher appreciation lunch she put on at her son's middle school was the "big event" that day. Getting the parents organized was a logistical nightmare but nothing one would call intellectually challenging—it occupied plenty of time but little talent. When the event was over, she dutifully completed carpool service for Phoenix and Nathan, returning home around 3 p.m.

While her teenage daughter studied with a friend and her eighth-grade son practiced soccer, she took a respite from parenthood to write in her journal. The calm and quiet on the patio of their San Mateo home put her in a reflective mood, opening up thoughts and ideas that she was never quite able to discuss with Johnny . . . or anyone else for that matter.

First her cell phone buzzed, interrupting her. A text had arrived from Johnny. His flight must have gotten seriously delayed—or maybe he somehow knew she was writing about their relationship in her journal. Then a second spasm hit her phone with a text from Phoenix. Then her phone actually rang. Clearly Maggie needed to get rolling, so she closed her journal and picked up her handset.

It was Johnny's assistant, Stephanie Ramirez. "Are you sitting down?" she said. "You better turn on CNN."

Maggie dashed to the kitchen, feeling a hole deepening in her heart. She turned the television on with a numb hand, lowering the remote slowly to her side. There was a long pause before she gasped.

What looked like a mobile-phone video of billowing smoke and fire rising above some rolling plains at twilight was on the news channel's split-screen next to a still photo of metallic ruins seen from a distance. She allowed her mind to go completely blank for a moment. Then she processed what the images meant. A plane had clearly crashed. The caption listed an airline and flight number that did not register. Stephanie had called . . . and that was all she needed to know.

Then she remembered the texts. Reading Johnny's message hit her even harder than the actual images of the crash and fire. "Forgive me for not being there . . . so many times. I hope you find a deeper love." He'd somehow found a way to apologize, say goodbye, and set her free all at the same time. Living up to his over-achiever reputation right up until the end. She slumped in the kitchen chair. She tried to cry, but found herself slamming her fist on the table.

Much later, on the flight from Chicago to Omaha, she'd made the mistake of pulling out her journal again, thinking that writing would calm her down. The accusing words of her last entry left her trembling:

> I watch Johnny pursue his ambitions and I marvel at his zeal, his tenacity, his sheer grit. But I've become a bit character in someone else's life play. Don't get me wrong. I love being a mother and even if there's only a bit of spark, there's certainly much friendship and respect with Johnny. But the reason I'm in the pity pit is that I want something more. I want a relationship that has his, mine, and ours. Organizing lunches for teachers is nice—but I want to teach the world.
>
> If Johnny is holding me back, what's next? Am I ready to take that big a step? How can I say "no thanks" to my predictable corner of the world? What would it mean for Phoenix and Nathan? Could I support myself?

Somewhere between her Harvard degree and the parking lot at Nathan's middle school, Maggie had lost her way. She got caught in the gravitational force of an immovable object named Johnny and woke up one day realizing her world revolved around his ambitions, his direction, his purpose in life. As the plane landed in Omaha, her final thoughts had been along the lines of *Oh God, what if he's crippled? I could never leave him then.*

Fear, uncertainty, and doubt.

Now, walking into the emergency room entrance, Maggie passed what looked like an idling camera crew and went straight to the hospital's front desk. Once the receptionist realized who she was, she took her back to a private waiting room where things seemed to proceed like they do in every television drama.

"Mrs. Humboldt? My name is Christina Jacobus. I'm a family counselor at the hospital. I'm here to support the families of crash victims, as well as to coordinate things with the medical staff."

Maggie didn't seem to have an appropriate response other than to ask if she had any information on her husband.

"All I know is that his injuries are quite serious and he's been in surgery through the night. I wish there was more I could tell you, but we won't know anything until the doctors come out. What can I get you? Some food or something to drink?"

"No, thank you."

"You must be exhausted after the overnight flight. There's a private restroom just around the corner if you'd like to freshen up. I'll check in with you later and will come back when we have news from the surgeons. If you need anything, just knock on the door in the back." The counselor left the room, leaving Maggie alone with the cheap furniture.

She slumped down on an old couch that lined a wall under a draped picture window. A window that now looked out into the morning haze of her unknown future. Two table lamps at either end of the couch attempted to bring her some light, but there was no breaking through the gloom in her mind. Her thoughts shifted wildly. The last time she saw Johnny. Their final phone conversation. The look of fear on Nathan's face. The sound in Phoenix's voice when she heard her father was in surgery. And now back to the clock on the wall in the dull waiting room. Nothing to contemplate but her life.

After an hour of handwringing, Maggie's mind had slipped into a waking sleep when she was startled by the hallway door opening. A doctor and the counselor. Maggie felt a strange combination of fear and adrenaline surge through her body. They held her uncertain future in the balance.

A defendant in front of the jury.

•　•　•　•　•

"I have to be honest with you, Mrs. Humboldt. From a clinical perspective, I don't really understand how your husband is still alive." The balding doctor with horn-rimmed glasses said this with a look of wonder while sitting on the edge of a white, laminated table. They were in a windowless room outside the Intensive Care Unit. Maggie sat across the table and tried to conceal the whirlpool of emotions running through her head.

"Doctor . . . what exactly does that *mean*? Is he going to live?"

Quickly wiping the bemusement off his face, he proceeded. "Ma'am . . . I'm sorry, but we're in uncharted territory here. We've been able to address the external injuries, but he lost a lot of blood and the effects of the severe concussion are impossible to forecast. We're still sorting through a collection of internal injuries and the risk of infection from those is high. We just don't have any guideposts for assessing his prognosis." The look on his face said "clueless" and yet he seemed to be enjoying the wonderment of it all.

"So . . . I'm just supposed to sit here and wait?"

Probably sensing trouble, Christina Jacobus stepped out of the conference room shadows. She sat down next to Maggie and gently grasped both of her hands, turning her away from Dr. Horn-Rimmed and his bedside manner. "They're going to keep your husband in a controlled coma—probably for a few days. They want to let his brain rest and any swelling to subside. Once that's happened, they can pursue some of the other issues and we'll have more information."

"And where does that leave me?" Maggie pulled her hands from Jacobus's and ran them through her hair, looking at the counselor and then at the doctor. She realized there wasn't a real good answer to that question. Succumbing to the reality, she simply mumbled, "Thank you. Thank you for saving his life and for everything you're doing." Then she walked out. And she kept walking, down the hall . . . past the nurse's station . . . into the elevator . . . down to the lobby . . . around the fish tank . . . through the sliding glass doors . . . and out into the cool, murky air. She paused, realizing she was outside. She found a bench—a metal affair intended for those waiting for the hospital center shuttle bus—and sat down.

"God, how did I get here?" she asked out loud.

The memories came back quickly and easily. Pleasant memories that she now had to view through a different lens. Beginning with how she and Johnny had finally taken the plunge.

Johnny had stumbled home to Maggie's New York apartment the afternoon of 9/11—a traumatic day that seemed to change him. Perhaps for the first time in his life, he'd had no idea what to do. Humility had not been an easy concept for him. Nor was the idea that he'd needed someone to love and someone who'd love him back.

A few weeks later, he finally took her on that trip to the Hamptons— and this time he didn't let anything get in his way. They didn't go on a crowded commuter train, but rather in a chauffeured limousine. And they didn't stay at a B&B, but at investment banker Jerrod Midgley's private beachfront estate. She rubbed the engagement ring on her finger and smiled at the vision of the romantic, fireside proposal where Johnny tried to share a bit more of himself. Wrapped in a warm blanket, together on the beach, with seemingly nothing between them. "Yes" had been such an easy word at the time.

Literally the next week, Johnny announced he was leaving investment banking to go back to business school. "Mags, I'm tired of working my ass off so someone else can build something great. Paul Hayek is doing the real thing—I know it won't be easy, but I want in on that action." *Classic Johnny*, she thought. There was always a bigger mountain to climb, and he wanted to do it without training or ropes. Or discussing it with her first. Stanford was the logical school to attend, and like many things in Johnny's life, his relentless efforts brought him an acceptance letter—and a way to leave New York and 9/11 behind.

With their marriage planned, Maggie had followed—again.

What she had underestimated in this orbital whirlwind romance was the driving force that made Johnny tick. In a short phrase, he worked his ass off. His blind pursuit of performance and perfection was beautiful to watch in one sense, but when Johnny's success metric became the money that came with a "unicorn startup," Maggie knew she had lost him and herself.

God really was messing with her. For the second time in her life, she'd made up her mind to "move on" and a plane crash had interrupted her plans. How was that possible? Nobody was that unlucky. Before this latest disaster, she'd decided that things needed to change—both in their relationship and in her own sense of mission and direction. Divorce? Maybe. That was a painful thing to contemplate, much less act on, with her husband half dead in a room five stories above her.

As an ambulance pulled up to the emergency room entrance, lights flashing, she pulled up Johnny's "last text and testament" on her phone. How would he react if he woke up? Where would his head be? Did the slow descent toward death enable him to see the real depths of his heart—or was his text just a knee-jerk reaction to the reality of the end?

"Christ, I'm right back where I started. I need to get off this damn merry-go-round." Watching the shuttle bus pull away for the second time, she got off the bench and went back inside.

# Chapter 23

# THE AFTERNOON TRAIN

ALTHOUGH AMTRAK'S ACELA service between Boston and Washington, DC, was America's fastest train route, Obaid bin Latif saw a symbol of American decay. Discussions for high-speed rail service in the US had begun in the 1980s, but Acela's first revenue run did not take place until 2000. In contrast, Japan's highly successful Shinkansen trains first ran in 1964, and France's equally popular TGV service first ran in 1981. Those trains run on dedicated tracks with speeds significantly above those of the Acela, which operates on a mishmash of tracks and conditions and shares tracks with local services like MARC and the northeast regional trains. But despite its shortcomings and low profile, bin Latif selected it because it finishes its run at the heartbeat of the nation's government. The perfect next target.

He boarded the blue-trimmed, silver train at 1:15 p.m. in Newark. He climbed up the steps, turned left, and went through the sliding glass doors that led into the "quiet car" in business class. Bin Latif was dressed as a businessman, including a blue suit, red-striped tie on a starched white shirt, neatly trimmed black-haired wig, and wire-rim glasses over a prosthetic nose which jutted out over a freshly shaven chin. The clothing was uncomfortably new and far too western for his taste, the fake nose even more disagreeable. But he needed to blend in with the rest of those traveling up and down the northeast corridor—and the camouflage from video security cameras was crucial.

Having taken an aisle seat, he placed his backpack in the seat next to him. He stared vacantly out the window, avoiding the eyes of other passengers. Sitting in the quiet car ensured that he would not have to talk with anyone during the trip, both reducing distractions and adding to his security screen. A conductor came down the aisle and scanned his ticket. He'd brought a fake ID with him that matched his disguise but didn't need to show it. A train blew by the window going the other direction. It reminded him of their speed. *Shit.* All those people going that fast without even a seatbelt. The scale of death and destruction would be impressive.

Forty minutes into the trip, with rolling countryside sliding by the windows, he casually got up from his seat. He grabbed his backpack and traced his steps back through the glass doors at the back of the car. He knew exactly what he would find. He pulled the metal lever over to the left to open the sliding door to the restroom—the one place on the train he felt confident would not have any surveillance. It wasn't really a "restroom"—more like an oversized port-a-potty on wheels with everything lined in faux steel for ease of cleaning. The important part was the small maintenance supply cabinet built into the sink unit.

He slipped on plastic gloves, always protecting against the FBI's eventual investigation. He was through the rudimentary lock quickly. Then he attached the device on the back wall behind the sink pipes. He verified that the settings were correct and powered up the attached burner phone. He double checked that all was in working order.

Yes . . . the proverbial four bars.

He closed and relocked the cabinet. Tossing the gloves in the backpack looped over his shoulder, he left the bathroom. He remembered to flush the toilet and adjust his zipper so that anyone seeing him come out would think nothing of it. Returning to his previous seat, he put the backpack down and waited for the next station.

He'd made it look easy, but he knew better. He'd scouted the train six months in advance so that nobody would find him on video footage later. To further avoid FBI forensics, he'd purchased two unused burner phones in different locations using different disguises. He'd also had to find the right hiding place that was accessible and surveillance-free. The device had to be equipped for remote detonation, small enough to fit in the supply cabinet, but still capable of derailing the train. He had even verified that no janitorial service would take place en route.

Ironically, the one thing that was easy was getting the bomb on the train. No metal detectors, no searches, no nothing. Supposedly there were dogs that swept the cars, but he'd never seen one.

When the Philadelphia stop was announced, he got up and left the train. In a little less than two hours, he would take credit for his second attack in two days . . . and the chaos would begin.

• • • • •

Senator Regan boarded the Acela Express at Philadelphia's 30th Street Station, a squat, Roman-columned structure that would have fit nicely into DC's government architecture. The plane versus train tradeoff was about a toss-up from Philly, but going by rail would make it easier for herself and her two staff members to confer during the trip. In any event, given events at Offutt the previous day and the knock-on effects delaying and canceling flights, she felt more secure taking the train.

She spent the better part of an hour debriefing with two staffers on the security conference speech and then preparing for the set of meetings scheduled for the late afternoon and evening. Regan loved the back-and-forth with her team and was addicted to the go-go nature of her job. But getting anything productive done in Washington had become an incredible grind over the last four years. She could feel the physical and emotional wear and tear shredding at her dedication to service. Still fit and healthy at age seventy, with flowing gray hair and the creases of experience across her face, she was coming to the end of the track. But she was unwilling to get off while the country was in such a divided state. Unfortunately, she was not confident in the people waiting in the wings, ready to take her place.

As they approached the Maryland/District of Columbia border, she placed a call to Tamika, hoping to provide both some comfort and encouragement to her staffer-on-leave.

"Hello, Smith here," came the military greeting as her call was answered.

"Tamika. This is Senator Regan." She spoke in quiet tones, respecting the privacy of those around her.

"Good to hear from you, Senator. I should have checked in with you sooner, but things have been a little crazy here."

"No kidding. I can't imagine what you've been through. I read the stories and the team showed me the photo and social media reporting. The crash was so tragic . . . but from where I sit, you and your team were amazing."

She could feel the emotion in Tamika's voice as she answered. "The internet reaction just blew me away. So many people made me out to be some sort of Superwoman—and then there was some of the vilest and most racist things I've ever read. It reminded me of so much good and bad going on in the country. I don't know how to think about the future, but it's going to be different."

"Tamika, I know you have thick skin, but this is definitely going to test you. I cried at the end of your press conference. You've never spoken much about your family. I'm so sorry to learn about your brother. I called to make sure you know I'm here to help in any way I can."

"I really appreciate you taking the time, and your thoughts about Alex. I always wondered how you maintained your cool in front of the press—I wish I'd been able to hold it together."

"Hmm. Someone once gave me some good PR advice. When the emotion is real, when it's genuine, when it comes without warning, then it's your most powerful way to communicate. I thought that was the best part of the whole press conference. I got to know the real Major Smith— not the superhero, not the military poster-girl, but the daughter, sister, and woman." She paused briefly, choosing her words carefully. "The most important thing for you to understand—to really internalize—is that you were incredible on all fronts. In the field and in the press room. I'm beyond proud to say we work together."

The line went quiet. Then, slowly, "Thank you, Senator. That means a lot coming from you."

Regan rushed in to fill the void. "After the dust has settled, let's get some time to really chat. I have some ideas to discuss with you, perhaps a new role you can . . . oh SH—!"

A rocking explosion and horrid screeching of metal cut off her words as a wave of heat washed over her. Then the world turned sideways.

•   •   •   •   •

JJ sized up his new best friend from the FBI. Special Agent Aaron Phillips was short and stocky—built in the fireplug model with a big barrel chest—but he moved with an athletic grace that belied his build. Ex-football player, JJ guessed. He was in his mid-thirties but already going bald with wisps of graying hair above his ears. Perhaps this was genetic or maybe more a reflection of the job. Either way, he was both imposing and unassuming at the same time. JJ decided to plan for the worst and course correct later.

They were talking early in the evening over a secure connection. JJ was in the base's Sensitive Compartmented Information Facility—called a SCIF—and Phillips in a remote equivalent at the site of the Amtrak explosion and derailment. "I was planning to be in Omaha tomorrow, but obviously that's not going to happen now," commented the FBI agent. "I know our bosses are arguing about jurisdiction, but it looks like we're going to tag-team this for the time being."

Fine. Whatever. "What do you know from your end?" questioned JJ. "Looks even worse there than here."

Phillips panned the camera around so JJ could get a better view. "The train was just pulling into Union Station when an explosion ripped apart the fourth and fifth car. Killed seventy-two people right off the bat. Another ninety-four were injured in the derailment, including a US senator, a DC city councilman, and a CNN anchor." He stopped with a sigh. "I'd guess that a few of those won't make it."

"Goddamn it," was all Jessup could say. He walked away from the screen.

"That's just the train damage. The bomb also blew out windows in the main building and brought down part of the station canopy—that killed another seventeen and sent forty-plus people to the hospital." Phillips turned the camera back around to his face. "Colonel, this was not a homemade explosive. This was a bomb designed to kill on the train *and* in the station."

JJ came back to his screen. "Any other intel on the device itself?"

"Still way too early. We've got forensics on-site, but the place is a war zone so it's going to take a bit for us to sort it all out. My guess is it was triggered by a cell phone. The timing of the train coming into the station was too perfect. We'll obviously track that down. Probably burner phones, but sometimes we can get some data anyway."

Captain Washington entered the SCIF and put a video up on JJ's second screen.

"Fucker!" was all JJ could say as he slammed his hand on the desk.

Phillips's image jerked up saying, "Who?"

"It's our newfound friend Obaid bin Latif. He's posted another video taking credit for the train explosion. Jesus . . . two days, two attacks, almost two hundred dead." He rubbed his eyes hoping that would somehow change the picture. "Do you have any information on him or on this IBF organization?"

"We've got nothing. Bin Latif and his organization didn't exist two days ago as far as we can tell—suddenly they're on our most-wanted list."

"What about the video forensics and the flag? I'd never seen that before."

"Neither had we. Black background with swords on both sides—that seemed consistent. But then there's the shattered ball in the center—we've got our symbologists working on that but nothing so far."

"This is going to scare the shit out of everybody. You think they're gonna close things down?" JJ remembered the last airline shutdown all too well.

"The president's meeting with Homeland and the FBI director right now. This second attack will put them over the edge for sure. They'll declare a state of emergency—probably means shutting down the whole transportation system." He paused to yell a command to one of his people. "Well, I'll keep pushing from here. Keep me posted on developments at Offutt. 0800 your time tomorrow—if not before?"

"Roger that." JJ cut the connection. He thought about the implications of closing down the country's transportation system—planes, trains, ferries, and more. The concrete, smoke, and dust he'd seen on the screen took him back eighteen years.

But this time the prick was still alive.

## Chapter 24

# RIVERVIEW

WHEN A LARGE-SCALE disaster happens, people turn to their TV sets or mobile phones, drawn to the fire, smoke, uncertainty, and the stories of heroism and sadness. And carnage. A good bit of this is genuine concern and anxiety, albeit mixed with a tinge of morbid fascination. But there is also the thought, *What if that had been me?*

Ford Wilkes was glued to CNN, watching the coverage of the two crashes from his family room in Riverview, Michigan—a nondescript suburb of Detroit. But he was more focused, more attentive than the average looky-loo or typical couch potato. And he certainly wasn't thinking, *What if that had been me?* He was adding up the body count.

The plane had crash-landed at a damn military base—one that actually specialized in intelligence gathering. Somehow, he found the irony amusing. But it was also super frustrating because the Air Force wasn't allowing the press access to the carcass of the plane. None of the graphic images he needed people to see. The footage from Union Station was more explosive—but that had just happened so the details were also pretty skimpy.

"Shit!" yelled Wilkes, throwing his mostly empty beer can against the wall. "How are people supposed to know what's going on if you don't show them anything?" The can bounced harmlessly across the floor as he let out an irritated grunt. "I can't trust these fake-news clowns anyway." Unfortunately, the other networks were showing the same useless information. Even the wimps at Fox.

And that was a problem for Ford Wilkes. For him, the media coverage wasn't about some perverse itch for the macabre. This was business.

He got up from the raggedy couch that was his primary perch in the living room and walked around the small house that served as his current home. The couch was flanked by a beat-up leather recliner chair that faced a flat panel TV circa a decade ago. The TV itself was standing on top of a cheap old dresser that had once belonged to his parents. The dark-paneled walls created a cave-like atmosphere, making the room seem even smaller than it was. He liked the cozy feel. There was a small galley kitchen with an opening in the wall that looked out over the couch directly at the TV. A breakfast nook, two bedrooms—one of which was his "office"—and a cramped bathroom from the 1960s completed the architectural wonder.

He wasn't much for decoration anyway, didn't need a lot of sleep, and was a shitty cook. So why did he bother with a house? For starters, the price was perfect. He had millions, but the plan required that he spend his funds carefully. He'd diligently allocated money, time, and other resources to each stage of this project. He was driven to achieve his mission but realized patience and discipline were his friend. He wasn't about to squander funds on trivial matters like fine homes or renovations.

In addition to cost, the humble house provided privacy. He'd found it at the end of a cul-de-sac that had mostly been abandoned during the housing crash of 2007. If he had neighbors, he hadn't met them—and that was just as well. He left the yard to nature's progress, giving the impression that the house was empty. Being "unnoticeable" was part of the plan. Appearing to be ordinary enabled him to hide his extraordinary efforts in plain sight. There was also the reality that he'd just had too much nomadic work in his life, and the physical structure gave him some sense of permanence.

Was that Jung or Freud? Ha.

Back to CNN, where some blond chick seemed to be reviewing the timeline of every airplane and train crash in US history along with an explanation of the National Transportation Safety Board's role. "Pleeease . . . get the hell back to your kitchen and let the professionals tell me something!" he yelled at the TV.

He was checking social media too. Twitter was news he could count on—especially to gauge how people were reacting to the crash. He had already unleashed a series of bots and fake social-media posts to amplify the effects of the attacks. He could see the momentum building online as people forwarded his "news." He was dying to see how long it would take President Trump to post some xenophobic response. Now that would start a shitstorm that would support his work "bigly," as the president was fond of saying. There had to be a QAnon conspiracy opportunity in here somewhere . . .

Wilkes thought Trump had several screws loose but had voted for him anyway. He certainly wasn't going to vote for Clinton. For him, the 2016 election had been all about the establishment—its money, its control, its ideas—and what could be done to bury them once and for all. Wilkes didn't believe any of Trump's promises to "drain the swamp," but the president's willingness to attack almost any institution made his candidacy the perfect foil for Wilkes's mission. The very act of casting a ballot was unusual for him. Then again, Wilkes thought of himself as a patriot. Voting was small potatoes compared to the actions he had put in motion to reclaim the country.

He caught a glimpse of himself in the slightly cracked, framed mirror that had been hung in the hallway by a previous owner. He indeed looked "unremarkable," which of course, worked to his advantage. At five-foot-ten, and in the neighborhood of 185 pounds, a passerby would have forgotten him before the next street corner. His bland, brown hair with wavy curls ensured that he needn't bother with a comb very much. And despite an admittedly horrible diet, he was reasonably fit and could pretend to be "buff" when necessary. Basically, he looked like a white, ordinary, working-class stiff.

He liked the fact that the cover hid his inner genius. While he looked ordinary on the outside, he saw the truth behind the smoke screen that was today's rigged system. He recognized liberalism, and the paternalism that came with it, as intellectual bullshit. And he was more than clever enough to figure out how to expose that reality.

All of that brainpower had almost gotten lost in the quagmire that was the Detroit public school system. All through elementary and middle school, teachers questioned his work ethic, misreading his boredom as slowness. Then, during his freshman year in high school, he discovered the magical logic of computers. His mother raised holy hell at his school getting him into a special program that opened doors to programming classes. It was the one and only gift she was able to give him, but it was enough.

He flourished.

A white, lower-middle-class kid with a "climb the ladder" future. He graduated with highest honors from Wayne State University in 2006 with a degree in computer science and took a job in data security at a regional bank.

But when the financial crash hit in late 2007, he was laid off and couldn't pay back his pile of tuition loans. The ladder was kicked out from under him—his path out of poverty and debt blocked by the greedy bastards on Wall Street. With no immediate job prospects, or even any on the horizon, he stopped looking for work and began figuring out who was to blame.

His dad seemed to have all the answers. "You put a negro in the White House and the whole country falls apart. There are spics invading over the border taking our jobs—and the ones they don't take get shipped off to Mexico or China or get replaced by some machine I can't operate. Union is for shit . . . no backbone at all. We get brushed aside like trash." His dad's solution was to drink and then take his frustration out on his wife.

As much as Wilkes hated his father's abuse of his mom, he understood the disillusion. His dad had been fifty-seven years old, with no job and no future. The entire system sucked. The schools, the economy, the government, all of it. Then they bailed out the very banks who caused the problems in the first place.

*Fuckers.*

By mid-2008, Wilkes was unemployed, had over $25,000 in college debt, felt shitty about his life, and didn't see a future in his hometown. So he hitchhiked his way west on I-94 through the Rust Belt, then on into the Grain Belt, and eventually into the Frack Belt. He knew now, with hindsight, that this migration changed his life forever.

The oil boom was just hitting North Dakota and that meant one thing—jobs of all shapes and sizes. Given his background in programming, Wilkes was able to find work quickly. Work that paid well, especially for a single man with nothing to do but save. Williston, North Dakota, was going from a sleepy 12,000-person crossroads to a 40,000-strong, self-proclaimed "Boomtown." And everything needed technology infrastructure to run well. For the first time, he was happy—with the money, with himself, and with the friends he met in The Brotherhood. It was the start of his true calling.

A calling that was finally beginning to show results.

Still unable to fill his appetite for information on the plane and train attacks, Wilkes went down the hall to his bedroom office and put his talents to work. Over the next two hours, he'd hacked into the FAA and NTSB websites and intranets, but they were still clueless about what had caused the crashes. When he discovered that more than a hundred were dead, he paused. Not everyone—but enough that people would take notice. Still, he craved more information.

He was sure the FBI would now be on the case—and he'd already heard from that poster-boy colonel in the Air Force. A year earlier, in a technical triumph that had surprised even himself, he'd cracked into a portion of the FBI's network. He was tempted to look for some clues there but thought better of it. Going there ran the risk of leaving his tracks for them to find. He could not afford that just yet. Instead, he tapped into a commercial geo-satellite that gave him an idea of the breadth of the destruction at both locations. His partner Obaid bin Latif had certainly delivered.

Everything was going according to a carefully curated plan. He could settle in and watch those smug bastards begin to squirm.

## Chapter 25

# FROM OFFUTT TO MAXWELL AND BACK

TAMIKA RETURNED TO HER quarters, after-action report drafted and tasteless dinner consumed. She turned on as many lights as she could find. Maybe they would bring some illumination to her soul. But the dark events of the past two days had all become too much. She could not escape the images that crowded out everything else. She relived stepping into the fiery plane. She thought about Johnny Humboldt and his faint moans. And she heard the sound of Senator Regan's labored breathing through the open cell phone line.

The news coverage of both attacks was shocking—the images of the body bags at the morgue, the destroyed train, and the damaged station flashing across every news network. She could feel the anger and hatred welling up inside her. The immediate thought was that this bin Latif was a cowardly asshole. But that idea quickly triggered memories of Alabama and Afghanistan—again, and again, and again.

Realizing she hadn't really slept in almost forty hours, Tamika went to her bed. She took off her boots and laid down without bothering to remove her clothes or pull down the cover or sheets. Even as the exhaustion washed over her, sleep did not come easily. She just couldn't distract or turn off her brain. No chance she was watching any TV or looking at her computer. She tried reading the spy novel sitting on her bed stand, but that felt too real. So she just looked up at the ceiling, letting the energy slowly seep out of her body. She drifted off—not to a deep sleep but to the nightmares from Alabama.

She was commissioned as a second lieutenant in May of 2001 and had reported to Maxwell Air Force Base. Just a week into her training there, she was asked to join five guys and two women for a night on the town in Montgomery. Barhopping really wasn't Tamika's scene, but she felt safe given the crowd and was a little excited about the "adventure" of her first off-base evening. The guys seemed nice enough, everyone was an officer of some sort, and the mood was light and chill.

Derrick Tomlinson, who had invited her, was a bit of a smack-talker, and when they finally got to Sheldon's Pool Hall, a little friendly competition broke out. She had learned to play pool from her father—on reflection, he must have visited more than a few places like this during his time in the Air Force—and she was never short of competitive drive. By that point in the evening, the group had dwindled to four. Tamika paired with Derrick to take down his two friends in three straight games.

"Now *that's* how you play pool. You guys got your asses kicked by a hick from the country and a girl. You're definitely buying."

The "girl" comment was a sign to Tamika that the night was coming to an end. This was their third bar, which was probably one too many. "Derrick, I'm wiped. I've got an early bell tomorrow morning so I'm gonna grab a cab back to the base."

"Whoa, whoa, you can't do that. We've gotta collect on our victory. At least stick around for a final round so they pay up."

*Great. Now I'm playing pool pong*, thought Tamika. Being new to the crew, she didn't want to be an ass, so she gave in. "Okay, I've got to hit the head . . . then one drink and back to the base."

She walked down the length of the bar into a poorly lit hallway. She entered a door labeled "Bitches" (which was naturally paired with the one that said "Bastards"). As she looked into a murky mirror in the bathroom, Tamika sighed. She had taken the leap to go out and meet new people and it had mostly been a waste of time. She had only had a couple of beers, reflecting her Olympic training regime, but the group was all about drinking, yelling, loud music, and fraternity games. *Definitely have to add that to my list of achievements*, she thought. *I need to ask Dad how he met Mom on this gig.* Into the stall, flush the toilet, back into the scrum.

When she returned to the table, someone handed her a glass of beer. They all toasted to the pool gods, spilled a little of their drafts, and took a good drink. "I always say, you've gotta know how to pick your partner— and I picked the perfect one tonight." Derrick was clearly satisfied with himself and the opportunities ahead.

And that was the last thing Tamika remembered from that fateful bar crawl.

She had woken up the next morning with a sudden start and a bad headache. She jerked her head. She realized she had no idea where she was. What the hell had happened? She got out of bed and suddenly realized she had no clothes on. Oh God. She found the bathroom in what looked like a Motel 6ish room and gave herself a full inspection. There were no visible marks on her face or upper body. Good. But then she looked at her arms and realized her wrists were red and raw. And when she bent over to see the bruising on the rest of her body, all she could do was scream.

She was moving at light speed, as only she could. Not even thinking about what she was doing. She frantically searched the room. She found her clothes crumbled in a pile at the bottom of the bed. She put them on, found the door, and ran out. The parking lot had a few cars scattered in various spots in front of a double-decker set of motel room doors. She looked around wildly and realized she was inside a courtyard parking area at The Sunshine Inn. Metal railings, trash swirling around the cars, and the incessant flashing of a vacancy sign under the name. By now the tears were flowing—and Tamika hated crying—and panic had fully set in.

Twenty minutes later she was back on base in her quarters, not even knowing how she'd gotten there. As the fear and helplessness subsided a bit, they were quickly replaced by sheer anger.

"Where the *fuck* is that shit Derrick? I'm going to find him and string him up by his balls."

Turning from an empty threat to action, Tamika called the base operator asking for the office number for Lieutenant Tomlinson. No lieutenant by that name? Derrick Tomlinson? Oh, great—it's *Captain* Tomlinson. In the weight room where they had first met there were no uniforms or insignias and they had all gone off-base in jeans and t-shirts. *That fucker lied to me, then he drugged me, and then he . . . shit,* she couldn't even think it. With panic returning, the word *rape* hit her between the eyes. Back to the operator.

"How about Harrison and—" *what was the name of the lousy pool player with the Popeye arms? Jefferson . . . no, Jamison.* "—Jamison?" They were both captains too. So now the picture was complete. Three captains on the make, preying on new arrivals at the base.

"I'm such an idiot."

"Pardon me, Lieutenant? Do you want me to connect you with anyone?"

"Sorry to bother you." The phone bounced off the cradle, suffering the wrath of Tamika's anger.

*Maybe it was just Tomlinson . . . or maybe . . .* she could not finish that thought. She just had to block it out.

Somehow, her mind moved on to what she should do next. She could go to the police. And tell them she had been drugged and gang raped by three superior officers. In a motel where they probably had no names on the register. Oh . . . and that was after barhopping with them for four hours. That would be a tough interrogation for a white woman, much less a biracial one in Montgomery, Alabama.

She could take it up on base with the MPs or even with OSI. Going to the Office of Special Investigations would be a big deal. How would it look when a newly minted Air Force grad accused three captains—who had probably seen combat duty—of rape? Would anybody listen to her? She hated being weak, but she cared about perceptions and her career.

And then deep down, she started to have doubts. Maybe it was her fault. Did she do something to egg them on? Was there some secret code she had emitted? She certainly didn't think so, but some guys were so stupid about understanding what was a green light and what was a red light. To them everything started as a yellow light about to turn green. The more she thought, the more she blamed herself. She could have left earlier. Could have said no to the last beer. Could have been smarter. What if she got pregnant?

Shame and helplessness were soon to follow. Thankfully for Tamika, those were two emotions she just could not live with. Her first stop was the shower and the sink. There was not enough washing and scrubbing that could remove the scum from her body—but she washed and scrubbed until her skin was raw beyond the bruises. When she was done, though, the stains were still there, emblazoned in her psyche in places the soap and the brush could never reach.

Instinctively, she put on her running clothes and went for a workout. Exercise had always been her sanctuary, and more than anything right now, she needed a place to feel safe. She quickly realized that her body was not right. The injuries were more than just superficial and deeper than just her self-esteem. But she ran anyway. And not wind sprints—she ran along the base trails for over an hour. Running let her mind go blank, an emptiness that would become a steady companion in the coming months. She just felt the ache from the bruises, the burn in her lungs, the pounding on her legs, and the impact as her shoes hit the ground.

• • • • •

Tamika woke from a fitful sleep in a cold sweat. She took a moment to realize she was in her quarters at Offutt. The nightmare was not always the same—but it always had Derrick Tomlinson front and center. Even though she had no memory of the act itself, she could never forget his face, always leering down at her. She had listened to all the Academy bullshit—Integrity, Service, Excellence—followed by honor and brotherhood. When she graduated, she'd figured she was part of the fraternity. She'd learned in a Montgomery bar that it was still a "fraternity" and women were just a prize to be shared among the brothers.

She tried to block it out, but her mind went to the next time she had seen Tomlinson.

"Lieutenant, where've you been? We've missed you in the weight room . . . and I sure need a pool partner." They had run into each other behind one of the barracks.

Anger rose quickly. "Get out of my fucking way before I rack you."

"No salute? I might have to report you for that."

Middle finger salute for a reply.

"Look, Smith, I don't know what you think happened. We both had too much to drink, or at least just enough to make it interesting. As I recall, you enjoyed it. Actually, I think you enjoyed it three times as much as I did."

No words—just the flash of a right fist, straight for his face.

He slipped the punch, grabbed her arm and swung her around in an arm bar. Now at her back, he pushed her up against the building. His hot breath right in her ear. The wood cool against her cheek.

"Listen, bitch. What happened, happened. This is the Air Force, not the Academy. I thought you always wanted to play with the big boys. Welcome to the game. If you so much as whisper about this to anyone or ever take a swipe at me again, I'll bury you. White captain versus a Black woman—how do you think that ends up?"

Tamika felt the weight of his body pushing her deeper into the wall. She wanted to vomit. All she could do was twist and grunt through gritted teeth. She'd never felt so helpless. He knocked her head into the boards a bit as he pushed away.

"First time I've had chocolate. Sure was sweet."

She crumbled to the ground, feeling the pain of defeat as he walked away.

But as the minutes passed, sitting alone watching the afternoon shadows begin to lengthen, she also experienced a strength and courage settling in her soul. For Lieutenant Tamika Smith, spiritual grace met her tears and anger, mixing in a way that ultimately proved powerful. As her head cleared, she rose to her feet. She brushed herself off, leaned back against the wall, and whispered words of thanks to any angels listening.

Then, "Fuck you, Captain. You're right about one thing. I will beat the big boys."

That night, September 10, 2001, she'd written a letter to the one person who had always been there.

Her brother Alex.

## Chapter 26

# IN THE GRILL AND BAR,
# THURSDAY, APRIL 18

RETIRED GENERAL FRANK SMITH sat quietly reading a letter he had not looked at for at least a decade. A letter the Navy had forwarded to him with his son's personal effects. A letter he wished he could forget but knew he never would. Reading it again took him inside the mind and heart of the most important person left in his world. And it reminded him of so many of his shortcomings as a father.

*Dear Alex,*

*I tried to call you tonight, but I guess you're on assignment. I really need your help and advice and want to talk as soon as you can. Hopefully by the time you get this, we'll have already connected, but this will have to do for now.*

*My little world of sprinting for the Air Force and serving my country as a public relations Vanna White at the Olympics has fallen apart. I'm down a deep hole and am trying to figure out how to climb out. I don't even know how to talk about it. So maybe it's better that I have to write you first.*

*Damn. Let's get to the point. I was raped. At least by one guy but probably by three. It was a group pub crawl that ended with me in a bed naked. I went upscale . . . they're all captains. Unfortunately, I have no evidence. No proof that they drugged me, no proof that one, two, or all three of them raped me. But I've been over and over that night in my mind, and there is no way I did anything wrong.*

*I can deal with the physical scars, but that night changed me. I dreamed about serving, about protecting others, about fighting for what is right. I dreamed of running to represent my country. I dreamed about finding someone to hold me—a soulmate—whom I could trust with everything. Someone who would respect and value me for who I am and what I can achieve.*

*What do I do with all of that now?*

*You've always been the smartest one in the family—always the person who could figure things out. How do I find justice, prevent it from happening again, and continue my commitment to the Air Force? How do I get my dreams back?*

*I know this is a pile of shit to place at your feet, but you're my big brother, my shining light, my beacon for what is right and good about people. I need your help.*

*I love you and miss you.*

*Tammy*


The general put the letter down and pulled out his cell phone, hitting the first speed-dial number. She picked up on the third ring.

"Hey, Tammy. I was just thinking about you. I tried to call yesterday but you were probably pretty busy." He got up from his seat, grabbed his bag, and walked out the door and down the metal stairs. "I'd ask how you are, but I bet you're tired of hearing that question."

With a long, deep breath, Tamika said, "I saw your call and should've called you back, but I never quite got a chance to sit down and think. I have so much to tell you. And a lot of questions, too."

"You and me both. The video from the Union Station attack was devastating. How did the bastard bring down the plane and then attack the train? I can't believe the senator was on board. What do you know about her condition?"

"I heard from her assistant that she's in ICU at Walter Reed, stable but still at risk. That's better than I'd feared. I've thought about asking for leave to go see her—or to go chase after this guy."

He could tell that his daughter was struggling to keep it together. She finally continued. "But you can imagine what things are like here. I guess all I can do is pray."

The general wasn't sure what to say, so he shifted gears a bit. "Hey . . . I saw the press conference on CNN. You made me very proud. That was not easy and you were awesome."

"I'm not sure that's a good thing. The Air Force now wants me to do an exclusive on *The Today Show* on Friday. Maybe Fox News too. Daddy, I'm just so emotionally drained—I don't know if I can do that. I have to keep reliving the whole thing, which brings back other memories that I want to forget. And then they figured out the connection to Alex and that opened up even more wounds. I just feel like the entire universe is . . . I don't know . . . targeting me." He heard frustration, desperation, and a bit of fear in her voice.

"Would a burger and a beer with your dad help?"

"Now how's that going to work? Is there some type of suds edition of FaceTime I should be using?"

"Actually, I'm on the tarmac at Offutt right now."

"How did you . . . ?"

"I'm retired from the Air Force, but they still consider me family—and their planes are still flying."

Thirty minutes later, Tamika and Frank Smith were sitting in a corner booth at Billy Frogg's Grill and Bar, a plate of buffalo wings and some chips and salsa on the way. The bar was situated in an old warehouse building and was full-on neon, with a variety of store emblems, traffic signals, subway signs, and beer trays decorating every surface in the joint. The bar area was stocked with a full assortment, liquor bottles lining the wall against a long mirror. The sensory overload could have been a problem, but it created a noise-cancelling effect that drowned out everything except the two of them. Now with beers in hand, they settled back for a more serious conversation.

"After my last letter to you, I made a decision," began the general. He was fidgeting in the corner of the booth, trying to find a way for the wood to feel comfortable. He resigned himself to a long drink from his beer.

"Imagine my shock that a general in the Air Force was able to achieve that lofty goal."

"Watch your mouth, young lady," he said with a soft laugh. "I can still have you put on report."

"Not for much longer. I've reached a decision or two as well. But since you're so proud of your achievement, you go first."

The music seemed to blare just a bit louder in the background, country twang filling the silence between them. Another sip of beer and then a clearing of his throat. "I've certainly made my share of mistakes in the Air Force, but I've made even bigger ones as a parent. And that's going to stop right now. I flew out here because I had to be with the daughter I love, to support her after another difficult mission."

"That's the big decision you made? Really?"

"Enough with the sarcasm already. I'm not finished." He knew it was time, but that didn't make it any easier. "There are things you need to know. Things I've kept to myself for too long."

Tamika gave him a deeply puzzled look. "Come on, Daddy . . ."

"I read your letter to Alex. And I read it a long time ago."

A barely audible moan came from her lips, and she moved instinctively to get up from the booth. Frank Smith gently grabbed her wrist and eased her back into the dark wood.

"Daddy, why didn't you tell me? I've had nobody to talk to for almost twenty years." The tone was a bit nasty but with accents of both sadness and curiosity.

"I could say the same to you," he said quietly. "I just assumed it was something between you and Alex, so to speak, and you didn't want to share it with me. I've never been very good at understanding when I should talk to you. That was always your mother's role."

"How did you get the letter?"

"When Alex died, the Navy went through all his personal effects, removed anything remotely related to his work, and sent the rest to me. Including your letter. Some intelligence screener is probably the only other person who read it. I'm sure you know that Alex never got it."

The waiter interrupted and dropped the food on the table. "Here are your wings and chips. Let me know when you want to order lunch."

"No way he could have. I only mailed it the night before the attack." Her head tilted back and she stared up to the ceiling, perhaps looking for inspiration but only finding more beer trays. Then her searching eyes came back to his. He felt an uncomfortably penetrating stare that seemed to burn straight through to his innermost thoughts.

The general decided he'd better continue. "I should have told you, talked to you about it, gone after the bastard . . . something. But I was so obsessed with Alex's death. So depressed over the holes in my own heart. And I lost my connection to the most precious person left in my life."

Now they both needed a long gulp of beer as they picked at the food, trying to bridge the gap that had opened between them.

He finally took the leap to her side of the chasm. "I want you to know, I eventually did something. Maybe not enough, but something. I kept asking myself how a base commander could let that happen? I knew Chase Weber well—we served together. I always thought he was a good man and a very capable leader. So, I flew to Maxwell and told him about the letter."

"Was I still there?" asked Tamika incredulously. "Why didn't you see me?"

"You were already in theater with the Taliban." He looked away. "God, Chase was mad. I don't know if I've ever seen someone that pissed off. Turns out he has three girls. We talked about a bunch of ideas, but we didn't know the names of the captains involved. And post 9/11, almost everyone at that level had shipped out. It was a dead end."

"That's exactly why I never mentioned it to you or anybody else. There just wasn't anything anyone could do. And the Air Force certainly didn't want to hear about it."

He loved the service but was glad she was finally being honest with him. "Sadly, I think you're right. When the sexual assault scandal hit the

Academy a few years later, Chase and I both forced ourselves onto the investigating committee. I didn't retire from the Air Force until the changes we recommended were implemented. It was bittersweet for me. The Air Force was my life's calling and to leave it on such a pathetic note hurt—but at least that work was done."

Tamika didn't seem to know what to say.

He cut back in before she could respond. "I'm so sorry I couldn't rescue your honor, but I hope I honored your commitment to the country."

She looked past his shoulder with a questioning look, her lips parted slightly, and then seemed to come to some conclusion. "Daddy, I'm grateful for what you did. Truly. I'm positive it's made a difference at the Academy and hopefully saved others from . . ." She couldn't come up with the right words for her experience. "But there's so much more to the story. I think it's time you knew everything."

# Chapter 27

# HELMAND PROVINCE

KANDAHAR.

The very name would come to mean "rebel stronghold" or "god-forsaken wasteland," depending on which side of the war you fought. Second Lieutenant Tamika Smith had reported to Kandahar in the late spring of 2002 and was assigned to the 451st Air Expeditionary Group. The 451st controlled the airspace in southern Afghanistan, managed drone deployments, and was responsible for all combat search and rescue activities in the country. Her training at Maxwell had been accelerated, and she quickly became a fully qualified CSAR specialist. In hindsight, she would wonder what it meant to be "qualified," as she certainly hadn't been prepared for what she found there.

The airbase near Kandahar was originally built by the United States during the Cold War, used by the Soviet Union when it occupied Afghanistan, and then secured by the Taliban as a jumping-off point back and forth to Pakistan. After 9/11, the airbase and the surrounding desolation was captured by the US Marines and Army. In retrospect, that background explained everything Tamika had experienced during her tours in Afghanistan. A typical clusterfuck.

Honor. Her father had used that word a moment ago in their lunchtime conversation at Billy Frogg's Grill and Bar, and it had hit Tamika right between the eyes. What does it mean to serve with honor? What would her father say when he'd heard the whole story? Sitting in the booth, trying to look up at him but failing miserably, Tamika inched up to the real point of her story, reliving the pain that was already showing on her face. "Kandahar made desolate look like civilization. The wind-worn rocks, shitty terrain, dusty desert, dry stream beds—all of it was just my little part of hell. And I was still earning my CSAR stripes, making mistakes and trying to cover them up by working my ass off. I guess I thought of it as my Olympics and I still wanted to be a champion."

The look she got back was one of patience and understanding from a father who had been to all points of hell on the military compass. He waited in silence for her to continue.

Tamika hesitated but knew the time had come. "Everything about that day is embedded in my mind, coming back more vividly each time I go there. The day started like an oven and progressed to blistering quickly. The walk from the barracks to the ops center had to be a run . . . the ground burned. The call came in at 1207 local time—one of our Pave Hawk's was returning from a ground insertion when it went down in the hills above Helmand Valley. Now that is *not* a place you want to go down. Rugged, tribal, and Taliban infested. But the initial intel was that this was a mechanical problem—so they sent up a CSAR team in another Pave. Me."

"No gunship cover?"

"Like I said, they didn't think it was necessary. It was the middle of the day—not a time when much is moving in that part of the world—and this just looked like a rescue operation. In hindsight, stupid, but this was Afghanistan in 2002. The Army used their Apaches for ground support and there weren't a bunch to spare. We learned our lessons the hard way."

Tamika paused again as she thought about how to tell the real story. Being honest with herself was not easy.

"We came in low around a ridge and saw the wreckage down by a stream. There is a bunch of irrigation in Helmand and the Pave had crash-rolled down the hill to a flat area next to one of the channels. They'd hit hard—sure didn't look like a controlled landing to me—but I guess I was still green and didn't really know a crash from a landing. Then we saw the gunfire from the ridge above and in front of the helo."

More memories flooded in, and she went into replay mode.

"Wilson 0-3 base, this is Lynchpin 1-2 over the crash site. Bird is down—likely damage from enemy fire. We have unfriendlies on the ridge to the north moving in. 50-cal fire coming from the downed helo. At least one survivor. Requesting gunship support."

"Roger, Lynchpin 1-2. Stand by."

"Captain, get me down there. Put us to the south back behind the crash site." Tamika had trained for this moment. She'd been on a number of missions already, but this was a chance to save someone from the killing and she was not going to let it get away from her.

"Lieutenant, our job is search and rescue, not firefighting. We wait for orders."

"By the time Wilson 0-3 figures it out, there won't be anyone to rescue. Put me the fuck down there. I'll get to the Pave, no problem. I can extract back to your position." She said it with the conviction of someone who hadn't seen much combat.

The pilot and copilot looked at each other, shook their heads, but wheeled the helo in a hard circle maneuver, the left cargo door looking straight down to the ground, putting some distance between them and the insurgents.

"You've got five minutes, Lieutenant. I won't lose another bird. Get in, get 'em moving, and get out."

"Roger that. Keep me posted on the gunship support."

The rescuing helicopter came to a rest on a slab of rock some 500 yards beyond the crash site and behind a dirt-brown outcropping—leaving some buffer and cover from the advancing enemy.

Tamika hit the ground and ran her Olympic race. Wrong distance with the wrong shoes and too much equipment. But she set a record in the CSAR dash, across open ground exposed to the fire from the hills above. She crushed the curve around another pile of rocks with her best lean and crossed the finish line smash-sliding into the back of the damaged helicopter amid a flurry of bullets. When the dust settled, she squeezed around a badly bent cargo door and dove inside the carcass.

*And then she froze.*

*It wasn't the dead gunner she stumbled over or the blood splattered around the interior of the crippled bird. It wasn't the incessant crackle of the ship's 50-caliber gun firing up into the hillside. And it wasn't the sound of bullets ricocheting around the outside and exposed openings.*

*No, it was the face of the man firing the gun that shut her down in her tracks. And for a brief instant, her world stopped spinning. The audio muted. Nothing but silence amid the cacophony of war. Her brain locked up, seized by anger, hatred, and sheer shock. Through the dirt, sweat, and blood, she recognized Captain Derrick Tomlinson, who seemed to be yelling something urgently at her.*

*The radio buzzed in her ear. "Apache on station in six minutes, Lieutenant. I don't think you have that long. Get who you can and get the fuck out of there."*

*"Roger that." Brain rebooted. Audio back on.*

*"They got us with fucking ground fire if you can believe that. Both took fragments in our legs," screamed Tomlinson, pointing over to his copilot, who was huddled speechless. "Jesus, where's our support?" He clearly didn't recognize Tamika. Maybe out of context. Maybe fighting for his life. Maybe he never noticed her at all.*

*"Lieutenant . . . NOW!" screamed the voice in her ear.*

*Tamika paused to look at Tomlinson, his leg bleeding through a makeshift bandage, and the injured copilot, who looked even worse. She made a choice. "Gunship inbound!" she yelled. And without a second thought, she dragged the copilot out the back of the helo and hoisted him on her back. As she stood to run the second lap of the race, her radio came alive again.*

*"Covering fire, Smith—haul ass." The Pave Hawk popped up over the outcropping and unleased everything it had on the hillside to protect her retreat. With the rapid-fire sound of Tomlinson's gun fading in her ears, she made it to the first curve and some protection from the rocks there. But she felt the sting of a round in her arm as she ran the exposed straightaway. She stumbled to the right, more*

*from the shock than from the wound, and bounced off the rocky ground on her side. The unnamed copilot was now screaming as they moved. This was not how they taught extraction at Maxwell.*

*Run, bitch, run! was all she could think.*

*Adrenaline and primal forces took over, pushing her body beyond itself. When she finally hit the protection of the rock wall, the Pave settled to grab the wounded flyer. Tamika hopped in yelling, "Go, go, go!" The Pave Hawk wheeled back and away from the action to climb out of range.*

*"50-cal has gone quiet, Lieutenant. What's your sit rep?"*

*"Pilot was badly wounded and couldn't move—just sat there firing. He told me to take the copilot. They were closing in when I evac'd. He must be dead. Tell the Apache to light the bastards up."*

*"Roger that." He paused and looked her up and down. "Gotta say, I've never seen anyone run like that. Fucking Carl Lewis with a redwood tree on his back. You are one crazy woman." A minute later, she felt the explosions as the Apache did its work—the Pave Hawk shook as the bombardment reverberated through the air. She looked away feeling nothing.*

*She would be called a hero for saving the copilot's life. She would be awarded a Purple Heart for the wounded arm. Her epic run would be a story retold on the base. And the only thought in her head was, You finished first, but you lost the race.*

Now back in the Omaha bar . . . music, smoke, and noise . . . Major Tamika Smith looked up at her father, tears running down her face. "I never thought twice about it, Daddy. I left him there to die, and I didn't give a shit."

General Frank Smith looked her straight in the eyes, searching for the words to heal her soul, and said what he felt deep in his heart, "Better him than you."

# Chapter 28

# PAUL HAYEK'S HOME

AL QAEDA. TERRORISTS. Assassins. Paul Hayek could come up with any number of descriptors, but he kept coming back to the one that was burning a hole in his soul. Muslims. Perhaps in some sort of war-torn, implicit peace treaty, his Christian father and Muslim mother had always left religion and faith up to Paul to decipher. Born into a Judeo-Christian-Islamic shitshow in Lebanon, he'd originally chosen to follow science rather than a God that could not make up his mind. The logic of Spock had been his guiding light. The idea that there was some supreme being orchestrating things had been banished from his lexicon. Then eighteen years ago, 9/11 had happened and Paul's outlook on life and faith had changed.

He knew Maggie was in Omaha now and that his lifelong friend and business partner's survival hinged on some surgeon's skill and one of God's coin flips. He was pacing his Menlo Park living room, blazing a new hiking trail in the hardwood floors. It was foggy outside, the living room lit by a single standing lamp in the corner by the stone hearth. His footsteps echoed deeply in the silence. The décor was modern bachelor—a bit sparse and austere but well beyond the fraternity. The house seemed to appreciate Paul's grim, helpless mood.

He'd watched the online video of Obaid bin Latif taking credit for bringing down Johnny's flight and blowing up the train—all in the name of Allah. With great anger, it brought him back to his conversion moment in 2001. He had been reading news accounts of the 9/11 attacks as well as watching CNN's coverage. And in the horror of reliving those accounts, he'd had a rather shocking revelation: At some cultural, anthropological level, he was Muslim. He had had no idea what that meant at the time—he certainly hadn't thought about observing Salah five times a day—but he had known it was an important epiphany in his life. The call with his mother that followed had confirmed it.

On that morning after 9/11, Nayla Hayek went right to the point. "Paul, I'm so glad you called. For the first time since Beirut, I'm scared. All those people killed—how could someone *do* that? And then they claim it's part of an Islamic holy war. It makes me sick. People here are so angry that I'm afraid to go outside."

"Ommi, that's why I called. I couldn't sleep last night. You know how I get when I'm agitated. I'm angry, too."

"We should all be upset, Ibni. Murder is murder. Mothers and fathers, sons and daughters . . . gone." There were tears in her voice.

"It's more than that," continued Paul. The words came slowly for him. "They did it in the name of Islam, and that . . . that's blasphemy." An anguished pause. "How could they?"

Paul rarely used Arabic words like *ommi* with her, believing it should be left in his past, and he never, ever had cared about Islam or any other religion for that matter.

His mother must have sensed this. "Paul, we've talked often of the civil war in our homeland. The war that never seems to end. The war that has been going on for thousands of years. Jehovah, Jesus, Allah—they're not the cause of this war. Hatred is a human creation. It takes hate-filled people to murder the innocent. Yesterday is yet another example of the dark side of humanity."

"But you said you're scared and afraid to leave the house. The hijab will label you as one of them. As one of us. They'll make us all out as murderers."

"I'll overcome my fear—we must all overcome our fear. We must proclaim the true meaning of Islam. We must make people understand that *salam* means *peace*."

"And how can I do that? I'm just an engineer trying to build something."

"My son, are you Muslim? Is that who you are?" She said it gently and Paul let the words sink in for a minute. She continued. "Does anyone else know? You have nothing to fear if you have the courage to face it. The courage to tell others what you now know."

There was a long silence, one that Paul didn't know how to break. As she always did, his mother had found just the right words to make him think beyond the math of his daily life.

"I love you, Ommi," he concluded. "Be careful." And he hung up.

Later that day, he wrote an editorial that would be published in the San Jose *Mercury News* as part of their ongoing 9/11 coverage. He had closed the editorial with an attempt at solidarity between his Islamic faith and his love for America:

And I am a Muslim. I may not practice all aspects of Islam, but it forms the fabric of my principles and beliefs. It shapes who I am and how I care for others. Islam is a faith based in modesty, forgiveness, tolerance, and morality. There are those that use violence as a tool of our faith. They are not my brothers or sisters and their actions have no place in Islamic life. Their hearts are filled with murderous hate and they shall be judged.

On this day, in the shadow of the 9/11 attacks, I say to my fellow Americans that I am your brother, your neighbor, your friend. I share your anger, I feel your sadness, I join you in prayer. A homeless refugee, a hard-working immigrant, a grateful American, a peaceful Muslim.

Please accept me for who I am and what I will become.

For Paul, the editorial had been about personal catharsis. But for others, it singled him out as "one of them." That declaration of his Muslim faith and heritage had cost him the next round of funding he needed for his first startup. In the anger and fear after 9/11, Silicon Valley and its venture capitalists had shut him out. It killed his dream for a company he'd founded called VidEx—a video streaming service years before Netflix.

Now back in his Menlo Park apartment after "jihad attacks" on a plane and a train, he still felt the pain and anguish . . . and could not deny the anger. The pacing back and forth was not erasing his shock that nothing had changed. He scanned through a number of articles online, all of which covered the sensational press conference, Johnny's miracle rescue, and the horror of Union Station. He felt his hands tighten and his heartbeat accelerate as he processed the implications of an Islamic terrorist group operating in his adopted homeland.

Paul Hayek was not a liberal Democrat by any stretch of the imagination—he fully embraced traditional conservative principles—but he was tired of months of anguish and haranguing across the country as the border crisis escalated. He hated Trump's message blaming immigrants and refugees for everybody's problems, but he didn't see others offering viable solutions either. He knew the real process of moving to a new country. He knew the real sacrifices people made. Paul's own immigration journey had begun because of a violent, well-documented war—a fight with no end in sight.

He knew things were different on the Mexican border, but he still felt a kinship and compassion for those trying to improve their lives. He contemplated the US becoming a more difficult place for immigrants to get a fair shake. What would that mean for the country and for future immigrants? And for himself as someone who had been given great opportunities but maybe had underachieved?

As an engineer, he distilled his anxiety into two concrete decisions. He would figure out how to save the failing Cybernoptics. It was his baby, and nobody was going to take the company away from him. And for a second time in his life, he was reminded that God's gifts were meant for more than just making money.

He decided those gifts required more of him—and actions that were more personal.

## Chapter 29

# RECOVERY, FRIDAY, APRIL 19

"HEY, WELCOME BACK to the living," were the first words he heard as he returned to something like full consciousness. The room was still swimming a bit, but Maggie's smiling face greeted Johnny, and he reflexively smiled in return. *Wow*, he thought, *I survived. How the fuck did that happen?* Out loud but in a whisper, he rasped, "I never thought I would see your smile again."

Soon there were tears on both their faces. No hugs could penetrate the equipment tangle surrounding his body, but a tight grip of the hand was enough emotional connection for the moment.

"Are the kids here, too?"

Maggie dabbed at her eyes with a tissue and cleared her throat. "No—you can see them on FaceTime later. Stephanie is trying to keep them focused on school. They've yelled incessantly about wanting to come, but that didn't make any sense while you were snoozing."

"Am I going to be all right? I feel like shit." He tried moving his head around, but his range of motion was limited. "It looks like I've collected some plaster, wiring, and electrical connections since my last flight."

"You were too stubborn to die. The doctors now think there's a good chance you're going to make a full recovery, which by the way, they would have bet against when you came in. You know, you bounced down the runway like a rubber ball." She added the appropriate motions as if the words might not sink in for him.

"Last thing I remember was the first jolt of the plane hitting the ground . . . then nothing. Absolutely nothing. How many days have I been out?"

"We're just starting day three. They kept you sedated while you were fighting some shitty infections and brain swelling." She pointed to the fluid bag and tubes still delivering antibiotic drips. "They're still a little worried about the infections, I guess because they have a way of sticking around."

And with that bit of cheery information, Johnny drifted back off to dreamland.

• • • • •

Tamika moved purposefully into the main lobby of Nebraska Medical Center. It had been three days since her rush from the helipad into the lobby with her miracle rescue and she now had a chance to really notice her surroundings. Like so many other hospitals she had visited, the architecture was from at least four different decades, with enough connecting hallways, elevators, and wings to make a Habitrail proud. She followed a color-coded path that led to the ICU, hoping to finally meet the man she'd pulled from the ditch.

The ICU nurses had seen her on the ward several times visiting other crash patients—her notoriety bought her a bit of unauthorized access—and they had been quick to notify her when Johnny woke up. She walked down the stark, white hallway, past a number of computer stations, wheelchairs, and a bed on rollers. She paused before knocking on the door, feeling the emotions of the last few days wash over her. *Time to get yourself together, girl.*

Her knock was met by a woman's voice saying "come in" in a tone that was as much question as command. Tamika pushed the heavy door in. Her eyes focused immediately on the man lying in a mechanical bed surrounded by an impossible amount of machinery. The Frankenstein-like image made her want to look away. Johnny Humboldt's leg was elevated, clearly in a cast. His head was heavily bandaged, and an entire side of his face was badly swollen and discolored. His arms were seemingly sprouting miles of tubing with the connected equipment continually beeping. Computer monitors lit up the room, redrawing graphs with each breath. And all of this strangely set among a menagerie of fresh flowers and plants, presumably sent by all sorts of well-wishers.

Regaining her composure, Tamika shifted her attention to the attractive, blond-haired woman just rising from a vinyl chair on the opposite side of Johnny's bed. She was a few inches shorter than Tamika, wearing dress blue jeans with a white blouse under a patterned blue sweater. Both fatigue and relief were written across her face. As much as Tamika had talked about Johnny's rescue over the past few days, she honestly hadn't prepared herself to meet him. Much less his wife. She hoped the awkwardness didn't show. The words finally came out.

"Please excuse the interruption, Mrs. Humboldt. My name is Major Tamika Smith. I work in search and rescue at Offutt Air Force Base where your husband's plane crashed."

"Oh my God . . . I should have recognized you from the pictures. You're his rescuing angel!" Maggie jumped up and gave her a huge hug, catching Tamika a bit off guard. "Please, please, sit down. Johnny will wake up again here at some point."

"Ma'am . . ."

"My name is Maggie. Should I call you 'Major'?"

With a nervous laugh, she said, "Tamika will do just fine. Technically, I'm in the Air Force Reserve, but the sooner I get rid of the title, the better." *Why am I blathering about that?* "But Maggie, I was just going to say that, if this is an intrusion, I'll certainly understand."

"Are you kidding? It's just me, Sleeping Beauty, and these hospital machines. I could use the company."

"How's your husband doing?"

"Well, where to start? He has some external wounds that are a hassle—a broken leg, a badly sprained wrist, and enough bruises in various stages of discoloration to fill a Crayola sixteen-pack. But the doctors tell me it was the brain trauma and internal injuries that should have killed him. When he was thrown from the plane, he fractured his skull, punctured a lung, and broke two ribs—with a grade 3+ concussion to wrap it all up."

"Good grief. I still don't understand how he survived the initial impact."

"Well, that's just like Johnny. Everything is a prize fight and he's the underdog. He always manages to outwork and outthink everyone and somehow end up on top. I'm not sure how that works when death is on the other side . . . but he seems to be winning that fight too. The doctors are now pretty optimistic."

Before Tamika could respond, Johnny opened his eyes and asked for some water.

"Honey," Maggie said, pouring him a cup of water, "I want you to meet Major Tamika Smith. She's the one who dragged you out of the ditch and brought you to the hospital."

Johnny looked up and actually managed a smile. "Nice to meet you, Major."

"Good to meet you too, Mr. Humboldt. How're they treating you here?" She couldn't place the unease she was feeling. He was the one in the hospital bed, for Christ's sake.

"Pretty well, I guess. I'd love to lose some of the wires and beeping machines." He paused as if fully appreciating her for the first time.

After a moment, Maggie cut in. "Johnny, honestly, you're such the Detroit boy. You might want to say something that approaches 'Thank God you were there to save me.' And Tamika, if you call him Mr. Humboldt ever again, I will cut off your visiting privileges." They all laughed—Johnny with some effort.

Maggie continued to fill what was a strangely awkward silence. "Johnny, you know that you and the major are quite the famous couple now. What's the latest tally, Tamika, something like 300 million views?" She pulled out her phone and showed the photo to her husband.

Johnny fixated on the image, staring long and hard. "As usual, Maggie's right. I'm deeply grateful for what you did, Major. I'm not speechless often, but I don't really know what else to say." Then as if reconsidering, "God, I look more dead than alive . . . and I don't have any idea how you found me and pulled me out of that ditch."

"The good news is that I've had a lot of training—and this time nobody was shooting at me. The real heroes are the doctors. When I brought you in, I didn't think you were going to make it." Now, all things considered, Tamika thought he looked pretty darn good.

The conversation turned to more mundane topics and then Johnny nodded off.

Maggie smiled quietly. "He just sort of runs out of gas in mid-sentence."

"That's all right. I'm just glad to see him alive and making progress. I've brought back way too many that didn't make it or ended up a shell of what they were. Angels were watching over us that night."

"He did the same thing when that older husband and wife came up to see him earlier this afternoon. They said they were sitting next to him on the plane. Brought Johnny some chocolates."

Tamika smiled. "The Roscovitches. They're such a cute couple. When I pulled them from the wreckage they were so worried about your husband. I visited with them yesterday—so good to see them recovering too."

After a longish pause without much to say, she continued, "Well, I've got to get back to the base. The Air Force wants yet another set of reports—it's like the investigation can't move forward fast enough, and yet they want every 't' crossed and each 'i' dotted properly." Tamika grabbed a pen and quickly wrote something on some scrap paper next to Johnny's bed. She handed it to Maggie. "Here's my cell phone number. If you think of it, I'd love to get an update on how he's doing. I don't get to track many of the success stories, and this is one I'll never forget."

"Of course, I'll make sure Johnny gets it. Thank you so much for coming by. There is no way we can ever show how much you mean to us now." Maggie gave her a hug, complete with a soft pat on the back as Tamika left the room.

*I really like them*, thought Tamika as she walked back down the stark hallway. Then out loud to nobody in particular, "Too bad I'll never see them again."

# Chapter 30

# A WEEKEND WITH FAMILY

STEPHANIE RAMIREZ FLEW out with the Humboldt kids after school the next day, and together they stayed the weekend. The family reunion was as joyous and raucous as you can have in a hospital. The medical staff met Phoenix and Nathan and shared in their joy, for this was truly a celebration of life and a reward for their lifesaving work. There were balloons, some desserts, a bit of singing, and plenty of laughter in and outside of Johnny's corner room. Only a few hospital rules were broken.

All of it was a much-needed elixir for Maggie, reminding her of the meaning of family and the wonder and importance of her kids. Patience was going to be very important for both of them, as Johnny recovered physically and began to sort out the inevitable emotional challenges. Yet, in some twisted way, it also forced her to think about the difficult decisions ahead. While she had missed being able to share her day with him, she could not set aside the deep problems in their relationship. Why did she feel trapped and unfulfilled? Where had the fire and intensity gone? She caught glimpses of Johnny smiling or laughing and wondered where his head was at. How could she be selfish when she saw all of this? Was this more about her or about him?

Sunday began much the same way, until Maggie called a halt to the festivities. "I need some fresh air and a walk. Honey, why don't you and the kids have some time just to talk and catch up. You can certainly ask Nathan about his chemistry test and Phoenix about the dance last weekend. I think they need some daddy time before they head back home this afternoon."

"I'll come with you," Stephanie said. "I need much more than a walk after all this food, and we have some house things to discuss anyway."

The women grabbed coats and hustled off. Two elevator rides and a few switchbacks brought them to the front of the hospital and a brisk north wind. They walked in silence for a bit, mostly just trying to catch their breaths in the cold air and build up a bit of exercise-momentum warmth. Traffic was light as they got to Saddle Creek Road, and the sidewalk was empty except for the barren trees planted between the sidewalk and the street by a city planner run amok.

"Now this is something I don't miss in California," said Maggie breaking the ice figuratively and perhaps a bit literally. "We had some cold days in Boston, but this wind is no fun at all. I thought spring was here."

"Well . . . I'm a Latina from Arizona, so this is just bullshit as far as I'm concerned." Stephanie looked sideways at Maggie and laughed. "I have to say it feels good to blow off a little steam. I know I've been on a razor's edge with work and the kids—and I can't possibly imagine what you've been going through."

"I've been asked 'how are you doing?' so many times—and there really isn't anything I can say. I thought my husband was dead, I waited while he knocked on death's door, and now he's back. Ta-da!" Maggie shook her head violently, as if to knock some sense into herself.

"I'm sure that's tiring—but at least he's alive and we're all together."

Realizing that "family" included Stephanie, Maggie reacted quickly. "Jesus, neither of us have taken the time to thank you properly for everything you've done. It's like having one of our parents there to fill in. I know the kids love you—and they probably tell you things we'd never hear. What can we ever do to make it up?"

"First off, you don't need to do anything for me. I love Phoenix and Nathan and would do anything for them. I've never had any kids myself, so I love the role of Aunt Stephanie."

They had reached a stoplight that was flashing the "Don't Walk" sign, but Stephanie stepped into the metaphorical traffic. "But if you really want to thank me, you and Johnny can start being honest with each other."

"What's that supposed to mean?" Maggie stopped, mid-crosswalk, turned at Stephanie and gave her a "butt out" look.

"Relax, Maggie, I'm on your side. And I'm on Johnny's side, too." They stepped up onto the next sidewalk and continued walking, Maggie wondering where Stephanie was going with this.

"I've worked with Johnny through thick and thin for thirteen years— and I know everything he does and almost everything he's thinking. And even though we're just friends, I feel the same way about you. In many ways, I'm a part of your relationship. The crash was a horrific thing, and I know it was like reliving 9/11 for both of you. It had to expose those old wounds."

"I thought we had left that behind," interjected Maggie as they reached the next intersection.

"Maggie, you know we can't run from our history. This crash certainly made me cry and left me sleepless, but it also forced me to step back and think about how much I treasure both of you and what you've done for me. Watching the kids also made me think about the meaning of family and what I've missed."

They continued straight into the wind along some apartment buildings. "I never understood why you didn't have kids—you're such a natural with them."

"Maria and I chose not to get married, and we chose not to have a family. Maybe we were too self-conscious about the double whammy of being Hispanic and lesbian. But it was the choice we made. And married or not, we still know what being in a loving relationship requires—the sacrifice it demands. It's not about the ceremony, not about the living together, not about the sex itself." She stopped short there.

"What?" Maggie was now feeling agitated.

Stephanie dove in. "In the last five years, I can count on one hand the number of times either you or Johnny has shown real, emotional affection for each other. Friends, partners, and parents—absolutely rock solid. But I don't buy 'lovers.' I don't buy 'emotionally connected.'"

Maggie's first reaction was to deflect. "You're kidding, right? You pick now to have this conversation? Like I said, my husband almost died."

"There has always been *something*—some reason to postpone facing what you both know. *Of course* the timing sucks, and I feel rotten bringing it up. But I also saw the text Johnny sent to you. I see you guys pretend with the kids. And I see that look in your eyes."

"That's just the grind of work, kids, and life speaking," she said defensively. "It squeezes the juice out of the love until sometimes there's not much left." Another empty intersection, more crosswalk, and up the curb onto the other side.

Stephanie stopped walking. "You and I both know that love is about the deep, impossible-to-describe feeling of holding someone's hand and knowing that they are the mirror reflection of your soul. Maria is my soulmate—I know that with a certainty that I can't explain. And I think you know that you and Johnny will never play that role for each other."

Maggie turned her head up to the slate gray sky, and then back down to the ground, saying with a tone of acceptance, "I keep asking myself, 'How did I get here?'"

As they turned back toward the hospital, Stephanie filled the void, "In your heart, you know you want something different. That doesn't mean you don't love your kids or respect Johnny for all that he is. But it's time that you became the person you were meant to be."

"I have everything—great kids, plenty of money, a trustworthy man—and it's just not damn enough," Maggie continued, some irony mixed with resignation. "I can't even believe I just said that."

"Because it's true. And there's nothing wrong with that."

# Chapter 31

# A BASEMENT IN VIRGINIA

MUNCHING ON A PEANUT BUTTER and jelly sandwich, crumbs sneaking their way into one of his several keyboards, Bryce Roscovitch sat quietly contemplating the front page of CNN.com. Mainstream media was not his usual home on the internet, but it was an easy way to understand what was going on "above ground." In the real world. The world he tried to avoid as much as possible. Bryce's comfort zone, his specialty, his home, was in the proverbial darkness of the underworld. A place where there was no establishment structure, societal pressures, or parental expectations.

The dark web.

In a literal sense, he lived in a two-bedroom house in a small town in rural Virginia, but even there, he spent most of his time in the basement. He'd built an office—more of a cave, really—complete with blackout curtains on the windows with light provided by the four 28-inch, 144hz monitors that formed a semicircle around his worktable. The room had electric baseboard heat, but he never had to turn that on. His four tower computers sitting under the table hummed 24/7, generating plenty of heat for the room.

Since he was in the "security" business, he had custom built each of the computers utilizing full disk encryption with terabytes of local and backup disk storage. He mostly ran Windows and Linux but he also utilized more eccentric operating systems like Solaris and QNX. LUKS and TrueCrypt provided his Linux and Windows encryption—and he even had physical measures in place that destroyed his real encryption keys if they detected movement or tampering of his desktop machines.

He capped this digital security with a complex system of hardware and software firewalls and compartmentalized network zones.

He'd done all the special electrical work himself, including installing a diesel generator that would kick in should the power go out for longer than his uninterruptible power supply could handle. He'd also acquired a non-traceable prepaid SIM card that allowed him to have a 5G connection for emergency purposes. The only exception to all of this custom work was the two T1 high-speed internet connections (one fiber and one cable) he'd had installed.

This was command central for his business—an operation that uniquely suited his talents and had made him wealthy enough.

Of course, he didn't think it was really about the money. He'd watched his father pursue the capitalist dream and felt the sacrifices firsthand. Bryce had abandoned that path for good. The overdose in college that almost killed him had ended up being the lifesaving wake-up call he needed. He left home, left his family, and, most importantly, left the burdens and expectations that came with being the firstborn son of a self-made billionaire.

The only person he could trust in this world was Angela, and even she didn't know exactly where he lived or what he was doing. They communicated sporadically through an untraceable email connection, which was essentially an encrypted digital "blind drop" protecting both Bryce and Angela. Still, she was a physical and emotional lifeline to the real world beyond his computers—and he missed her deeply.

And with that longing came a lingering sadness, especially when he occasionally received his mom's retyped letters from Angela. He knew Shea had tried to help while he was growing up. But he'd felt alone and trapped—and, like a caged animal, had to escape. He'd embraced a new life, one that allowed him to be "productive," accountable only to the standards of excellence held by his fellow dark-web dwellers. For despite all the youthful dysfunction, Bryce had discovered that he was talented.

Extremely talented.

He found solace in the world of programming and realized that writing code was as natural for him as counting from one to ten. He'd heard of people who had perfect pitch and could reproduce a piece of music without any professional training. Bryce was the equivalent savant programmer—hidden in his autistic spectrum attributes was the programming manifestation of Beethoven.

Sure, he had to learn some languages and conventions, but that came easy. Once appropriately armed with those basic skills and his uniquely wired brain, he could create almost anything. The irony, of course, was not lost on him. "Jesus," he'd said to no one in particular one day. "I've got the same skills as my father . . . except I'm much better than he is." Exponentially better.

He could have become a university researcher, sold his skills to the highest corporate bidder, or latched on to a unicorn startup. And that is where any similarities with his father ended. Working with people was deeply challenging for Bryce, a combination of extreme shyness, physical awkwardness, difficulty reading social cues, and outright fear. Puberty and early adulthood had scarred him so severely that he had to run and hide.

Fortunately, today's digital economy was stocked full of opportunities for someone with Bryce's skills. His specific talents were doubly valuable in the world of the dark web. He could hijack his way into any number of schemes, and then use those same tools to mask his identity from everyone else. He never called himself a hacker—he found that term strangely nondescript and offensive. Nor was he a Julian Assange or Edward Snowden character who pirated information to leak it for some supposed social purpose. Bryce didn't know if those two were criminals or activists with a cause, but he did know they were technical nothings. Setting aside labels or job titles, Bryce was proud of the fact that he pursued his profession with the dedication of an artist and the zeal of a fanatic who valued the challenge of being the best in the business.

Of course, his career came with some ethical challenges. If someone wanted information, he provided it. If they needed materials or goods of any type, he procured them. If they asked for network access, he opened the firewall doors. And he did all of this with the digital equivalent of hands over his eyes and ears so that he knew nothing of the plans or end goals. He was a digitally minded, passionate agnostic, indifferent to the intent of others. He valued only the challenges laid in front of him and his ability to stay hidden in the dark recesses of the underside of the connected world. His basement home.

Wiping some PB and J from his cheek, he brought his mind back to CNN. As he watched the continuing coverage of the investigation of the airplane and train crashes, his attention shifted to one of his previous clients. A large supply of explosives . . . the timing involved . . . the likely trigger mechanisms . . . these all matched a series of "requests for purchase" that he'd fulfilled over the past eighteen months. He certainly knew that some of his contracts led to bad outcomes, and he had long ago accepted that people might get hurt as a result. "But that's just bad guys killing bad guys," he'd rationalized, never allowing himself to evaluate that moral conundrum logically.

"Who cares?"

But this felt different. Too many people had died—too many innocent people who'd done nothing wrong. Parents. Children.

He pulled back from his computer screens and turned toward the dark expanse of his basement office, the glow from the monitors creating shadows across the sparse furniture and concrete block walls. Was this just the price for what he did? Did he need to start "qualifying" clients? Was there business that he should turn down? Maybe claiming to be agnostic was just a cop out. Should he be a full-on atheist—or did he have to believe in some set of principles? Perhaps he was just another criminal trying to justify himself. A partner with a terrorist?

He turned back to CNN's website and looked at the names on the manifest for Flight 209. He read each and every one out loud and tried to picture them in his mind, searching their virtual faces for feelings and answers to his questions. And then as he scrolled near the bottom of the list, into the Rs, his world stopped.

•  •  •  •  •

Now that her parents were out of danger, Angela Roscovitch Kilmer had some time to herself—or at least as much time as any mother gets when caring for a new baby. She had just gotten the latest medical update from her own mother. Her dad had a grade 2 concussion, and they both had whiplash injuries and a number of bumps and bruises, but nothing that wouldn't heal eventually. Their age and Charles's concussion would keep them in the hospital for another day or two. Then they would finally be able to fly to California to meet their newborn grandson, Bryce.

She obviously loved her husband, but her baby boy was now the ever-present joy in her life. By naming him Bryce, she'd both honored her brother in the best way she knew how and created a constant reminder of the challenges she and her husband might face in helping their son grow into a man.

She nearly missed the email as she was cleaning up her inbox. With the birth, the plane crash, her mom and dad's recovery, and the rush of parenthood, she'd barely had any time to keep up with her digital life. It was tempting just to flush all the unread mail and start fresh, but she knew she couldn't do that—the fear of missing something important overcoming the chance for a clean start. Instead, she did a quick pass through her inbox attempting to weed out the trash that had accumulated. In the process, she saw the one address she knew was important. "Blind Alley" was Bryce's untraceable email handle, and the subject line grabbed her attention.

**From:** Blind Alley
**Sent:** Sunday, April 21, 2019 2:30 AM
**To:** Open Window
**Subject:** I'm in Trouble City
**Importance:** High

You should know that I've been following you from afar to make sure you're safe, and I'm so excited about my new nephew. You named him Bryce! I would come to see him if I could, but there's still a dead spot in my heart that just won't go away. It may sound strange, but I can do more to protect and help you and the baby from where I am.

In any event, I'm now the one who needs help. I've never told you what I do—I suppose partly because it would be dangerous for you to know—but I'm also afraid you would judge me. The truth is that much of what I do is illegal, and the rest is in a gray area that isn't much better. I've always rationalized that I'm just a supplier, a go-fer, a middleman who never does anything himself. And if I stopped doing what I do, my customers would just go someplace else. But now I'm in deep trouble and I need your help—or your advice—or your forgiveness.

The blood of innocent people is on my hands, and I can't ignore that any longer. You know that I've been in dark places before and tried to make the darkness permanent. My pain isn't like that now. I don't want to kill myself, but I am looking for a way out. Nobody will ever forgive me. I don't expect that. But I need to know that I tried to make it right. I hope that somewhere in the cosmos it's never too late.

I have some work to do now, work to understand exactly what is going on. Fortunately, for once, I am the best in the world at this. When I figure things out, I'm going to come to you. There is nothing you can or need to do right now. Just know that I will be in touch, and I hope you'll help me then, as you always have.

I love you very much. Give a hug to Baby Bryce. I loved the pictures you posted.

As Mom would say . . . pray for me.

Bryce

She stared at the email for a long time, not knowing what to think or do. Dear God, what had Bryce done now? What did he mean by "the blood of innocent people?" Did he kill someone . . . and why? In the back of her mind was a thought she just could not bear, but it would not go away.

"Peter!" she screamed. "Peter!"

Her husband came running back to their shared office. "Angie, Angie, calm down. What's wrong?" He pulled her up from the desk chair and hugged her. He wiped at the tears that had appeared on her face.

"It's Bryce . . ."

"The baby is fine. I just checked on him," came the reassuring response. She felt the warmth of his hug and was tempted to just soak it in, but right now she needed him to understand.

"Not baby Bryce—it's my brother." She pointed to the email, unable to keep her hands steady.

"What the hell?" was all Peter could say after he'd read the message. He drew back from the computer and held her close again.

"What am I going to do?" Angela asked, leaning back in his arms to look him in the eyes. "I don't know what happened—but *killing* people? How can I believe Bryce could do that?"

"You know he's been troubled. And how much pain he was in. Maybe it just became too much for him."

"I know, but I just can't believe he'd ever be violent." She paused, not sure she could verbalize the real fear in her heart.

"What? There's something more. Tell me."

Now whimpering, her body rejecting the words. "Do you think he bombed the plane? Did he try to kill Mom and Dad?"

# Chapter 32

# THE INVESTIGATION

IN THE DAYS FOLLOWING the downing of Flight 209, Colonel Jerry Jessup had taken maximum advantage of the "interagency cooperation" with the FBI and effectively declared himself in charge of the Offutt crash investigation. He drove his team and the local FBI agents hard to follow the terror trail farther upstream. Each time they came back to brief him, the news wasn't good. The bin Latif video postings were untraceable, with no clues on where they were recorded. Facial recognition came up with nothing.

The Offutt team concluded the bomb was placed inside the aircraft door, probably in the escape slide mechanism using an altimeter and timer to set off the charge.

"Sir, escape slides aren't opened or checked with any great frequency. Based on the remains of the door and an analysis of the burn patterns, we believe the bomb was actually inside the mechanism."

"So, this should be easy to trace, right?"

"Yes sir, but—"

"But what? You should have the guy on video putting it in the slide."

Sweat began to appear on the lieutenant's forehead. "Sir, the path to the repair facility was straightforward, as was tracing the door through its last servicing. Everything was catalogued, numbered, and tracked. But the trail went cold there."

"Cold? You better not tell me that a ghost put a bomb on our plane!"

"Sir, the tech who last touched the door has disappeared. One day he's on the security video attaching the slide to the door—and the next day he's AWOL from work."

"Well, what do we know about this vanishing tech? Is he a jihadist? Did he skip the country?"

"That's just it, sir. We've gone over his life with a fine-toothed comb. He's a white guy who barely posts on social media, lives by himself in a small house, and shops at the local Piggly Wiggly. Has been with the maintenance company for five years. Mostly Mr. Vanilla."

"What does 'mostly' mean?"

"Naturally, we checked his bank records. He missed his last house payment. The funny thing is there was a $50,000 deposit made a month ago, still sitting there in his account."

"So he has the money but misses a payment, and doesn't show up for his job? I'd bet my next paycheck he's dead."

"We're following up with the local police, but they haven't found him or his body yet."

"Fuck" had been the last word in that briefing.

Now JJ was meeting FBI Special Agent Aaron Phillips who had flown to Offutt to see the crash remains personally. They were standing in a hangar filled with the carcass of the nearly demolished jet—pieces of the aircraft laid out on the floor in front of them as though ready to be reassembled Humpty-Dumpty style.

"You've made a bunch of progress in just a few days. I'm impressed, Colonel," Phillips said with what sounded like genuine admiration.

"Thanks, but it's been way too easy. At first, I thought this guy was pretty smart. Then he leaves a trail so obvious a cadet at the Academy could follow it. And then suddenly it goes perfectly dark."

"Most of these guys don't care if you can figure it out afterward. Hell, they're usually dead anyway."

"That's exactly my point. This guy is alive and well, which I suspect is more than can be said for the guy he used to insert the bomb. Who is bin Latif and what's his relationship with these IBF Abdullahs? The bomb was damn sophisticated, but—"

"I see where you're going," interjected Phillips as he looked over the bomb report. "This C-Textrate is hard shit to get. Highly compressed and more powerful than its C-4 cousin—exclusively produced for the military. The tech guys also think the device had a double altitude switch

on it. Armed the bomb and started a timer when it went over some altitude and would have detonated automatically if the plane came down
too quickly."

"If all that's right, our bin Latif probably didn't even know which
flight it was going to be on or when exactly it would go off. And still
he was able to execute the train attack the day after." JJ let that sink in.
"I'll say what I bet you're already thinking: We might be dealing with
more than a lone wolf here. In fact, given the complexity of these two
attacks, I'd say it's a damn high probability. Anything useful from the
DC investigation?"

"The bomb was remotely detonated by a cell phone—like we suspected—and it was the same C-Textrate as on the plane. We're doing
some serious digging to figure out how he or his group got their hands
on so much military-grade explosive." Phillips jotted a note on his tablet
for follow up.

"Makes you wonder how much more of it they have."

"I know, I know. We need to get to the bottom of that. Did your
team get anything from the second video?"

"Other than the guy is a cocky, arrogant prick? Nothing. Room was
exactly the same as in the first video. My guys think it might have been
filmed at the same time. What do you know about how the bomb got on
the train?" JJ was hoping for a break, any break, that might give them
some way to identify the man called bin Latif.

"First, we think it was in the fourth car's john, in a closet or in the
towel dispenser. That means someone probably had to be on the train
recently to place it there—too much risk it would be found accidentally
otherwise."

"If he's a lone wolf, I guess that means his film studio is on the East
Coast somewhere. No other way for him to get on the train so soon after
the first attack. If he's part of a cell, who knows? There must be some
video from the train, right?"

"The bomb and fire took the video system with it. Nothing survived
from the train itself. You'd think they'd have it uploading to the cloud
automatically, but the damn Acela is ancient. We're going through video

from every station between Boston and DC, but since we don't know where he got on or off, that's a needle in a haystack. We'll get it done, but it will take some time." He looked straight at JJ. "Of course, if we're dealing with a terrorist cell and someone other than bin Latif planted the bomb . . . hell, we won't even know who to look for."

JJ paced back and forth, thinking through the possibilities. "Do we have any way to trace the phone call that detonated the explosives? My bet is that he wasn't on the train very long. Again, too much risk. If we knew where he was when he called the detonator, we could narrow down the video search."

Now it was Phillips's turn to think. "Depending on how smart he was with the phones, we might have a shot with a trace. I'll get the digital team on it. Not sure how to isolate the call, but if we can narrow down the location, maybe we can ID burner phone calls in the area. The team is still trying to piece together the device itself, but that's a long shot too. Either way, we gotta get a handle on who this asshole is and if he's working with others."

"Now you understand why I'm so pissed. For all we know, he's planning another attack for tomorrow, the next day, or the next week. And we've got next to nothing."

"Jesus. So, we've got a non-suicidal Islamic terrorist who leaves plenty of evidence but still can't be traced . . ." Phillips's voice trailed off.

"With lots of technical skill, advanced planning, and promises of more attacks. And he doesn't care who he kills."

They both paused and looked out over the hangar at the airplane debris. Something was nagging at JJ, bringing 9/11 back in waves. He knew there was more to these attacks than an Islamic surrogate on a jihadist binge. But just like before, he couldn't see clearly through the haze.

"Shit, Colonel, can you remind me why we wanted this case?"

Without hesitating, JJ replied, "Because it's our watch. And this time I'm going to hunt this fucker down—and anyone else he brings along with him."

# Chapter 33

# LAST DAYS IN NEBRASKA

WHEN THE KIDS HUGGED Johnny one last time on that Sunday afternoon, there were some tears shed all around. "The doctors think I'll be out of here soon, so I'll be back before you know it," promised Johnny. "And I'm going to be working from home for a while, so you'll be sick of me quick enough!" The laughter made him feel better, but Johnny suspected there would be more than a few bumps in the road before things returned closer to normal.

He was now alone in his room, a sterile, bright white, plastic- and metal-filled prison. The environment left him with lots of time to evaluate himself and his second life. It occurred to him that as the plane was falling to earth, he had sent what he thought would be his final communications to his family. And in that moment, Johnny knew that "Forgive me for not being there . . . so many times," and "I hope you find a deeper love" were the clearest expression of how he really felt. Maggie had been a conquest, who became a friend, and who was now a partner.

So, what now? Did that realization matter? Was saving the relationship the goal? Maybe Maggie and the kids deserved more? He hated giving up on someone who had been such a central part of his life. He just couldn't imagine facing his kids and explaining to them that their daddy had failed. Was there still a way to win?

It didn't take long for that problem to come front and center. On the Monday after the kids' visit, Maggie came into his hospital room with an all-business look on her face.

"We need to talk, Johnny."

This was not the Maggie he'd come to know—either before or after the crash. The transformation was a bit shocking, almost like she'd put on a mask to perform in a Kabuki play. "There's no easy way for me to say this, but we need to face some serious realities." Johnny examined one of the tape patches covering a needle in his arm as if it had just arrived.

"Look at me please." It was a demand, not a request. "Look, this isn't easy, and I know the timing is shitty. But even before the crash, I realized that something was missing—certainly from our relationship but also from my own life. And I'm finally facing the honest truth."

"How can you be unhappy?" Johnny interjected, surprised at his own rising anger.

"It's not that I'm unhappy or ungrateful. I'm sure people think I have the perfect life, and in many ways, I do. But I'm just . . . I don't know . . . unfulfilled. Incomplete. I do whatever needs to be done to support you and raise the kids. And those are great things, except that they leave no room for me and my own dreams. Maybe that's selfish . . ."

"You should have your own dreams, Maggie—nothing selfish about that. You just have to reach out and grab them for yourself. Nobody is keeping that from you." It came out in a scolding and critical tone. He was finding it difficult to let go.

"You know as well as I do that if I took that attitude, the kids would get the shaft and you'd be unhappy." A raised voice, anger just over the horizon. "Maybe I could accept the latter, but the kids absolutely come first. You're never there to help with them, and even when you're there physically, your mind is on Cybernoptics."

With some effort, Johnny managed to strike a neutral reply. "You do know that our relationship has been good for us, right? We've both gotten some portion of what we wanted. I've always provided for you and the kids—I work my ass off for that."

Maggie jumped on that. "You do work hard, but is it really for *us*, or just for *you* and *your* ego?" The redness of anger spread over her face.

He shrugged. "I guess I deserved that. But it works both ways. I'm too self-obsessed and focused on success—and you're a bit too enticed by the brightness of the flame. If your point is that we have to change, I guess I agree."

The horizon arrived, and Maggie took the final leap first, clearly tense but committed. "This is about more than change, Johnny. I need my freedom."

Her words dangled in the air, suspended by a thin thread.

And then, maybe for the first time in his life, Johnny admitted defeat. "It's okay, Maggie. Relax. I meant what I said in my crash-text. I want you to be happy."

Maggie's body went visibly limp as she let the tension out and collapsed into a chair. "Jesus, Johnny, how can two people who know each other so well communicate so poorly? Should we try counseling? Is it worth it for the kids?" Her questions may have been sincere, but they sounded obligatory.

"Lord knows I probably need counseling. If someone really got into me they'd find enough psychoses and afflictions to keep me busy for a long time. But that's more about me."

Maggie sighed, "I don't want you to be someone you're not."

Johnny cut in, "I wish I could promise I could change, that I could turn off one set of switches and turn on another. But I don't think it works that way, and I'm just not sure how much I can change. I've always been this way and probably always will." Resignation and acceptance all in one.

"Pretending really hasn't gotten us anywhere. You've been a good partner, but I need more from a husband. And if I'm honest, I need to demand more of myself. I've gotten lazy and lost my own compass."

Those words caught his attention. "And we both love the kids. I really saw it this past weekend. They need you as a father, now more than ever. Especially Nathan. That's so important to me."

"Of course. Agreed," said Johnny. He looked away. He'd thought through the facts of the situation and the logical conclusion, but the enormity of the conversation was just hitting him.

And it hit hard.

New home, time away from the kids, no companionship. Starting over.

"So, what do we do next?" she asked.

As always, rallying to the challenge, he replied, "We get my ass back to California, hire a lawyer, and figure it out. Sometimes shit happens . . . we have to move on." Cold and harsh was not his intent, but the decision was made.

"And the kids?"

A gentleness entered his voice, a new note that even he noticed. "Let's think it through first—there's no real rush. We can be partners in crime for a little while longer."

"God, the timing of this is really shitty. The cash crunch . . . then the crash . . . then this. All at once. Is Cybernoptics really going to go under? Is there any hope?"

Johnny looked straight up, noting the antiseptic look even on the ceiling, and his lips curled up a bit at the sides. "I've been doing a lot of thinking about that, too. I have some work to do but I have a plan—one that could do more than just save the company. I'm not sure Paul is going to like it and it may not pan out. But I can get the ball rolling from here. And that is another reason to wait a bit on the relationship front." He couldn't bring himself to say the "D" word. Divorce meant failure.

"So . . . we fake it for a while?" said a skeptical Maggie.

"Isn't that what we've been doing for a long time?"

• • • • •

A day after their heart-to-head conversation, Maggie had said her good-byes and flown back to California. Stephanie couldn't take care of the kids forever and there wasn't much more she could do for Johnny. That left him time to think—and not just about the coming changes in his personal life.

Cybernoptics was in no better shape than before the crash, and with Johnny's convalescence, the money was burning, with no replacement in sight. Despite his newfound appreciation for being amongst the living, he was still compelled to complete his startup quest. Paul's original concept was a good one—in fact, a truly inspired approach—and it was worth seeing through. His hospital room was slowly transforming from a wired-up medical ward to a WeWork cubicle as he turned from surviving one crash site to preventing the next one.

He sat at a table next to his bed, still connected to some drugs. A laptop screen was open in front of him, which for once was for his writing, not his vital signs. The whole premise for Cybernoptics was to be the industry-defining, end-to-end virtual reality platform. Paul's vision involved producing a more natural, free-motion VR experience that had no cords. This technical triple backflip off the three-meter diving board was ambitious, audacious, and inspiring, but now not possible given their missed deadlines, established competitors, and lack of cash.

Johnny knew it was time for a different approach, one that would change Cybernoptics's technical and business strategy. He spent most of the morning working on a one-page summary of a new "North Star" goal and clarifying some thoughts on how to transform the culture and team dynamics to compensate for Paul's brilliant eccentricity. His key insight was that they needed a way to make money from the success of Oculus, Sony, and Microsoft, the current "leaders" in what was still a nascent industry. Rather than get caught up in their cutthroat competition, was there a way to the promised land no matter who won?

The second lens he used was Cybernoptics's demonstrated skills. As much as Paul was in love with hardware, he was more a software guy—and the team's skills reflected Paul's expertise. They had already done some great software work, which would all go to waste because of the failure of their hardware platform.

He took a pause to eat some hospital food lunch. The menu was growing tiresome, especially now that he had enough energy to notice the difference. To distract himself from the blandness, he browsed on his laptop to find an interview Maggie had mentioned—an interview with the major who had saved his life. He'd been in a fog when she'd visited him, but now he had a better opportunity to consider her in full. For the first time, it dawned on him that she was Black and quite beautiful. But there was much more to his impression than just the superficial things.

Her words were confident, thoughtful, and brought real emotion to the challenges she'd faced during her service.

He finished his lunch and returned to his Cybernoptics task. He fleshed out a memo to Paul that ended up being a bit over three pages, which was about as much as Paul would read. When he finished writing, Johnny realized that none of this was rocket science. As messed up as the company looked, a few difficult but self-evident decisions could change their course for the future. If they stayed focused on the new North Star goal and kept it simple by working on five newly defined priorities, they had a chance.

Doctor Horn-Rimmed Glasses finally released him from the hospital on a sunny, chilly Friday morning. But Johnny's return home was more difficult and emotional than he'd expected. Beyond the complexities of traversing the airport with his broken leg, just getting on the plane in Omaha made him pause and reflect. The challenge wasn't only about how to overcome his fear of flying. The last time he'd done this, people had died. Mothers and fathers, husbands and wives, sons and daughters. That last one really hit home as he thought about Phoenix and Nathan and the game he and Maggie had agreed to play.

As he waited for his flight to take off, he thought about the memo he had emailed to Paul. His mind raced between the terrors of flying and nervousness over Cybernoptics's future. Emailing an explosive memo was not exactly an ideal way to drive strategy change. Paul would stew about it the whole weekend. But they had a meeting scheduled for Monday that would determine the future of the company, and Johnny wanted Paul to be prepared for radical change. If Paul was open to that, the whole process could move quickly. If not, Johnny needed a backup plan.

During his final days in the hospital, Johnny had collected all the cards from the flowers and gifts in his hospital room and sent off some quick email and text thank-you notes. One of the names struck a bell in his steadily healing brain, generating some further research.

Interesting.

Not exactly a VC, but someone with plenty of resources and just maybe some willingness to help. He had sent an introductory email—it was a long shot, but one he felt he had to take.

# Chapter 34

# THE WILLISTON YEARS

FORD WILKES SAT in his living room watching the memorial montages for those on Flight 209 and the Acela train. Perhaps that was voyeuristic, but he preferred to think of it as a tribute to those who had died for the cause. He knew that his mission required great sacrifice—certainly he had sacrificed along the way—and he recognized that others would pay the ultimate price. Willingly or not. After all, every war has its casualties.

"It really is a second Civil War," he said aloud to no one in particular. "I'm now a general and I'm mobilizing my troops." He could see his reflection in the TV screen. "General Wilkes has a nice ring to it." He brushed at some wayward hair and straightened his clothes.

He knew that wars were usually the result of many factors, but they all seemed to have a flashpoint. In Wilkes's War of Anarchy, the Great Recession of 2008 was the ignition. It was a bubble-bursting plunge that brought the nation to the economic brink. In hindsight, it was the classic speculative asset buildup—the buying of the proverbial "swamp land in Florida"—followed by the crush of reality. Subprime mortgages packaged into financial instruments nobody understood but everybody willingly bought, combined with an out-of-date regulatory system and financial firms willing to stretch and break the rules.

A market ripe for disaster.

Wilkes had watched as the recession crushed thousands of individual families, including his own. That was when he realized the truth: This financial fuck-you was the result of collusion between government bureaucrats, Wall Street fat cats, and the elected politicians who took their money. Some government agency said the recession officially ended in 2009, but Wilkes knew that was bullshit. Entire swaths of the country had never recovered. Left by the side of the road as the technology sector thrived, manufacturing died, and the financiers made off with even more money. And as The Brotherhood reminded him, nobody was ever held accountable.

Psychologists would call it a "stressor"—Wilkes now called it his "epiphany."

He had been introduced to The Brotherhood during his years in the fracking lands of the Dakotas. While the name might evoke a cult or an alt-right, white supremacist group, the reality was more nuanced. He was attracted to The Brotherhood because it, too, believed the system was rigged—rigged to keep certain people in their place and protect the wealth of the one-percent. But instead of being racist or neo-Nazis, The Brotherhood swung the political door in a different direction—one that was anarchist in concept but also strongly opposed to the radical feminist agenda. To Wilkes, it was a male-dominated, working-class-centered outgrowth of the Occupy Wall Street movement.

Wilkes remembered his first meeting vividly, in part because it was so . . . unusual. And because it clarified so many ideas that had been swimming around in his head since he'd left Detroit. Even now, he could almost smell the basement of the local labor union hall. The floor was old school, linoleum tile, stained from some years-ago water damage. The low-ceilinged room had three concrete pillars across the middle, holding up the main auditorium upstairs, forcing attendees to peer around the corners or hedge their folding chairs over to one side. Thirty-some men sat on those metal chairs facing a speaker. The leader of The Brotherhood was at the front of the room, pacing back and forth as he spoke. The cramped space and human bodies added to the heat of his declarations.

"My Brothers, we must not get distracted by our financial successes in fracking-land. These are just tools provided for us to achieve our ultimate objective. We also must not get distracted by feminist, equal rights, and gay-pride ideas that pollute the minds of our children. Instead, we must focus on three critical goals as we plan for the future."

Wilkes lingered in the back of the room as the speaker began his call to action.

"First, we must bring down the walls of the Establishment—the Establishment that sucks the life from us in so many ways and prevents us from being truly free. In short, government must *die*." Anger was in the air as he said this. Wilkes remembered his father's diatribes about "bullshit government," and as he looked around the room, he could see the same fury on the faces of his newfound Brothers in the movement.

"Second, we must be dedicated to the twin ideals of Freedom and Equality. We all must be free to pursue our own desires, to ply our own labors, and live as we see fit. And we must each be able to do that equally, with a sense of solidarity and unity of purpose. It's our challenge to do this without creating the very structures which we fight against." Wilkes liked the mental backflip being described, even if he couldn't figure out how to perform the trick.

"Finally, we must be willing to do whatever it takes to achieve success. There will be times when voluntary association, maybe with some labor groups, will be sufficient to bring about our short-term goals. But we can't be faint of heart. Let me be clear that there will be times when more forceful measures are required." This was met with a mix of applause, shouting, and banging on the chairs.

Looking back, Wilkes could congratulate himself on taking this last principle further than any member of The Brotherhood had ever dreamed—and to devastating effect.

While he was only an official member for one year, The Brotherhood's meetings and rallies had shaped Wilkes's political views into a concrete ideology grounded in an ideal state established and led by free-thinking men. And by men alone. He knew that women were too weak and cattish to lead—give 'em an inch and they would take a mile.

When some of his fellow Brothers' Facebook pages started getting flagged for rule violations, he knew his commitment to the ideology would be tested. The last straw was the flagging and removal of a series of his own anonymous social media posts. Censorship. Mind control. Proof that the unholy trinity of big tech, big media, and big government were in cahoots as the enemy of freedom itself. He knew he needed to act.

The Brotherhood had never talked about taking armed action against others. But Wilkes knew there was an implied violence underlying the group's commitment to "freedom and liberty." If the goal was to destroy the establishment, bystanders would be killed along the way.

So be it.

In his mind, nobody in America was an innocent anymore.

Now preparing for the next phase of that plan, Wilkes knew he'd been lucky. In finding Williston, he'd stumbled into one of the few places in the world that hadn't suffered during the worst of the 2008 downturn. He had fed at the trough of big oil. After almost four decades of angst over OPEC embargoes, energy dependency, and protecting Middle East oil, technology had come to the rescue and turned the United States into a net exporter of energy. The price of oil crashed, with repercussions felt everywhere from Caracas to Riyadh to Moscow. And little Williston, North Dakota, had stood at the metaphorical epicenter of this energy turnaround.

His own personal boom-period was reflected in the bank numbers he was reviewing—an update that was important given the regular supply of money required by his special form of "venture capital." During his five years in Williston, he'd managed to save by living simply and staying off the "buy-some-toys" train. His timing was doubly fortuitous because he'd invested that savings at record lows in almost every financial market. And if he'd also increased his windfall by using his "skills" in not quite legal ways, well then, he deserved it, given how the deck was stacked against people like him. As he looked at his accounts, he'd turned his nest egg into a fund worth millions. Not that he was going to invest in startups. His entrepreneurial efforts were of a different nature.

Studying the numbers also reminded him of the sacrifices that had been made. Even though General Motors was bailed out by the government, his father never got his job back. His parents were evicted from their home in 2009, unable to pay the remaining mortgage. They went from a house, to a tenement, to the street. At some point, Jefferson Wilkes had decided his wife was the cause of his woes—she ended up in a hospital and he ended up in prison. Ford Wilkes knew he could have helped, but concluded that giving them money would have been like treating the symptoms. He wanted to conquer the disease. So he had consciously deleted them from his life in order to focus his resources on the ultimate prize.

Sigh.

Convinced that his financial house was in order, he went through his mental checklist for the next set of activities. He had a number of individuals he needed to support financially to create the desired impact across the country. Obaid bin Latif was clearly his most important "investment"—forming a major tentpole in his effort to frighten, panic, and destabilize Americans. But as the ultimate venture capitalist for domestic anarchy, his other activities effectively painted chaos across the country, adding to the cracks and divisions ripping apart the nation's social fabric.

His biggest challenge was managing his supply chain of people and materials—and doing that without leaving a scent that could be traced back to him. His solution to this conundrum, like so many things with his mission, required training, patience, and practice.

The internet is a wonderful thing, but the portion of that particular iceberg that is public is not a great place for terrorists to troll. The NSA, among many agencies, had a well-deserved reputation for using advanced algorithms to track threats and pursue suspects digitally. Edward Snowden had exposed a bit of this work. But in typical regulatory fashion, nothing had really changed and the NSA was basically unfettered.

Bad guys beware.

But Wilkes had done the research and slowly become somewhat of an expert on the below-the-surface part of the internet iceberg that was not indexed by search engines. He'd gravitated to a series of subnets where he could stay anonymous and not be tracked. The terms that went with it—Tor, Onionland, I2P, multilayered encryption, digital masking, IP misdirection, and the like—were his cloaking devices. Done properly, they meant he could pursue his activities in privacy and still ensure that his partners in crime got the right information and resources when they needed it. And in time, the right "authorities" could also be manipulated to support his work.

For now, he was concerned about two security issues. First, despite the anonymous nature of this part of the web, Wilkes knew there were those who could see in the dark, so to speak. His plan required materials, money transfers, contract hires, and more—and someone could conceivably back-trace his activities. Wilkes was a talented code jockey, but he suspected there were others who were far better at this than he was. If one of them came after him, trouble would follow. His best defense was to switch targets, partners, tactics, methods, and suppliers frequently. And if it came down to it, he'd already proved he was willing to be ruthless with those who might cross him.

Law enforcement was a more immediate concern. While the FBI had proceeded on a predictable pace, the Air Force colonel had moved further and faster than he had anticipated. Jessup was not directly on his tail yet, but as a VC supporter, Wilkes was concerned about bin Latif's safety. Enough so that he was going to have his partner pause his activities, both to create some distance and to let the pursuers stew a bit in their own juices. They would lose the scent in a few months. And then his star pupil could go back to wreaking havoc across the country.

And when Wilkes eventually allowed the authorities to catch up, bin Latif would be there for the ultimate act of self-sacrifice, anarchy, and destruction.

# Chapter 35

# FINALE AT OFFUTT

RECENT WEEKS HAD BEEN a series of "last times" for Tamika Smith. She had jumped into a burning plane for the last time. She'd hopped a ride in a Pave Hawk for the last time. And she'd made what she hoped was her last trip to a hospital to check on people she had saved. That last visit to see the Roscovitches had started out as a courtesy and had ended up as so much more.

On the runway that night, they'd been "the elderly couple"—now she was able to see them in a more complete light. Charles was striking in appearance, not because of his height or size, but because of his long, angular face, slightly unkempt hair, and outsized nose. The horn-rimmed glasses completed the look of someone who was clearly smart and didn't care all that much about the appearance of the book cover. His wife was almost the opposite. Shea had a round, pleasant face—mid-length, thick red hair, dimples, and a few freckles that seemed to say, "I'm Irish and proud of it." "Adorable" was the only word that popped into Tamika's head.

Shea had driven the conversation initially, having watched Tamika's interview on *The Today Show*. "I can't imagine doing what you do. And now that I've heard and read some of the stories about your tours of duty, I just don't know what to say. I know the expression, 'We thank you for your service,' but all of that must take a toll on you."

"I wish more people understood that. To be honest, I'm in the middle of making some career decisions. My dad is with me now—he was a lifer in the Air Force—so we've had some good conversations. But the crash shook me up. So many things are changing . . . another terrorist scare . . . the current gridlock in DC . . . old wounds from the Middle East. I just feel unsettled." And then there was the unspoken: public enemy number one, Obaid bin Latif, and the scars she carried from the 9/11 attacks.

The angst was not easy to hide.

Charles couldn't help himself. "It's so frustrating to see what's happening around us. Ever since the recession, it just feels like everything's falling apart. Mass shootings, police violence, and discrimination are no longer even news. Now planes are dropping from the sky, terrorists blowing up trains—and that idiot in the White House with his war on immigrants."

"Charles!" came the rebuke from Shea. "This is no time for politics, and certainly no time for presidential rants."

"Don't worry, Shea," calmed Tamika. "I may be in the military, but you can bet I'm no lover of what I see in Washington . . . frankly from either side." She shifted the discussion to what she thought was more neutral ground—their post-retirement life. "I've read a bit about Patterson Electronics. It's surreal to think that I used your products in Afghanistan and then we met on a runway in Nebraska!"

With some prompting, Charles gave her the CliffsNotes version of the Patterson story and then talked about how much he missed the pure challenge of the work.

"And now?"

"I do some private investing in technology companies and consult to up-and-coming entrepreneurs. I've done some guest lecturing at my alma mater, too." He turned to Shea, who took the cue.

"When we sold the company, I got involved in a few local nonprofits but just didn't think I was having any real impact. So we created the Patterson Fund. It's a family fund earmarked for organizations that can impact social and civic issues on a national scale."

"Wow . . . now that turns the whole DC dysfunction thing on its head. You're giving me all kinds of motivation to figure out my next steps."

Charles jumped in. "Major, the work Shea's been doing is amazing—and it makes the success we had at the original Patterson so much more meaningful. It sounds like you want to make a transition, too. I'm going to text you my contact info. If there is anything we can do to help, you just name it. We're so grateful for all that you've done."

She couldn't tell if Charles was being polite or serious, but either way, she'd found more conviction about her impending career change from their conversation.

And now, a few days later, she was meeting with her commanding officer for the last time. Her decision to end her reserve duty, effective immediately, had not come lightly. She'd known it was the right thing to do for a long time. But steeped in military tradition, committed to her country, and loyal to a fault, she had postponed the inevitable separation with the logic that it was something she could do part time while working for the senator.

Not so much.

So, she'd traded doing a series of press interviews and speaking engagements following the crash for an early termination of her reserve commitment. A deal the Air Force had been glad to cut. She knew that her dad's fingerprints might be on that agreement too, and for once she just didn't care.

Her final meeting with Colonel Jessup was part of the Air Force's discharge process. But somehow it didn't feel like the procedures were being followed at all. Instead of sending her an email or ordering Captain Washington into action, JJ had called her on an actual landline and asked that they meet. It was a bit surreal now to see Washington smiling at her from his wooden Air Force desk in the outer office—so much water had passed under the bridge in such a short time—and she gave him a half-salute for fun. She knocked on the door she'd almost destroyed a few weeks ago, entering when she heard the military command, "Come."

She stopped dead in her tracks.

Colonel Jerry Jessup—the officer who usually seemed to have a stick up his ass—was relaxing behind his desk dressed up as Jerry Jessup, the civilian. His workspace was clear of the usual pile of military documents and he was sipping on something that probably wasn't coffee. Liquid courage? Of all things, there was some music playing in the background from his computer. Bruce Springsteen?

"Good morning, Major Smith. Thanks for taking the time."

Now that really left her a bit speechless. All she could manage was a nod and a semi-formal "stand at attention" pose.

"Relax, Major. Come in and have a seat. We have a lot to discuss."

"Thank you, sir."

JJ got right into it. "First thing for you to know is that I'm leaving the Air Force as well."

Now that was a shocker. She thought JJ was a man of her father's mold—true to the wings until the end. Was he somehow discharged for his press conference stunt? "I had not heard the news," was all she could muster.

"In case you're wondering"—and there was a smirk on his face— "I'm going to work for the FBI. They've got so many 'acting' people over there that they decided to hire someone full time who has a deep intelligence background."

Tamika still wasn't sure how to react. How would it look if she expressed happiness? Was she happy for him or glad to see him go? With a straight face she said, "What will you be working on there, sir?"

"They've asked me to head up the counterterrorism group tracking this prick bin Latif," came the crisp reply. "Between my experience on the Counterterrorism Security Group around 9/11 and my work in surveillance here, I have more experience than anyone left over there."

Now that captured Tamika's genuine interest. In addition to her new-found friends from the Flight 209 crash, she was deeply concerned about her civilian boss, Senator Regan. The legislator was still in the hospital recovering from her injuries. The road back would be long and perhaps never complete. Truth be told, the bin Latif hunt was tempting for her too. Tamika's universe had been attacked so many times she didn't know how to express the level of anger she felt. Something between loathing and "string them all up."

She changed her expression to one approaching respect and asked JJ, "How's the investigation going?"

JJ's face went dark. "We've made lots of progress tracking leads up to a point . . . and then everything just evaporates. This bin Latif guy has no real history. He just suddenly appears and is a munitions expert, a murderer, a master thief, and a ghost all rolled into one."

"What about this IBF group?"

"That's the thing—I don't think he's connected to ISIS or IBF, whoever they are. I don't care what they claim. He's just not a jihadist type. But I also don't believe that one person could plan, orchestrate, and execute two successful attacks in two days. And he's stayed off our radar screen somehow, and that's damned difficult to do. Personally, I think we're dealing with a cell of some sort that doesn't run in the usual circles. Possibly a new breed of attackers. But maybe something worse."

Worse than al Qaeda or ISIS? Tamika could feel the anger returning.

JJ swiveled around in his chair and looked out the window for a good thirty seconds—long enough for Tamika to wonder if she should say something. He finally nodded his head and turned back around with a determined look on his face.

"Look, I know you think I'm an asshole and you're just looking forward to getting this meeting over with."

That line caught her by surprise . . . again. They'd gone from terrorist investigation back to the Air Force in one big jump, so Tamika went with the obvious. "Well, I thought we were doing my discharge interview?"

"Don't worry, I'll process all of your paperwork, no problem. Unless you have any questions, we'll let Washington do his real job for once."

"No questions, sir."

"Good . . . and let's cut the 'sir' crap. We're both leaving the Air Force. My name is Jerry or JJ—and I really want to talk to Tamika."

She paused as the confusion flashed straight from her mind and washed across her face.

JJ let out a nervous laugh. "I know . . . it's tough to see me as more than just your commander. I guess I'm trying to show you the other side."

She did her best to regain her composure. "I never made many friends as a team leader . . . I know it's not easy. And my dad tells me I can be a pain in the ass."

"True. And your dad is one of the good guys. It's part of the reason I wanted to talk. Although I suppose what I have to say is as much for me as it is for you."

Tamika had now concluded that she just needed to let him keep going. With a smile. "All right. So how are we going to kick off our new friendship?"

JJ stood up and walked back to the window. "I saw your press conference and some of the follow-up interviews. You were really good. I hate doing those types of things, but you were a total natural." He took a sip of something from his cup. "Anyway, when you talked about your brother at the end, I connected some dots." Now with his head down looking at the shine on his shoes. "I suppose I should have figured it out earlier, but Smith is such a common name. And he was in the Navy."

"Did you know Alex?"

JJ inhaled. Big exhale. "We met in person once, briefly, after the *Cole* bombing. But that's not the whole story. I was assigned to the CSG after bin Laden attacked the *Cole*. I spent the entire spring and summer of 2001 locked in a room looking at field reports and intelligence. Didn't do any good." Another breath. "I was in the Pentagon on 9/11."

"What?"

Tamika was now leaning forward in her chair—she saw something familiar in his eyes. Regret? Anger? Pain? Combination of all three? Some things she knew.

"I had a meeting scheduled with your brother the morning of 9/11. I got delayed and arrived in the west wing just as the plane hit. If I'd been on time, I would have died with him. I tried to save him. To save all of them . . ."

"Holy shit," escaped from Tamika's mouth before she could stop it.

Tears filled his eyes. "There were so many damn leads. So many fucking clues. A shitload of intelligence. I was close. I knew something was going on. Something in the US. And I didn't say anything because I hadn't pieced it all together yet. People died because I failed."

Tamika could feel the emotion. The pain was tangible. The anguish a familiar friend. She stood up, not knowing how to console a man she'd hated for too long. Her brother's death was still raw after all these years. She paced the room at first, grinding one hand into the palm of the other, trying to comprehend his words. In the end, all she could do was walk behind him and put her hands on his shoulders. She managed two words and whispered, "You're forgiven."

They stayed like that, seemingly locked in time. Two people caught in the crossfire of war. The irony of painful loss bringing them together. She finally gave his shoulders another small squeeze and pulled away.

"Proud to serve with you, sir." And with a last salute, she was gone.

# Chapter 36

# BOARD GYMNASTICS

HAPPY MOMENTS CONTINUED all through Johnny's first weekend home in California. Precious time spent with his kids, a celebration dinner put together by Stephanie, and a steady stream of friends and well-wishers. It all reminded him about the second chance he and Maggie had been given. They both put on a great show—and in truth, only part of it was a performance. Johnny still cared for Maggie, and he knew she felt the same way. Hugs and kisses came easily and focusing attention on Phoenix and Nathan was heartfelt.

The friendship was real. It was the rest of the relationship that was a lie. In the back of his mind, Johnny was thinking about the future—both the cloudy, painful parts as well as the freedom and new opportunities. An emotional schizophrenia that was difficult to navigate.

Paul was at the celebration, too, and they managed not to talk about business. Johnny thought it was nice of Paul to let him have his day, and when he told him that, Paul just smiled and said, "You and I will always be friends, no matter what happens." He took a long swig from his beer, looking away. "Besides, you've earned a break from work."

As the weekend died into dusk on Sunday, Johnny finally took his computer out and rejoined the grid to prepare for his Monday return to Cybernoptics. In the midst of a flood of "welcome home" emails, he found two notes that set off alarm bells:

**From:** Paul Hayek
**Sent:** Sunday, April 28 11:45 AM
**To:** Johnny Humboldt
**Subject:** Meeting Shift
**Importance:** High

I had a chance to read your strategy memo. The good news is that it didn't surprise me, given our last conversation and your airplane text. But I'm sure you realize I disagree with almost everything you said (except the part about needing money), so we have to figure that out. I know we were planning on meeting with the team to discuss next steps tomorrow morning, but I don't think we can do that, given our lack of alignment. Let's meet at the Starbucks on 4th tomorrow around 4:30 so we can chat away from the team. Besides, you must want some more time with Maggie and the kids.

Welcome home.

Paul

While that seemed innocuous enough, an email from Gary Clifton, chair of the board for Cybernoptics, put things in a clearer context:

**From:** Gary Clifton
**Sent:** Sunday, April 28 12:30 PM
**To:** Cybernoptics Board
**Subject:** Special Meeting
**Importance:** High

We are all grateful for Johnny's return to California, and amazingly all in one piece. With the management team now back together again, I thought it would be important to gather the board to get a status update on the company's progress. I know this is short notice, but I'd like to call a meeting for this Tuesday at 9 a.m. at the Petersen & Glover office in Menlo Park. Probably will last 90 minutes. My assistant will send around a meeting request with all the particulars. We'll arrange for a dial-in number for those who can't make it in person.

Please do your best to be there, and if not, participate by phone. We don't do these types of meetings often and this is an important time for the company.

Again, to Johnny, welcome home!

Gary

Johnny read the emails three times to make sure that he understood— or at least thought he understood. Paul never sent carefully constructed emails, never used complete sentences or punctuation, and was never, ever calm when he disagreed. Getting the board together for a special session was equally unusual. In fact, this would be the first non-scheduled meeting in the company's history. It was not that kind of board.

Paul was up to something. Perhaps his comments about Johnny needing "a break from work" had a different meaning. If his friend was scheming behind his back, he would need to use all of Monday to get ready for both meetings.

He feared that things were about to get ugly.

• • • • •

Johnny rolled into the Petersen & Glover office in Menlo Park on Tuesday morning knowing that the day would be difficult but also feeling like it was time to confront the issues squarely. His meeting with Paul on Monday afternoon had gone about as he'd feared. The memo had pissed his partner off, and Paul had clearly been busy working the board over the weekend, almost certainly trying to position himself as the person with the right plan for the future. At their coffee shop meeting on Monday afternoon, Paul asserted his rights as the CEO and primary founder, causing a close-to-blows public fight in a Starbucks.

It started with Paul's suggestion that Johnny take a leave of absence. "You didn't even share my strategy write-up with the rest of the board, did you?" Johnny had accused with plenty of invective and volume. Heads had turned, but Paul had chosen not to respond. "I didn't think so," Johnny had continued, knowing that eventually he would get to Paul. "Now I see why they say you shouldn't go into business with friends."

After some more back and forth, Paul got agitated, jumped up from the table and stood as close as he could to Johnny, crowding the space and leaning right over him in his wheelchair.

"For you, this is just about the damn money. I knew you never really believed in the dream. A real friend would have fucking understood that." And with that, he pushed himself back from the table and stormed out of the coffee shop.

Friends forever, indeed.

Johnny now shrugged at the memory as he wheeled himself into the glassed board room at P&G with some door assistance from the receptionist. He thought about how formal and official this would make the occasion. Sort of like having a knife fight at the Ritz Carlton. The room could easily seat twenty people around a table that was wider in the middle but with a traditional "head and foot" giving the impression of inclusion while still having power seats at either end. Pads of paper and pens were arranged at each seat, along with a leather "placemat" reflecting a bygone era when such things were actually used. Coffee, scones, and a selection of drinks were arranged on a sideboard and an assistant was making sure the laptop on the table was projecting correctly onto the two screens on either end.

Contemplating the sweeping views toward the hills to the west, Johnny stared out the wall of windows opposite the door and tried to absorb the importance of gathering the board. Meeting at P&G was a necessity, since they didn't have a conference room at Cyber House, but it also was somehow symbolic of the issues they were going to discuss. Their P&G partner, Daniel "Danny" Thompson, would join them for the meeting, as well as his junior associate, to take minutes and keep the conversation "privileged."

Board members came into the room like entering the ark—two by two—chatting about the latest Trumpian declaration on Twitter or the ridiculous valuation that some VC competitor had paid for an invest-ment. Although they'd been "sourced" by either Paul or Johnny, the board wasn't really divided along those lines. They all knew each other from previous board meetings, of course, and several of them had per-sonal and professional relationships beyond Cybernoptics.

But most importantly, they all cared about the money.

Johnny rolled across the room to greet them. The Red Sea parted, and he went down the length of the table, shaking hands and getting more than a few chair-hugs. Nobody really knew what to say, but the volume of their words and the smiles on their faces were really what mattered. Somebody grabbed a chair and moved it away from the table to leave Johnny a parking spot. Paul entered the room last, organizing some papers he'd brought with him.

After a few minutes of chitchat and coffee mongering, Gary Clifton asked everyone to grab a seat. The entire board had made it—there had clearly been a lot of phone chatter over the weekend and on Monday. With Johnny's welcome home over, everyone put on their business faces quickly, knowing well what was at stake.

"Paul," began Clifton, "why don't you update us on where the prod-uct stands and how the schedule's shaping up." In an apparent attempt to control the conversation, Paul had created a series of technical slides—an unusual spasm of organization that caused Johnny to chuckle under his breath. The papers were Paul's notes for the presentation.

"I've talked to all of you over the last few days, so I don't know that I need to say too much," began Paul. "Johnny and I both know that Cybernoptics's issues are of our own making. We slipped off the rails and will pay the price for those mistakes." He talked about the changes he was making on the team and the solutions in development to get the chipset and other hardware efforts back on schedule. "So," he concluded, "the product work is clearly now on track, and I'm sure we can raise the next round of funding if we can bring some focus to that activity."

He paused there, apparently to make sure folks were following him—and also to sneak a look at Johnny. He learned nothing from the glance, as his business partner was intentionally distracted, tapping away on his cell phone.

Johnny decided he had better look up so that Paul would continue.

"Johnny and I have also discussed him taking a leave of absence to allow a full recovery from his scary ordeal and to give him some time with his family. With the product work on track, I can devote the time required to finally make some progress on the next financing. Of course, we hope all of you will participate in helping us bridge the shortfall."

And that was as far as he got. Without saying anything, Johnny spun his wheelchair all the way around the table—all eyes following him like a tennis ball headed across the net. He handed Clifton a thumb drive, saying calmly, "Could you please put these slides up on the screens?" Johnny kept his voice level, knowing that this was not the time to show emotion—he'd gladly let Paul play that card.

He dove in.

"Before we go any further, I have some important questions and answers for the rest of you. Everything you've heard so far this morning has been carefully prepared and curated to give you confidence and bring out your checkbooks. I find myself in the unusual position of telling a group of investors to say 'no.'" He paused briefly to let that thought settle in.

"I know Paul's comments implied that he and I agree on the path forward, but nothing could be further from the truth. I disagree with almost everything Paul just said and will demonstrate why you're all about to throw your good money after a bad plan."

Paul interrupted, almost knocking his water all over the table in the process. "We had that argument yesterday, Johnny, and it's *over*." His characteristic temper was getting the better of him, which was part of the plan. "If you think I'm going to let you screw up this company with your MBA ideas, you're fucking crazy. *I* control this company."

"Well . . . that's just another way in which you're mistaken," Johnny said evenly. "I'm a shareholder and board member. I don't agree with your plan. And I'm going to have my say."

That got everyone's undivided attention, along with a few raised eyebrows.

"More than that, I'm going to present a plan that is better for the company, better for our employee shareholders, and better for investors. Oh, and my plan actually has a chance to succeed."

"For SHIT!" Paul pounded the glass table hard enough to rattle everyone's coffee cups. "That crash screwed with your head—we don't need to listen to this."

Nervous glances were shared around the room. Nobody on the board was expecting a brawl. None of them had ever seen the two friends go at it like this, and certainly not in a formal setting. Lots of fidgeting and people looking anyplace but at Paul or Johnny.

Clifton jumped in. "Paul, please settle down. Relax." Glancing at the P&G lawyer for confirmation, he continued, "We should hear from Johnny and then we can see where that takes us." They all looked to Johnny, who knew they were wondering if he really had lost it. Gary Clifton was now leaning in, sensing that there was more to the story. "Your slides are up now, Johnny. What are you proposing?"

Paul couldn't help himself. "Are you seriously going to consider this? No damn way I'll let this happen." He got up as if to leave, then veered over to the windows and turned his back on the table.

Johnny was now just ignoring Paul. "I have a slightly longer write-up on this that I can forward to all of you. But honestly, it's not that complicated—fixing really hard problems requires incredible focus and simplicity." Johnny took them through three slides that summarized the purpose, principles, and priorities he'd proposed to Paul. The same ideas from his memo that had never been forwarded to the board.

"Paul's right. Our situation is complicated, and this will simplify things for the team so they can really make progress. It will certainly change the focus of the company, and yes, it does flush much of the investment. And that is precisely the point. Throwing your money at a losing proposition is just another way to waste even more money. This takes a huge element of risk and uncertainty out of our future."

Nobody in the room said anything. They were just looking up at the slides, knowing they were significant, but wondering if there was more to the story. Paul turned around and under his breath just said, "Fucking unbelievable."

Johnny wasn't done. He was now ready to play the card that really mattered.

"Of course, none of this means anything if we don't have the funding. Which brings me to the last thing Paul said that wasn't quite accurate. I've *already* had success on the funding trail. I have two new investors who will buy into the company at the same price as our last round. And they are in for five million each, with an additional five million if we meet certain development milestones."

Johnny avoided Paul's look of disbelief and went right to Thompson, the lawyer. "If you could signal to your admin, I'd like her to bring in some guests, which by the way is why I was texting during Paul's little speech."

A few seconds later, a woman and a man walked into the room, both looking a bit awkward, as they'd likely heard the yelling through the glass. The woman was in her early forties, her black hair worn short and cropped, and simply attired in a longish pencil skirt, blouse, and blue jacket. The second person was much older and dressed for a trip to the grocery store. Johnny introduced both of them, and board members stood up to shake hands and offer them places at the table.

"Well, it's really quite simple," began Madeline Nicoletti, who Johnny had introduced as the Managing Partner at Lifeline Family Ventures in New York. "We're a family fund that's trying to expand its coverage into new, technology-oriented areas. In doing that, we're only willing to invest if we have a high degree of visibility. So, as part of our investment, we'll require that you add me to the board of directors." This generated some nods from the rest of the board. Any new investor at this scale would not only get a board seat, but also a significant amount of influence.

The second investor was also from New York but was not your typical VC. "I'm an engineer through and through," he began. "And I know the power of software—in fact, I built my entire fortune on it. It seems to me that the real opportunity here is using software to find profitable areas that the big boys won't or can't serve. So, my funding requirement is a series of board resolutions that refocus the company on its software stack and shut down the hardware portions of the work."

"Oh fuck," was all Paul could say.

Charles Roscovitch just smiled.

# Chapter 37

# RECONCILIATION

HER FATHER HAD ACCOMPANIED her to Washington, DC, where they were now staying together in an Airbnb in Georgetown. Their lunch conversation at Billy Frogg's in Omaha had begun a reconciliation process for Tamika, both with her father, but more importantly with herself. They had long talks about her tours, her feelings about the Air Force, her future, and most importantly about the rape. As they walked together down the National Mall toward the Washington Monument on a Sunday afternoon in mid May, Tamika returned to the guilt that would not leave her.

"How many times have we been over this, Tammy? You were the victim of an attack—a planned, coordinated attack by a group of sexual predators. How can you blame yourself?"

"I know it's not really logical, but it makes me feel dirty and unworthy. How do I find someone for the rest of my life with that on my mind? How . . . what do I . . . how do I cleanse my soul?"

They walked in silence for a bit, crossing the street and climbing slowly up the rise to the monument. Her father finally pulled up and held her in his arms. "I wish I knew the answers to those questions, Tammy," he whispered in her ear. Then he looked away, searching for an answer that wasn't there. "But I think that's out of my league. You should get some real help."

"You mean a shrink?" What the hell? The great General Frank Smith recommending that someone see a Sigmund Freud?

He gently turned her around with his arm on her shoulders and continued the walk down the other side toward the Reflecting Pool. "We all need help sometimes, Tammy. When your brother died, I finally had to go into therapy."

"You did?"

"I was useless on the job and empty as a parent, and I needed help to fix that. I still talk to my therapist every few months. She's part of the reason I opened up with you."

"I had no idea, Dad. I should have been there for you."

"No. You were shipping out to Afghanistan and had more than enough on your plate. And you have way too much Catholic guilt as it is, my dear. Everything is not in your control and certainly isn't your fault. I just needed help . . . and I found it. It's brought me a bit of peace. I just want the same for you."

"I'll think about it, Daddy. If you can do it, maybe I can too."

That same evening, she got an email from Charles Roscovitch with his contact information and a link to what looked like a blog post. The message read, "Contact me whenever you need help. I sense greatness in you. Make it happen."

As nighttime fell, Tamika got her PC out and read his post, which had been written during the 2016 presidential campaign. Charles had begun with great passion describing the many challenges surfacing across the country. None of this was new for Tamika, but what was different was his intense focus on leadership:

And we've lost the ability to debate issues in a civil and productive way. That starts with our government leaders on both sides of the aisle and carries all the way through to pundits, the press, the influencers, and the blue check marks on social media . . . even among our families and friends.

Franklin Roosevelt, Winston Churchill, George Marshall, Harry Truman, Rosa Parks, Dwight Eisenhower, Martin Luther King, the list goes on. A group of exceptional leaders from the past century (complete with human flaws) who rebuilt a world recovering from the scars of totalitarian dictators. A world reeling from the threat of nuclear destruction and the trauma of class and racial bigotry. They carried us forward to a more equitable society in their time. At the heart of our problems today is a *lack of leadership*. We need a new set of leaders with concrete ideas, the skills to communicate those ideas, and the trust and respect from others to make them happen.

She'd thought Charles was just a businessman who had made his money and retired. As Tamika read through the rest of the post, she realized he was a firebrand who cared about his country deeply. He was actively engaged in solving difficult problems.

Interesting.

Then the end of the post drove the point home and made it very personal:

Amid today's challenges lies great opportunity. People who might never have seen a role for themselves in politics and civic issues— whether on a local or national scale—are considering taking part. When the world is coming unglued, when each new piece of news seems to knock us off the track, we can panic, point the finger at others, and become reactionaries who turn back the clock. Or we can pick ourselves up, dust off our pants, and take action. There is no room for whining, blaming, or wishing it were not so. Just a race to be run. A race that absolutely must be won. And the runners can come from anywhere.

Tamika sat very still when she finished reading. There in the darkness, with the glow of her PC screen shining on her face, she thought about how she'd spent her last eighteen years. She admitted to herself that she went to Afghanistan to avenge Alex. And then she stayed there to atone for Tomlinson. Did it all add up to anything? Had she really served her country, or had it been something else? The last few weeks had indeed unglued her world. It was time she put it back together again.

Yes, she was leaving the Air Force. But there needed to be more than that. She had to stand up, dust off her pants, and find a better way to serve. A way that would enable her to counter the forces that were dividing her country. She couldn't take on bin Latif and the paranoia he was creating directly—no one knew where he was or even who he was. But she could fight him in a different way.

Time to honor Alex, forgive herself, and move on.

•  •  •  •  •

In one of life's simple ironies, Major Smith's first official day as plain old Tamika was Memorial Day. She woke up on that Monday with no great plan—just a visit with her father to Arlington National Cemetery later that afternoon.

Her thoughts were all on Alex.

She wondered what he would have said if he could be there—if her brother could somehow reply to her letter that he never received. She thought about everything her father had told her over the last few weeks, and how much she'd learned about herself. She took her laptop out on the veranda overlooking the small backyard in Georgetown, surrounded by the walls of other homes but still filled with privacy and privilege.

She let her mind go back. Back to all the times she spent with Alex. She opened the PC and became his ghost writer.

*Dear Tammy,*

*Somehow, I've been given one last chance to write to you—to share with you everything I need to say. I've watched your trials since 9/11. I know why you went to Afghanistan. I watched over you in Kandahar—I saw the fragile humanity and towering heroism in the choices you made. I saw you jump into the fire to save the lives of people you didn't know. I was with you in the ditch, rescuing that man. I share in the pride that Dad feels for the way you've served your country. A job well done.*

*Charles is right. Some fights must be fought. There is no way to ignore evil. When the fighting's "done," Shiites and Sunnis may still disagree, Jews and Arabs may still hate, and bigotry will still live on. I have no illusions that any war will settle those disputes. Perhaps that's the human condition. But the outright evil in the air must be dispelled and that can only happen if we stand united. Evil taunts humanity, but you proved that humanity is alive and well every time you came to the rescue. Don't ever stop doing that. Don't ever regret your sacrifices.*

*You've lived your adult life in search of two things: revenge and forgiveness. I've seen it in all that you do. The desperate need to punish someone, and then the need to punish yourself. For the first, you don't need to avenge my death. Life is too precious to be consumed by so much hatred. You served your country, you fought for what was right, and that's enough. Let it go.*

*As for forgiveness, no amount of energy, of lifesaving, of sacrifice will buy your freedom. I can't and won't judge whether you did the right thing. I don't think anyone but God has that right. You made a choice, you saved two lives, and sacrificed another. I'd guess Tomlinson would have done the same. You are a good person who tries to do what is right, and forgiveness is within your grasp. You have to ask a simple question: Can you accept your own failings, your own weaknesses, your own humanity? That will have to be enough.*

*You were put on this earth to do more than just win a race, fight a war, or save the ones doing the fighting. You have untapped talents—the ability to lead, the compassion to inspire, the toughness to make difficult decisions, the perseverance to fight through obstacles, and the commitment to serve others. I know you thought I was the special one, but you are the perfect combination of Mom and Dad. A combination that can do tremendous good. Get on with it.*

*You know how much I loved history. Well now you have a chance to make history. I watch as generations grow up that don't really understand what happened in World War II. Dictators, fascism, fear, bigotry, repression, slaughter. As it always does, history is repeating itself. Don't let that happen.*

*There is more I could say but you will find your way. Know that I will always be there—just trust yourself and you'll feel my strength.*

*With love,*

*Alex*

Tamika finished typing. She leaned back and took several deep breaths. She felt a soft shudder of release go through her body.

The recent attacks had tempted her to stay in the military or join Jessup at the FBI. Domestic terror was the story of the year, accelerated by headlines featuring gun violence and mass shootings, raising more questions about whether anyplace in America was safe. But Alex and Senator Regan were pointing her in a different direction. She printed a copy of the letter to share with her brother at the 9/11 Memorial later that day. It was more than a letter to herself. It was a commitment and a promise made in her brother's name to move beyond her service in the Air Force.

Tamika could not deny the lure of a new, life-affirming mission—one that would replace her former Olympic dreams. Now she felt a certain amount of fear tinged with great anticipation and excitement, a feeling she recognized from her days in the starting blocks. It was time for the gun to go off. Time to run a more important race.

To find a new way to serve.

# PART 4

## DAYS OF FEAR AND COURAGE

Feel the rain on your skin
No one else can feel it for you
Only you can let it in
No one else, no one else
Can speak the words on your lips
Drench yourself in words unspoken
Live your life with arms wide open
Today is where your book begins
The rest is still unwritten

**—Natasha Bedingfield, Danielle Brisebois, and Wayne Rodrigues**

# Chapter 38

## ESCALATION, OCTOBER 2019

"PRAISE ALLAH!" Saying the words out loud surprised him but brought deep pleasure. The time had come for Obaid bin Latif to spring back into action. Six months had been a long wait. But stepping back into the shadows had been the right course of action. The twin attacks on Flight 209 and the Amtrak train had been wildly successful, especially given his unique motivations.

Air and train travel had ground to a halt for almost a week as security procedures were re-evaluated and updated. The FAA had issued new requirements for maintenance companies, and airport-type screenings were instituted at train stations across the country. None of those facilities were designed for this type of passenger management, creating a predictable amount of chaos. President Trump and Congress had argued for weeks over who was to blame for the attacks and how to prevent them in the future. Both sides had fallen over themselves trying to project a tougher stance on terrorism. This only served to raise the level of Islamic paranoia—an environment ripe for the anarchist's picking.

So much for the good news.

Bin Latif also had learned from Wilkes that the FBI was gaining ground and doing it faster than either of them would have liked. They had managed to track his actions on the train and had distributed some photographs that showed various oblique angles of his face. His paranoid insistence on disguises had saved him for now. Barely. But he knew the time would eventually come when they would close in on him. During his six-month terrorist sabbatical, he'd reached the conclusion he would have to use their aggressiveness to his advantage.

Now as winter approached, bin Latif was anxious to strike again. He planned to hit them in a way that would cut deep and hard. Sitting in a white panel van at a Nevada Pilot truck stop, he went through the plan once more in his mind. His marching orders were unconventional, but the scale would be impressive. The visuals shocking. The social disruption epic. There were similar structures that were more famous and others whose destruction would kill more people. But his chosen target would bring the most populous and economically important state in the union to its knees.

Electricity. Agriculture. Commerce. The military. Thousands of lives. Everyone would feel the devastation.

"Delicious" was the word that came to mind.

The site was surrounded by fencing, some video cameras, and other simple barriers—but still relatively unprotected. Architectural and engineering plans had been acquired over a year ago, giving him plenty of time to choose his insertion point precisely. As before, his tactical approach enabled him to do his dirty work and then easily evaporate back into the ether. He had already recorded the all-important video and selected a few clues to draw in and mislead his pursuers. Thinking it through, he concluded that in many ways this would be his easiest attack—fewer moving parts and intangibles to manage. It would certainly create the most turmoil.

But mostly he craved *fear*.

Bin Latif was smart enough to know that casualties were helpful, but ultimately just statistics. It was fear that would drive the country over the edge. Fear to go to work. Fear to travel. Fear to walk in public places. Fear of neighbors. Fear of strangers. Fear of anyone who was different. His job was to sow that terror deeply enough that people stopped believing in the system. If he could make that happen—if he could break people's trust in basic principles—victory was his.

He turned the keys to the van, rolling out of the gas station onto Interstate 80. Then he headed up into the mountains north of the Sacramento Basin where lake waters awaited.

• • • • •

Fingers flew across the keyboard. Breaching the firewall at the travel agency was pedestrian work for Bryce Roscovitch, but it was an essential part of his ongoing efforts to protect his parents. Sitting in his basement cave, unsure if it was even light outside, he took a break from the keyboard concert.

"That should cover it for now—God, I wish they wouldn't travel so much."

The realization months ago that he had almost killed his parents had been a shock to Bryce's conscience. It made the consequences of his work extremely personal—and with that came a level of accountability he'd never felt before. He couldn't say with certainty he "loved" his parents but he definitely "cared."

His first step had been to secure his family as best as he could. While there was nothing he could do physically, he put a digital safety blanket over their lives. Angela and her husband Peter Kilmer lived in Rio Linda, California, a small farming town that had turned into a bedroom community and suburb of Sacramento. Charles and Shea were back home in upstate New York. He regularly did threat assessments based on their locations, travel habits, and work routines, trying to identify risks he could mitigate.

It didn't surprise him to learn that his mother and father were investing their money—anything less would have betrayed their capitalist genes—but at least Shea was dedicating her work to the social concerns of the Patterson Fund. Charles was off doing technology venture capital work, which in Bryce's mind was just a new phase of his single-minded focus on business success. Both were traveling extensively, making their safety a perpetual concern.

Angela and Peter were easier to track as their lives revolved around Peter's work as a finance manager at a trucking company and Angela's part-time efforts on behalf of the Patterson Fund. His new nephew, baby Bryce, kept them close to home as well.

Bryce had also followed the FBI's investigation into the terrorist attacks with great interest from his basement cave. Hacking into their system was within Bryce's skill set, although he had to do some fancy keyboard foot-work to make sure they didn't know they'd been penetrated. Once "in," he was impressed that they had produced some photos—even if they were a bad, inconclusive set of images. Someone had done a great deal of video analysis to find the *specific* person who had been in the *exact* car on the train at the *right* time to plant the explosives. And that realization had set Bryce off on a hunt of his own.

So, on one particular evening, he talked himself through what he knew so far—sometimes finding it helpful to have an imaginary friend with whom to compare notes.

"Well, Bryce, we have the unique advantage of knowing just how much C-Textrate you supplied our terrorists. That could shed light on their future plans." His friend was certainly thoughtful, although the word *terrorists* annoyed Bryce.

"Hmm, you're right." He said it like he was talking to a co-worker. "Exactly how many bombs can they make from that amount?"

It was a painful question, and since his knowledge of explosives was hardly extensive, it had taken some research and time to estimate how much had been used in each assault. The conclusion was not good. "Shit. They still have a bunch left. What the hell were you thinking when you sold that to them?"

Of course, that just reminded Bryce that he had *not* been thinking about the use of the material at all. And that thought brought him full circle. With a sigh, he readdressed his partner. "Okay, smarty pants, so they're going to attack again—and probably with another bomb. How can we isolate the target?"

"Well, Bryce, so happy you asked. Let's start by looking up- and downstream of the explosives transaction and see what other things they may have purchased. Let's also search for other work orders, resource requests, or open contracts that could be related to our client."

That had sent Bryce off on several weeks of analysis, using his dark web talents to trace the explosives sale to a specific person, location, or entity. His client-turned-adversary was too smart and too good at his digital craft to make that easy, but ultimately, Bryce had been able to narrow his search to fifteen possible purchases.

Those items included everything from an electrical grid schematic to a corporate firewall breach to a denial-of-service proposal, with things like a power generation security plan and highly specialized military sniper rifle thrown in for good measure. Bryce had been involved in some of the transactions, but he had competitors who were also in the market—and his client was likely spreading his business around. As summer turned into fall, he had begun the laborious process of trying to back-trace each of those sales, being particularly careful to mask his presence.

With every passing day, the absence of any bin Latif activity made him increasingly nervous. Based on his illicit access to FBI communications, he knew the silence and lack of information was driving them crazy, too. Bryce was making progress on identifying his client/terrorist, but he feared not quickly enough. And that brought him back to intensify his family monitoring, looking for targets and hoping he wasn't too late. With no way of knowing where or how bin Latif and his compatriots would strike next, he had no assurances that the few people still in his life wouldn't be affected again.

And this time the consequences might be deadly.

# Chapter 39

# IN THERAPY

*GOOD LORD, SHE'S TOUGH, but I hope she knows what she's getting into.*

Frank Smith sat at his temporary desk at Beale Air Force Base, in the flatlands to the east of Sacramento, thinking about his daughter. The two had discussed Tamika's plans for the future at some length, bringing a mixture of pride and trepidation to the General. He was proud of her continuing commitment to serve the country, albeit in an entirely different field with a whole new set of landmines and enemies to navigate.

He knew her motives were genuine. But he also knew that might not matter once she entered the political fray. The infighting had reached epically absurd proportions. Impeachment hearings, refusals to testify, subpoenas, lawsuits, and Twitter tantrums were all part of the daily news.

As a matter of principle, General Smith had never voted in a presidential election—and he knew many senior officers followed a similar approach. Since the military was by design apolitical, he had always believed that he should reflect that in his personal behavior. But now he was a civilian. With one of the most important elections in recent memory coming up, he knew he would have to make some decisions. The country had real problems and the federal government wasn't doing anywhere near enough. When you added the pressures of domestic terrorist attacks, racial issues, and regular mass shootings—well, in his mind he was worried about the future of the republic. And that brought him back to Tamika.

Beyond concerns about her future career, he was most worried about her emotional health. She had recently promised him she would see someone to help her deal with her trauma symptoms, and he knew that would be critical in the pressure cooker she was entering. He'd been concerned enough to write her a second letter. A letter that was part advice for his daughter and perhaps partly about his own therapy. Toward the end of the missive, he got down to the nitty gritty.

> . . . As I've reflected on my career, my therapist helped me realize I was often literally and figuratively flying above the fray, trying to insulate myself from the reality of the death and destruction I caused. I know your experience was different. You saw the pain and suffering on the ground in a way that I rarely did. You watched a war go from being a noble crusade to another Vietnam, up close and personal.
>
> I also suspect that these experiences changed you in fundamental ways. How could they not? But deep down, I hope and pray that my Tammy is still there. The little girl who dared to compete with and beat the boys. The high school student who loved math and science and could have gone to almost any school. The woman who chose to serve with honor even when others showed her none. The leader who pulled others from the wreckage. That is my Tammy.

Lost in thought, he walked over to the window. He looked off toward the Sierra Nevada mountains in the hazy distance and wondered idly when it would rain again. The Sacramento Valley was parched after a long, hot summer and the base was a concrete, sun-reflecting oven. Some water would sure help.

• • • • •

"I wake up in the middle of the night screaming."

Saying the words out loud felt foreign to Tamika, even as they spoke to the truth of her PTSD. The realization that she had to "get her shit together" was part of her commitment to a new mission. That meant tackling some deep, dark issues. She found it strange but somehow liberating to share them with someone she had just met.

She was sitting in a comfortable armchair in the office of one Dr. Elizabeth Stromwell, and the occasion was Tamika Smith's first visit to a professional therapist. The sun was sneaking through some clouds and shedding a bit of light into the office through a set of floral curtains. Stromwell sat in a matching chair placed in a group on an area carpet along with the proverbial couch and coffee table. The décor was warm and traditional, matched by bookcases, two diplomas in frames, and a colonial-style desk in the corner, a variety of papers strewn across its surface.

A silence immediately set in. Tamika stared straight ahead, eyes locked on a spot over the doctor's left shoulder as she tried not to see certain images that crept along the edges of her mind. She finally bowed her head down, wiped her eyes, and looked back up at Stromwell. The psychologist took off her owl-like glasses, placed them carefully on the table. "I bet that's very scary."

"I've done things that should feel a lot scarier. The first time I jumped out of a perfectly good airplane, I nearly peed in my pants." A flash of a smile appeared for an instant. "But this is so different. I just can't control it."

Her father's letter had been more open than Tamika had ever expected possible. If the General could get help, so could she. Was that some weird version of her competitive streak again or just common sense? Tamika turned back to the woman recommended by an Air Force doctor friend.

Stromwell started with the basics. "Tell me what it was like when you went out on a rescue mission."

"I suppose it depends on how many times you do it. I remember my first mission in Afghanistan . . . man, I was ready to roll. When the call came in, I was the first one on the flight line, in full gear, itching to get in the game. I'll never forget the helo pilot walking up, taking one look at me, and saying, 'Popping your cherry isn't all it's cracked up to be.'"

"And how was it?"

"Like he said. We flew into some tiny village in the backcountry to pick up a wounded gunner off a Pave Hawk. The villagers just glared at us, I tripped getting out of the bird, and not a single shot was fired. Sloppy first sex."

"What about the times after that?"

"The excitement disappeared quickly. I spent a lot of time on base waiting for something . . . anything . . . to happen. At one point, I went three weeks without flying a combat mission. Then, just as the boredom was setting in, *BAM!* I was off trying to pull a bleeding guy out of a firefight on some worthless pile of rocks. The adrenaline rush never went away—I guess getting shot at'll do that to you—but the rest of it just became my job."

"Have you had the dreams all along or did the Offutt crash bring them back?"

"I nearly froze on the Offutt runway—that was new. And then the nightmares came back and worse than ever. The more I think about that bin Latif asshole on the loose, the more I see the Offutt victims in my dreams."

The conversation continued, covering much of her time on deployment. They talked a bit about Alex, but beyond the sadness that came from the loss of her brother, Tamika didn't think they were getting anywhere. After thirty minutes, Stromwell went in a new direction—and the wound became more raw. "Tell me about the Purple Heart. I have to admit I've never met anyone who's won that. Honestly, I'm honored."

Tamika didn't say anything—just put on a lost puppy look, as if to say, "Do I really have to?"

"Major, I know none of this is easy, but I've watched your interviews and read your fitness reports, and you blow me away. I can see the tenacity and the passion. But as I talk to you, I can also see the pain that's there just behind the brave face."

Exhale. "It was just another mission. Just part of the stupidity at the beginning of the Afghan fighting. We weren't well prepared yet—didn't really understand what we were up against. I saved someone—but another pilot died."

"You were wounded in the rescue, right? That's not just another mission."

Tamika got up and walked over to look out the window, feeling Stromwell's eyes following her steadily across the room. Her voice trembled with a mixture of anger and despair. "I should've died that day. I should've stayed there with him and fought. I can't even look at the Purple Heart. I think it's in a moving box somewhere."

Gently. "Tell me."

# Chapter 40

# NORTH OF SACRAMENTO

BIN LATIF SAT IN THE driver's seat of the white panel van on a road turnout overlooking Oroville Dam in north central California. It was just past midnight, with a waning moon slowly moving across the horizon. Through the trees that lined the hillside, the face of the dam was well lit, both along the top of the wall as well as around the entire property. He knew a great deal about this particular concrete barrier.

Oroville was an earth-fill dam on the Feather River, and by any measure it was a massive structure. At almost 800 feet, it was the tallest dam in the United States. At capacity, it contained over 3.5 million acre-feet of water and drained over 3,500 square miles of rugged, mountainous terrain.

The scale was impressive, but more important to bin Latif was its destructive power. The dam supplied water and protected important agricultural interests in the Sacramento River Valley. It was also a significant source of electricity, diverted irrigation water to the San Joaquin Valley, and provided drinking water for cities as far away as Southern California. He knew that people would die—which was meaningful in a certain way—but the attack was designed to do much, much more. There was no government "backup plan" to recover from the loss of this dam.

The explosives were in place. That part of the mission had gone off without a hitch. Now, just a few touches to some buttons and tens of thousands of lives would disappear. It was a heady proposition. Years of planning. So close to fulfillment. Bin Latif opened the glove compartment. He took out the phone. Slowly and precisely, he dialed in the fateful call number.

With eyes pinned on the face of the dam, he hit send. Then he carefully placed the phone on the passenger seat. His gloved hands left no fingerprints, but the phone was definitely a bone for the FBI to chew on. There was no visible explosion. But he had researched the engineering and knew the dam was terminal. He got out of the van and climbed into a black Ford Escape he'd parked nearby. He changed clothes carefully, turned on the lights, and drove away. He pulled a hat down low over his eyes as he rode upriver into the mountains.

He certainly wasn't going the other direction.

•  •  •  •  •

"No, please God—*no!*"

The panic in Bryce's shouted voice echoed through the dark basement, reverberating back at him. It reminded him who was to blame. Although it was almost daybreak in Virginia, he'd been up much of the night continuing his back-tracing exercise of the explosive-purchasing client. The breaking news flashes from California had triggered a number of alerts he'd created in his efforts to track and protect Angela and her family. All he could think of now was baby Bryce and the possibility that he had somehow killed or hurt his namesake nephew.

He immediately flew into action on his keyboard, accessing news feeds, satellite imagery, the FBI's information network—any source he could use to understand what was going on below Oroville Dam. The video he saw was devastating. Anything in the water's path was washed away. He found some projections on water flows and possible flood zones. Rio Linda was on the edge of the onslaught. The fate of his loved ones would all depend on how big the breach was and how fast it would spread out into the Sacramento Valley. From the satellite imagery, it looked like Peter's business was caught in the deluge—hopefully he was not working the night shift. The FBI reported that an Air Force base was evacuating personnel due to flooding. The entire infrastructure of central California was in deep trouble.

After an hour of frantic hunting, including checking traffic cams near Angela's house, Bryce was tempted to call her. He didn't own a traditional cell phone—way too easy to trace—and the secure communications link he had from his computer could implicate Angela in ways that he just could not risk. As his mind slowed down, he realized there was nothing he could do. Nothing for Angela, Peter, or his little nephew.

Damn those sociopathic fucks. If there was one thing Bryce hated, it was feeling impotent—useless. Fumbling alone in the dark.

• • • • •

The Washington, DC, setting was totally familiar, but now Tamika was on the other side of the table. The morning meeting was held in Room 418 of the Russell Senate Office Building, complete with the big rostrum for the senators and the pathetic wooden tables for those testifying. By design, witnesses had to look up at the legislators, creating an intimidating environment. Stone walls, casement windows, and a small gallery behind the tables for viewers and the press completed the scene. At the back, cameras were rolling during the hearing, reflecting Tamika's heightened public profile.

She was appearing before the Committee on Veterans' Affairs. The topic of the day was whether the US government was providing for the care and well-being of men and women who had served the country in active war zones. Senator Regan had arranged for Tamika to testify, knowing that the hearings would play well in her home state of Washington, which had many military installations. The fact that the "hero of Flight 209" was on stage—with clips to air on news services across the country—wouldn't hurt Tamika's reputation either. After a series of pointed questions to one of Tamika's counterparts on the panel, it was her turn to testify.

The ranking member on the committee opened the discussion.

"Major Smith, this is going to sound like pleasantry, but it's a serious question. Exactly how are you doing?"

Tamika paused, knowing that she was there at the request of the Air Force and conscious of her family's proud history in the military.

"Senator, my family has served this country for several generations. My grandfather and my father were both Air Force combat pilots. I served three tours in Iraq and Afghanistan, and my brother died on 9/11 while serving for the Navy. We're honored to be part of the military, and my father and I both know the military cares about our well-being. I was exceptionally well-educated at the Academy, received good medical care when I needed it, and got my law degree while in the reserves. I'll never forget any of that."

"But you decided to leave the reserves early. Why?"

Tamika wasn't prepared to talk about her new career ambitions just yet. Still, her motivations were never far from the surface. "I'll never forget the support I received—and I'm proud of my service. But our efforts haven't kept the terrorists from coming to our shores. And they're spreading hatred, fear, and division across our country. To me, that's the greatest danger. That's what we must stop. That's where I'll focus my energies."

"I fully agree with you about what threatens this great nation, Major. But in your tone, I sense there's more to the story. Tell me about that. We're here today to assess our veterans' needs. Tell me about the effect military service has had on your life."

Tamika shifted her gaze to meet the questioner head on. "The bottom line, Senator, is I never got to say goodbye to my brother. I will never be able to talk to him again. I will never be a bridesmaid in his wedding, or an aunt to his children. My father can't do the things he always promised his son he would do when he was on-station in some godforsaken place. I still wake up at night in a cold sweat having relived one or another of my missions. I see the faces of some of the people I saved. But mostly I see the faces of those I lost. That never leaves you, and I don't know what anyone can do about that."

Senator Regan met her after her testimony was complete. "That was simply perfect. The right balance of patriotism, service, and sacrifice—and said in a way that left everyone speechless. I can count on one hand how many times that's happened."

"Thank you, Senator. I know I'm going to have to be more intentional about those types of things, but that was just pure instinct and honesty."

"All the better, my dear. Authenticity is in short supply these days. We're going to keep pushing you in the media and online—it will be subtle but consistent. Your brand is growing and that has to continue."

The concept of a "brand" and the hype-machine antics annoyed Tamika, but for the time being, she was trusting the senator's instincts.

As the two walked out of the hearing room, a gaggle of reporters with cell phones, recorders, and cameras pushed forward, almost pinning them to the wall next to the door.

"Senator Regan!" shouted the lead dog in the pack. "Senator, what are your thoughts on the dam attack in California?" Tamika looked up in surprise. What the hell?

Microphones from all directions, shoved toward their faces. A security guard pushed in, saying, "Give 'em some room, folks." He stretched his arms out to force them back into a semicircle.

"Senator!" demanded the same reporter.

The seasoned politician barely missed a beat. "We are, of course, monitoring developments through the FBI and law enforcement. I can't comment on what caused the dam to fail . . . that is still under investigation."

"CNN is reporting that Sacramento is in danger and that Beale Air Force Base is under water," chimed in another reporter on the left.

That was all Tamika needed to hear. She bolted through the throng, sprinting down the hallway. In her gut, she knew dams didn't just implode on their own. Blood pounded in her head with the same repeating thought:

Her father was at Beale.

He was all she had left. If anything happened to him, she'd kill bin Latif with her own bare hands.

# Chapter 41

# FBI OFFICES, SAN FRANCISCO

"TURN THAT THE FUCK OFF." Special Agent in Charge Aaron Phillips had watched the video three times and that was three too many. "I assume we learned nothing from the video or where it was posted." It was more of a statement than a question.

"Whoever he is, he's not stupid. He knows how to cover his tracks," came the agent's reply.

"Maybe. But then you gotta explain the van with the cell phone. The driver didn't exactly cover that up. And the Ford Escape tire tracks plus the headlights on surveillance—that gave us at least a lead. Narrowed it down to about . . . half a million cars."

"Well, somebody understood how to create a delayed reaction at the dam. It took four hours for anyone to know something was wrong. By that time, it was too late."

Aaron turned to a screen up on the wall showing one of his agents standing knee-deep in water. "Fowler, what's the latest downriver?" He'd already watched some horrific video on CNN—haunting images he thought he would never see in America. Disaster area did not begin to describe it.

"Oh God . . . it's a total wipeout here, sir." He moved the cell phone camera so that Phillips could see the power of water unleashed. "Thermalito, Oroville, and Yuba City are basically gone. They had to evacuate Beale Air Force Base, which took some serious damage, and the suburbs outside Sacramento are under two feet of water. In a way, we were lucky—the levy saved most of the city itself. Power and roads are out everywhere. First responders can't even get to the flooding without a boat or helo."

"How many?" Aaron didn't really want to know, but he had to ask the question.

"How many what?"

"Dead."

"Officially? A little over 5,000. But it's chaos here so we won't really know for a while. The number is going to go up. *A lot.* Everyone was home sleeping and got no warning. My guess is north of 35,000."

"Motherfucker!" yelled Aaron to no one in particular. The scale was beyond anything he'd ever imagined in all his training and years with the FBI. Something that made 9/11 look small.

A voice from near his office. "Sir, it's the Assistant Director—he's on the secure line."

"Shit," was all Phillips could say, but he hurried back across the maze of desks to a conference room in the rear. He'd flown into the San Francisco office as soon as the news of the attack was confirmed. He was the agent in charge of the FBI's continuing investigation into the Flight 209 and Amtrak bombings, and now the challenge was going to escalate with a vengeance. Obaid bin Latif was alive and very much active.

They'd quickly turned the largest, windowless conference room into a war room. Maps of the Sacramento River Valley, photos of the dam before and after the attack, and shots of the tire tracks were posted on three of the walls. Video monitors clogged the table and the remaining wall. Four agents were coordinating responses, communicating with others in the field, and following up on possible angles.

Aaron looked up and immediately saw his new boss, the Assistant Director of the FBI's Counterterrorism Division, glaring at him from the largest screen on the fourth wall. Although they had developed a good rapport during the early days of the investigation, newly minted Assistant Director Jerry Jessup did not appear particularly pleased at the moment. He was an intimidating presence in person, and the screen magnified that into an ogre-sized image of anger.

"What the hell do we know, Aaron? I assume we've authenticated the video?"

"Oh, it's definitely him, Director. As best we can tell, everything mimics the first two videos. Same background, clothes, same everything. Starts in Arabic, finishes in English—and now he's clearly taunting us."

"I know. I watched it and had the same reaction. But our perp in the video doesn't look much like the businessman schmuck carrying a back-pack onto the train. How many of these pricks are out there and where the hell did they come from?"

"Well, that's what's interesting. We've managed to trace the name Obaid bin Latif to a refugee program through the UN out of Syria. Doc-umentation says he's Kurdish but there's nothing upstream of that. And our ethnic folks aren't buying the Kurdish thing—the facial markers and language accents don't fit. The paper trail in that part of the world is for shit, of course, but even by their standards, there's not much. He was sent to Michigan in an asylum program and then just disappeared. Like smoke in a windstorm. He blows things up, ships a video, and then evaporates."

Jessup seemed to have calmed down a bit. "Let's slow down for a sec. He claims he's responsible on the videos, but I would bet my pension he's not the one doing the damage. Like I've said, we could be dealing with a sophisticated, well-funded, IBF terrorist cell. A new organization right under our noses. What do we know about the dam explosion?"

Aaron walked over to a side table to hold up some items. "Not a hell of a lot yet. We assume he remotely detonated the bomb, but that's still a guess. We traced a phone call from the cell in the van. One time use, burner phone to burner phone again. We think he called the bomb . . . but could have been a call to a partner, a whore, or a holy virgin for all we know. The phone had no forensic evidence—but still interesting that he left it there."

"Forensics on the explosive itself?"

"We're still working on that. From the scale, it looks like the same C-Textrate but millions of gallons of water washes things clean. We've been back-tracing the material to see where things went missing. That's a long shot but we're doing it anyway."

"How the fuck did he get the bomb on-site? There must be *something* on video, some visible sign of a breach."

Back to the set of screens on the wall, all flashing through various views of the dam. "We just got all of the video feeds from the thirty-plus cameras on site. We'll plow through all of that. Not sure what we'll learn but we'll see. It's not like our dams are security-hardened targets."

Jerry paused, clearly thinking through the scenario. "We've got a plane from New York, an East Coast train, and a dam in California—and we've got a bad photo, some burner cell phone data, a panel van, and a missing Ford Escape. So basically . . . we've got shit."

There wasn't much for Aaron to say, so he just waited for JJ to continue.

"I just can't believe we're dealing with one person who is doing all this damage. It must be a cell—and maybe bin Latif is just the mouthpiece. Or maybe he's the leader and lets others do his dirty work. I don't know. We've never seen anything this organized, this persistent, and this focused on our blind spots domestically."

JJ wasn't finished. "The security cam video is absolutely key. If we can match an image at the dam site with the bullshit he's sending us or with the videos from the train stations—even if it's just the damn gait of his walk—at least we'll get some intel on whether we have a lone soldier or something much worse. Let's start there. If you find anything, blow up the picture and show it at every airport, hotel, motel, truck stop, gas station, campsite, and anyplace else you can think of. We gotta get a line on who he is and who he's working with."

"Got it. We're also working the money trail. Three attacks mean some serious dough is moving around. Anything else you think we're missing?"

"Other than everything else . . . no . . . that's all I've got. I've heard from everyone from the director up to the president. They want bin Latif and his team strung up in Times Square. We can call in a damn airstrike if we need to—resources will not be our problem. Look, I'm coming to San Francisco later today. We're going to go through this from top to bottom and figure out what else we need." Then JJ leaned in, his face practically jumping through the screen into the conference room. "Aaron, these guys just killed more people than any terrorists or natural disaster in US history. And they're not going to stop. Unless we get 'em, this'll get way worse before it gets better."

JJ made the signal to cut the secure connection. But before it dropped, Aaron heard him utter the bitter, angry words of regret.

"This time, these fuckers are mine."

# Chapter 42

# THE LINCOLN COALITION

CHARLES WAS GRATEFUL that his daughter's home was ultimately spared. But their neighborhood was uninhabitable—no power, no water, no gas, no nothing. The Roscovitches arranged for an Airbnb for the family, so Angela and Peter packed up their Chrysler minivan and managed to drive to Vallejo just north of Oakland.

The federal government's FEMA response to the crisis was mixed at best. Certainly, there were good people who tried to provide assistance, but FEMA's budget and leadership had already been depleted by other disasters and political shifts in spending. California was not on the "best friends" list of the administration in any event, and a paralyzed Congress struggled to pass legislation that could affect the outcome. The net result was many expressions of support, some actual assistance, and a sheer inability to change the course of the disaster. Charles could see the housing shortages, energy rationing, and rising food prices coming. Wall Street was in a tailspin.

And all of that was unacceptable to Charles—not just the insufficient response to the current cataclysm, but the entire political and social meltdown that was engulfing the republic. The fallout went beyond partisan gridlock in Washington—common decency among the general public was dissolving as well. Social media was a shitstorm. People were getting into fistfights in grocery store parking lots. At their sons' baseball games.

In Charles's view, the US was again at war with itself. Not a true Lincolnesque Civil War, but a conflict of historic proportions, nonetheless. It was a fight between urban and rural, coast and heartland, whites and people of color, privileged and disenfranchised, and the old and the young. It was a fight between those who wanted to protect their wealth and those who wanted to support economic mobility—a simple haves/have nots financial premise that was destroying the country's sense of self.

The country was at a crossroads, and Charles knew that if something wasn't done, Obaid bin Latif was going to rip the country apart like no army could. So he *was* doing something. In the best way he knew how—the way that fit his entrepreneurial skillset. Over the course of a few evenings, he'd written a plan—a manifesto of sorts—that outlined an approach to changing the political course of the country. Not a new political party exactly. But rather the foundations for a powerful movement.

He and Shea were now on a walk late in the afternoon along the shores of Onondaga Lake, the water reflecting the late afternoon sunshine. Their dog, Sadie, took a flying leap into the lake, chasing some ducks away from the shore. Charles barely noticed, lost in thought processing what needed to be done.

Shea broke through his reverie, using that tone she'd use when broaching a topic she'd been waiting to bring up. "So . . . I see you've been doing some late-night writing again."

"You know I only think well in the shower or in the dark."

"Hmmf" was Shea's immediate response. "I read what you left on my desk. You realize that more than a handful of groups, foundations, and think tanks have tried to do what you're suggesting? And they've all basically failed."

"I know . . . but things have never been this bad. At least not since the Great Depression or the Civil War. I think the average American is looking for a path forward. One that's about transparency, honest debate, and principled choices rather than hidden agendas and extremism."

"Yes, but that doesn't mean it'll work."

"Any good startup idea is following in the footsteps of other failures, and this is definitely just a start. Besides, we have your leadership, our money, and our network to get it all started."

"My leadership? When did you lump me into this?"

"Well, I assumed the Patterson Fund would bankroll my proposal."

"What proposal? Fill out an application and get in line."

Charles laughed as he threw a stick for Sadie. He knew Shea agreed with him. He knew this was an opportunity to do more than just support some nonprofits. He knew it was a chance to change the way the game was played.

And he knew they would do it. Together.

·  ·  ·  ·  ·

Tamika's computer screen was providing the only light in her DC apartment. A week had passed since the devastation at Oroville. She'd called her father in a panic the morning of the attack. Luckily, he'd been safely evacuated with the rest of the military personnel at Beale, and she was thankful the CSAR team there had been prepared. But it was the *third* time that Obaid bin Latif's actions had touched her life in a meaningful way. With all of her other challenges at the moment, that was unnerving. The media had somehow caught wind of the connection—she suspected Senator Regan's staff talking behind the scenes—and that had generated a few stories speculating that she was being targeted for some reason.

The idea was outrageous. Yet, paranoia was building in the back of her mind. This feeling was different from being shot at in Afghanistan. So much more personal. Occasionally, she found herself trembling . . . and just a bit afraid.

She stood up from her couch, longing for a long run to burn off the energy, but having to settle for the view east from her studio out across Arlington National Cemetery. Her apartment was tiny, even by her prior military standards. She'd picked this unit for the huge picture window and the view. Not of DC itself or of the Potomac. What she cared about was the view toward the Pentagon and the two memorials that were sacred to her. From her aerie on the hillside, she could see the spotlights on the Arlington Cemetery marker where her brother and other unidentified remains were buried. Further in the distance, she could see the 184 lighted benches at the Pentagon that honored those who'd died in the attack there.

She picked her laptop back up and continued reading an email she'd received earlier in the evening. While she and Senator Regan had discussed many aspects of her future career, they'd never actually talked point-for-point about Tamika's personal views on issues or policy. Early on there'd been a general conversation confirming Tamika was on board with the senator's work, so the unstated assumption was that she would just continue down the senator's well-worn path. The email from Charles Roscovitch was forcing her to consider her own ideas.

His message contained a memo laying out a civic and political coalition he was starting. She reread the last few paragraphs, trying to imagine herself dealing with those types of issues:

> We can work together to create equal opportunities without the prejudices of gender, color, religion, economic status, or ethnic background. We can use our creativity and technical know-how to create new solutions that reshape our country, just as they did in the Industrial Revolution, opening doors to a bold and better future. We can educate our children and retrain our adults to prepare for that future and enable them to support themselves and their families. We can grow our economy and protect the earth—in fact, we can grow our economy by protecting the earth. And we can play a positive role in ensuring public health and safety, continued economic development, and social progress around the world.

> We need a deep and respectful national debate on what is truly important to the country. We need a coalition of leaders working across government, business, and civic organizations. We certainly don't have all the answers. But like our greatest president, we seek to unify a country increasingly being pulled apart at the seams.

> We are the Lincoln Coalition, and we are here to unite and serve.

The buzz of her cell phone made her jump. She reached across to the bedstand to see who was calling, then pressed the button to answer the call as she shook her head at the man's dedication.

"Charles—what are you doing up so late?" Probably writing policy positions.

"Tamika, it's so good to hear your voice. Sorry for the late hour, but I suspected you might still be up."

"I don't sleep much. Old habits die hard."

Charles continued, with a purposeful tone in his voice. "First, I was glad to learn that your father got out of the flood unhurt."

Tamika responded instinctively. "Thanks. Dad was lucky. Almost makes me wish I was still in the military. I'd gladly go after the bastard myself."

"Ahh . . . but I understand you're taking your career in a very different direction."

Not knowing how to respond, she took the safe road at first. "What do you mean? I'm still working for the senator."

"I understand that, but I want you to know you can trust me, Tamika. It's not a well-kept secret that you're going to run for office. And I have a hunch you're going to win."

"That's very nice of you, Charles, but I haven't announced anything yet." Tamika's curiosity was piqued by both the email and the call, but she still wasn't sure how to handle her unannounced candidacy.

"Well, that's why I phoned. I hope you had a chance to read my memo."

Tamika had to laugh—straight to the point. "I was just rereading the last part when you called. Do you think there's room for a third party?"

"The Lincoln Coalition won't exactly be a party. My vision is that we'll support both Democrats and Republicans. People who are willing to debate across the aisle to develop legislation that tackles the real issues we face—whether that's social issues or reinvesting in our infrastructure or stopping people like bin Latif and the fear he's spreading."

"That sounds remarkably rational. It's about time someone stepped up with something tangible to fight the partisan bullshit in DC. I'm sure the senator will be very interested in your ideas. Can I put you in touch?"

Charles cut right in. "I want *you* to be the first candidate we support."

That brought Tamika up short. She knew having someone as important and wealthy as Charles fall into her lap was a huge opportunity. After all, fundraising was going to be a permanent part of her new life. And yet she just wasn't prepared to make any commitments at this point. She kept rolling down the safe road.

"I'm flattered, of course, but . . . well there isn't anything to support." After a pause for effect, "I should probably discuss this with the senator."

"Tamika—enough about the senator. I like her, too, but we both know her time has passed. I've watched all of your interviews and your testimony on the Hill. It's *you* we believe in and it's *your* campaign Shea and I want to support. And we can do that with both on-the-ground activity and serious money. I'm quite sure the senator will understand how that works."

And Tamika realized her life was never going to be "normal" again.

# Chapter 43

# EAST COAST,
# EARLY NOVEMBER

BRYCE ROSCOVITCH LIKED jigsaw puzzles—so that was the good news. The bad news was that this particular puzzle had the digital equivalent of 10,000 pieces, all in shades of yellow and orange, representing a sunset reflecting off the water. It also had no edge pieces or box cover art. Needle, meet a farm's worth of haystacks. Any normal person would have looked at the pile of pieces, thrown their hands up, and walked away.

But Bryce was not a normal person. He had just the right amount of ADHD, carried a bag of OCDs with him, and had no sense of how time elapsed. It was the perfect combination for solving null-set problems. The Oroville Dam bombing had sent him into a tailspin worrying about Angela and her family, until he traced Charles's Airbnb transaction and realized they were safe. Nevertheless, Bryce was more motivated than ever to find his rogue client—even if he wasn't sure what he would do when he did. He spent less and less time on his regular business, passing up what would have been "easy money" in exchange for more time to investigate and explore the world of Obaid bin Latif.

He'd started with what he saw as the richest source of information—and the weakest link in the security chain. The FBI. Sitting in his basement cavern in Virginia, lights out and dark in the middle of the day, he talked himself through the information he found in their files, looking for an angle they had missed.

"Okay, where do you wanna start?" he asked his imaginary friend.

"Let's see what our brilliant partners at the FBI have learned from the videos our terrorist posted. By the way, why would someone post videos anyway? Doesn't that just make you a target? If I wanted to bomb something, nobody would ever find a trace." His friend was smart *and* opinionated.

"Hmmm. You're right about the video posting, but the guy is not a complete boob. The FBI couldn't back-trace his IP address. Not brilliant but better than your average code-jockey."

"We'll have to look at that more. But hey, Bryce . . . here's something more interesting. It seems they don't think the guy is Kurdish. They're not sure this Obaid bin Latif is even Arabic. Wow. So, what does that mean?"

"Duh. It means the guy is a convert—could even be an American. Hell, he could be from anyplace."

"What about that Ford Escape? There must be some type of trail there somewhere." Bryce could never quite picture the face of his alter ego, but the ideas that came from these conversations in his head helped him sort through difficult issues.

"Good point. The FBI says a black Ford Escape was stolen in Oroville a week before the explosion, and they found it on the side of the road outside Lake Tahoe yesterday. And you gotta love this—the plates on the car were fakes. That's obviously the car he drove away in from the dam."

"So, someone steals the car, changes the plates, and then the bomber uses it a week later. Not bad." His friend was impressed.

"They got the driver on a street cam after the theft, but nothing that gives us a good look at his face. Don't see anyone else in the vehicle either, but the angle isn't great for that. Can't be sure."

Bryce paused to think through the problem. The FBI had the right vehicle but had lost the trail at that point. The SUV had turned down a side street into a neighborhood that didn't have consistent public camera coverage. This guy was no slouch. He knew exactly where to go.

His invisible friend offered a possible solution. "Let's assume he's not just driving through. He's smarter than that. He's gotta be doing the plate switch and changing cars. No way he's driving a stolen car around for even a few hours."

Now that was good thinking.

"We can map out possible paths through the area and then cross-reference them with the camera assets we can grab." The "Internet of Things" was a godsend to someone like Bryce. He had ways to access bank ATM, school, and private business cameras—and more importantly knew how to crack into most home security cams. Best of all, he didn't need warrants or permission. He did whatever he wanted to do, when he wanted to do it.

He spent the rest of that evening writing some AI code to analyze possible paths for the SUV, cross-referencing with underground garages or similar structures. He then wrote a bit more code to compile the relevant video and search for a vehicle exiting the area that fit his parameters. Given the number of cameras and the size of the area, there were terabytes of video to access, catalog, and scrub.

Two days later, Bryce's efforts were rewarded. The driver had stopped in the neighborhood and pulled into a small, covered garage. A lone red pickup truck emerged some ten minutes later headed in the opposite direction. Since the Ford Escape never exited, Bryce concluded his target had switched to the truck. And this time, Bryce got a clean look at a face through the front window. A single face.

"Not bad looking . . . but sure doesn't look like an A-rab," his imaginary friend said. "Let's see if you can enhance that a bit." More software, more typing, and a bit of swearing.

"Hmmm . . . doesn't look that much like the guy in the terrorist videos, and nothing like the businessman on the train."

"Well, that fits the FBI theory that it's a new terrorist faction. You should do a little facial recognition search—will take forever but might tell us some more."

Bryce got several machines working to match the picture from the traffic cam with photos from databases around the world. It was a long shot—and with an almost unlimited number of photos to evaluate.

But worth the time. He figured he had a virtually unlimited supply of that.

• • • • •

Ford Wilkes thought of himself as a son of The Brotherhood. But now he was taking their philosophy of anarchy to a new, extreme level. His attack plan was squarely aimed at the capitalist, pluralist society that was destroying the traditional American way of life. A life that in a free America should be a goddamn birthright for hard-working men like himself. As he sat at the kitchen table in his Detroit house, everything seemed to be going pretty damn to plan.

If there was such a thing as DEFCON for anarchy, the country was moving from 5 to 1 in a hurry. In response to Obaid bin Latif's work at the dam, the Department of Homeland Security had declared a state of emergency at sites they deemed "critical to the national infrastructure." Guards with M4s became a regular part of the landscape at many facilities and businesses across the country, and active police patrols in armored gear increased in larger cities. Best of all, the politicians couldn't agree on the basics of a unified approach to the problem.

Chaos fed on itself, and he and his plan accrued the benefits. Less travel, less entertainment, less eating out—more anger, more finger-pointing, more profiling. Wilkes found the gun debate particularly enjoyable—while the politicians were fighting about gun control, the nation was arming itself to the teeth. New firearm applications had increased by three hundred percent and ammunition sales were through the roof. Baltimore, Charleston, Charlottesville, San Bernardino, Orlando, Las Vegas, and many other cities were hit by smaller terror attacks that Wilkes just watched and enjoyed. Of course, he was selectively using bots and AI techniques to spread both real and fake news about these events through Facebook and Twitter, further raising the level of anxiety across the country.

American society was in full retreat, bringing out the worst in people.

Amazingly, nobody had any clue who Wilkes was. His digital foot-prints were old and faded. And his focus on security was paying off handsomely. While the FBI was off chasing Obaid bin Latif and his band of IBF terrorists, Wilkes was orchestrating the next wave of attacks—enjoying his own cleverness in taking The Brotherhood's ideas and cloaking them in the "Islamic Brotherhood Front." He was way ahead of the authorities and had the tools, resources, and protections in place to do whatever was needed without being detected. His project plan would rely on that advantage—right up until the end.

In addition to his FBI surveillance, Wilkes was paying close attention to both mainstream and social media outlets, using them to gauge pub-lic sentiment. He saw the articles connecting bin Latif's attacks to that Black Air Force major from Offutt and those close to her. That piqued his interest.

With a little internet surfing, he realized that this Tamika Smith per-son had become a bit of a media darling. And he almost understood why. She was definitely hot (okay, that was interesting)—but also articulate and tough. Unfortunately, she was already talking about "ending divi-sion" and "unifying the country"—ideas that threatened Wilkes's plans.

"She's a woman, for Chrissake. How can anyone take her seriously as a soldier?"

He'd never done well in the woman department. But really, who could blame him? If only women were a little more like his computers and would just follow the *fucking path* he'd set out. But no, they had to be irrational and fickle. Always challenging him. Never falling in line. As he stared at Tamika Smith's picture on his screen, he sensed she fit the type.

"Shit."

He had soon turned her interviews, a series of coincidences, and media innuendo into an issue that needed to be addressed. He did exten-sive background research on Tamika, her family, and her friends. The more he thought about it, the more he convinced himself she could be a significant threat to his efforts. Apparently, there was a political event planned in Seattle.

"Fuck me! People think she's going to run for office. Who does she think she is?" He had to do some pacing to calm himself down.

"All right. Let's be strategic. There's gotta be a way to use this event to turn the public against her. Reduce the threat." Better yet, eliminate it.

That would require a major change in plans—and a new target in a beautiful glass house.

# Chapter 44

# UNDER GLASS

"ARE YOU READY, MY DEAR?" came the question from over her shoulder.

"Always," was Tamika's immediate response. A reflexive reaction from her helicopter days. But deep down, she felt a bit less confident than she was willing to admit to Senator Regan. For Tamika, this wasn't about cashing in on her fame and developing a second career—it was about driving positive change in a country that seemed to be slipping into an abyss. And yet, the whole idea of running for office was uncomfortable and daunting. There was the small matter of winning a primary, much less a general election. And even if she eventually won, did she really have what it took in the cutthroat world of politics?

Tamika looked out from behind a door across a patio that bordered the giant glass atrium. The Glasshouse, as it was officially called, was the centerpiece of the Chihuly Garden and Glass exhibition in Seattle. Dale Chihuly was a world-renowned glass blower whose exhibits had been featured in venues ranging from London's Kew Gardens, to the canals of Venice, to the Louvre in Paris. The fully glass-enclosed Glasshouse was shaped like two half semicircles that met in a peak at the top. It featured a massive, hundred-foot-long burnt-orange and red collection of blown glass pieces that ran like a serpent down the length of the building's ceiling. With the lights shining up through the glass five hundred feet to the neighboring iconic Space Needle tower, it was an impressive, remarkable venue for important announcements.

The senator continued, "Well, I'll take the lead and make my announcement—and then introduce you. Just stick to the script and everything will be fine. This should be short and sweet. Just the first mile of a marathon."

Tamika gave her a forced smile while stretching her legs, almost as if she were getting ready for a 400-meter sprint.

The senator laughed. "Well, 'old habits' as the saying goes, right? Remember—marathon, not sprint."

And with that Tamika let out a breath of air. She was ready. Her face relaxed into a natural smile. Together, they both walked through the door and across the courtyard. Then she stepped into the far end of the Glasshouse to embrace her future.

•  •  •  •  •

Obaid bin Latif was apprehensive for the first time. Turning the van left onto 5th Avenue, he knew this mission had been slapped together haphazardly. For someone who was dedicated to careful planning and advanced research, that was a disaster in the making.

The instructions were clear—but this attack was fundamentally different from the others. It wasn't conceived or designed to maximize anarchy, disruption, and fear. Instead, it was an assassination. A targeted, preemptive strike to eliminate a potential enemy before she could even enter the fight. He understood the logic but hated the risks it created.

He'd managed to get a secondary source for the explosives. Not as powerful a material as he'd been working with, but it would get the job done. He'd tried to cover his tracks as best he could given the lack of time to prepare—and his disguise and the deception around the rental van would give him some cover to escape the scene. But deep down he knew the potential for exposure was high and success far from assured.

Despite his misgivings, he couldn't deny that elements of the attack suited his needs. Bin Latif hated American politicians for their hypocrisy and graft. To bomb a room full of politicos and sycophants? A room made of *glass*? He could envision thousands of shards raining down upon the exposed audience, slicing their way indiscriminately through the crowd. The death toll would be relatively small given the size of the event, but the graphic nature of the destruction would be both vivid and dark. The media optics would be off the charts. And in a voyeuristic society, who could stay away from those bloody images?

Besides, even if he missed his target, he had set her up to get blamed for the attack. These days, just a single, well-placed, fake clue—and some subtle social media manipulation—was enough to sway large swaths of the population to buy it hook, line, and sinker. That would tear down her precious public image and credibility.

He turned right onto Thomas Street and showed the security guard an access pass he had forged. He drove a few hundred yards down the tourist complex's driveway, avoiding pedestrians milling at some of the street shops, and parked next to the Collections Café entrance.

Just to his left, the glass structure was lit up like a Disney World ride. He reached into the back of the van to check the cell phone. Power on and batteries charged. He carefully pulled a hoodie over his head, put on dark glasses, and adjusted the rest of his disguise. Then he stepped out of the van, turning his face away from the exhibit's collection of security cameras.

He walked as quickly as his adjusted gait would allow, finally entering the passageway behind the Museum of Pop Culture. He stayed in the shadows beneath the World's Fair monorail that ran overhead. When he stopped to pull out another burner phone to make the fateful call, a group of half-drunk college students walked up the steps toward him.

*Shit.* He kept walking.

• • • • •

Tamika was a bit surprised by the hectic scene inside the beautiful glass building. Fifteen rows of chairs with an aisle down the middle had been arranged across the center of the room, with five cameras on their tripods encamped at the back. The senator's team initially had been worried about filling the room in the middle of the Christmas season, but that hadn't been a problem. In addition to the usual gaggle of reporters and Democratic Party officials, the social and financial upper crust of Seattle had turned out and were milling about in small groups. The invitation had promised an important series of announcements, and there was a buzz in the crowd. The senator was clearly a draw, but it slowly dawned on Tamika that people might be there to see her.

A standing glass podium had been placed at the head of the room and was adorned with a number of microphones. The US and Washington state flags were stationed on poles like sentries behind the rostrum. The mayor of Seattle met Senator Regan and Tamika at the door, shook their hands, and walked with them to their chairs between the flags. Tamika took her seat alongside the senator, noting that the hum in the room had faded quickly.

Mayor Judith Magid adjusted the coat of her deep blue pantsuit and went to the podium.

"Ladies and gentlemen, please take your seats." A pause ensued as everyone settled in. "Thank you for joining us this evening in this beautiful, iconic Seattle setting. Tonight, we have several announcements important to the future of our state and its elected representatives. Our country finds itself in very challenging times. More than ever, we need great leadership. And Senator Marianne Regan has been just such a leader for over twenty years. She has consistently responded to the needs of our state, as well as led policy initiatives important to the entire country."

Tamika found herself eyeballing the assembled crowd, wondering how they would react to her candidacy. Usually, she could control the outcome of a contest simply by outworking her opponents. It dawned on her that politics didn't always work that way. Perceptions would now be just as important as her actual actions.

The mayor had finally gotten to the end of her preamble. "She truly needs no introduction to this group, so I will simply welcome you and turn the evening over to an outstanding public servant . . . Senator Marianne Regan."

Amid appreciative applause, the senator rose to walk to the podium.

Tamika felt on a knife's edge as she watched the scene unfold, her life about to change.

Suddenly doors on three sides of the atrium burst open. A large group rushed in, led by a man in a dark blue suit and red tie.

"This is the FBI!" he shouted in a loud, crisp voice as he ran toward the head of the room, flashing a badge in his left hand raised high in the air.

"I'm Field Agent Franklin Higginbottom. Everybody has to exit the building immediately through the doors to the right of the stage. The police will escort you to a holding area. Remain calm but move quickly, please. Thank you very much for your cooperation. Come on, folks . . . let's get moving."

His little speech did not exactly achieve "calm," but the audience started toward the exits. While that was in progress, the agent pushed up to the confused trio of speakers and ushered the ladies out the other side door.

"Hurry, please," he said with urgency. "We need you out of the area immediately." The women all tried to run, which was no easy trick in heels. The mayor stumbled and Tamika grabbed and steadied her to prevent a fall.

Higginbottom guided them toward an SUV while he pressed his other hand to his earpiece. "Moving Sprinter to the car. Site is now clear." Two more men in suits jumped out of the vehicle and opened the doors to the Suburban.

"We're taking you to our offices downtown. We'll get you up to speed on the situation there."

The senator stopped dead in her tracks.

"Young man! I don't care if you are from the FBI. You'll tell us what's going on and you'll tell us right *now*." The senator had her bossy voice on.

As he held open the door to the Suburban, clearly a little annoyed, Higginbottom replied tersely. "Ma'am, a white van was found parked and abandoned on the service road just behind the atrium. It's filled with explosives and a cell phone."

"Shit."

# Chapter 45

# LATE INTO THE NIGHT

"WELL DONE."

Jerry Jessup's first words were a rare compliment. He was hearing Agent Higginbottom's initial report from Seattle on a secure PC at his home in Alexandria, Virginia. Aaron Phillips had joined them from San Francisco, where he was still working the dam investigation.

Deactivating the cell phone before the bomber could place the fateful call had prevented another disaster, but in the back of his mind, Jessup knew they'd been lucky. His agent had been posted at the Glasshouse event on a whim. Higginbottom had walked to the back of the venue to close a door that had been left ajar. If he hadn't looked out into the night, noticed the van, and done the right thing, JJ would be watching another fucking video from bin Latif's band of bombers.

"I assume you guys have everything locked down?" continued JJ.

"Yes, sir," said Higginbottom. "Seattle PD has closed off the entire Seattle Center. We're interviewing event staff, attendees, and anyone who was on the grounds. It's a busy place at the holidays so that's going to take a while. There're a bunch of cameras in the area and we're collecting all the video."

"Seriously, first-class work, Frank. You should drop off the call and keep digging, especially on the videos. More agents coming your way to help you with the interviewing. Contact me directly if you get something."

"On it, sir." And with that, he cut his connection.

Phillips jumped in. "The security videos should be particularly interesting. We may get multiple looks at our friend, bin Latif."

"Or another of his friends," corrected JJ. "I'm still convinced this is a cell. Based on what you told me about the device, we can't even be sure it's the same group."

"Yeah. The bomb was definitely different—different material for one thing—so I suppose it could be a copycat," responded Phillips. "But I know you don't really believe that. Odds are it's our terrorist friends."

"Then why the amateur hour with the device and van? This group has been so buttoned up—everything carefully planned and executed. All low-risk, high-reward targets, relatively speaking. And now they use a crude device, a van parked in plain sight in a restricted area? That's a huge risk to attack a small group of people."

"It was at the Glasshouse next to the Space Needle," countered Phillips. "It's a major tourist attraction."

"Sure, but that bomb wasn't going to do much more than shatter all the glass in the atrium. Lots of people hurt—maybe a few killed. That's small potatoes for these guys. Bin Latif and his crew are higher end than that."

They looked at each other across the digital connection, a virtual stalemate as they tried to sort through the evidence.

A text message popped up on Jessup's phone. He went from thoughtful to pissed in an instant, slipping back into military role. "I need to talk to Major Smith—she's got some serious questions to answer."

"I'm sure Higginbottom is already interviewing her—"

His temper and impatience cut in. "Damn it, Aaron. I've got new information. Now. It's time I found out what's really going on."

•  •  •  •  •

It had been a long night and yet it was only 10 p.m. Tamika was walking back from the ladies' room in the FBI's Seattle office when Agent Higginbottom ushered her briskly into a small room with a desk, chair, and a phone. No explanation—just an uneasy feeling that she was now on the other side of the proverbial table. The sudden exit from the

Glasshouse had rattled her at first, but those nerves were quickly being replaced by confusion.

She was startled by the ring of the phone.

"Jessup here," came the crisp response when she answered.

Why was *he* calling her? As she took in her surroundings a bit more carefully, she realized she was sitting in an interrogation room, complete with what was likely a two-way mirror.

"Colonel Jessup, what the hell's going on?" Tamika demanded.

"Dial it down, Major," came the reply. "And we should probably both remember we're civilians now."

Tamika took a deep breath. "Sure . . . but why are you calling me? Shouldn't you be focused on finding whoever tried to take us out tonight?"

"That's exactly what *I'm* doing. You're in the middle of some serious shit and you've got some explaining to do."

"You're kidding, right? What the hell do *I* have to explain to you? Is this an interrogation?" The confusion had now turned to anger.

"With all the news coverage after Omaha and DC, you and Senator Regan have been on our radar. We've been tracking some online chatter—mostly the usual anonymous whack jobs—but we determined that some of the threats were credible. When the invites went out for the Seattle event, I sent an agent to be there." No emotion in his words.

Tamika wasn't sure whether to be pissed that they were tracking her or thankful that they had. She went with the latter. "Well, thank God you did. So, you think this was a random attack or is this that scumbag bin Latif?" Her words might have betrayed her own feelings.

"That's why I wanted to talk," interjected Jessup with a darker tone of voice. "We just got the rental information for the van with the explosives. Does the name Blair Haba ring a bell?"

"Dear Lord—he's one of Senator Regan's campaign aides."

"Yeah, I know. I need straight talk, Smith. What's the story on this guy?" Back to interrogation mode.

"Not much I can tell you. We've only done a few events together." She paused, now realizing where this was going. "I guess he's now one of my aides, too."

"Come again?"

"The senator was going to announce her retirement tonight. The train bombing was the last straw. And she was also going to endorse me to run for her seat."

"Hang on. So this whole thing was just a big campaign stunt? Trying to generate some press? You gotta be fucking kidding me."

Tamika could feel the ire in his voice.

She responded with a bit of her own. "Give me a damn break, JJ. Nobody would be stupid enough to use their actual name on the rental. I'm very close with the senator and her team. They might be spreading rumors about my candidacy, but they'd never do something this crazy. Jeezus, I can't believe you'd even consider it."

"Even if I believe that—and we *will* chase it down—something is still off. This could be our Omaha-Acela-Oroville terrorist cell, but why would they attack the event and then point the finger back at your people? I don't believe in coincidences—not this many anyway. You must have some connection to this bin Latif guy. Anything from your time in the Air Force?"

"Other than I want him dead, nothing I can think of." She looked into the two-way mirror, wondering if Higginbottom was back there watching. "I'd never heard the name until the Offutt attack. I suppose you could check my records from Iraq and Afghanistan—maybe there's something there. I can't think of any reason our paths would've crossed."

There was silence on the line. A long silence.

"Did I lose you?" Tamika questioned.

"No. I'm still here. Just thinking some things through." Another pause. "Listen, we'll look into the Haba thing, but I'm going to assume for now you're being straight with me. This may not have been bin Latif. Given the amateurish approach, it might have been a random attack. Or a copycat. But I'm going to assign Higginbottom to you for the time being. I want people to know the FBI is protecting you."

"You know I won't like that . . . but I get it. Again, thank you for what you and your team did today. Believe me, we had nothing to do with this." Then with a different, more urgent tone. "And c'mon, JJ. You and I both know this was him. What can I do to help?"

"You need to leave this to us, Tamika. My command, my responsibility."

"I hear that, but this guy's getting closer and closer to me. Offutt, the senator, my father—and now me. I feel like a target. And I'll be damned if I'm going to let him have a free shot." Bin Latif was now *her* public enemy number one. She waited for a response—an order from her commanding officer. What she got wasn't quite what she wanted.

"I'll talk to Higginbottom. Keep your cell phone close."

"JJ, let's get this guy. And fry him."

And with that, she hung up.

## Chapter 46

# FROM RIVERVIEW TO SEATTLE

"IDIOT!" FORD WILKES was beyond pissed—mostly at himself—and was delivering a thorough personalized tongue-lashing while pacing in the living room of his Michigan house-turned-headquarters. He had to avoid the couch cushions he'd thrown on the floor as he marched in anger.

"I had a plan and it was fuckin' working. Then I got distracted by that stupid Air Force wench and bin Latif almost got caught." He turned abruptly.

"Now they have even more video and all my secrets are at risk." He spun around and went back the other way, kicking a cushion in the process. "I should've stuck to the plan." Another turn.

As he made for the other end of the room, he said it louder. "I should've stuck to the plan!" When he reached the coffee table, he shouted at the top of his lungs, emphasizing each word, "*I . . . should . . . have . . . stuck . . . to . . . the . . . fucking . . . plan!*"

With his anger spent—at least for the moment—he collapsed into the couch facing the television across the room. CNN was running extensive coverage of the failed bombing in Seattle, complete with speculation about who was behind it and the brilliant work by the FBI to spoil the attack.

"Brilliant work, my ass," huffed Wilkes. He had taken a digital trip into the FBI network and knew the full story. "Shit, some waiter leaves a back door open and an FBI agent is there to discover the truck. Now that's gotta be karma coming back to bite me in the ass." Because he should have stuck to the plan, of course. Damn it, he couldn't let it go.

Then the TV screen caught his attention again.

There was a press conference going on in Seattle. He scrambled for the remote and cranked the volume.

"Good afternoon," began the woman at a wooden podium that was mounted on a simple table. The seal of the City of Seattle was featured on the wall behind her, flanked by the ubiquitous flags. "My name is Senator Marianne Regan. As many of you know, I was preparing to speak at Chihuly Garden and Glass last night when someone attempted to bomb the building. While no one has taken credit for the attack, and the police and FBI investigations are ongoing, I want to start this morning by making several things perfectly clear."

Wilkes knew the bitch's face but could not quite place why she seemed particularly familiar.

"First, I want to extend my thanks to the FBI for their quick action to avert the attack and also thank local law enforcement for their help in tracking the perpetrators. Many lives were saved last night—my own included." With that she gave a nod to several people to her right, and applause broke out in the room. As the camera panned the venue, Wilkes saw about twenty-five people in uniforms and dark suits sitting in metal foldout chairs—authority figures there to support and protect her.

"Second,"—and with this she looked straight into the camera and pointed a finger—"I want the perpetrators to know that every resource of the US government is being brought to bear to track you down and bring you to justice. The end of the line is coming for you, and it's coming soon. That's a promise."

Wilkes almost laughed. Typical woman. She was going all Rambo on him over the TV, but was hiding behind the protection of her precious FBI. *C'mon on, girl, bring it on*, he thought to himself. And then it hit him. She was the senator who almost died in the Amtrak attack. And yet she didn't look the worse for wear.

Christ, how could he miss someone twice?

"Third, last night's attempted attack didn't change anything. We're

here today to make the same announcements we had planned for yesterday. We all must resist the temptation to react to events like this with fear
or by changing course. In fact, it's even more important that we move
forward with discipline and determination. So, let me be the first."

"Go for it, baby!" jumped in Wilkes, the knee of one leg now bouncing with adrenaline. "I guess I'm going to have to come for you again."

The senator continued. "I have served the citizens of Washington
State for over twenty years—and almost my entire life has been spent
in public service. I'm proud of that work." She paused to hold back a
bit of emotion. "But over the past year, I've concluded that a new generation is needed to deal with the challenges we face as a country. New
ideas, new points of view, and new energy. And as much as I'd like to
continue being a light driving through the darkness we face, there are
others who should carry the torch forward. Leaders who can do it with
power, courage, and determination."

"Hah! Just as I thought. She's quitting. I scared her off." Wilkes
smiled for the first time that day.

"So, today, I'm announcing my plan to retire later this year. I've
informed Governor Chancellor so that he can call a special election this
coming November to select a new senator who will complete my term.
I want to thank my supporters for continuing to place their trust in me
over the years." Again she paused, and more applause broke out.

*Why are they applauding?* thought Wilkes. *Good riddance.*

Signaling for quiet, Regan continued. "But today involves more than
just my announcement—in fact that is the least important thing we'll
discuss. I've given a great deal of thought to who could pick up where
I'm leaving off. It needs to be someone who can take the progress we've
made and lift it to even higher levels. Someone with policy experience,
of course. But we also need someone with life experience. Someone who
has been battle-tested. Someone who has great compassion for people.
Given the nature of politics today, it needs to be someone with courage,
integrity, and an iron will." She looked around the room and smiled.

"Please allow me to introduce the person I'll champion as the next
senator from the great state of Washington—Tamika Smith!"

Wilkes just stared at the screen.

Well, shit. The rumors were true. At least his extra efforts had been justified. He leaned forward as he listened to Smith's short speech, splitting his attention between her good looks and her message.

Her words were a warning shot right across his bow. ". . . and let me close by making it clear that we have to fight to stay together. We can't let terrorists change the way we act. The partisanship, the bigotry, the deep fake media posts—these are all things that drive blind anger and hatred. As someone who has served this great country my entire life, I will not let that happen on my watch." She paused to collect herself. Then tipped her chin up a notch and continued.

"And I have a message for you, Obaid bin Latif. I'm tired of your smug videos and hit-and-run attacks. We're going to find you in the shadows, pull your cowardice out into the light, and then bury you in the darkness of a cell."

Wilkes fell back into the couch. Now he *was* convinced she was a serious threat. He took a deep breath, thought for a moment, and then smiled. *Well, I may have missed her this round, but I won't make the same mistake again.* It was time to go back to the plan. Time to unleash Obaid bin Latif in new ways. Time to create more havoc and destruction. And then, with a little sleight of hand, I'll get back to my Black beauty here.

And the next time, she *will* die.

# Chapter 47

# RECONNECTING, JANUARY 2020

"GOOD GOD, WHAT THE HELL am I doing?" she said right out loud as she rummaged around for something appropriate to wear. With the campaign in full swing in the new year, Tamika Smith had officially resigned from her job with Senator Regan and moved to Puget Sound to focus on the primary election. She had moved into a small bungalow in Burien, just south of Seattle. The house was on a quiet street, only a few blocks from a park along the Sound where she could run to her heart's content. While it was as reasonably priced as the Seattle market could offer, her self-imposed austerity plan meant that the space in the cramped "master bedroom" closet was minimal. And the clothing selection was . . . well . . . selective.

She continued to banter with herself, looking for some therapeutic effect. "I'm going to dinner with a guy I barely know, who is even older than I am—oh, and he's divorced and has kids in high school (!). I swear, Shea is going to hear it from me. I know she's pulling the strings on this somehow. 'You need to get out there . . . you're so beautiful . . . you can't go through life alone.' I'm in the middle of a campaign. I don't have time for a relationship. Heck, I don't even know what *kind* of dinner this really is. The last time I saw him I was in uniform. What am I supposed to wear now?" Nobody in the empty room answered.

Johnny Humboldt had called her office earlier that week, a few days after attending a campaign fundraising event. His call had caught her off guard, raising the daunting, haunting question, "Am I emotionally capable of a relationship?" and the more practical, "Is there room in my life for a man right now?"

She recalled the somewhat awkward conversation. "Hello, can I please speak with the future Senator Smith?"

"Uh, who's this?" Probably another donor, Tamika had thought.

"Obviously, I made a big impression on you. I'm the guy you lugged out of a ditch—and then shared an epic Facebook post with courtesy of the US Air Force." Oh shit, it's him. She and Johnny had only spoken briefly at the fundraiser.

"Johnny . . . I'm so sorry. I've been a bit off center with the campaign rolling into high gear. I think I'm on the phone with maybe thirty people every day, most of whom I don't even know. And hearing the 'senator' thing is just . . . weird."

"Don't apologize—I can't imagine what your life is like. I guess living in the big lights is tough. I hear they're bright and there's a bunch of glare to go with 'em."

"You'd think I'd get used to it, but I really never have." She paused, not sure where to go next. She went with the first thing that came out. "It was great to see you hiding in the back of the crowd at the fundraiser last week. Shea Roscovitch told me you were in town, but I wasn't expecting to see you."

"I have Shea and Charles to thank as well—they invited me to the event. I love her to death but sometimes . . ."

"Exactly. I was halfway through my speech when I saw you in the audience—did you see my little double take in mid-sentence? I'm sorry we couldn't talk more afterward, but the damn handlers kept me busy shaking hands and collecting money."

"Trust me, this is not a lobbying call—but I do want to ask a favor. Seeing you the other night reminded me that I owe you at least a nice meal and some conversation, even if it's almost a year too late. So, I was wondering if you'd join me for dinner later this week?"

She put her hand over the phone and mouthed "shit" again . . . but then a little smile came across her face. With some panic thrown in for good measure.

"Hellooo? I don't know how I should take the silence, but I think I'll assume you were speechless with excitement."

"I'm never speechless . . . at least not these days," laughed Tamika. "And yes, I'd enjoy getting together for dinner. But I have campaign events on Friday and Saturday night, so that only leaves Sunday."

"No problem at all—that works great."

"Where should I meet you?"

"Well, I'm kind of old fashioned about these things, so would it be okay if I picked you up around seven?"

Her smile widened just a bit more.

And that's how they ended up sitting in a small, quiet restaurant in Wallingford just north of downtown Seattle. The menu was farm-to-table, the décor featured brick with wrought iron tables, and the hubbub at the bar filled the pauses in the conversation. She'd resolved the closet panic by choosing some comfortable jeans, a white button-down shirt, and a blue sweater to keep out the cold. "Nothing fancy" had turned out to be the right choice. Johnny was almost in the same uniform—for the first time, she could fully appreciate his midwestern good looks, now with a little gray around the temples that added character.

They'd jumped right into the "what have you been up to" talk, and Johnny was explaining his ongoing connection to Charles Roscovitch.

"Charles was a savior for the company, certainly with his funding but also with his ideas and advice. Cybernoptics was within a month or two of running out of money when he agreed to finance a major shift in strategy. I had to take over as CEO—and I was definitely not ready for the job."

"Tell me about that—Senator Regan keeps saying I'm doing fine, but I feel like a fish out of water most days."

Johnny smiled in sympathy. "Charles tried to warn me, but I had no idea how lonely I'd be in the job or how difficult it would be to lead a team. I felt the weight of every decision, lost sleep over the employees we had to let go, and was totally unprepared for the complexity of the work."

"But Shea told me you just sold the company successfully—and I bet it's not easy saving a company that was on the rocks. Sounds to me like you should be really proud."

"Thanks. I suppose there's some truth to that, but the biggest thing I feel now is relief. We got incredibly lucky. Facebook needed our software stack and a series of patents and bought us out at a good price. I'm living here for now, integrating our team with the Facebook engineers in their Seattle office. Going back and forth to San Francisco is a pain, but the day-to-day pressure is mostly gone."

Tamika wanted to ask how his kids were doing but was afraid that would be too personal, especially on a first date (wait, was this a date?).

As if reading her mind, he said, "And I can spend a bit more time with the kids now that work is more predictable."

Tamika chose her next words carefully given what Shea had told her. "That all must have been very difficult." She tried to say it without any pity, angst, or concern. Just a human reaction to what she knew must be a sadness in his life.

"The last nine months were definitely no fun. Crash . . . Cyber-noptics . . . divorce . . . upset kids. Kind of a cluster for sure. It's been a rocky road for Phoenix and Nathan, but I see signs that they're making progress."

"I bet they look up to you—I know I always looked up to my dad, even when he wasn't there."

"I hope I can keep that close bond, even with the separation. I guess if I'm honest, the divorce felt like failure for a while. But Maggie—oh, by the way, it's now Margaret—and I have stayed good friends. So, I've concluded that's the way it was meant to be."

"Shea told me that the Patterson Fund is supporting something Margaret's doing?"

"Yeah, she founded a really cool organization called Fifth Year. It's a nonprofit apprentice training school—except they have no buildings or campuses—everything is done online and through mixed reality technology. It's designed to help kids who don't need a traditional four-year college. But everyone still needs some training to make a living wage, you know? They're using some of the tools we created at Cybernoptics. Funny how some things come full circle."

Tamika smiled in appreciation but wasn't sure where to go next.

The conversation paused—each pretending to enjoy another bite particularly well.

Johnny moved things along. "Well . . . I'm blabbering. That's just about enough of me. You've got to tell me how you ended up running for senate. From major to lawyer to staffer to senate candidate in what . . . five or six years? That must be some kind of record!"

"I promise you that wasn't the plan. I'd decided last summer my future was in politics and was doing the groundwork to run for a state position first. But then the senator told me she was going to retire."

"So, you decided to run for her seat? I know about the courage and bravery thing but that takes real balls."

Tamika was beginning to relax. Johnny was confident without being pushy and had a natural way of moving from topic to topic. More of a "normal guy" than she'd expected—not some rich, self-centered entrepreneur.

Back to his question. "Ha . . . it wasn't like that at all. The senator suggested the idea and it caught me completely off guard—I didn't know what to say. I asked her why on earth she was pushing *me* to run. I thought I was too young and too inexperienced."

Johnny jumped in. "But you've done more than most—served your country, led teams under pressure, saved lives, made sacrifices, worked for an education. You know law and policy, but you aren't some trained politician or a party-line follower. I wish there were more people like you running."

Tamika smiled. "Funny, the senator said something like that, almost word for word. She told me I should never, ever doubt myself again."

"Amen to that. You're perfect for this. Decorated war veteran . . . check. Trained lawyer . . . check. Thoughtful and excellent speaker . . . check. Liberal enough for the state but not Bernie Sanders . . . check. Female *and* of color . . . double check. And . . . well . . . frankly, good looking and famous . . . checkmate."

She glanced up at Johnny, feeling a bit self-conscious about the compliments and curious about the good-looking line. "I really don't know what I was thinking when I said 'yes.' I have no idea how to run a campaign and raising money's just a complete pain in the ass. Thank God for the Lincoln Coalition." The Roscovitches were financing the lion's share of her candidacy, and they talked together regularly about policy ideas and campaign strategy.

"I think you're just being modest. The Coalition's lucky to have you on their roster. I know from listening to you the other night that you have strong ideas and a confident presence. Once people get to know you, they'll trust you."

"Well, it's good to know I have one voter on my side. I mean, you are going to register here, right?"

"Don't worry, you'll get my vote. And it's not just because I want to see you again."

Well . . . now she knew it really was a date.

• • • • •

Flattening the curve. Social distancing. Shelter-in-place.

Ford Wilkes marveled at these new phrases—ideas nobody could have put in any advance plan—and yet he embraced them as his own. On January 21, 2020, the first Covid-19 case was confirmed in Washington State, bringing with it generation-defining images that would change everyone's view of the world. While reports of the outbreak from Wuhan, China, made widespread news, nobody was prepared for the pandemic that would assault the globe. The perfect spice to add to an anarchic stew.

So Wilkes let it cook. In a few short weeks, the tiny virus took down the mighty US economy and exposed dramatic shortcomings in the country's health care preparedness, supply chains, and emergency response capabilities. A chaotic federal government response made matters worse, leaving many life-defining decisions up to the nation's governors and mayors. Predictably, they responded with varying levels of proficiency.

Wilkes knew how this story would unfold—his worldview had been shaped by the last recession. For people with resources, it would be a strange and surreal set of circumstances, but mostly one that had to be endured. And there would be those that would prosper or even profit off the suffering—the rich would absolutely get richer.

For those on the other side of the economic divide, the fear, anxiety, and pain would be more immediate—a question of survival rather than inconvenience. They would fall further and further behind.

While all of that pissed him off, Wilkes took it for what it was. An opportunity of a lifetime. No careful planning. No assignments for Obaid bin Latif. No munitions required. All he needed to do was let nature take its course and watch the chaos ensue.

Naturally, he wasn't willing to stop there.

# Chapter 48

# ZOOM DATING, MARCH

"FUCKING UNBELIEVABLE!"

Johnny could somehow feel the frustration and anger coming through the Surface laptop sitting on the kitchen counter in his Seattle condo. He and Tamika had squeezed in a few outings in person in February, but as the country shut down, they'd reverted to virtual dates—not very satisfying but still a way to stay connected. As she pounded the table, he could see the lights of DC in the background of her Alexandria apartment.

Tamika had put her senatorial campaign on hold to return to Washington, DC, to support Senator Regan and her team's near 24/7 efforts to provide badly needed help to those in peril. It was yet another call back into battle, this time using her policy and communications skills rather than her CSAR training.

"I thought the bill got passed? And two trillion is nothing to sneeze at." Johnny knew Tamika was exhausted but he was genuinely surprised by her reaction.

"Oh, the outcome is a great first step—no question about that," came her reply. "But the bullshit that went on to get us there was ridiculous."

"Well, I suppose each side had some things they wanted—isn't that pretty typical?"

"Hell, you know I'm all for difficult conversations and negotiations. That's how you get constructive, well-tested policy done. But so much of this was politically motivated—people throwing in their favorite initiative, even if it had nothing to do with Covid or the economy. The small government crowd couldn't make up its mind—first they blocked a bunch of social services funding, claiming there had to be 'means testing'—then they turned around and pushed for a huge pile of corporate support with no requirements or provisions. The progressives think we should just print money and ship it to everyone. Shit—" She paused to take a giant gulp of wine.

"Well, at least the final outcome—" Johnny went for the presumptive close, but Tamika wasn't done with her rant.

"And by the way, why did it take us so damn long to respond, to begin with? It's March 27th—this bastard bug has been in the US for almost two months and we've known about it for almost three. You'd think we could get ourselves organized. We're just now getting national resources called up, releasing emergency supplies, and the rest. First responders have been working their asses off without the proper equipment. And don't get me started on the testing fiasco. We have no idea how many cases there are or who's infected. How is that possible in the most technologically advanced country on earth?"

Johnny wanted to do the Zoom version of a hug but that wasn't a feature—at least not yet. Instead, he tried to turn her (again) to the positive side. "Hopefully, you'll be in one of those senate seats yourself not too long from now. What would you have done differently?"

He could practically see the wheels turning in her head.

"Look, I'm CSAR-trained. I can't help but think in terms of preparedness. Gates and others in public health have been sounding the alarm pretty consistently. What we really need is a clear strategy. My dad used to tell me there was an emergency response plan for nuclear attacks back in the fifties and sixties. I think some of that still exists today but it's probably light years behind where we need to be. We need to revamp our entire preparedness system. I suppose that could start at the CDC or at FEMA, but it really involves a whole bunch of government agencies and NGO leaders. It also has to include state and local bureaus as well."

"That sounds like a ton of work—I wouldn't envy that group."

"If you got the right bipartisan leaders and some of the key policy people organized, I think you could make it happen. Heck, if I get in, I'd want to work on that." Tamika brushed a wisp of hair away from her eyes. "What's really eating me up is that people are super afraid right now—I can feel the fear when I'm going to the Capitol and I can see it in the TV interviews. First bin Latif, now this. It's too much. We've got to fight back."

She looked away from the camera toward the lights of the city. "This is a war and that is one thing the federal government should be great at doing. We need to give the people reason to hope. To believe in each other. But my conclusion from the past three weeks is that we don't have much of that in DC right now."

"Well, isn't that what the Lincoln Coalition is all about? Principled leadership. Selfless decisions. Definitive actions. Once you get back on the campaign trail, you'll have a message to send to voters and the resources to reach them. If we're going to fight a war on multiple fronts—if we're going to take down bin Latif and beat this virus—you're a leader people will follow."

She was fighting for what was right. And that was just one of the reasons his love for her was growing.

• • • • •

Ford Wilkes had considered himself at war for several years now. He watched with almost orgasmic pleasure as the stock market dropped over thirty percent, unemployment skyrocketed, and the US economy went into a sudden, and potentially deep, recession. The stockpiling (and hoarding!) of food and goods, the closing of businesses, and the rationing of resources were all parts of the anarchy report card. And while the virus was doing its dirty work, he concluded that he should support its efforts.

Since he couldn't afford to get infected—and he certainly needed to protect Obaid bin Latif—he chose technology as his primary weapon. In early February, he'd made a particularly prescient decision to buy up a massive supply of medical protective gear, including the all-important

N95 respirator masks. Instead of selling them at high prices like the typical asshole, he'd covered his financial tracks, faked manifests, and then shipped them circuitously to a storage facility. There they were, resting comfortably, unavailable to the hospital workers who needed them. He continued to monitor the availability of critical goods and resources throughout the crisis and intervened to subvert supply chains. Silent actions that killed.

His second weapon was social media. He'd already been using a variety of bots to enhance the level of anxiety brought on by bin Latif's attacks—now he applied the same tools to the pandemic. He could work both sides of the aisle on this by vilifying any politician, red or blue, every chance he got. The more distrust in the government, the better. He also offered up conspiracy theories about the virus risks being exaggerated, while spreading false information about how the virus could infect others. Either way, he won another battle in his efforts to drive social division.

Looking up at the TV screen one afternoon in late April from his secluded home, he had the satisfaction of watching CNN and realizing a startling truth.

"Shit . . . look at that. Entire parts of the country have stopped. Wall Street is in chaos. Right wing protests in state capitols. People are either paralyzed with fear or full-on ready to riot."

He was winning.

# Chapter 49

# MEMORIAL DAY

"JUST HOW MUCH TEXTRATE did they steal?" JJ's frustrated voice echoed across the conference room in the FBI's main office in Chicago. He didn't care at this point about minimizing the volume. Four months after the aborted Seattle attack and just as parts of the country were heading back to work from the Covid-19 quarantine, Obaid bin Latif and his crew had successfully taken out a critical part of the interstate highway system. The ensuing bedlam was getting all too familiar. If JJ had yelled much louder, the folks on Dearborn Street below would have looked up.

Special Agent Aaron Phillips spoke, clarifying what JJ already suspected. "Actually, more likely he bought it on the black market. Military contractors sell this stuff to allies all over the world—and, downstream, some of our partners aren't so good about keeping track of it. Our cyber team's been working since day one to trace any transactions, but I'm pretty sure that's going to continue to be a dry well. Between the dark web and cryptocurrencies, it's getting damn hard to identify purchases or track the money."

"Well, I'm glad we got that straight . . . I feel so much better." Jessup didn't try to hide the sarcasm dripping from his lips. Struggling with the lack of progress and his simmering anger at bin Latif, he turned away from Phillips to look out the window.

This terrorist cell had hit an airplane, a train, a dam, and now the interstate system. How could there be no real leads? How could the FBI be no closer to catching these fuckers after four successful attacks and one near miss? How could he, Jerry Jessup, be failing . . . again?

Finally, facing the large, tinted glass window and looking out, he spoke. "What do we know?"

"He used multiple charges, placed on each of the Eisenhower Expressway overpasses at the Jane Byrne Interchange. Remote cell phone detonation. Just like the train and the dam. The overpasses fell on the Dan Ryan Expressway below—forty-five people killed, twice as many injured. That intersection is the heart of the commute. Chicago's ground to a halt—again—and probably will be stuck there for weeks. Disrupted some gas lines, too. People were just getting used to going back to work, and now they're pissed. It's starting to boil over."

"Please tell me we have something on video. There must be twenty cameras on that interchange. Somebody must have seen something." In his mind, he was doing the math on shutting down transportation in a city like Chicago. The economy was in the toilet from the pandemic and commerce needed to move. This was going to mean hundreds of millions—maybe billions of dollars—in additional losses. *Damn it.*

"You're right about the video. We're going through all of it from the past two weeks. We're canvassing the neighborhood too, but it's not exactly a place where you hang out to watch the cars go by. Thing is, we don't know when he planted the bomb. Could've been that day, a week before, or a month before. Doubtful anybody saw it."

"And the fucking video he posted?" JJ was beyond pissed about the footage claiming responsibility. He'd nearly destroyed the computer screen when he saw it the first time. Bin Latif's taunts were getting more personal. "Come on FBI, I'm trying to help you out, but you've got to keep up. Are you afraid you might get infected?" Jerry had thick skin—it came with the territory—but these scumbags had burrowed way deep.

*Breathe*, he said to himself. *You can't let them do that to you.*

Phillips continued. "You know, the video thing is weird. No way to trace the first three posts but our guys are making progress on this one. He's either getting careless or someone on his team's just lazy."

"Sirs . . . you gotta see this," came a call from the doorway.

Both Jessup and Phillips slipped around the conference table, past the walls that were filling up with photos, maps, and diagrams, and went into the main squad room. As in its San Francisco office, the Chicago bureau featured a maze of desks, screens everywhere, each playing some form of video, and a steady buzz of activity from people talking on phones. A small group was huddled around a screen. Six-foot distancing rule be damned.

"What do you got?"

"This was two days before the bombing. 0300."

The video was operating on infrared, so everything had a dingy, orange glow like the sun was shining through some smog. What looked like a dark-colored Ford SUV rolled slowly down a side street and parked near an overpass. *The* overpass. A man in full Arab garb hopped lightly out of the driver's seat. He went to the trunk and pulled out two back packs and an extension ladder. He looked straight up at the camera, gave a slight nod and then moved out of sight under the overpass. Ten minutes and thirty seconds later, he sauntered back into view. He gave a little salute—again looking directly at the camera—and put the ladder into the trunk. He casually climbed into the SUV and drove off.

Performance completed.

Nobody around the cubicle said anything. Everyone just turned to look at Assistant Director Jerry Jessup. But instead of the explosion he knew they expected, he gave them a stone-cold stare.

"I want everyone to get this straight. Nobody fucks with the FBI like that. They're leaving clues in the open, which means they're either taunting us, setting a trap, or both. Regardless, I want *this* particular Arab bomber on a platter. They seem to be sacrificing him anyway. When we're done with him, he'll tell us how to get the rest—including Obaid bin Latif. Trace the car—that is the second time with a Ford SUV. Facial recognition on the photo. Carpet-bomb that picture until somebody reports him. Figure out where he bought the cell phones. Dig, dig, and then dig some more. Nobody goes home until we find him."

He stopped there to look around the entire set of cubicles. Ironically, people were tired of being at home.

"But hear me *clearly*. Once we find 'em, we stop right there. I don't know what their game is, but we're going to figure out the rules before we play. These guys are very smart and don't care who or how many they kill. That's a very dangerous combination."

•　•　•　•　•

Obaid bin Latif had to admit that the performance in Chicago had been tremendously satisfying. Sitting on the sidelines during the pandemic shutdown had tested even his patience, but he knew postponing the attack had been the right move. Finally getting the chance to snub his nose at the FBI was a giant ego massage, especially after his failure in Seattle.

That assignment had been screwed from the beginning. Not enough time to plan properly or to backstop the Senator Regan campaign head-fake. No way to get the proper explosive material in the right location. Too many people, police, and cameras. He'd gone several extra inches (and pounds) on his disguise—and actually managed to get the makeshift bomb in decent position. If those damn drunks hadn't interrupted and stared at him like they did, he would have detonated the device while he was walking down the alley. But his number one priority was always survival—and in Seattle he'd been damn lucky.

Chicago was completely different. Getting back on plan had made executing the attack significantly easier. Resources were in place, the explosives ready to go, and the risk of detection limited. He'd even had extra time to prepare.

Chicago also represented a turning point for him—one he knew was necessary and part of the plan. The time had come to lure the FBI in, and to do it in a way that would send them down the wrong rabbit hole. Unfortunately, that would require taking even more risk—and Obaid bin Latif knew his neck would be on the line. It would take all of his special talents to get through to the other side safely.

Perhaps the salute and staring at the video camera had been a bit over the top, but he couldn't resist the temptation. If he was going to let the FBI track him, he wanted to have some fun in the process. He'd especially enjoyed the words in his video post. He'd done some research on

Assistant Director Jerry Jessup and would have loved to see his face and hear his reaction to the taunting. The dolt was still under the impression that this was some big terrorist cell at work.

Well, that was probably a good thing for Obaid bin Latif *and* Ford Wilkes.

· · · · ·

Redemption. Atonement. Salvation.

These were all ideas Bryce was taught when he was young. All part of the religious dogma his mother had tried to instill in him. He could never understand how someone from two thousand years ago could offer the solution. How did one man's execution at the hands of a foreign invader provide solace to the rest of the world? It was all just too abstract for him. But now with the blood of thousands on his hands, Bryce Roscovitch was an agnostic in search of forgiveness. With nobody there to act as confidant or confessor, and much of the world still in some form of lockdown, the God that was his computer system would have to provide some solutions.

His original facial recognition search had yielded some potential clues. He had a partial match with a photo from a driver's license database. And yet the person on the license didn't really look that much like any of the other photos or videos. But his facial recognition program was an AI-based piece of technology that, to date, had never failed—and it clearly had detected some similarities.

The Chicago episode added to the mystery—an Arab-looking guy with different features from the others, and someone who clearly wasn't worried about being identified. Bryce's search needed to confirm whether the FBI's thesis about the terrorist cell was correct—or if he was dealing with just a few assailants, or even with a solo attacker.

He was also pondering the Seattle failure. Why would someone who was clearly smart and calculating pursue something so poorly planned? He couldn't dismiss the copycat theory completely, but his instincts said this was the work of the artist known as Obaid bin Latif. He knew the FBI was asking the same questions—and they didn't have any better answers than he did. He'd watched the video of the attacker parking the van and escaping down the alleyway over and over. Something about it was off, but it took him a long time to realize the problem.

The driver had adjusted his clothing in an awkward way when he closed the van door, and his walk across the lot seemed somehow unnatural. Almost stilted and clumsy. Bryce Roscovitch thought he knew why—and that sent him back to his computers in search of a different set of code that could help solve his visual riddle.

He also had not given up on back-tracing the fifteen transactions he'd identified as possibly relating to his client/terrorist. He had zeroed in on three different IP addresses that could connect the dots between the various transactions necessary to pull off the attacks. Now he was trying to connect those IP addresses with the video postings—without much success for the time being.

More stalled parts to his investigation. To his search to atone for his sins.

"So what do we have, Bryce?" asked his imaginary friend.

"Well . . . we have a bomber who claims he is from the Middle East but could just as easily be from Texas. We have at least three IP addresses but can't connect them directly with the terrorist. We have pictures and videos that don't match but have some similarities. He's smart enough to use the dark web exceptionally well, but stupid enough to leave a cell phone and tracks that lead to a car. And now he's taunting the FBI in a video. It's even possible we have a team of two. Maybe even a cell."

"Bryce," came the sympathetic response, "you've got a big pile of shit. If you want redemption, you better dig deeper."

# Chapter 50

# ENDINGS AND BEGINNINGS

CYBERNOPTICS'S SUCCESSFUL EXIT was a watershed event for Paul Hayek. He'd suffered through painful, public failures as well as his share of perceived and real persecution. He would always have the hot temper and strong opinions that were the granite stones of his personality. But the sale of his "creation" made the chip on his shoulder a bit smaller and a little more difficult to knock off. Paul could thumb his nose at the Silicon Valley folks who had snubbed him.

He was now in the club, whether they liked it or not.

In their on-again, off-again friendship (which was "on" at the moment), Paul and Johnny had talked for many hours (and across several days) about their newfound status as successful tech startup leaders. "I woke up this morning," said Johnny over another pizza dinner, "and realized I'd won. And then I asked myself 'won what?'"

They were sitting in the dungeon conference room of Cybernoptics's now-empty warehouse, eating pizza and hashing out their future. This dinner ritual had become a regular affair during the darkest days of the company. The interior room had one door and a picture window that only offered a view of the rest of the warehouse and its cubicles. It all seemed to deny the existence of the outside world. Tunnel vision on work. When the company was in trouble, it had sucked . . . and they both had known it.

Paul took a big bite of pepperoni and pineapple and wiped the grease and cheese from his chin. "We've both been trying to prove something for years—but I'm beginning to wonder if anybody else really cared."

Leaning back in his chair, angled against the wall, Johnny replied,

"I think I told you I went to a Lincoln Coalition fundraiser that Shea Roscovitch corralled me into—and I gotta say I was inspired. Some of it was political blah, blah, blah, but these people really believe in serving the country and making things better. And the bombings and Covid mismanagement make that even more relevant. Our startup ego trip kinda pales in comparison."

"Are you sure it was patriotism—or were you just turned on by seeing your guardian angel again?" Paul looked sideways at Johnny to sneak a peek and was rewarded with a bit of a blush.

"Very funny. And yes, we've been dating. A guy has to do what a guy—" and then he stopped dead. "Oh hell, Paul. I don't think I've ever felt this way about someone. When I listen to her speak . . . she has a completely different sense of purpose."

"I know what you mean. I'm struggling to find a sense of purpose myself now that I've—correction—*we've* conquered the startup buzz saw."

Paul was aware that as his faith had deepened, so had his desire to contribute to something greater—perhaps to help or support those "like him." The prosperity that came with the sale of Cybernoptics only heightened the inner tension he felt. As did the increasing public discord. For Paul, the question was simple but somewhat existential: Did a successful executive, or a successful company for that matter, have obligations and responsibilities beyond their own achievements?

Johnny packed up the pizza box and crushed it into a little square. "Shit. I've been completely hung up on this unicorn startup dream, and Tamika and Margaret are trying to help people living a nightmare. I've been fighting to prove that the kid from Detroit could make it—and they're trying to help the people stuck in Detroit." He pushed the pizza box into the recycle bin with a little too much effort.

"We've made a lot of sacrifices along the way, that's for sure." Paul thought about the wife he didn't have, the kids he couldn't enjoy, and a social life that revolved around pizza in a conference room. The Muslim immigrant had done good. But what did it really amount to?

"We need to shut down this room—for good. Now that Cybernoptics is done, it's time for both of us to declare victory and decide what to do with the spoils." Paul waited for Johnny to get up. They both looked around one last time to lock in the memories. Then Paul turned out the lights and closed the door.

On the way home, Paul called his mother. She was still his confidant and guide. He was driving a new Tesla through the side streets near his house, twilight settling over the bedroom community, and he wanted her advice.

"Something's bothering you, Paul. What's going on in that head of yours?"

"Ommi—I feel like I climbed up the Empire State Building and when I got to the top, there was no view. Why did I work so hard to get here?"

She let the silence sit while he processed what he'd just said.

"When I pray," Paul continued, "I feel the silliness of my pride. I always felt inadequate, and now that I've succeeded, I feel even more inadequate. If that makes any sense?"

"You should celebrate your achievements, Paul. Being proud when you've accomplished something after great effort is a good thing. Our faith encourages us to feel that joy. You shouldn't feel guilty."

"But what's the real point? It's great to have the money, and I can certainly help you and Dad and buy nice things for myself. But is that what it's all about?"

"The problem with pride is it can cloud our vision—it can confuse us into believing that we alone achieved success. Maybe Allah has a plan for you that's bigger than this little plateau you've found. You're now one of the more successful Muslim immigrants in America. Successful in the hallowed ground of Silicon Valley. Successful in a place that tried to shut you out. Allah has gifted you a platform and rejecting a gift from your God is a sin worse than pride itself."

Paul sat there with the car silently humming in the dark, mulling over her words and hoping for inspiration.

They talked for another thirty minutes, some of it serious, some of it small talk. But the entire time they were chatting, Paul was framing in his mind some next steps. He couldn't deny that along with everything else now driving him, the fact that the serial bomber who had almost killed his friend and continued to wreak havoc was purportedly Islamic and on a jihadist crusade. That burned at Paul's sense of Muslim identity.

So as he had during his time of conversion, he sat down the next evening to declare his beliefs. Paul's last "letter to the editor" had cost him the funding for his first business. But he was free of that pressure now. He could once again say what he felt and do it knowing he had nothing to prove. He closed his letter to the *New York Times* with a challenge to his fellow business leaders:

> *Obaid bin Latif is a fraud as a Muslim. But he has shown a great light on our fatal weakness—he has exploited our communities' economic and social divisions to drag us into a world that lacks the basics of common decency. To the men and women who are my fellow business leaders, this is a call to action.*
>
> *Authentic leaders don't just watch the share price, calculate what is best for company value (or for themselves), and then act accordingly. Even in a land where capitalism reigns supreme, we must have a moral compass. We must use our positions of influence to do what is right for our local communities and society as a whole. This is not abuse of power or putting our values above others. Instead, it is called citizenship, something the founding fathers exercised every day. America's modern business leaders need to follow their example.*

As his mother had pointed out, he was now on a path to something more meaningful than making money. He was still an engineer, but now going to work for his community.

No longer just a "founder." Now a proud "civic engineer."

# Chapter 51

# MICHIGAN TO VIRGINIA

OBAID BIN LATIF KNEW that localized power outages due to weather conditions happened quite frequently. The disruptions were a hassle, leaving people without electricity for hours and sometimes days. But large areas of the US power grid had also experienced major outages that had nothing to do with violent storms. From software bugs to technician mistakes, large parts of the country had been thrown into darkness multiple times, primarily because of the way a highly distributed system was poorly connected.

And Obaid bin Latif knew exactly what to do with that information.

As the heat of the wilting hot summer of 2020 reached a peak and with the chaos in Chicago in his rearview mirror, he returned his attention to the East Coast, where a massive power outage would surely lead to more anarchy. One of bin Latif's first "acquisitions," now some two years old, was a software hack that exploited a control system used by many electric companies, including Baltimore Gas and Electric. BGE served a community that was a racial powder keg. All the better to magnify the effects of an unexpected blackout in a city already overheated, both physically and emotionally.

He also knew this would be his penultimate major attack—and that required a careful orchestration of the particulars. For one, he had chosen his timing meticulously. With public order and resolve ping-ponging between panic and anger, now was the opportune moment to smash the ball and score some points. The good news was he could execute this incursion remotely—literally from the comfort of his Detroit apartment.

He had planted the malware knowing that it would take several days to go into effect, giving him time to film his video missive and make the final preparations at the apartment.

While he was confident about the attack's success, he had other goals to meet. He planted the code with a subtle trail attached—breadcrumbs that would suck the FBI into a trap that would make so much more damage possible.

Recording the video itself was easy. He followed the same recipe as before, making sure he provided the appropriate FBI motivation at the end. "I am tired of playing with my food. If you can't make this more interesting, I'm going to have to escalate my efforts. The time has come for the infidels to pay in a way they could never imagine. Like the coronavirus, you will never see me coming and, by the time you realize it, I'll be gone."

After all, he needed to drive up the scope of the threat. And this time, he needed them to find him.

● ● ● ● ●

Knowing that the Baltimore situation was in the capable hands of Obaid bin Latif, Ford Wilkes turned his attention to the next wave of attacks—a planning process that revolved around drone technology. The US military was using drones to fight the war in the Middle East without putting pilots at risk, and Wilkes was amused by the level of ethical debate it had been generating. In one dimension, you had a whole series of discussions about what it meant to attack a US citizen acting as a terrorist in the Middle East. What if that citizen was on US soil? Who got to be judge and jury? He smiled smugly at the thought of "due process" being an actual concept in this debate.

On a completely different level, military scholars were debating the implications of fighting a war without having to consider the safety of the combatants. What would constrain people's ambitions? What would limit the carnage? How do you think about time-honored attributes like courage, bravery, and patriotism when the "soldiers" could be behind a desk and series of screens, directing machines to kill others? The one thing that had ever mitigated the horror of war was the nobility found in humans sacrificing to protect others. When that was gone, the only thing left would be the horror.

And that was fine with Ford Wilkes. The more horrific, the better.

He moved from his Riverview, Michigan, kitchen to the couch and pulled his laptop off the coffee table, where he propped his feet. Of course, drone technology could be put to many other uses—search and rescue, mapping, remote security, automated delivery, aerial photography, and even monitoring shelter-in-place decrees. The list of socially acceptable applications was almost endless. But what would happen when the buzzing of a drone brought visions of destruction and mayhem? It was an opportunity to turn society against the very technological advancements that offered a better future.

That was irresistible.

Naturally, there were drones and then there were Drones. Wilkes needed something compact that could be controlled from considerable distance. He also needed a device that could carry a reasonable payload. And he wanted something that would be difficult to detect and impossible to shut down by interfering with the signal. He had crossed over into a military-grade device. Special preparations and precautions were clearly necessary.

As for his target, he was going for the triple backflip off the low diving board—two simultaneous attacks in two different cities. Bin Latif would be the bait in Detroit—that part of the plan was fixed. But he had intentionally left his second target open so that he could assess the state of the nation and adjust accordingly. Now he was evaluating several options.

DC was his primary focus—the proverbial center of the country—a location that would have a symbolic impact in addition to causing large-scale death and destruction.

"So, is it the Capitol? Or the White House?" Both were obvious choices.

But he was concerned that these sites were now carefully protected from aerial attack after 9/11—and even more so after his own recent contributions. Smirk. He pulled up a map of DC and looked over some other possibilities.

"Arlington Cemetery?" That was full of symbolism, but blowing up people who were already dead didn't seem very satisfying.

"Maybe it should be Reagan National Airport?" He liked the presidential connection, but he'd already done the plane thing.

"The Supreme Court?" Definitely appealing—who were they to restrict his liberty? He'd have to check on when those old stiffs in the black robes would be on-site.

Clearly, he had more planning work to do.

The irony in all these preparations was that Wilkes ultimately wanted bin Latif to be caught—but only on his terms. That, in fact, was becoming his biggest challenge. How was he going to let authorities get to bin Latif and yet still deliver the Detroit attack and drone-enabled fatal blow? Wilkes also had the small but important matter of a certain Air Force major turned political adversary. He still needed a plan to eliminate her and the Lincoln Coalition from the playing field.

He smiled. Everyone should have such problems.

• • • • •

Once he'd narrowed down his transaction search to the three IP addresses, Bryce had written a protocol that would watch each address, in the event that there was more activity. The silence from this work over the past nine months had led him to believe the terrorist (or the cell) had purchased all his weapons "up front" and was using them one by one. So, when his computer emitted an audible "bing," he jumped reflexively. It was late in the evening and he was doing more work on the video recognition problem. The protocol alarm told him that one of the sites was active—and after some investigation, he realized that his customer was back on the market and looking for some very advanced equipment.

There was no way for Bryce to determine if this was his original client, but not believing in coincidences, he followed the transaction carefully. This latest "request for purchase" included detailed specifications that were very high-end. Bryce knew these devices only had a few uses. And none of them were good.

He had to assume this was his target.

The question now was, what the hell should he do about it?

He got up from his desk. Using the screen glow to find his minifridge in the back, he grabbed a beer. His first instinct was to pursue the letter he'd sent to Angela and ask her for help. There had been something cathartic about writing to her. Something that lifted a bit of the guilt. He'd never been to confession after that first time, but now he thought the sacrament might be more about sharing the burden. Less about the cross and more about the resurrection. Of course, the conundrum was, what would he ask her to do? Sending her to the police was not going to be productive without all his information, and there was no practical or safe way to get it to her. Even then, what he had wasn't conclusive. That avenue would have to wait until he had more.

His second idea was to gather up the evidence and "anonymously" ship it over to the FBI. Unfortunately, contacting them would expose him to being back-traced. Putting his angst and shame over his role in the attacks aside, Bryce was still a survivor and had no intention of getting caught. Besides, why would the FBI assign any credibility to the information? There was no guarantee they would follow up. More likely the information would join a stack of other leads sent in by the goody-two-shoes and the crackpots. It might get pursued—eventually.

Still, he had too many questions and too much desire to atone for his mistakes to just walk away from this nutcase. The risk in allowing things to move forward was that the terrorist might find someone to sell him the weapons he wanted. Once that process got rolling, there was little Bryce could do to stop it.

This was not a friendly game of cards. This was high-stakes poker played in the dark recesses of the internet with knives out on the table. In this game, there were no rules and people played to kill. He decided to take out some insurance by acquiring some equipment of his own, exposing himself to discovery in the process.

"Fuck it," he said out loud, and made the purchase.

# Chapter 52

# DARKNESS AND LIGHT

THE LIGHTS WENT OUT in one quick cut—and with them, everything electrical went down. Annoyed by the outage that followed but oblivious to its scope and the damage to come, Tamika and Johnny sat in the tiny living room of her Alexandria apartment, now turning a late-night dinner into a candlelit affair. Not only had they been dating for six months, but Johnny had come on board as one of her senior campaign strategists. It was a fitting way for him to apply the lessons he'd learned in business to the challenges of politics and elections.

"Wow . . ." was all Johnny could say as he looked out the window.

"Wow what?" Tamika came over from behind and put her arms around him.

"I've never seen anything like that. The glow from the fading dusk, car lights on the roads . . . and then nothing but darkness."

"But look at the monuments—beacons of light in a dark city."

With a wry chuckle, he said, "I was just going to comment on the backup generators." He looked back over his shoulder to kiss her. "You really are a romantic patriot, aren't you?"

"Anything wrong with that?" she answered, a certain edge to her tone.

"Whoa there . . . I meant it as a compliment, Tamika." He spun around, looked into her eyes, and kissed her again quickly, but only on the cheek as she turned her head.

"Sorry . . . but you know I'm a little sensitive about that." She navigated in the low candlelight to the kitchenette to organize their take-out dinners, while Johnny seemed to sulk back into a dark corner.

*Shit*, she said to herself. *Why do I always snap like that?*

She still didn't know how to define their relationship. It had started in a dark ditch—not exactly an attractive metaphor. Now she wasn't sure how to think about the boundaries between friend, confidant, lover, and "forever."

Dr. Stromwell had asked her about their dates. That had at least given her something positive to discuss. "We've had to squeeze things in around the pandemic and the campaign, but I guess when we go out, mostly we do things that are just fun. Bars and bowling, some road biking. Hell, he even surprised me with a skydiving afternoon for my birthday. Shit, they made me jump with an instructor!"

The doctor continued down the path. "You've talked a few times about wanting to have a family—how do his kids fit into that?"

"I was terrified the first time I met them, but somehow they seem to like me." Tamika noted the look on Stromwell's face. "Okay. I think Nathan has a crush on me and Phoenix thinks I'm some kind of role model."

"Is that enough for you?"

Tamika had no answer for that.

Stromwell took the final step. "Have you told him?"

"That I love him?"

"No . . . not that." She gave Tamika a long, hard look.

It did not take long for the tears to well up. Quietly, she answered, "I don't think I could ever talk to him about that."

"That's up to you. But there are so many things you've not said to him. Until you do, how can you be sure if it's love?"

Sighing at the memory of that recent session, Tamika grabbed their plates and walked back into the main room. The plan had been to watch a movie while they ate but now they just sat on the couch next to each other waiting for the silence to break. Not a fight just yet, but there was knife-cutting tension—something that happened every so often. For Tamika, it was the little things that set her off.

After a few moments, Johnny seemed to decide that staring at a blank TV was not that interesting and the candlelight was not very romantic. "Can you please tell me why you got so upset? You served your country with incredible distinction and saved so many lives, including mine. Your whole campaign is based on the idea that we need to bring the country together. Why does being called a patriot hurt so much?"

Tamika just couldn't let it come out.

Johnny went all in. "Tamika . . . I love you . . . I *love* you. But Jesus, I can't love the secrets, whatever they are. These episodes drive me crazy. I need to know all of you—the best and the worst. Part of you just won't be enough."

His gentle plea was met with an angry response. "Do you *really* love me? Or am I just the person who saved your life when your marriage was falling apart?" *Did I just say that?*

"What? Are you shitting me? My failed marriage has nothing to do with this. And at least I can talk about that and share my kids with you." Blazing eyes locked to hers. "I have to know . . ." The "or else" was left unsaid, suspended between them.

"Fine. You really want to know? Well, I'll tell you, Mr. Love Boat. Would you still love a woman who was raped and then killed the person who did it to her? Is that your idea of a 'patriot'? Is she the one you want to spend the rest of your life with?"

For ten or fifteen seconds, Tamika thought Johnny was going to lose it. Or worse, just get up and walk out. He stood up and did a short tour around the apartment, brushing back his hair and rubbing his eyes. But then he took a deep breath, walked back to the couch, grasped her hands . . . and faced the uncertainty of their future. "Tell me everything."

So she did.

She told him all of it. From beginning to middle to end. No tears or emotions. Just a cold, expressionless narrative from the *Washington Post* war desk. Johnny said nothing for almost thirty minutes, just listening to her and absorbing her words. Then, when it was clear she'd told him everything—the good, the bad, and the ugly—he reached out and held her close.

Tamika began to tremble and the tears finally came. He asked no questions and needed just a few words. "I love you completely. All of you. Forever."

•    •    •    •    •

They shut the world out that night, with lovemaking on the couch that made up for the dying light of the candles. For the first time, Johnny felt like he could really experience Tamika. Not just the badass fighter and determined leader that he admired, but also the person with a tender, sensitive heart that he knew he loved. This was not a conquest or an acquisition. He'd met a kindred spirit. A soulmate.

It was a surprising revelation for Johnny Humboldt, the perpetual solo artist.

When they woke the next morning, their cell phones told them what they'd missed during their night off the grid. When the power had gone out, the violence that ensued was more than the highest hopes of any terrorist. The outage spread from its epicenter in Baltimore south through Washington, DC, to Richmond—north through Philadelphia to Newark—and finally as far west as Cleveland and Cincinnati.

The electrical disruption set off a chain reaction of "enough is too much." Temperatures in the high nineties, ongoing racial tensions, the worsening economy, and pent-up pandemic overhang led to an outpouring of both genuine anger and random rage. Downtown Baltimore was soon ablaze. Looting was reported in big cities and small towns. The president was evacuated to Camp David as a security precaution. For the next few nights, American streets on the eastern seaboard would be under curfew, patrolled by military reservists with automatic weapons.

For Tamika, this was the last straw. Society was falling apart. And she knew Obaid bin Latif was to blame.

# Chapter 53

# ELECTION DAY 2020

"I CAN'T BELIEVE WE'RE ALL HERE," Tamika said to Johnny as they looked across the room. She realized it was the first time they'd all been together since the demise of Flight 209—and on that fateful night at Offutt Air Force Base, the balancing scales of life had shifted for all of them.

Johnny had lost his wife but had discovered the sanctity of life. Margaret had found herself but had to give up on the security of Johnny in the process. Jerry Jessup had abandoned his military career but was still chasing redemption with a new enemy. Charles and Shea had realized they might never find their son Bryce but had inherited a whole new family to nurture. General Frank Smith had left the Air Force but reconnected with his daughter. And Tamika had traded a pile of bad baggage for a new opportunity to serve. Eighteen months was such a short time, yet, for all present, it seemed like a lifetime of change.

The penthouse hotel suite at the Seattle Fairmont was a strange venue for a reunion, steeped in tradition complete with carved moldings from the 1920s and furniture that was on the dark and heavy side of the flapper era. It was election night, and the Democratic Party had picked the location to celebrate what they hoped would be a big shift in the House, the Senate, and the White House.

In contrast to the Fairmont, the group was more of a W Hotel crew—a younger progressive group supporting the Lincoln Coalition and Tamika's platform for a positive future. Only the security check, health screen, and face masks reminded everyone of the current time and place. And then there was FBI Agent Higginbottom, standing at attention in the corner.

Tamika looked across the room at the Roscovitches. "Charles and Shea have really changed our lives. They've given us tenfold for what little we did—simple gifts repaid with uncommon dedication and care. I love my dad dearly and miss my mom and brother, but somehow God decided I needed special guardians." She continued, "You know, they have everything they could want except the one thing money can't buy. A lost son and a chance to relive the past. I'm never sure if they're truly happy. If I win—"

"When you win," corrected Johnny.

"*When* I win, Charles wants me to be the face of the Lincoln Coalition."

"Is that what you want?"

"I need to forge my own way, I suppose, but he's building a platform that I believe in. When we first discussed Lincoln Coalition support, he asked me one question: 'Are you willing to vote for something that you know could lead to losing the next election?' He doesn't care whether you're a Republican or a Democrat—all he cares about is whether you'll do what's right for the country. The Lincoln Coalition is becoming a voice of reason, a sign of hope—a real stabilizing force. Charles has created a platform to fight the terrorists *and* the extremists without the violence and incivility. And that's exactly where I need to be."

"Well, I'm now available to help."

Tamika looked over at him, realizing that was both a personal and a professional statement. Instead of replying, she just put her arm around him and leaned in.

They saw the first results flash up on the room's screens, telling them little more than the vote counting had begun. For Tamika, this was a new type of race. There was no tape for her to cross and no clock to provide immediate results. There was a stirring buzz in the room as everyone tried to interpret what nine percent of the precincts could tell them. She and her opponent, Governor Richard Chancellor, were neck and neck. And with the Covid-19-related challenges to voting, ballot counting was going to be slow.

News flash: Acceptance speeches were a long, long night away.

• • • • •

"Thank you for coming, Margaret," said Tamika graciously as she came over to say hello. "And I must be the tenth person to tell you how great you look in that dress. I get stuck in this middle-of-the-road garb to keep everyone happy!" The woman of the hour was conservatively attired in a knee-length blue sheathe dress, with just a bit of jewelry for an accent—feminine but not glamorous was apparently the goal.

Margaret Humboldt had formalized her first name believing it was more professional, but she'd decided to keep her married name to match with her children's last name. She tried not to notice Tamika's compliment, but she'd liked the look in the mirror earlier that evening. Green was definitely her color. With all the meetings and events for Fifth Year, appearances now seemed to matter so much more.

"I have to admit, this is a first for me. I've never been to a 'campaign celebration.' Charles and Shea invited me, thinking I needed some experience in advocating for my organization. Take this the right way, but it's kind of weird."

"Oh, I know exactly what you mean. I had that feeling about twice a day on the campaign trail. I kept saying, 'You want me to do what?' It's another world for sure." Pause. "So tell me more about Fifth Year. Johnny goes on and on about what you've accomplished—it sounds amazing."

"So how much has he told you?"

"Last night he was saying that you're getting incredible results, but I'd love to hear the full stump speech."

Last night . . . hmmm. But easier to talk about her new baby than to deal with thoughts of Johnny and Tamika together. "Well, he's probably been infected by my bias. But our graduation rate is over seventy percent, our placement rate is over ninety percent, and none of our students leave with any debt. We're capable of serving tens of thousands of kids because it's online and we don't need to add many teachers as we grow. It's still super early, so we'll have to see how well our graduates do in the job market."

"It must be tough to expand when you have to do everything locally."

"It's a bit of a mixed bag, to be honest. We're up and running in three cities—San Francisco, Seattle, and Houston—and because we have no physical buildings, we can go to any city where there is opportunity. So we drive our programs in places where local government and business are willing to support us—where the jobs are. That means our growth comes in spurts, one city at a time."

"I hear from Johnny that Detroit is next up on your list?"

"That's right. Detroit is a really a difficult environment, but we're launching with the help of Paul Hayek's new immigrant job-training organization. He's an absolute bulldog about getting corporate support, and Johnny has some connections there, too. They're both pushing to get some serious political attention."

After another long pause, Tamika seemed ready to move on to other guests. "Well, let me know how I can help. There are billions of dollars in pass-thru education and job-training funds that go from DC to the states. We should figure out how you can tap into that. And thanks again for—"

"Tamika wait. I want to say something—although I'm not sure if I can get it to come across the right way." This was not in Margaret's plan, but she'd opened Pandora's box and was wondering what would come out of it. Tamika turned back toward her with a curious look in her eye, and perhaps a touch of 'oh no, are we really going to go there now' thrown in.

"I know that Johnny truly loves you—and I don't say that lightly. Coming from him, that makes you a very special person."

"Margaret . . ."

"Please let me finish—this is important to me. I want what is best for Johnny, so I'm happy for him—and for you. I'll never forget that you saved his life. And you've been great with Phoenix and Nathan. Truly great. At the same time, I guess I'm a little jealous or angry or something. When you feel that from me, I want you to know it's not aimed at you or even at Johnny. It's just a choice I made—a choice we both made—and the right choice for sure. But . . . shit, I'm rambling. I guess I just want to be able to talk with you without some big, unspoken barrier."

Tamika's relief was evident on her face. "Thank you for saying that. We may not know each other that well, but I completely understand a jumble of emotions that can't be explained easily. I seem to live that every day." She stopped to look around the room. "When I see so many people from the crash here, I marvel at how things worked out. There's no real reason for our paths to have crossed, but somehow you and I are two ships that were meant to meet. We'll figure this out. And it'll be good."

Margaret gave a small smile. "If it weren't for the Johnny thing, I think I'd *really* like you." They both laughed.

The latest results were in. Chancellor, by more than they would like.

More waiting to follow.

• • • • •

"You must be Paul Hayek." Tamika was continuing to work the room and had long wanted to meet Johnny's business partner. "I feel like I know you so well. I get the stereo version from Charles and Johnny and . . . well . . . I suppose you're one of the few people in the room I don't recognize."

"So, that's two things we can agree on—Charles and Johnny in stereo can be quite the experience—and I only recognized you from your campaign photos!"

"Congratulations on Cybernoptics. I've always worked in big organizations and can't imagine what it's like to start something from scratch and then see your baby grow up."

"I suspect it's the business equivalent of diving into a burning plane," countered Paul with a tip of his glass. "I'm a fighter by nature, but I have no idea how you did that."

"I think the big difference is you had to use your brain, and I had to turn mine off." That brought a good round of laughs and a clinking of glasses.

"So what are you doing now that Cybernoptics is part of Facebook?"

"As you know, Johnny's been doing all of the transition work with the Oculus folks. That's freed me up to focus on a longtime personal passion. I'm working with leaders in the business community to take on aspects of the immigration issue. Something has to be done before it pulls the country completely apart."

With a slight smile, Tamika said, "It's good to know Johnny was right—you're not afraid to take on a challenge. Every time I think about immigration, my head starts to explode. I don't know if I should begin by talking about discrimination, labor policy, religious persecution, border restrictions, virus mitigation, or political asylum. And then this bin Latif idiot blows something up and we have to start over."

Tamika had apparently hit a hot button squarely on the head—and with a sledgehammer. Paul's reputation for volcanic anger surfaced, hot lava now spitting out. "He's an *abomination*. A disgrace to Islam and to everything we stand for," he hissed. There was an uncomfortable pause as heads turned in the room and Paul took a long drink, clearly not sure how to resurrect the conversation.

Charles walked over quickly and tried to bring Paul back to center. "I heard someone say 'immigration' and thought I should join in. Our team has debated the topic back and forth on about a weekly basis. There's so many ways to attack this—where are you going to start, Paul?"

Paul managed to relax a bit as he continued discussing a topic that was clearly important to him. "We think there are three prongs. There is a protest and activism effort that really must confront the neo-Nazis, the hate groups, the Proud Boys, and their sympathizers. There's an underground war being fought, and it's about as clear a case of good versus evil as you can get." He paused to gauge their reaction.

"Amen to fighting evil," said Tamika quietly. "I know a bit about that. How do you draw the line between fighting the battles that must be fought and not turning into one of them?"

"I wish I had a good answer for that. Was Malcolm X right or was

MLK? We're still struggling with another shade of that same battle." Paul took a long drink.

Charles continued probing. "You mentioned three prongs?"

Shifting his gaze from Tamika to Charles and then back again, Paul continued. "There's definitely a policy element to this. Our immigration policy is a shamble—laws, presidential executive orders, department policies and procedures—just a mishmash of ideas that have accumulated over time. As business leaders, we can have an influence here, and there is a subgroup that is going to push this aggressively." With a smile at Tamika, he said, "I'll put you on the list for them to come see."

"Well, let's hope that I matter in the conversation. I've run races all of my life, but this slow-motion finish is killing me."

Paul surprised Tamika by just plowing ahead. "I saw you talking with Margaret earlier—she's actually a part of our third initiative. In the end, so much of this comes down to economics. I was fortunate. My parents were well-educated and spoke English. They found jobs and slipped into the productive mainstream. For most immigrants, that's not how it works. And when you're stuck in the poverty cycle, only bad things happen."

*Socially awkward but super passionate. I can work with that*, thought Tamika.

"Margaret mentioned that you're joining forces in Detroit?"

"Yes, there'll be a march in support of minorities and immigrants that will end at city hall. The politicos will do a bit of pontificating on the policy work they're doing and what they'd like from Washington, DC, and then we'll announce our support for the Fifth Year program in Detroit. We've got the CEOs from GM and Ford, the mayor, several members of Congress, and Senator Studebaker coming to speak. We think we can turn out five to ten thousand people. Maybe more, if folks can put their virus fears behind them."

"When is your Detroit event?"

"December 7th."

Tamika looked at Charles and smiled.

December 7th was going to be a big day for all of them.

# Chapter 54

# THE FINAL PLAN

THE BITCH ACTUALLY had a chance to win.

Ford Wilkes sat up and paid close attention for the first time all evening. He had always been a bit of an election junky, dating all the way back to watching results with his usually drunk, always belligerent father. He had tuned into CNN on the TV and had AON and Newsmax streaming on his laptop to see how the balance of power would shift in Washington, DC. A lot was at stake in Congress and legislatures around the country, to say nothing of a momentous presidential election—he wanted to see what both sides had to say about the results. The coronavirus was an added wild card, creating challenges and frustrations for both voters and election officials.

For Wilkes, the more chaos in the actual election process, the better. He was excited to see that the Trump-Biden outcome was hanging by a thread. He fantasized about the legitimacy of the outcome being called into question. That was an anarchist's dream. But no matter what, he knew this day would be significant for him. When the counting was done, he would take the final steps in his arduous but patient journey. And he'd settle on the site for his DC attack.

For now, he chose the BarcaLounger chair in his Riverview home and used the side handle to prop up the footrest. With a beer in hand and a bowl of chips on his lap, he turned his attention to the networks that were calling winners and losers. The polls closed by time zone, so the early discussions that evening were from the East and Midwest—although the counting of mail-in ballots was making it tougher to evaluate the early results. The presidential race was going to go down to the wire with Wisconsin, Michigan, Pennsylvania, Arizona, and Georgia (of all places) deciding the outcome. Congressional districts in his hometown of Detroit were a complicated jigsaw puzzle of boundary lines that crisscrossed the city. He couldn't keep track of whether his old house was in the 13th or 14th district—either way the winner was going to be a Democrat he would have hated. Even gerrymandering couldn't change that.

"Hot damn," he said out loud as the first returns came in from West Coast senate races. "My pretty little Air Force chick with the nice ass might win." He actually had mixed emotions about the outcome of her race. He hated seeing a woman—any woman—taking a position of power. And Tamika could clearly be a threat to his goals if she won.

But his ego would not let go. She'd rescued people at the Air Force base and had slipped through his fingers in Seattle. How sweet would it be to get her in the end—a famous elected senator with a military background—*and* a woman? Oh, and she was dating the guy she'd saved. If she won the election, Wilkes knew their paths would cross again. There was an irresistible sense of destiny.

He knew the sound of Opportunity knocking.

Later, he was watching real-time results projecting from his laptop to the big screen. For the next four hours, he sat and hit refresh every once in a while to get the latest tabulation. He had no clue who Richard Chancellor was, but he looked like an old fart who definitely needed to lose.

"Yes, yes, yes!" he yelled, like he was at a Red Wings game, punching his fist in the air. Smith was now beating Chancellor (he really must be a loser) by a little over 2,500 votes. "Pick the winner," he screamed at the screen—but none of the news services were projecting the outcome just yet.

He set aside his laptop, got up, and ran around the counter into the kitchen to get another beer. He stood next to the couch to take a few good gulps, chasing some satisfaction. The next voting update had Chancellor back in the lead.

"Shit."

One minute he was winning the lottery and the next his whole plan was shot. And so went the rhythm for the rest of his evening and well into the morning, East Coast time. At some point, he finally drifted off to sleep, chips falling into the creases of the seat.

That damn chair was just too comfortable . . .

• • • • •

"Thank you, Washington!"

Ford Wilkes woke with a start to the image of a Black woman smiling broadly and waving from a podium as a crowd applauded wildly. It took him a moment to come back to his senses. Then he realized Christmas had come early, and his present was gift wrapped with a nice, tidy, black bow. The caption on the screen made it clear that Tamika Smith was the new senator-elect from the state of Washington. She was speaking to her supporters in the ballroom of some old hotel in Seattle.

After she'd said "thank you" the requisite number of times and complimented Richard Chancellor on his campaign, she turned to the national election results. "We won't know the outcome of the presidential election for a few days—and the race for the Senate won't be decided for a number of weeks. But personally, I'm very hopeful we will have a new leader in the White House soon!" That brought cheering from the mostly partisan crowd.

He watched her take a deep breath, as if to gather herself for something significant. "As a retired major in the Air Force, I care deeply about protecting our country—and as I watch Obaid bin Latif kill thousands of innocent people and a pandemic virus infect the nation, I understand the desire to point fingers at others. It's natural for people to huddle with those of a like mind, to divide, to choose sides, to discriminate, and ultimately, to hate. This is an all too common human reaction to the pain and challenges we all feel—and we certainly have real challenges in our country.

"To be sure, these reactions are also in response to leaders and influencers who say that it's okay to point fingers, to bully, to shirk responsibility, and to blame others. It's precisely this misguided leadership, this selfish leadership, this lack of leadership, that we must resist. And we must fight it together." That brought a wave of cheers and shouts.

She looked across the audience and then straight into the camera, eyes blazing with fiery intensity. "We must all step back, take a breath, and look within—like Abraham Lincoln did—and understand how we can bring our country back together. We must use *every* tool at our disposal to bring leaders to the forefront who will fight for that unity of purpose. Indeed, Democratic and Republican leaders who will fight for the very survival of the country."

"Shit," was all Wilkes could say.

"But no matter what, tonight was a turning point for the citizens of Washington and hopefully for America. I'm happy to report that the Lincoln Coalition now includes five senators and twenty-five elected representatives—again, both Democrats *and* Republicans. With my fellow members in Congress, we have the opportunity to truly make a difference. On our watch, we will fight the battles that must be fought. We will rebuild and advance economic opportunity at home. We will create a resilient public health and emergency response system that can protect all Americans. And we will defeat the evil we see here and abroad." More yelling and applause.

"We're going to kick that effort off at a Lincoln Coalition rally in Washington, DC, on December 7th—an important day in our country's history when our homeland was attacked. Now we face a similar threat, and we must respond with the same unity and resolve. We want thousands to join us. Thousands to make a statement about what we expect as citizens. This is our opportunity to come out in force—our opportunity to make our voices heard—our opportunity to show that we care about our communities and our great nation. On December 7th, we march to the Lincoln Memorial. Regardless of your party of choice, I look forward to seeing *all* of you there . . ."

Back at the cul-de-sac, Wilkes nearly fell off the recliner.

The perfect date and location.

In an instant, plans clicked into place in his mind as he thought through the logistics of making the ultimate attack a reality. He knew that the God he regularly defiled must somehow be on his side.

And he was going to make sure that nobody would ever forget December 7th again.

# Chapter 55

# THE APARTMENT, LATE NOVEMBER

JERRY JESSUP KNEW THAT most investigative work was in the realm of mundane. Evidence was gathered. People were interviewed. Research was conducted. Leads were followed. And to paraphrase Yogi Berra, "Ninety percent of the work was mental and the other half was physical."

The task force tracking the Obaid bin Latif cell had been going 24/7—chasing down black Ford Escapes, interviewing anyone who might have seen something somewhere, researching bin Latif's hazy background in Syria, tracing internet traffic around the world, and generally following any possible lead. The team was physically worn out. But just as in baseball, the key hit could come at any time—and the FBI's cybersecurity team was fairly certain they'd hit a home run in the ninth inning.

JJ now sat at the head of the table in his SCIF, getting briefed on their research. The investigation had clearly taken a toll on him. His jet-black hair had thinned and turned a ratty shade of gray. He'd put on almost twenty pounds—a shocking development for an ex–Air Force Academy grad—and he realized he'd gone from being a demanding leader to a bit of an asshole. At the beginning of this goat rodeo, back at Offutt Air Force Base, he'd seen the investigation as an opportunity for redemption and career advancement. Now it was a source of daily frustration and misery.

He was failing—and it was killing him.

His team was talking about some IP triangulation they'd done between the videos and the malware power grid hack. "Get to the damn point. I don't care about your brilliant technical work. It couldn't be that good if it took you eighteen fucking months to find him. Do you have him or not?" *Shit.* He'd lost his patience again.

"We have him, sir . . . or at least the location he's been using to access the internet."

"*And?*"

Aaron Phillips jumped in. "It's a corner apartment in a third-floor walkup in Detroit. We've got it under digital surveillance as well as with a team on the ground."

"So . . . you don't have him and we might be scaring him away as we speak."

Special Agent Phillips gave JJ a look that could kill. "We've gone very light—haven't talked to the super, the leasing company, or anyone. We're just watching every entrance—mostly cameras and drones—waiting for him to pay a visit."

"Then get your ass out there and sit on him. I don't want his apartment, his furniture, his mail, or the name of his girlfriend. I want him. I'd like to string him up personally, but if you happen to wound him first, I won't complain. I want his name and his photo off my board—forever."

•  •  •  •  •

Two weeks had passed since the meeting with Jessup. As the calendar blew through Thanksgiving, Phillips was on the verge of the most important FBI arrest since Eliot Ness put away Al Capone. Bin Latif had finally come home to his roost, and the operation to take him was on. This was going to be a little more complicated than the Capone tax evasion plan.

Phillips was prepared for a fight.

"Radio check . . . Team 1?"

"In position—top of the stairs, visual on the doorway."

"Team 2?"

"In position. Back stairs are blocked."

"Sniper team?"

"In position—sight lines on windows and both alleys. No place for him to run."

"Team 3?"

"In position—back of the building covered."

"Detroit police?"

"In position—ready to seal off the block."

"Choppers 1 and 2?"

"Standing by."

Agent Phillips paused to go through the mental checklist in his mind. What was he missing? They'd seen bin Latif enter the building earlier in the day—or more precisely, they'd seen a man go into the building who was a partial match for the guy under the Chicago freeway.

Close enough. The guy had stayed put. Showtime.

"Teams 1 and 2, move in."

Phillips trailed behind Team 1, hearing his lead agent send a civilian down to the lobby. Agent Cole escorted an older woman quickly down the stairs, almost knocking Phillips over in the process. If only she knew what she was missing.

Phillips caught up with his team at the door. They knew the layout of the apartment and exchanged final signals on who was going where.

No knock, no warning.

They used a battering ram and flattened the door to a chorus of "FBI" shouts as the team rushed in. Phillips pushed through as he heard the calls of "Clear, clear, clear . . . all clear."

The place was empty.

"Fuck. Goddamn it. Where the hell'd he go? Johnson—you saw him come in, right? There's no other way out—keep looking." Phillips kicked the cushions off a chair for their insolence at being empty.

"Agent Phillips, you better come here and see this."

Phillips followed the voice into what looked like a bedroom converted to an office. "Holy shit." Another attack. "Seal this off and get the Director on video. NOW!"

Back into his radio, "Detroit PD . . . close down the streets. Cole, make sure they search anyone inside the perimeter. Hell, search anyone standing by the perimeter. He *has* to be here."

Seconds later, an explosion reverberated through the building. "What the hell was that?" yelled Phillips. His triumphant day had quickly become a clusterfuck.

# PART 5

## A DATE WITH DESTINY

People know this world is a wreck
We're sick and tired of being politically correct
If I see through it now but I didn't at first
The hypocrites made it worse and worse
Lookin' down their noses at what people say
These are just words and words are okay

Racism lives in the USA today
Better get hip to what Martin Luther King had to say
I don't want my kids being brought up this way
Hatred to each other is not okay
Well I'm not a preacher just a singer son
But I can see more work to be done

The money's good and the work is okay
Looks like everything is rollin' our way
'Til you gotta look the devil in the eye
You know that bastard's one big lie
So be careful with your heart and what you love
Make sure that it was sent from above
It's what you do and not what you say
If you're not part of the future then get out of the way

Come on baby take a ride with me
I'm up from Indiana down to Tennessee
Everything is cool as can be
In a peaceful world

—John Mellencamp

# Chapter 56

# SETTING THE TRAP, DECEMBER 6, 2020

"YOU'RE ABSOLUTELY *SURE* you found it?"

Assistant Director Jerry Jessup was doggedly questioning his team on the ground in Detroit over a secure video line. He had decided to stay in his office in DC to quarterback the command post there. Still, he was used to being in on the action—flying amid the fray—and it grated to be so far removed from his team when this many variables remained. "You realize we're taking one hell of a risk here?"

He was still burning about the hidden-door trick with the little old lady walking out right under their noses. Or more accurately, under Aaron Phillips's nose. Although their target had escaped, the Detroit apartment was a treasure trove of information. They'd found the "video room," complete with its black flags and plain white backdrop—no surprise there. But the room had much more to offer. Maps, photographs, research, everything. Bin Latif's next target was set. And time was short.

The sun was going down on December 6th and there was no more room for error. What if there was a second bomb? What if they couldn't block the cell signal? What if bin Latif set it off some other way? What if his field agents missed something again?

Phillips seemed to read his mind. "Look, it's not my favorite strategy either, but we have to catch him and his cell in the act. If we announce we've found the bomb, fuck with it, or cancel the event, they'll just go underground again and blow up something else three months from now."

"So, go through it with me again—and let's make sure we understand how he doesn't walk right past us this time. Where is this circus going to take place?"

Phillips was sitting in a mobile command trailer parked in an alley in downtown Detroit. JJ had asked him to clear the room given the sensitive nature of the conversation—so it was just his lead agent and a bunch of electronics gear on the screen. Phillips slid a couple of feet over to consult a digital map. "It's gonna go down at Hart Plaza—which is smack in the middle of what is left of downtown Detroit—right on the river. Ten a.m. It's a good-sized space, but they're going to march there down Woodward Avenue from another park. That will be tough to protect."

Jessup consulted his own version of the map. "You said they're expecting how many people?"

"That depends on who you ask. The permit filed by the event organizer, something called Businesses for Workers Rights, says 10,000 plus. The mayor's office has told us 'thousands,' and the Fifth Year organization says their openings usually only draw a few hundred people. The wild card here is that BWR is led by Paul Hayek—he's a Muslim businessman who's pushing immigrant rights. We could get protesters ranging from the Proud Boys on one side to the Antifa groups on the other. It might be a typical publicity event—or it could turn into a riot."

"Great. So we have thousands of people coming to an event in a constrained area where we know a bomb has been planted. Most people will be wearing masks so facial recognition is for shit. There could also be a race riot. Several CEOs, the mayor, the governor, and a US senator will be there. And we're using all of this as bait to catch the deadliest terrorist in American history. Is that *really* our plan?"

Phillips just looked at him in silence. There wasn't much to say. They were out of time.

"Fuck" was all JJ could come up with. He turned away from the camera on the conference table of his wood-paneled office to find a good answer in the photos on the wall. As a combat pilot, he still wasn't comfortable with the shelves filled with scholarly books, the nice carpeting, and the expensive oak conference table in his FBI office. It just never felt "right" to him. Now he had the same feeling about the Detroit setup. Something was off, but he couldn't put his finger on it. Déjà vu.

Phillips finally broke in. "What do we tell the big shots?"

This time it was JJ's turn to go mum.

"We have to tell them, right?" repeated Phillips.

More silence.

"Holy shit, JJ. You can't seriously be considering having them go in blind?"

Coming back to his seat in front of the camera. "You're right, it's for shit, Aaron. But just how do you propose we tell some people but not others? If I tell one politician, he cancels. Same with the others. Pretty soon it leaks out that they have security concerns. And then our trap is no longer set. Anyway, how could I tell them and not tell all the people in the crowd? I'm supposed to sacrifice them but save the politicians? Now that *would* be ironic."

Death stares—neither of them able to blink.

JJ finally took out his decision-making knife to cut through the dead quiet of the call. "Here's what we're going to do. You need to track down this Hayek guy and the school woman. Make sure they understand the risks. If they want to cancel, we cancel. If not, we tell everyone that the FBI is going to provide heavy security because of the riot risk. That will have to count as our 'notification.'" Back to his feet again and over to the window. He paused with a long look across DC, the lit Capitol to his left and the equally bright tip of the Washington Monument to his right. He knew there would be no sleep that night.

Now muttering to himself, his gut twisted in knots. "Bin-fucking-Latif knows we found his room. He knows we'll be there. And he still plants the bomb. Could be a trap—or maybe the guy has brass balls."

· · · · ·

"Bring the asshole on," had been Paul Hayek's initial response. "We won't be intimidated by some chicken-shit terrorist who won't show his face." Margaret Humboldt knew that Paul Hayek had done his job and then some. He'd brought out the heavy hitters for the Fifth Year announcement in Detroit. The immigrant, class-struggle angle, and the protesters that came with it, was an unexpected side effect that raised the stakes significantly. Now she was meeting with the FBI. And her newfound fear had nothing to do with stage fright.

"Mr. Hayek," said Special Agent Aaron Phillips, "I appreciate your commitment to what you're doing, but bin Latif has killed thousands. If this bomb goes off, God knows how many he'll add to his terrorist scorecard."

"That's the FBI's problem. You said yourself you know where the bomb is and can prevent a cell phone from triggering it. It's about time you guys caught the bastard."

Phillips took a deep breath, somehow resisting the temptation to yell at Paul. "Well, that's the plan. But you need to know that this guy is smart, and we don't know exactly how he'll react. The risk is real."

For her part, Margaret was speechless for the moment. She was rocking back on her chair, unsure how to process the idea that her little nonprofit was on some sort of terrorist hit list. They were sitting in a conference room in the Detroit FBI office, complete with dingy lighting, a conference room table that must have been war surplus, and an old school clock on the wall that told her it was almost midnight. The huge mirrored window across from them indicated that it was probably an interrogation room. And then she noticed the light on the camera in the corner of the ceiling was off. Apparently, Agent Phillips was not interested in recording the evening's festivities. As her feet landed back on the ground, she jumped in during a pause in the testosterone exchange. "What about everyone in the crowd? Are we really going to put them in danger?"

Margaret was forcing Aaron Phillips to deal with the other side of the coin. She thought Paul was being reckless. But deep down, she also suspected the FBI wanted the event to go ahead. Their profound hatred for bin Latif was understandable, and this was a golden opportunity to catch him at his game.

Aaron Phillips took up the challenge. "Mrs. Humboldt . . ."

"Ms. or Margaret," she corrected him.

"Sorry. Ms. Humboldt, we're definitely taking precautions on that front. The bomb is targeted at the stage and the dignitaries sitting there. We're putting up a barrier that will keep the crowd well back in a safety zone—and with social distancing they won't be packed in tight. And we're confident we can prevent the bomb from being triggered."

"But you can't guarantee it."

"That's certainly true—which is why I'm here. This is a real opportunity to nail public enemy number one—everyone from the president down to my pet goldfish wants this guy taken down. But the folks at risk will be those on the stage speaking. That's where an explosion would do the most damage. You're private citizens and deserve the right to choose. It's really up to you."

Margaret looked at the defiance in Paul's face and knew his answer. She thought about all the suffering bin Latif had caused, including nearly killing her ex-husband. She thought about her children, knowing they would want the bastard caught. But how could they comprehend sacrificing their mother for the good of the country? For them, that would never compute. So, she considered a hero's death—the risk she would have to take. Did making that choice boil down to peer pressure, stupidity, or courage? Or was it a mosh-pit mix of the three?

She nodded her head in both defiance and resignation.

●　　●　　●　　●　　●

Three hours deeper into the night, Tamika Smith was facing her own set of demons. She was sitting at the standard-issue, built-in desk at the JW Marriott in Washington, DC, less than a half mile down Pennsylvania Avenue from Jerry Jessup's outpost. Her room was pitch black, except for the glow of her computer screen and the outlines of city glare around the white vinyl blackout curtains she had pulled across the sixth-floor window.

She contemplated the coming day—one that would lay the foundation for her professional future—and tried to reconcile the possible risks and rewards that lay ahead.

With no sleep in her future, she had opened her laptop. In years past, she would have written another imagined letter to Alex. Now she turned to someone living who she knew could help her channel the crush of fear, excitement, anticipation—and anger.

With fingers poised, she began to type.

*Dear Dad,*

*Tomorrow is the most important day of my life.*

*When I think about my crazy journey, with all its twists and turns, with the gifts and the pain, with losing mom and Alex, and finding Johnny, it feels like it all comes down to tomorrow. I know in my head that's silly. But in my heart . . . deep in my soul . . . I know that tomorrow at the Lincoln Memorial will be a defining moment.*

*It seems like I'm always fighting for something. At the Academy, it was for the respect of the men. On the track, I raced for the glory of the podium—to prove I was better than the rest. Then I fought in Afghanistan for Alex's honor and to reclaim my own. Every time I jumped into a bird, I was there to rescue others. When I came home to the US there was the PTSD and an uncertain future. And then the campaign with fundraising challenges and policy issues.*

*But my current fight isn't really about any of those things. The real battle is with an enemy in our midst. He is clothed today as a terrorist, but the real source of his power is grounded in ignorance, poverty, hopelessness, fear, and anger. He is the enemy that lies deep within all of us, preying on our insecurities. When we allow those emotions to fester, they open the door to worse—and suddenly the chasm gets very wide and deep. Anarchy is just around the corner. The last year has shown us that.*

*Tonight, I'm feeling the net result of that anger. I don't know if it's rational, but I fear for my life. Obaid bin Latif is still out there . . . and somehow I know he's coming for me. It's the ultimate question: Will you risk your life for something that you believe in very deeply? I'd like to think I've answered that question emphatically already. But I realize now that my actions were motivated by other emotions—very human emotions that were more about retribution than they were about salvation.*

*I'm left with difficult, existential questions I thought I'd answered in the Middle East. Am I strong enough to stand up for what is right, when so many others have taken the easy way out? Am I prepared to sacrifice everything so that others may lead a better life? Am I willing to die for the principles of democracy?*

*I pray that innocent people won't die. I pray that this won't be my last night's rest. I pray that our work and dreams will grow. I pray that we'll live on to fight another day. And I pray that the next generation will reap the seeds we sow. Good seeds with strong roots.*

*In all of my doubt and questions, I know one thing for certain. You'll be there for me. And I feel your power and courage.*

*With love,*

*Tammy*

When she took her fingers off the keyboard, the clock read 4:30 a.m. She heard a rustling behind her and soon felt the comforting hands of Johnny rubbing her shoulders and reading her innermost thoughts on the screen. His words mirrored her father's love and support.

"You're not alone."

# Chapter 57

# PEARL HARBOR DAY

JERRY JESSUP HAD GIVEN UP on sleep that night. If an attack in Detroit was successful, his career was over—and then some. He'd chosen to withhold information from elected leaders and intentionally put them in harm's way. They were bait in a trap. If the bait was injured, he was finished and headed to prison. But telling them guaranteed a leak . . . and the prize would slip away . . . and the lives of tens of thousands would be in danger of future attacks. He couldn't let that happen.

He paced the small living room in his two-story Alexandria, Virginia, townhouse, grabbing some papers from the adjacent kitchen counter. He was hoping that a lightning bolt would strike if he looked at the data for the twentieth time. A pot of coffee shared the counter with leftover food—the reheated remains from last night's dinner. His wife was out of town helping her parents move into assisted living, so Jessup had their little castle to himself.

When the deepest of the dark was receding through his living room window, he set the papers aside to take a quick shower. Then he poured another cup of caffeine and ate a scrounged-up bagel. He went back to the documents littered around the floor and over the couch of the living room.

"Shit, I know I'm missing something. It's right here in front of me." He took off his reading glasses, rubbed his eyes, and took a beer-like swig from his oversized coffee cup. He'd been here before and feared a repeat disaster.

Back to the evidence. All he could do was go over it again. He grabbed a legal pad and bulleted out what he knew.

What makes this group tick?

- Five surprise attacks, perfectly executed; one badly aborted effort.
- Advanced planning, sophisticated technical work, strategic targets.

Conclusion: SMART.

- Hazy background. Arab? American? Muslim?
- Killers? Yes . . . but no glory-seeking suicide bombers.

Conclusion: SURVIVORS.

- Big ego, careful, patient.
- Flags, threats, and taunts. A performance?

Conclusion: WHAT?


Two hours later, now in his DC office on Pennsylvania Avenue, JJ was still no closer to connecting the puzzle pieces. He picked up the pad of paper with his bullet points again. Something was bugging him. These were not your typical jihadi terrorists. As he thought about it, they weren't really jihadists at all. They had all the trappings but none of the substance. All they did was spread chaos. That was the key word, wasn't it?

He dug into his pile of notes and pulled up the research on the Islamic Brotherhood Front. Aside from a smattering of references on social media—all of which had been tracked down as false flags thus far—the IBF basically had no footprint. Phantom terrorists except for Obaid bin Latif and his videos. The media search also referenced a series of similarly named groups, including one the FBI had tracked for a number of years called The Brotherhood. Now those clowns were way out on the fringe right. Outright anarchists.

*Shit.* Now that he thought about it, Obaid bin Latif and his crew were more like anarchists—the attacks, the videos, the threats, the taunts—all designed to scare the shit out of people but without any clear political agenda. And it was working.

So how did Detroit fit? Did they just get lazy and leave a trail to the apartment? Now bin Latif "knows we know" and yet he's still going ahead with it? That didn't fit at all. A smart, patient survivor would just move his team to the next attack.

"IBF: Continues with Detroit attack. WHY?" he wrote on his legal pad. Then he underlined it.

Then almost idly he reversed the letters on IBF.

"Well, fuck me."

In spite of himself, JJ smiled. You had to respect the guy's craft. Detroit was a trap all right. But not for Obaid bin Latif or his Brother-hood. The FBI was being played. An attack was coming, probably one of epic proportions. But Detroit would likely be the safest place in the land. The main target would be elsewhere.

Of course, "elsewhere" could be anywhere. These assholes had shown a remarkable willingness to strike almost any target in any part of the country. This was the anarchist's version of a *Where's Waldo?* puzzle. With no time to scan the pages.

So where?

It was a career-defining—no, a lifetime-defining question.

●　●　●　●　●

Wilkes wanted to see it happen. Technically, he could control a drone from anywhere, but sitting in a conference room someplace directing angels of death no longer appealed to him. For the first time in his orches-trated drama, he wanted to see the destruction and chaos in person—to experience for himself the devastating effects of his precision plan. He liked to think he was motivated by strategic considerations like evalu-ating the target in real-time and analyzing the effectiveness of his work firsthand. But deep down he knew there was a sick desire to experience the pain up close.

And he especially wanted to see Tamika Smith die. It was the dirtiest side of his ego exposed in a way he couldn't deny.

So be it.

Without much reflection, he concluded that someone else would have to evaluate his soul.

The more pressing question had been how to get close enough to the speech without attracting attention from the crowd as he directed the drones? In his advanced scouting, he'd noted there was a bus and shuttle van waiting area to the south of the target. It was a one-way loop with angled parking that would limit his exposure and provide a convenient, quick getaway. Hacking into the system to register to enter the area had not been complicated. Now he could sit in his van, direct the attack, and still have a ringside seat for the destruction. The more targets he pursued, the more he realized how open and unprotected they really were.

He knew that this vanity exposed him to a bit of risk. He was going to be "on scene" for the first time and that undeniably raised the stakes some. But then what was the whole point of his entire security plan if he couldn't enjoy his finest hour of triumph?

From the beginning, his goal had been to distract the FBI, keep them in his back pocket, and know what they were preparing for next. Giving them the Detroit attack plans had ensured just that. Exposing bin Latif would enable Wilkes to hit a much more important target *and* continue into the future unfettered. He knew from his own digital incursions into the FBI ecosystem that they were totally focused on Detroit. Whatever happened to bin Latif . . . well, Wilkes was no longer worried about that.

With the FBI distracted, Wilkes had the leeway he needed in DC. The license to destroy a symbol of American government, attack a bullshit political coalition, and terminate the only woman he feared. All while watching it himself.

The best part of using a more advanced drone for his work was that he could launch it under the cover of darkness and keep it in the air away from the target until the appointed time. It was now around 10:45 a.m. and the two SHX-Diamond drones were on station, awaiting the digital commands required to bring their payloads to bear.

Wilkes entered the controlled traffic loop and took a forward parking position. He had a clear view of the gathering crowd through the tinted windows of his generic, white van.

He was a bit surprised to see that a security fence had been installed around the speakers' platform, complete with airport-type metal detectors. Little good that would do them. He could also see the health monitors reminding the growing throng of supporters to wear masks and socially distance. And he smiled as he saw a few protestors who had decided to put their Ringling Brothers Circus stamp on the event.

For Wilkes, it was all just perfect.

# Chapter 58

# THE CAVE, 11 A.M.

VOYEURISM WAS AN ESSENTIAL part of Bryce's profession. The internet was indeed dark where he trafficked, and he was constantly creating new and better ways to spy, snoop, or otherwise watch what others were doing. But in his quest to track Obaid bin Latif and his cell of terrorists, he'd had to be extra careful. His opponent, while not at Bryce's level, had sufficient technical skills. And perhaps help from others. Avoiding detection was an imperative. The cost of getting caught was exceptionally high, given what Bryce suspected was coming next.

Sitting in his work cave, he had watched the Detroit apartment raid as if it were on TV, having hacked the FBI's video and audio feed. But Bryce got to the conclusion much faster than the Bureau had. The moment he realized bin Latif was "not home," he went back and looked at the video prior to the raid and noted the woman leaving the apartment next door. As it turned out, that snippet of video was the key to breaking his entire investigation wide open.

Bryce's work had followed two trails of evidence. The first was an ever-growing collection of videos and photos of people connected with the terrorist attacks—some of which not even the FBI had. The bin Latif videos claiming responsibility, the train photo, at least three different views of someone walking across the Space Needle parking lot, the Chicago interstate performance, and now a woman walking out of an apartment. Plus he had footage he'd "acquired" from private cameras of the Ford Escape driver. Every photo looked different—facial features, skin tone, weight, dress, accessories, and now gender. He'd already noted the strange walk of the bomber in Seattle—and thought he might be wearing lifts in his shoes and padding to add to his heft. He found the woman exiting the Detroit apartment equally convincing, but just slightly off.

His "friend" had provided some inspiration and extra motivation. "Bryce, if you think the dude is wearing disguises, you need to unmask him. Use your superpowers against him. You're a maestro programmer—you can catch him using software." With that, Bryce had hijacked some Linux code that specialized in taking photos of young people and aging them based on facial structure. He wrote an entire new module that could transform multiple photos, strip various elements, and create an AI probabilistic composite of the real face.

Days later, Bryce had both answers and more questions. He'd done yet another facial recognition search across every database he could access using the composite, computer-generated photo. The satisfying, if much delayed, response brought a seventy-two percent probable match with an expired driver's license in the state of Michigan. Ironically, he got a second match from the FBI's own database—a surveillance photo from a group called The Brotherhood. His target was there in the third row, on the far right.

He could now put a name with one specific face. The bin Latif in the terrorist videos, the businessman on the train, the man in the stolen Ford Escape, the bomber in Seattle and Chicago, and the lady leaving the apartment were likely all the same person. The disguises were good, but bone structure and ties to anarchist groups didn't lie.

Bryce's second investigative angle revolved around the three IP addresses he'd identified earlier and the recent inquiry to purchase military-level equipment. While the Baltimore Gas and Electric malware clue and the IP mistake posting the Baltimore video had enabled the FBI to find the Detroit apartment, they had also opened Bryce's eyes to his most hated client's identity. The original explosive material, the schematics for the dam, the malware attack, and the weapons purchase all matched a single IP address at the apartment in Detroit. Bryce had immediately stepped up his tracking of the weapons purchases from that internet connection and yesterday evening had traced a shipment to a farm in Virginia.

With that realization, the curtain obscuring the whole damn charade came down.

The intersection between the expired driver's license, The Brotherhood photo, and the IP address could not be a coincidence. He was almost certainly dealing with one man. A clever man who had gone to great lengths to mislead many people—but just a single terrorist. No cell. Probably no IBF connection. And certainly not an Arab. The disguises were a way to protect his true identity. The multiple IP addresses for the videos were just a deflection—a way to keep the authorities off his tail and running in circles. The adjacent apartment and escape hatch were an emergency exit.

At first, the deceit seemed cunning—a wild goose chase that would keep authorities busy running down blind allies and chasing shadows that could shift and re-form on command. But on closer inspection, Bryce realized all the work was seemingly without much purpose. Sure . . . the FBI was looking for a cell of Arab jihadists. But if the guy calling himself Obaid bin Latif wanted to stay hidden, why leave so many clues? Why post the videos? The trail to the stolen car, the obvious salute to the camera in Chicago, and the rest of the clues allowing the FBI to find his apartment? What was the point of all that?

As he sat in his basement cavern, oblivious to the mid-morning sun shining outside, Bryce went back to his alter ego for advice. One question was still gnawing at him—a steady anxiety that told him to pay attention. "Why did this terrorist go to so much trouble to both conceal and expose himself?"

"Well, Bryce, the obvious answer is to avoid getting caught."

"How does leaving clues help someone *not* get caught?"

"When the clues are misleading."

"But they've been way behind him all along—he's hit all kinds of soft targets and there are hundreds more for him to go after. Why not just keep doing that in secret without drawing any attention to himself?"

His "friend" was thoughtful for a long time. "There's only one answer that makes any sense. The soft targets were never his real objective. They've created chaos, spread fear, and grabbed attention, but your enemy's after a bigger prize."

Now *that* would explain so much.

Suddenly the misdirection made perfect sense—and was in fact deceptively brilliant.

The FBI had found the secret door into the second apartment, figured out the connection to the lady in disguise, and realized how badly they'd fucked up. But they still had no idea who Obaid bin Latif really was. Nor in fact what he looked like as a white man. Their mobilization for the event in Detroit was equally misguided. Or at best a side show.

"He wanted them to find his apartment. Wants them focused on Detroit. He's gonna use the drones to hit a hard target next, isn't he?"

Bryce stood and anxiously grabbed a Coke from his refrigerator. Returning to his chair, he ran his hand through his hair and readdressed his friend. "I know I joke about the FBI all the time, but this guy really has tied them up in knots."

He paused as another, less pleasant thought crossed his mind. He'd lost track of time again in the cave. *Fuck.*

"The Detroit event starts in an hour. If that's a diversion, he's going to attack soon—maybe even before the Detroit gig. And I now know a hell of a lot more than the FBI does." They were missing two critical pieces of evidence—two partial facial matches and a shipping confirmation for the military equipment. Virginia must mean DC. *Double fuck.*

They didn't just have the wrong picture on the wall of their public enemy list.

They were trying to catch him in the wrong place.

# Chapter 59

# 9-1-1 CALLS

WHEN HER CELL BUZZED at 8:30 a.m. on the West Coast, Angela couldn't help but be annoyed. She was feeding the baby, getting dressed, and preparing for a busy day all at the same time. She was planning to stream the Lincoln Coalition event and only had thirty minutes to get her life sorted out. Hindsight would put all of that into proper perspective.

She grabbed her cell phone off the counter. "Hello?" she answered, but her tone said, "What the hell do you want?"

"Angela . . . this is Bryce." It was her brother's quiet voice, but tinged with anxiety at the edges.

Her surprise settled back into annoyance for just an instant. Then Angela processed that her brother *never* called her. Back to panic.

"Bryce . . . what's wrong? Why are you calling?"

"I told you this day would come . . . and now it has."

"Are you okay? Did you get sick? Where are you?"

"Ange, we don't have time for any of that. None of us have enough time. Get a paper and pen. Now." The urgency in his voice shocked Angela into action.

"Hold on a sec . . . I've gotta get to my desk."

"Hurry." He was acting like seconds mattered.

Down the hall. Rustle around the drawer. Find a pen. "Okay, I'm ready."

"You have to call Jerry Jessup at the FBI—he's the Assistant Director for Counterterrorism. His cell phone number is 639-976-5352."

"Wait a sec. How do I know that name?"

"Ange—shut up and write." This was a Bryce she'd never met. In charge and demanding. "Tell him the guy's name is Ford Wilkes. W-I-L-K-E-S. And his photo is in the Michigan DMV database."

"Whose name is Wilkes?"

"Angela . . . *write!* He's the terrorist. He's one man—acting alone—and the target isn't Detroit. Tell him there'll be a drone attack in the DC area."

"A what? Where? Bryce, you're scaring the shit out of me."

"If he gives you any trouble, tell him the C-Textrate serial number is 563249-837822. And there's enough left to blow up a good-sized building. Did you get the name and number?"

"Yes . . . but Bryce, what the hell are you talking about? How do you know this stuff?"

"Repeat the numbers back to me!" Now he was yelling. Angela did as she was told.

"Ange, I have to go. You may never hear from me again. I love you more than you'll ever know. Thank you for everything. I love Mom . . . and . . . you can tell Dad I love him, too." Then he told her his best guess on the attack target.

"Bryce! Wait . . . stop . . . how . . ." But he was gone.

Peter walked into the kitchen. "Who was that on the phone?" Her husband was still working from home in the aftermath of the flood and pandemic.

Angela reached quickly for his hands—panic setting in. "That was Bryce. Remember the email he sent me a while ago saying he was in trouble? He just told me to contact some guy at the FBI named Jerry Jessup."

"Wait a minute . . . that's the guy leading the Obaid bin Latif investigation. I saw him on the news after the blackout in Baltimore."

"Sweet Jesus. What has Bryce done?" She held up the notepad to show Peter. "He wants me to get a warning to Jessup about an attack at the memorial."

"Shit! Your parents."

Three hours' time difference. They were almost too late already.

More than blood drained from Angela's face as she realized what was at stake. She grabbed her phone and dialed her mom's cell.

Fucking voice mail.

• • • • •

"Aaron, Jessup." No verbs. JJ had no time for pleasantries.

"We're all set, Assistant Director," said Phillips, using his official, formal voice around the rest of his team. "No sign or indication that our friend is here. The event's just about to kick off. More people than we expected—around 15,000." Agent Phillips was back in the Detroit command post truck monitoring the action as they'd planned.

"Aaron, I think we've missed the whole plot. There may be an attack in Detroit, but I think that's a sideshow. They're going to hit us hard someplace else."

"You think they've been playing us?"

"Like a Fender guitar. Too smart to give us so much information. All that shit in the apartment was a plant. Just cheese in the trap."

"So what do we do?"

"You stay put. Keep the team focused. We can't assume what will happen in Detroit."

"If you're right, whatever their big target is, for damn sure it must be today. They'd want us tied down here for a reason."

"I just sent a high priority alert to the Secret Service and every FBI office in the country. The president is in Florida all week. The vice president is attending a funeral in Argentina. I suppose there are senators or reps who could be targets. But that puts us back in the small-potatoes category. Nobody really cares about Congress, right?"

"What other events are we tracking? Are we providing security or support anyplace else today?" As Phillips said it, Jessup's private cell phone rang. Not one of his programmed ring tones. *Nobody* had that number.

"I gotta go, Aaron. Let me know if you come up with a target."

Sliding the screen on his angrily buzzing cell, he yelled, "Jessup!"

"Jesus, I didn't think I'd get through. I have an urgent message for you."

A woman's voice.

"Who's this and how did you get this number?"

"His name is Ford Wilkes—Michigan driver's license."

"Whose name?"

"The terrorist. The guy who's been calling himself bin Latif. He's going to strike with a drone in DC today. The Lincoln Coalition event . . ."

*Shit, shit, shit.* Then out loud. "Who's this again? How do you know?"

A quick pause. "You just have to believe me. I was told to tell you that the C-Textrate serial number is 563249-837822 and there's enough left to blow up a large building."

A drone. The Textrate. The Lincoln Memorial. Now that was a first-class target.

"Anything else?"

"Hurry." And she hung up.

# Chapter 60

# HIGH NOON

A LARGE ROSTRUM HAD BEEN installed on the middle landing of the Lincoln Memorial staircase looking out toward the Reflecting Pool. The steps behind it were full of speakers and staffers, and a passionate crowd spread out over the grounds stretching back along the pool toward the Washington Monument. Some were waving flags, some were chanting slogans, most were socially distanced. The turnout was gratifying. And the Lincoln Coalition was streaming the event live to thousands more.

Tamika had urged Charles Roscovitch to kick off the noon event, but he'd insisted on staying in the background—a committed leader but not a headliner. So, Avery Bradley, the newly elected mayor of Charlotte, North Carolina, was the lead-off hitter. She was currently sharing the podium with Glenn Usinger, another new mayor from Milwaukee, Wisconsin. A Democrat and a Republican, now both speaking on behalf of the Lincoln Coalition.

"Let's begin by addressing an issue that is fundamental to our democracy. We've just completed the sacred task of electing citizens to represent us—and the legitimacy of those elections has been called into question. We must be clear and united about this—the courts, our secretaries of state, and local elections officials have all certified the voting as fair and accurate." Bradley paused for her colleague.

"The conspiracy theories and fraud claims are nothing short of a challenge to the sanctity of our republic," continued Usinger. "They represent a political coup in sheep's clothing—and all elected officials, regardless of party or persuasion, must denounce these efforts firmly and clearly."

Bradley jumped back in. "We can all bemoan the gridlock and morass that is Washington, but we must also accept that the issues we face . . . the challenges that divide us . . . the inequality and unrest we experience. All of them *can* be addressed by starting in our local communities."

Tamika alternated between listening to the two speakers and scanning the crowd. Her senses were on military alert.

"When we talk about security, we must recognize that we are in a *war*," Usinger was speaking again. "It's a war against anarchy and those who support it. When airplanes, dams, and roads can be blown up at will. When terrorists turn out our lights and extremists on both sides set our cities on fire. When elected officials lie to the people they represent and allow a pandemic to kill hundreds of thousands of us. That is a war. If we don't fight back, none of us are safe."

Mayor Bradley jumped back in for the conclusion. "We must bring economic success and a meaningful way of life to those who are being left behind. They are the very people our enemies recruit for support. We have to fight the systemic racism and the bigotry that arises when people lose hope. We should never forget that creating opportunity is the best way to defeat those with twisted minds who prey on fear and hopelessness."

December in Washington, DC, could be anything from balmy to frigid, from sunny to gloomy. On this Pearl Harbor Day, the weather gods had chosen the cold and gloom option. Clouds had been rolling in since around midnight, now hovering over the venue, a low ceiling in a basement. Piles of snow from a Thanksgiving Day storm lined the venue. Tamika smiled as she glanced at Charles and Shea, seated at the top of the steps with Abraham Lincoln looking over their shoulders from his seated pedestal. With the temperature at thirty degrees, the Roscovitches were dressed like they were going on the Polar Express.

Tamika also caught a glimpse of Phoenix Humboldt. She was up on a ladder shooting photos from the memorial looking down the length of the Reflecting Pool toward the Washington Monument. It must have

been a dramatic view—the swelling crowd with a few snow flurries flying. Definitely worthy of the traction she knew it would get on Snapchat
and Instagram. Valley Forge without the guns.

Johnny was there too, of course. He was acting as Phoenix's escort
and security Sherpa, clearing the way for her to get the best shots from
unique locations around the monument. He caught Tamika's eye and
waved. A welcome warmth spread within her chest.

She went back to scanning the crowd, the apprehension from the
previous evening returning.

$$\bullet \quad \bullet \quad \bullet \quad \bullet$$

Wilkes waited in his van. His mission meant listening to the drivel from
the first few speakers. Everything was in place. His itchy trigger finger
at the ready. But this time he didn't just want another flawless attack.
He wanted this to feel . . . personal.

It was time for Tamika Smith to go down.

But where was her boyfriend? He couldn't see Johnny-boy on stage.
Somewhere close by, for sure.

Killing them both would bring his mission back to the beginning.
Only this time, the savior would be the sacrificed.

"Jesus, woman, will you please shut up," he yelled at the livestream
on the laptop in front of him. "I wanna see the hot-looking bitch come
to the microphone." He checked his watch and then rechecked the status
of the drones.

"Fucking finally," he whispered as the blond woman wrapped up.
The camera panned out and across the crowd. They looked like follow-
ers at a goddamn revival. He set the laptop on the adjacent seat and
switched to the drone controller.

Showtime.

$$\bullet \quad \bullet \quad \bullet \quad \bullet$$

As her speech approached, Tamika began to fidget like a kindergartner, practically having to sit on her hands to keep them from shaking. She did everything to project calm, the feigned smile plastered on her face with her eyes now locked on the speaker. Somehow, she knew she was failing. Charles's only requirement for the event had been that she would lay out the agenda and plans for the Lincoln Coalition as the event's featured speaker. There had been some resistance to having a freshman senator-elect with no political experience take on such an important role. But Charles had insisted. On reflection—and with the task now squarely in front of her—she knew he was straight-up nuts.

Tamika listened as Avery Bradley finished an introduction that was more elaborate than she thought was necessary. Then she took a deep breath. She stood up, straightening her coat. As she approached the podium, with the applause of the crowd rising, she heard another sound that she knew only too well from Afghanistan.

This time, there was no place for her to run.

# Chapter 61

# THE DRONES, 12:15 P.M.

NOT *AGAIN*, WAS ALL JJ could process as he ran down the hall to the command center. He'd put extra security on Senator-elect Smith, including insisting on the metal detectors for the Lincoln Coalition event. But a drone? *Shit.*

"Get Higginbottom on comms!" he screamed across the cacophony as he burst into the room. "Get him now!"

Agent Franklin Higginbottom had been shadowing the newly elected Senator Tamika Smith to major public events ever since the Glasshouse incident. Now, JJ's team scrambled, and within seconds the command center's flatscreens began projecting a live feed from the field agent's "eyes and ears." Images of the Lincoln Coalition crowd appeared, with the buzzing of thousands in the background. The official livestream of the rally up on some secondary screens as well.

"Get her off the fucking stage, Higginbottom!" JJ yelled over the open comm line.

"What the hell—?" Jessup saw his field agent hesitate.

"This is Jessup. Grab whoever is speaking—get 'em down *NOW!*"

Higginbottom charged across the stage like a linebacker intent on sacking the quarterback. His body cam showed two women in front of him near the podium. He was going for the double takedown.

The command center fell silent, as Jessup and everyone stared at the live feed. Two drones were screaming straight at the stage. Jessup saw Higginbottom darting in from the left. But it wasn't going to matter. The linebacker was no match for a drone loaded with explosives.

He'd had the information, missed all the clues, and now people would die. *Again*.

· · · · ·

Wilkes watched an aerial view from the lead drone. He couldn't wait any longer. He pivoted the birds high around the Washington Monument and sent them swooping down just above the Reflecting Pool water at maximum speed.

Two angry eagles intent on their prey.

One was targeted at the people on the podium platform and would likely take out part of the crowd—the other was aimed at the memorial itself. Wilkes saw the stage rising in front of him on the screen, two speakers squarely in sight. The crowd a blur on each side and the water washing up in front of the drone. "I'm sorry, my beautiful badass. But it's your turn to die."

· · · · ·

Buying the drone control system had put Bryce at personal risk—the likelihood of someone discovering his activities in a follow-up investigation was now much higher than he liked. But he'd made the purchase anyway. The only way to stop the madness was to stop Wilkes. And hacking into the drones' guidance control system was Bryce's best chance at redemption.

Despite his superior technical skills, he'd not had enough time to program his way past the full set of algorithms protecting the drones. The military took its security seriously and had the manpower and money to back up the commitment. Bryce had concluded that his best option was to give up on taking control of the drones—instead he'd focused on disabling Wilkes's ability to communicate with the birds. He wouldn't be able to direct the drones, but he might be able to interfere enough to limit Wilkes's accuracy.

Now, whacking away at his keyboard as he furiously typed in commands, he was in a race to put his theory into practice.

"Damn it, I'm gonna run out of time!" he yelled into the emptiness of his basement hideout. He was watching the Lincoln Coalition on the livestream. A woman was at the podium—and in the background he could see his parents.

Must . . . go . . . faster.

"Wait a second, I'm in! I've got video from one of the drones. Oh shit, here we go. Around the Washington Monument."

His fingers flew across the keyboard. All he could do was try to block the signal to the lead drone. And hope it went someplace safe.

"*Yes!* One down. One to go."

Then he realized he was going to be too late. He was only able to tap into the video of the second drone . . . just in time to see the memorial and the staircase full of people approaching all too quickly.

"Fuck me." He'd failed.

• • • • •

"Shit! What the hell happened?"

The screams from the crowd drowned out Wilkes's own profanity-laced cry. He jumped out of the van and ran up the short rise toward the stage. Through the dust storm and panic of people running to escape, he could see that part of the memorial had fallen. But the speaker's podium was still standing.

"How the *hell* did I miss her?"

He realized too late that he was going to be crushed by the tidal wave of humanity surging away from the memorial steps and the Reflecting Pool. Knocked off balance, he retreated to the van. He slammed the door shut and hit the lock button hard. Then he rammed his head against the steering wheel a few times. "Five years of planning! Five years of my life. The perfect attack. I'm gonna fucking . . ."

And then silence within the van.

The crowd was bouncing against his truck like a pinball machine. He looked up and realized he had to get out.

And fast.

• • • • •

Jessup was just as stunned. At the last minute, the lead drone had veered left into the Potomac. The second bird had lifted above the stage and crashed into the side of the Lincoln Memorial itself, missing the entire crowd. The explosion was deafening even through the command center speakers, as plaster and stone crashed down everywhere. The fire from the blast was a brief flash, with nothing to sustain the burn. But the smoke and rubble were testament to the power of modern explosives.

The FBI analysts in the room fell silent. Then *BOOM!*

JJ jerked his head around as another explosion rocked the sound system in the control room. He heard someone scream, "*What the fuck—*" through another live feed.

*Phillips.*

And Jessup realized a bomb had also gone off at the Detroit event.

His mind went blank, not willing to comprehend the enormity of what had just happened. If more lives were lost . . .

All he could process was failure.

The control room sprang to life—an explosion all its own. With some thirty computer stations, fifteen large video monitors mounted on the walls, and a squadron of staff, the eruption shocked JJ back into action. His first move, based on years of training, was to put out the proverbial fire in front of him. "Shut up, people . . . *quiet!* We've got two scenes to work. Let's calm down and do our jobs. Who's managing the Detroit feed?"

"Over here, sir," came the response. "Michael Kim."

"Kim, you and your team are now direct to Phillips on the scene. Coordinate with the local LEOs. Keep me posted on comms."

"Yes, sir." Kim turned back to his screens and got Phillips on his headset, confirming he was all right.

"Everyone else, we're on the DC attack. I want every camera up— live and on replay. Report anything suspicious you see directly to me. Get to Higginbottom and make sure he shuts it down and coordinates everything on-site. I want a full team on the scene to support him. We need all the forensics and without any interference. Tell him that the Sprinter Option is now in effect. I repeat . . . Sprinter Option. We gotta get this bastard before he gets away. I'll be on comms."

And with that, he ran out the door and was gone.

# Chapter 62

# SPEAKERS' PLATFORMS, 12:20 P.M.

AARON PHILLIPS WAS OUT of the Detroit command post trailer before the smoke from the blast cleared. He ran across the parking lot, straight to the Hart Plaza stage. "Team 1, secure the scene around the explosion. Get first responders in there. Get everyone else out."

"Roger, that."

"And Garcetti, I wanna know how the fucker got another bomb on our site."

"Yes, sir."

Phillips moved on. "Team 2, you're with me on the stage. Get the big shots off before they trample each other."

He fought his way to the podium, nearly running down Margaret and Paul as they tried to get to safety. Margaret had just begun her speech when the explosion hit and was still clutching her script. Horror was written on her face and in her voice.

"My God . . . was anyone hurt? We should have cancelled. It's our fault—"

"Ms. Humboldt . . . I've got you." Aaron literally grabbed her as she kept instinctively moving downstage in the direction of the explosion. "Where's Mr. Hayek?"

"Damned cowards—cowards in Lebanon, cowards here!" Paul's voice was screaming in response.

In his ear, Aaron was getting the first reports from Garcetti and

Team 1. "Looks like a suicide bomber. Ran straight into an Antifa group. Nails, pellets, and body parts." A long pause on the line. "Jesus, how can people—?" With a breaking voice, he added, "There's at least fifteen down, sir, and only a few of them are moving."

Instincts kicked in. Aaron now had Margaret and Paul in tow. "Suicide bomber," he said to both of them. *Definitely not the bomb bin Latif planted in advance*, he thought to himself. He pushed some people out of the way as he shepherded the two speakers into the command truck.

"I've been doing this for a long time," he said. "I just don't know how you stop someone willing to kill themselves."

Paul grabbed him and pulled him up short. "You stop it by dealing with the fucking root problem. I've been living this since I was a kid. These people are the evil that lies under the covers everywhere. They create despair. They breed anger. They feed off greed. Until we deal with that you're going to keep picking up the pieces."

Paul let go of Aaron's coat, muttering an apology. He turned from the agent to Margaret and pulled her into a hug. "This wasn't our fault. Certainly not your fault. We just have to try again. We can't give up."

Aaron turned away, knowing action would speak louder than words.

• • • • •

Tamika Smith and Mayor Bradley were buried underneath the considerable girth of Agent Higginbottom. Tamika could hear the screams of the crowd. She felt the rumble as people climbed over each other to get off the steps and away from the memorial. But it was the pounding of her heart that told her she'd survived. The agent looked down and slowly rolled to the left to let the two women breathe.

"Anybody hurt?" asked Higginbottom through panting breath.

"Not from the explosion," said Tamika, checking her body parts and climbing to her feet. "Nice tackle."

Sirens could be heard in the distance. The noise of the crowd seemed to reach a crescendo, with the screaming merging together into one, loud roar. "Mayor, you all right?" Tamika asked.

Bradley, still lying on the ground, answered shakily, "I'm fine, I think. But . . . oh, shit."

The woman was looking over Tamika's shoulder. And as the dust settled a bit, they both saw the emerging skeleton of the Lincoln Memorial. The drone had gashed the right side of the building, a glaring wound filled with debris falling forward toward the memorial's stairway. A cloud of smoke and dust still hid the area between the podium and the monument. Tamika moved toward the rubble but was grabbed by Higginbottom, a vice grip on her arm. She instinctively tried to pull away but was locked in place.

"Jessup trusts you," he said. And with that he pulled his backup piece from a leg holster—offering it to her. "Do what you need to do."

Some combination of training, duty, and fear flooded through her as Tamika sprinted around the edge of the steps to the area behind. Running to yet another rescue. But the scene that unfolded in front of her was like nothing she'd ever seen.

Four columns on the right side of the monument had collapsed, crashing forward down both flights of steps. A portion of the portico roof had also collapsed, but miraculously, the corner pillar stood strong. And in the background, Abraham Lincoln still stared back at her with his gaze seemingly defiant in the face of attack. *A house divided against itself cannot stand.*

She shifted her gaze to the mountain of debris in front of her. Her senses filled with the acrid smell of explosives and the dust burned her eyes, Afghan-desert style. The only relief was the absence of fire. She pulled her face mask up, now using it for a different type of protection. She shut her eyes, once again having to force out destructive images from her past. The echoes of agonized cries that were never far away. And then . . . real cries for help broke through.

*Phoenix and Johnny.*

She opened her eyes and dashed ahead.

Tamika climbed around the shoulder of the rocks, ignoring the cuts on her exposed legs and arms and trying not to slip on the slurry of ingredients that was mixing with the old, icy snow.

"Johnny!"

Clearing the top of the mound, she saw Johnny bloodied but alive. He was kneeling next to Phoenix, who was on the ground amid the remnants of the steps. He held her head up, whispering into her ears—he flashed a thumbs up and gave a weak smile. Tamika's new family seemed intact.

But seconds later, a high-pitched wail grabbed her attention.

She scrambled to the right down the landslide of rock—and her heart sank.

Shea Roscovitch was the one screaming. She'd collapsed next to the ashen face of her husband whose body lay partially buried under the rubble. As Tamika got to the bottom of the pile and knelt beside him, Charles opened his eyes. Just.

He looked at Shea, then up to Tamika, and finally back to his wife. A prayer in his eyes. With soft resolve, he told her, "The job's now yours. Show them how to come together. Rebuild." And lying in the rubble of something he loved truly and deeply, Charles Roscovitch closed his eyes.

With revenge again in her heart, Tamika got up and ran.

# Chapter 63

# ON THE MOVE

"SIR, WE'VE GOT A VAN." His comms chirped in his ear.

"This is Jessup. Go!" He was running to his car in the parking garage below the building. His feet echoed across the concrete followed by the beep of his car as he unlocked the doors.

"We're going through the DC video. A few seconds after the drone strikes, someone jumps out of a white van in the bus parking area just south of the monument. He looks pissed—not scared—runs toward the memorial and then gets swallowed by the crowd. A few seconds later, he's back in the van and screams out of there. Ran right through a few people. Plates are covered in dirt."

Jessup was still trying to sort through the attack in his mind. This could be the lead they needed. Bin Latif or Wilkes or whatever his name was had a clear opportunity to wipe out the entire stage, part of the crowd, and still hit the monument. Two drones were plenty of firepower. So what the hell happened? How did he miss? JJ didn't believe in luck—and now he wondered if this guy getting out of the van had been wondering the same thing.

"I need a facial recognition check on van boy with one Ford Wilkes—Michigan driver's license. That's 'Wilkes' . . . as in John Wilkes Booth. Get someone looking deeper into an organization called The Brotherhood—I want a full profile. *And find that damn van!*"

JJ hadn't waited for his driver or escort. He'd run straight to his own car and now screeched out of the garage, planning to make a beeline for the Lincoln Memorial.

Unfortunately, there was no beeline to be had. DC traffic could be bad at any time and the layout of the city made navigating across toward the Potomac particularly difficult. Add an early season snow, a drone attack, and emergency vehicles everywhere. Gridlock.

"Come on, come on. Get your ass out of my way." The horn got a workout as he ran through his full, rich vocabulary of obscenities.

His earpiece twitched. "Sir, the van driver is a perfect match for your Ford Wilkes. Must not have been our guy this time."

*Bullshit*, thought Jessup. There never was an Obaid bin Latif. Just an American named Ford Wilkes. "Stay on him—*he's the one!*"

"We still don't have the van, but traffic around the memorial is brutal. Three cars tangled in front of the Kennedy Center after the attack. He can't be far."

"He just blew up the Lincoln Memorial—you're going to have to do fucking better than that!" Jesus. Then, "What assets do we have in the air?"

"Metro PD has a bird up and ours is just leaving the heliport."

"Tell them this is our priority target and get the agency bird online ASAP. Put a BOLO out on the van and Wilkes with the picture—all agencies. I want road blocks up and down the GW Parkway and Ohio Drive on the DC side of the river. And tell them to screen *everyone*. He could be disguised as a man, a woman, a dog, anything. We gotta put a ring around him and keep him penned in."

"Yes, sir."

"And get me everything you can on this guy. Life history, bank accounts, family, second grade teacher. I want it all."

Enough of him. Assistant Director Jerry Jessup paused and took a deep breath. He stopped yelling at the traffic, pounding the horn, and screaming into his radio. He was finally closing in on his man. He needed to think.

Where was this guy going to hide? The traffic had Wilkes hemmed in. The Potomac was an immovable object, limiting the number of routes he could take. If he was smart—and JJ was sure he was—he would ditch the van. He could try to disappear into the crowds on foot. But he could have done that from the memorial. He obviously had something else in mind. The police and choppers would cover the obvious places. What was left? A hole in the traffic led him south toward the Pentagon, thinking he might head east down the river.

He turned and accelerated.

• • • • •

Ford Wilkes turned left into a large parking lot. He'd spent the last twenty minutes cursing at traffic. The attack had blocked his original escape route down the river past Georgetown and out to the suburbs. So he'd shifted his attention to the Virginia side. But by the time he got across the Potomac, paranoia about staying in the van with all his equipment took over. He could manipulate the FBI with lots of advanced planning, but a city manhunt would tip the scales to their superior resources. He needed cover. He needed a place to hide. Somewhere he could think.

"Well, there's certainly some irony in this," he said out loud as he tucked the van in a corner of the parking lot, out of sight from the entrance to a monument. He leaned back in the seat and took a deep breath. What the hell happened with the drones? After all the diversions, the dark web secrecy—after all of the extra expense to make sure he was in control. "Shit. Shit. Shit." The only positive news was from Detroit. A quick check of his cell phone revealed that the resources he'd funded there had been successful. Not the decisive victory he'd hoped for but another deadly attack.

He eventually reached under the seat to pull out a Beretta Px4 and a few clips of ammunition. He had a rule against carrying but today was clearly different. He hadn't even bothered with a disguise. He walked over to a chain-link fence that was bordered by a hedge, and slipped the gun through it.

Retracing his steps, he cut diagonally across the back side of the lot and walked around two corners to the venue's Welcome Center entrance. He went into the vestibule of a small museum, complete with a Washington-style stone colonnade at the entrance, but with a modern glass atrium over the top of the building. The main room contained a series of exhibits that described the area's significance in American history. He walked up to the main desk, bought a ticket, grabbed a map, and walked through the metal detector.

He had no intention of staying inside a building with armed guards, so he turned right and went back outside. His best bet was to retrieve his gun, find a remote part of the site, and wait for the dust (and snow) to settle. If he was lucky, he'd find an opportunity to escape out of this walled garden back into more open territory.

The weather was shifting from light flurries to a steady pelt of snow that was starting to accumulate. "That will slow them the hell down."

And then he saw his own footprints and was a bit less happy.

• • • • •

"Command for Jessup." His radio was back in his ear.

"Go for Jessup."

"Sir, the US Park Police have a white van off Ohio Drive, parked near the Jefferson Memorial."

"Yes! Make sure they sit on it but don't make any contact. Clear the area of civilians. I'm five minutes out." He cut across three lanes of traffic, with his horn clearing the way. He looped to the right where the Jefferson Memorial was in the midst of a much-needed facelift. Christ— now he was working with the park police to take down the most important criminal in American history.

As he pulled into the lot, he used his thumbprint to unlock his service revolver and shoulder holster from the security device below his seat. He wasn't even sure if the park police had weapons. Two officers ran up to him as he exited his car.

A sergeant, who did in fact have a gun, gave him a sit rep. "The van is in the corner, in the service spot. That's what caught our attention. We've got officers on the perimeter—area is otherwise clear."

"Anyone in the van?"

"Yes—just sitting there. Hard to see, but it looks like there's some electronics in the passenger seat."

"Okay . . . I'm going to lead on the passenger side. You trail on the driver side. Two officers in back watching the double doors." He pulled his Glock 23 and removed the safety.

Jessup approached the van from the rear, carefully squeezing his frame in between the van and the car in the next spot. "This is the FBI," he called out in his loud, Air Force voice. "Open the door with your hands out first. I want to see both of them."

Nothing.

After a second verbal attempt, Jessup reached the door and swung his weapon around into the window. "FBI!" he screamed. Then just "oh fucking hell."

The young van driver was eating what looked like a peanut butter and jelly sandwich and listening to some music on a pair of AirPods. He threw his hands into the air at the sight of the gun, and the sandwich went flying.

Jessup lowered his piece and tapped on the window. They'd have to search him, but all JJ could see on the seat was an Xbox console and a controller.

Damned gamers.

# Chapter 64

# A FINAL RESTING PLACE

"WHAT DO YOU HAVE FOR ME?" he said, pushing the comms in his ear to demand some new intel. Jessup's adrenaline was still pumping a bit after the Jefferson Memorial false alarm. And his frustration level had risen, too. He spent a minute in his driver's seat staring intently at the Michigan DMV photo of Mr. Ford Wilkes, thinking *where the hell are you?* and trying to divine answers from the lines of the face.

"We got nothing, sir. We've stopped several white vans at roadblocks, but zero hits so far. The city is pretty well shut down."

"Casualties?"

"One dead here with around twenty injured—as much from the chaos after the explosion as from the bomb itself." Then, "Detroit is . . . worse."

Goddamn it. I have to make him pay. "I want every agency on this. Let's get NSA and DIA assets involved. Satellites, choppers, digital surveillance, AI analysis. Anything else you can think of. I want people on foot, door-to-door, starting at the memorial and moving out in a three-mile radius. Nothing moves without us saying so. I want the van . . . and I want *him*."

"Yes, sir."

As he cancelled the call, a text message chirped at him. The two-word missive hit him right between the eyes. It pissed him off, but it felt right. It would be just like this bastard to hide there.

His text response was simple: *30 minutes out. Let's take him down.* He attached the photo.

Traffic blocked his path back down Ohio Drive toward the Lincoln Memorial. But with some quick maneuvering, Jessup crossed the Potomac into Virginia using the US1/I-395 bridge. A few more turns put him on Highway 27, keeping the Pentagon on his left. He hit his windshield wipers to clear the oncoming flurries. He looked up at his two o'clock to see the soaring Air Force Memorial, the steel vapor trails depicting three jets climbing into the stratosphere, reminding him where all of this had started.

He exited the highway near the Pentagon, but instead of looping around to the left to his former office, he turned right and approached the Arlington Cemetery service gate. He showed his badge to the guard on duty.

"FBI Assistant Director Jerry Jessup. Have you seen this man or a white van?" He showed him the picture of Ford Wilkes from his phone.

"No, sir. No activity at this post for the last hour."

"I need access to the cemetery."

"I'm sorry, sir. Arlington's on lockdown. Nobody in or out. We're processing everyone at the Welcome Center entrance."

"Look . . ." He glanced at the guard's name tag. "Look, Corporal Petersen, I can't get to the Welcome Center entrance. I'm the lead investigator on the bin Latif case. He just bombed the Lincoln Memorial. So you can call your CO if you want to, but I'm going in here, and you're going to let me do it." He said it with a look from his past as an Air Force Colonel. Without a word, the guard lifted the gate and Jessup drove through.

His phone chirped again with another text. No need to call for backup.

Soon he was out of his car and pacing down Eisenhower Drive. He walked steadily past the rows of tombstones on either side of the street. Eyes scanning in all directions.

Arlington was church-like on any day. But with the restriction on tourists and the snow now forming a further blanket of white, it was more of a sacred sanctuary than usual. Jessup could not help but think of the people—commanders, subordinates, teammates, friends, and relatives—he'd lost over the years.

Perhaps out of remorse, he found himself drawn to the right—to the memorial he'd never had the courage to visit. Not sure what to expect or even if he was looking in the right place, he followed his instincts down York Drive through the trees. There were tracks in the fresh snow. He put his phone on vibrate.

He heard a sound off to his left. Jessup crouched down below some bushes.

He pulled out his Glock and removed the safety for a second time. Poking his head around the corner of the hedge, he raised his gun . . .

And scared the shit out of a maintenance man trying to get his cart moving in the snow. "Sorry," JJ said in a hushed whisper after getting a good look at his face. He flashed his badge and asked the man if he'd seen anyone else walking in the cemetery.

"There's someone over in the courtyards. He told me he was headed for the exit, but he didn't look like he was in much of a hurry."

Jessup thanked him and continued down York, entering Courtyard 2. Shaped with long, low walls like pews in a church, each courtyard contained columbaria with the ashes of those who had fallen in service. At the head of these rows was a circular garden, like an altar at the top of the congregation.

And there in the gloom of the snow, JJ saw a lone figure walking slowly out of the garden.

Jessup lightly jumped over the curb and pressed himself against the trunk of a tree. He didn't think he'd been seen, but now was not the time to take chances. And with two false alarms behind him, he wanted to be sure. His target continued walking quietly along the sidewalk, measuring each step as he took them. The suspect turned right out of the courtyard and then left on Marshall Drive. Definitely *not* in the direction of the visitor's gate.

Jessup realized his target now had a straight line back to the service exit. It was time to end this.

He took four quick, running strides with the sound muffled by the snow. Then shouted, *"Wilkes!"* The ghost-like figure responded to the name. "FBI—get your hands up!" hollered Jessup, his gun raised.

Turning fully around, the man said politely, "Officer . . . are you looking for someone?"

"Shut the fuck up, Wilkes. Or should I say *Obaid bin Latif.*" Jessup was steadily advancing, gun pinned on his target. "I know who you are and what you've done. Get on your knees with your hands where I can see them. NOW!"

Wilkes began to raise his arms and at the same time glanced up over Jessup's shoulder, creating just a flicker of hesitation in JJ. Wilkes immediately pushed off the curb—jumping to his right—and took off into another courtyard, dodging Jessup's gun shots.

Jessup's foot had slipped in the snow on the first shot. Pissed at himself for being sloppy, he ran to the base of the courtyard wall, looked up and fired again. He was met with a wild broadside of shots coming from the back of the yard. He ran hunched over down the length of the wall, firing again at his quarry.

He saw Wilkes cut across an empty stretch of grass and vault around a large marble structure sitting by itself. A stone sentry on guard to honor others. Wilkes's gun peeked out from the edge of the masonry and spit several shots across the open ground in JJ's direction.

Jessup ran faster to catch up with the much younger fugitive, firing as he dove to the snowy grass behind the last line of tombstones. There he came to a halt, ignoring the two shots that flew into the snow just inches off to his right. He heard a soft whistle off to his left—an agreed upon signal. He knew where he was. He slammed a new clip into his gun, jumped to his feet and squared off, digging into the ground. The time had come to face his demons.

• • • •

Despite being in the Air Force for almost twenty years, most of Tamika's shooting had taken place on a gun range. She'd passed all her qualification tests with ease but now her heart was pounding as she raced along Patton Drive. Her last text to JJ had let him know she was coming in from the main entrance and heading toward him. As she removed the safety on Higginbottom's Glock, she searched for the calm of the starting line.

Hearing gun shots to her right, she ran along the trees past the outer edge of the columbarium area to loop around behind their perp. Two more shots now gave her some bearings. She sprinted across the road, down a dirt path and slid to a stop in the snow behind one of the many white grave markers. She raised her weapon and exhaled a long breath.

Then she let out a whistle.

Jessup's voice called out clearly, "I'm right here, Wilkes. No anonymous killing this time. Just you and me, alone . . ."

And that was as far as he got. Tamika saw the man from the photo raising his gun while twisting around the side of her brother's resting place. She squeezed the Glock's trigger. Gun volleys echoing through the cemetery.

The target went down, hit from two sides by multiple shots.

Tamika ran forward to make sure her nemesis was done. Jessup ran up at the same time and kicked away Wilkes's gun.

They'd both hit the terrorist in the chest.

"You good, sir?"

"Bastard nicked me in the leg . . . no problem."

Jessup fired off two more shots, plastering Wilkes against the marble amid the inscriptions of names, as though exorcising years' worth of torment. "No trial for you, you sick son of a bitch."

Then with another kick, Tamika knocked Wilkes off Arlington's 9/11 Memorial tombstone marker and onto the snowy ground.

"Get the fuck off our heroes."

# Chapter 65

# FALLEN HERO

JOHNNY HUMBOLDT WALKED slowly to the podium, trying to gather his emotions. Cheel Campus Center at Clarkson University in upstate New York was certainly not a solemn or religious building. Nevertheless, it was packed with people who'd made the long trip to honor Charles Roscovitch. A friend, a business partner, a competitor, a political activist, and most importantly, a husband and father.

The temporary stage—filled with flowers, a lectern, and seating for the speakers—was set at one end of what was normally a multipurpose athletic court. Foldout chairs were arranged in neat rows across the court and were filled with guests. Others gathered in bleacher seats on either side of the arena. Thousands in total. It felt a bit like a school assembly—until the speeches began. Then the words and feelings seemed to morph the environment into a cathedral of sorts.

Johnny stole a glance at both Tamika and Margaret for emotional support. He stopped to embrace Shea. Dressed in a dark suit with a bright red tie, he wore a purposeful look as he stepped up to the podium, removed his Covid mask, and arranged his papers. He had written his speech down to make sure he got through it.

He began by referencing back to earlier speakers. "Everything you've heard about Charles Roscovitch today is true in my book. He was the ultimate engineer, a true visionary, a man with a plan, and occasionally, a pain in the ass." A round of quiet laughter rolled across the auditorium.

But Johnny had deeper things to say. "Charles taught me the real meaning of purpose, the absolute necessity to make difficult choices, and the sheer will to persevere through obstacles. For these and many other reasons, he's responsible for whatever success I've achieved. He leaves a hole in my heart that will be impossible to heal." Johnny's voice broke on the last few words.

Not used to losing control of his emotions, he took a moment to compose himself.

"But all of that doesn't begin to describe the impact Charles was starting to have on all of us. Somehow, he understood the threat of the McCarthy-like paranoia, the Trumpian incivility, and the QAnon anarchy brought on by the waves of attacks in our country. He equally resisted the radical rhetoric from those who would turn us into a socialist state. While he recognized that we have enemies abroad, he firmly believed that our biggest challenges come from within—a point that Ford Wilkes demonstrated tragically when he murdered Charles and so many others."

The stark words were carefully chosen. Johnny gripped the podium with both hands, white knuckled as he continued. "Charles knew that the only way to heal division and find common ground is to respect each other and work together. He demonstrated that with me and my business partner from the start of our work. In his second career, he was a shining example of how business, philanthropic, and political leaders must engage in our civic and social challenges and provide the ideas required to bridge our country's divisions. I'm just beginning to walk in his enormous footsteps—work that has changed forever my definition of 'success.'"

He looked over to catch the eyes of Shea and Angela, the younger of whom was tearing up. He had one last thing he felt needed to be said. "But Charles was certainly not perfect. He made tradeoffs in his personal life that I know he regretted. He loved his family more than anything else but often didn't know how to show it. I've never met someone so focused on success who struggled so mightily to define it. And that's why I loved him so much. In his infinite humanity, he enabled me to see that life could offer second chances. That I could make good in areas where I'd failed the first time around. And with the grace of God and the love of his wife

Shea, he was becoming a great humanitarian—and inspiring me to try to become one as well."

Johnny stepped back from the podium, hugging Shea once more as she stepped up to the microphone. Dressed in a traditional black dress and wearing a few pieces of jewelry that Johnny suspected Charles had bought her over the years, she looked dignified. Resolved. Shea peered out across the conference hall. A silence came over the audience as she adjusted the mic and took a long drink of water.

"Charles knew how much I hate speaking in public, and he would find it most humorous that I'm here now to praise and honor him like this." That brought a few soft smiles from the audience. "I'm so grateful to all of you for coming. It's heartwarming to see so many of our friends here today.

"From the moment I met Charles, here at this very university, I knew he was mine. Not in a possessive way, but somehow, I knew God had put him there uniquely for me. And I suppose I was here just for him. I can't really explain that feeling. Whenever I talked to Charles about it, he would just laugh and say it was a good thing we stumbled across each other's path. I know I will never replace him in my life . . . but I will carry on his mission."

Tears and a smile came at the same time. She wiped her eyes with a white handkerchief, seemingly bracing herself for something more difficult.

"Charles was never someone to make a decision and then second-guess himself. As Johnny implied, regret was not a word my husband used often, but the few misgivings he had ran deep. He and I both regret the loss of our son Bryce—not to a terrorist or to a disease or to an accident. We lost Bryce years ago because we couldn't figure out how to reach him in life. Charles always believed you could accomplish anything with a good plan, lots of effort, and a positive attitude. And yet, somehow, he never could find Bryce. My own deepest sadness is that Charles will never have a father's closure." Unable to continue, her head dropped.

The auditorium was silent except for Shea's quiet weeping. And then there were footsteps coming from behind the curtain at the back of the stage. A lone figure, dressed in an ill-fitting black suit, stepped out through an opening. He walked to the podium and wrapped his long, lanky arms around his shocked mother. He held her in a deep embrace. Then, with more tears but without another word, mother and son walked off together.

• • • • •

The president of Clarkson had given Angela and Bryce access to his office. It was a quiet place where they could talk—complete with a bay window that opened out into a spacious backyard with bare, snow-filled woods beyond. The office was pleasantly warm, heated by a gas fireplace and surrounded by bookcases filled with leather volumes from the president's apparent passion for American history. Bryce paced softly around the office looking at framed pictures that had been inserted on the shelves between the books. Occasionally, he pulled out a volume to scan through the pages.

Angela, leaning against the formal double-pedestal desk with her legs crossed in front of her, finally addressed the elephant in the room. "How did you know about the attack?"

The tears came to Bryce easily and quickly. "I killed all those people."

"*What?* Bryce what are you talking about?"

"I sold him the C-Textrate."

"Sold who? What's with this Textrate stuff?" She walked around to the other side of the desk.

"It's a military grade explosive that Wilkes used in his attacks . . ." He paused, choking on the words, ". . . and to kill Dad."

"You're a terrorist?" The thought made her fall back into the president's desk chair with a thud.

Bryce was now at the window and turned back to face her. "No . . . technically not. I'm a supplier . . . an agent . . . a salesman . . . but what I sell and how I get it isn't always strictly legal. I live on the dark web, in places where very few people go."

Her brother—a criminal. "Why do you do it?" Her temperature was rising steadily as she pulled up from the chair and leaned across the desk looking straight at the brother she had protected for so long. "Why did you sell him the fucking . . . Textrate?" The menace in her look was real, as was the slam of her hand on the desk.

All he could come up with was "Because it's what I do. I provide things. And I'm the best in the world at it. I didn't *know* what he was going to do with it. I wouldn't have sold it if I'd known he was going to kill people."

"Well, what exactly did you think he was going to do with a bunch of military explosives?"

Bryce opened his mouth, then closed it again. He shut his eyes and turned away. There was no real answer to that question. "As stupid as it sounds to me now," he whispered, "the intentions of my clients didn't seem like any of my business back then."

Angela loved her big brother and she hadn't thought there was anything in the world that could shake that love. But maybe now there was. "Why did you call me that morning?"

"Once I'd learned of the first two attacks last year, I knew I'd fucked up—worked for the wrong customer. I started stalking him—trying to ID him and figure out his endgame. It took a long time. When I tracked the drone shipments to the DC area, I knew I had to do something. I called you. I love you, Ange. And I trust you more than I trust myself."

Angela thought about that for a long time. "It was you that directed the drones away from the crowd?"

"I bought a duplicate control system when he purchased the drones. After I called you, I hacked into the system and blocked his control over the drones." He looked away but continued to speak. "I didn't get to the second one in time, and it hit the memorial. I tried to save everyone—but killed Dad in the process."

"Jesus." She moved around the desk to be closer to him. Angela stopped short, now trying to sort out her own twisted emotions. For so many years she'd hoped and prayed he'd somehow return to the family. Now he was back, but it wasn't at all how she'd expected.

The brother she had protected was some sort of shadowy, pseudo-criminal. Maybe he didn't know what he was doing at the time, but he'd helped a truly evil person kill thousands. And yet he'd had the conscience to realize he'd been wrong and had risked his own freedom to save so many others. What would her father have done? What would her mom want? What did her faith demand?

"I can't save you this time, Bryce. Forget the law. Forget the FBI. Forget the cyber guys that will try to figure it out. *You* know what happened. *You* know what you did. You'll have to live with those *you* killed, and with *Dad's* murder . . . for the rest of your life."

Angela was like her father in this respect—she would make a decision and never look back. She knew what was right. She knew Bryce would suffer with this burden no matter what. But she also knew what she would do. What she had to do.

"Stay with us."

"What does that mean, Ange?"

"Stay with us. And . . ." The pause was uncomfortably long.

"And what?" asked Bryce.

"And we'll never speak about this again."

# Chapter 66

# THE REFLECTING POOL, MARCH 2021

THIS STARTING LINE DIDN'T look like any of the others in her life. There was no warm-up to stretch her legs and work out some of the nerves. No competitors to size up, confident that her heart was bigger and stronger than theirs. No white lines that laid out the path. No finish waiting for her to break the tape. Instead, over a hundred thousand people were stretched out around the Reflecting Pool all the way down to the Washington Monument. And somewhere in the back of Tamika's mind, she realized that tens of millions were watching on TV as well—all of them waiting for her to speak.

The Lincoln Memorial was still not fully repaired. Much of the rubble had been removed, some temporary stairways built, but the columns and rest of the original building were still damaged. The rostrum and seats were placed closer to the monument this time—with Abraham Lincoln looming in the background above the speakers, an imposing reminder of why everyone was there. Certainly not just to hear some political speeches. The huge crowd had gathered to honor a country that had been attacked from within—just as in the time of Lincoln—and to remember how he stood tall during those trying years. With a vaccine for Covid-19 in distribution, a new government elected, and Ford Wilkes dead, the time had come to look to the future.

Tamika was once again slated to be the keynote speaker.

She had asked her father to open the event by leading the crowd in the Pledge of Allegiance. It was the first time the two had ever worked together professionally, and she felt some chills as he stood and spoke about "justice for all." General Smith then asked the throng to observe a minute of silence to honor those who had died during the anarchist attacks and the pandemic.

For Tamika, this moment of silence, as she stood observing the entire throng, was deafening in its impact.

And with that, Senator Tamika Smith rose from her seat next to Johnny Humboldt and moved up to the starting line. She took off a warm, full-length winter parka as she walked to the podium. She tucked a loose lock of hair—which was pulled back in her usual style—behind her ears and adjusted a small American flag pin on the black dress coat she'd chosen to honor those who had passed. When the proverbial gun went off, her mouth went completely dry. The first words felt garbled to her, but they came out clear and strong.

"I want to thank all of you for coming today to help us honor and remember those who died at the hands of Ford Wilkes or fell in the grip of the coronavirus infection. There are no words sufficient to make up for the suffering loved ones experienced over the past year. I want to take a personal moment to remember my dear friend Charles Roscovitch, who died on these very steps. He was an amazing mentor, a trusted advisor, and a patriot. I will miss him desperately."

She paused for effect, but also out of necessity. Flags arranged on poles across the back of the stage whipped and snapped in the wind. As the emotions cleared, she squared her shoulders with resolve, glancing briefly at her father and at Johnny, knowing that the mission forward, and her role in making it happen, were now crystal clear.

"Charles was the eldest son of an immigrant to our country—a boy who grew into a man who loved the freedom and opportunity he found in America. Ford Wilkes tried to destroy that American dream. He tried to demolish an important symbol of our national unity. Then, a month later, a collection of anarchists and extremists stormed the steps of our nation's Capitol—an act of sedition and destruction that struck at the heart of our republic.

"But before he died, all Charles could think about was the sanctity of that union. As he was dying, he told those of us around him to 'Show the nation how to come together. Rebuild.' He meant more than just the Lincoln Memorial—more than the security of our Capitol—he wanted us to rebuild our belief in what it means to be American. Today we'll start that process in earnest, and I won't rest until we see it through."

Her voice got more forceful and determined as she reinforced that sense of purpose. "I want to focus my talk where we just began—with the Pledge of Allegiance." She took a moment to look at the flag nearest her straining against its weighted base with each gust of winter wind.

"So let's begin with 'I pledge allegiance.' That single phrase unites us all as Americans—regardless of our heritage, race, religious belief, gender, orientation, or age. In today's political environment, we rationalize points of view or behavior as 'American' even when those ideas reflect prejudice, hatred, and bias. Instead, when we pledge allegiance to our country, it means we put the nation first in our civic lives. Before our own self-interest, before the profits of our job or business, and certainly before our political party. That is what the Lincoln Coalition is all about."

Warming to the topic, she pulled the microphone from the podium and walked out on the top step, finding the eyes of a Black, college-aged man in the crowd. "'I pledge allegiance to the flag . . . of the United States of America.' Now we're getting to the nub of our issues—we are the *United* States of America." Her emphasis loud and emphatic.

"And later, when we say, 'One nation, under God, indivisible' we reinforce the absolute requirement to work together. Put simply, the entrenched divisions in our country must stop. If our allegiance is to the country, then we must find ways to listen to others, figure out what is truly important, and find a *united* path forward." This was becoming a gospel speech.

"My father, who you heard recite the pledge, is a descendant of the pilgrims. My mother's ancestors were slaves." She turned fully around to look at Abraham Lincoln, rising above the stage behind. "This is at the very core of the Lincoln Coalition. Our greatest president fought to keep us together as a country—from pilgrims to slaves—so *every* person could realize the fruits of our founding principles. And we must follow that example." Turning back to an applauding audience, she was greeted with a nodding head from the young man.

She moved to the left side of the steps and looked in the eyes of a middle-aged woman sitting in the fourth row, waving a small American flag. "'And to the Republic for which it stands.' America is in fact a democratic republic, where we elect leaders to *represent the people*. Not to prop up a king, entrench a dictator, or protect a demagogue. Donald Trump clothed himself in the trappings of a populist, but he's been the definition of a demagogue. Our democratic institutions barely held the line in the face of his assault on a free and fair election. We must address the horror of January 6th." There were equal parts of fear and thankfulness in her voice.

"Respecting the will of the people, graciousness in victory and defeat, and peacefully transferring power are essential parts of elected leadership. In the Lincoln Coalition, we are here to serve—not to be served." A smile to the woman. It was greeted with a smile back, and the flags waving up and down the Reflecting Pool got a bit stronger.

She continued by moving back to the middle of the steps and finding the eyes of an older white man. "We close the pledge 'with liberty and justice for all.' This is about human dignity and equity—that *all* Americans should have access to basic services and assistance—and be treated equally under the law. We've been fighting this battle since the origins of slavery, and the war still has not been won."

Her voice was now rising to a crescendo in pitch and pace—urging the crowd to join her movement. "Martin Luther King's dream expressed on these very steps over fifty years ago has still not been realized. Those of us in the Lincoln Coalition fight for that dream every day." As the crowd came to life with its approval, the white man in the audience touched his head with a small salute of approval.

She walked back to the podium and adjusted the flag on the pedestal to make sure it could fly freely. She returned the microphone to its holder, her hands now free to accent her words. "I'm embarrassed by the lack of progress we've made as a national government over the past twenty years. Time and time again, we've turned national challenges that threaten the health and safety of our citizens into partisan politics. Look around you today and ask yourself, where have all the real leaders gone? Is there hope for America?" That brought some quiet as people looked to her for a solution.

"Ford Wilkes lost hope. He decided to destroy a country where nobody cared about him or his family. I'm glad he's dead—he was evil in so many ways—but I also accept that we sowed the roots of his anger and insurrection. We've allowed our country to be divided, to become a land of 'haves' and 'have nots,' to be ruled by incivility, hatred, and bigotry. And we've left people behind."

She knew she needed to rally them back. "While I condemn Wilkes's traitorous actions, I will take up the fight for equity and opportunity to rebuild a nation where people believe in their future. We must protect ourselves from the Obaid bin Latifs outside our country—but, more importantly, we must provide opportunities for families like the Wilkeses inside our great republic. Because I believe in the America of *hope*.

"To bring that hope to life, we need strong, committed leaders. Leaders who are united in their purpose, who care about the country before themselves, and who will serve others first. In all their failings—in all their disagreements and missteps during our country's birth, the founding fathers demonstrated this type of leadership. Our country is great because of their example."

She took to the challenge with speed in her delivery. "Charles Roscovitch started the Lincoln Coalition because he believed such leaders still exist among us and can be powerful, positive forces for change in our country. We believe in courage, in sacrifice, in accountability, in making tradeoffs and difficult decisions. We deeply believe in the potential for greatness in the people of our country." Rising applause from the crowd, which was coming alive again.

Senator Tamika Smith continued her sprint down the back stretch. "So what does that mean exactly? What can we all actually *do*? Let me start with my partners in the Lincoln Coalition. Beginning today, we're declaring a 180-day initiative. We're giving our fellow leaders in

Congress and the White House 180 days to draft, debate, and approve legislation for Covid-19 response and recovery, a national emergency preparedness plan, expanded job training, and a massive national investment in infrastructure. Then we'll move on to the tougher questions around fiscal responsibility, criminal justice reform, racial bias, comprehensive health care, immigration, and the environment. And we have the votes to block anything else from moving through Congress until these issues are wrestled to the ground. The time has come to get serious about the things that matter."

A rumble began at a low pitch as people started to absorb the message. And like a preacher seeking "Amens," Tamika Smith studied the faces closest to the stage and saw that just maybe . . . they believed too.

Around the last curve she came—speaking with the steady rhythm that she knew so well from running the toughest of races. "I ask us *all* to make a promise as citizens: to engage fully across our government, our businesses, and our civic organizations to drive change. And if we invest in this promise, the return will be tenfold. Not just for ourselves, but for generations to come.

*"We CAN provide health care to all AND not bankrupt the country in the process.*

*We CAN defend ourselves against terrorists AND be a force for peace and justice.*

*We CAN protect our borders AND act with compassion to immigrants and refugees.*

*We CAN advance technology AND educate our citizens for next-generation jobs.*

*We CAN produce energy for growth AND protect the environment.*

*We CAN tax the wealthy AND ensure there are incentives to invest in the future.*

*We CAN grow the economy AND prepare for the unexpected.*

*We CAN fight bigotry and hatred AND be proud of our history.*

*We CAN advance equity AND provide a safety net for those in need."*

Senator Tamika Smith—byproduct of the melting pot that is America—walked with the microphone to the front of the stage. "I will not pretend that this will be easy. It will take dialogue, arguments, some fights, some compromises, some experiments, some wins, and some failures. We must stick to our common sense and dedicate ourselves to the long-term mission. If we pledge ourselves to a united country that provides liberty and justice—if we elect leaders of Mount Rushmore quality—then we can get it done."

She again turned herself sideways and addressed the statue of Abraham Lincoln directly. "To the president who guided us through our darkest hours, I can firmly say I believe in America the Beautiful. We fought long and hard to make it our homeland. But lately, some people have tried to take it away. It's high time we took it back."

She turned back around to the audience and finished simply, "We are the Lincoln Coalition and we're here to serve. Come join us." With the crowd erupting behind her, she walked back to her seat.

She sat down and couldn't help but soak in the moment. Huh. Maybe she'd been wrong about the race all along. Maybe life was less about the medals and more about the commitment. Less about the success and more about the people. Less about the destination and more about the journey. Her story wasn't defined by a series of once-around-the-track events, but rather by the long arc of a life committed to doing what was right.

The crowd was still cheering wildly.

Tamika stood again to wave. Then she whispered to Johnny, "Game on."

# ACKNOWLEDGMENTS

I FACED A DIFFICULT question in September of 2016. I'd been very busy marketing my first book, *Xbox Revisited*, and it was time to begin writing again. But what should I write? I contemplated a second nonfiction effort, thinking I had much more to say about innovation and leading through difficult circumstances. But I also wanted to grow as a writer—to learn new approaches to communications, emotional expression, and creativity. So I decided to explore fiction, along with the challenges of character development, scene description, dialogue, and plot lines worthy of a thriller. My natural skills and talents only took me so far down that path—so there is a long list of people to thank.

Let me start by being clear that while the plot is grounded in historical events, the characters in *The Wilkes Insurrection* are fictional. They are my own combinations and creations—some of them having swirled around in my head for many, many years. Any similarities or likenesses to actual people are purely coincidental.

My family was a constant source of support and energy. My wife, Pauline, was eternally patient with the amount of time I spent sitting in my office tapping at the keyboard. Phillip, Sabrina, Nicoline, and Madeline read multiple versions of the manuscript, sometimes while flying and not knowing what was coming. Our dog, Roscoe, was with me for almost every word, and our walks kept me in shape and provided key plot inspirations. Siblings, in-laws, nieces, and nephews have all provided ideas and suggestions. I love my extended family (now fifty strong) and *The Wilkes Insurrection* is a Bach-clan effort.

The plot has a tremendous amount of specific material that is well beyond my skill set. I have many people to thank for their subject matter input and efforts to keep me on the straight and narrow path. Any errors or inaccuracies are my failings or author's license.

I never had the courage to join the military—but Tamika Smith is my vision for service to our country. A number of decorated veterans helped me mold and shape Tamika and the rest of the Air Force context. They assisted with terminology, procedure, communications, and the ins and outs of life in service to our country. With great gratitude for their support and sacrifices, my thanks to General Darren McDew, General Chuck Wald, Lt. Colonel Jennifer Jensen, Captain Kari Granger, and Captain John Davis. Aim High.

Ed Fries graciously introduced me to the budding AR/VR community in Seattle. I want to thank Bob Berry, Nick Fajt, Todd Hooper, Forest Key, Alex Kipman, Mark Kroese, Sebastian Motte, and John Vechey for inspiring Cybernoptics. Some of our work together ended up on the cutting room floor, but the company you helped create took Johnny Humboldt and Paul Hayek to the next level.

Bryce Roscovitch grew and developed over the course of writing this manuscript. He went from a plot side note to a starring role—and his technical skills far exceed my own. My great appreciation to Francisco Domingo Santos and Leo Lens for their insight into the dark passages of the cybersecurity world. Likewise, I love airplanes but have a fear of flying. José Tomás Andreu Cooper cleaned up my pilot communications etiquette, and Michael Van Haaren walked me through the physics of gasoline-filled aluminum tubes crashing into concrete runways.

*The Wilkes Insurrection* has many cultural undercurrents that I hope I've addressed respectfully. A whole host of reviewers provided valuable input on racial and gender issues and filled in many of my numerous blind spots. In addition to being a lifelong friend and voracious reader, Elizabeth Conwell supported Tamika in her therapy sessions. I also appreciate the assistance of Ayman Aldahleh and Alex Morcos for their guidance with Arabic translations and the various elements of the Islamic faith.

Throughout this project, the author community has been a wonderful support group and source for perseverance. Justina Chen has long been my communications guide and muse. She provided incredibly insightful writing feedback, especially with scene description, and the Lincoln Coalition was all her idea. Kim Seely was the first person to read a full manuscript and offered great character insight and encouragement. Bob Dugoni and Greg Shaw were very gracious with their time, feedback, and referrals. And while many agents turned down my manuscript, they provided important input and incredible motivation.

My friends have patiently read through various drafts of *The Wilkes Insurrection*, well before it even had a proper title. My thanks in particular to Paul Aigner, Nick Black, Richard Butters, Brad and Judy Chase, Jack Fitzpatrick, Anne Francis, Mike Gallagher, Pete Higgins, Blair Rasmussen, and Paul Shoemaker for providing their thoughts, ideas, and critiques. Mike Delman, Jess Dollinger, Jason Grumet, Leslie Higgins, Susanne Lyons, Laura Midgley, Lorraine Orr, Patrick Spence, Jim Voelker, and Blair Westlake also gave important feedback that helped me prepare to market and sell the story.

Of course, none of this would have been possible without the dedicated support of publishing professionals. Bonnie Hearn Hill completed an early edit of a massive manuscript and helped me understand the importance of focus and point of view. Heidi Toboni did the really heavy editorial lifting, enabling me to turn a good story into a real thriller. Her attention to detail and commitment to the ultimate messages made *The Wilkes Insurrection* so much better. The entire team at Greenleaf Publishing has been incredibly dedicated to producing a polished, successful novel. My thanks to Justin, Jessica, Lindsay, Ava, Stephanie, Sheila, Kristine, and Amanda for all their energy and effort. And with gratitude to Matt Brown, Fauzia Burke, Adina Friedman, Andrew Gottlieb, and Heidi Toboni for their passionate creative work to promote and market the book to my most important audience—my readers.

Finally, I listened to thousands of hours of music while writing. I love pop music, so my personal soundtrack includes plenty of Ed Sheeran, Taylor Swift, John Mellencamp, Carrie Underwood, OneRepublic, the Eagles, and Train. My thanks to the Sonos team for producing amazing speakers and software that animated and inspired my work. *The*

*Wilkes Insurrection* has a soundtrack too. You can find out more at www.robbiebach.com and www.wilkesinsurrection.com.

Hopefully, team Tamika Smith has encouraged all of us to be more protective of our democracy and more committed to community engagement. Please join me in this important work as civic engineers.

My best,

Robbie Bach
Medina, Washington

# ABOUT THE AUTHOR

**Robbie Bach** joined Microsoft in 1988. Over the next twenty-two years, he worked in various marketing, general management, and business leadership roles, including supporting the successful launch and expansion of Microsoft Office. As Chief Xbox Officer, he led the creation and development of the Xbox business, including the launch of the Xbox and the highly popular successor product, Xbox 360. He retired from Microsoft as the President of the Entertainment and Devices Division in 2010.

In his new role as a civic engineer, Robbie works with corporate, philanthropic, and civic organizations who are driving positive change in our communities. He guest-lectures extensively at a variety of colleges and universities and speaks to corporate, civic, and trade association audiences across the country. In 2015, he published his first book, *Xbox Revisited: A Game Plan for Corporate and Civic Renewal*.

He is the current chairman of the board at the Bipartisan Policy Center and is a board member at Magic Leap, a leading augmented reality company. He also serves on the national board of governors for Boys and Girls Clubs of America and was the chairman of that board from 2009–10. He previously served as a board member of the United States Olympic Committee, Sonos Inc., Brooks Running Company, the Space Needle Inc., and Year Up Puget Sound. He is the co-owner of Manini's, Inc., a gluten-free pasta and flour company.

He was an Arjay Miller Scholar at the Stanford Graduate School of Business, where he earned his MBA, and a Morehead Scholar at the University of North Carolina, where he earned his degree in economics and was also named an Academic All-American on the Tar Heel's tennis team.

He and his wife, Pauline, reside in Medina, Washington, with their yellow lab, Roscoe. They have three grown children and one grandchild. Robbie loves peanut M&Ms, upholding heroic ideals, and those motivated to save the world—although not necessarily in that order. *The Wilkes Insurrection* is his first novel.

On social media:

    LinkedIn: robbiebach

    Instagram: @robbiejbach

    Facebook: @robbiebach61

    Twitter: @Robbie_Bach

    For more information, go to www.robbiebach.com

    or visit www.wilkesinsurrection.com